MONEYSHOTS

By Jonathan Asche

STARbooks Press
Herndon, VA

Published in the United States
STARbooks Press
PO Box 711612
Herndon VA 20171
Printed in the United States

Many thanks to graphic artist John Nail for the cover design. Mr. Nail
may be reached at: tojonail@juno.com.

Book and text design by Milton Stern. Mr. Stern can be reached at
miltonstern@miltonstern.com.

Cover photograph courtesy of Hot House Entertainment,
www.hothouse.com.

*Special thanks to Jim, Don, Jerry and Richard,
who encourage me more than they'll ever realize.*

For Tomé, again.

Also by Jonathan Asche

Mindjacker

MONEYSHOTS

PROLOGUE

Perry Snopes couldn't believe his luck — not one, but two gorgeous young men to keep him entertained for the evening. One — the one he was fucking now, the guy practically doubled up with his legs over his head while Perry pounded his cock up that tight ass — looked like that hot boy-band singer, the one who was dating that slutty-looking pop star who swore up and down she was a virgin. Cute face, not quite boyish but still lacking the hard-edge of manhood, naturally blond hair cut close to the scalp, and a compactly-built body. The other guy — straddling the face of the boy-band-singer-clone, getting his balls licked while he leaned over to slide his tongue between Perry's gasping lips — looked a bit older, but not by much. Maybe it was the goatee that made him appear older or the fact that a thin layer of brown fur accented the tight muscles of his torso. Perry wasn't too crazy about how the goatee guy had bleached the tips of his spiky hair, and the tattoos on his arms and the one sprawling across his back were kind of trashy, but Perry wasn't bothered enough to throw the guy out of bed. God, no. Not now.

The experience made enrolling in that goddamn seminar worth it.

Perry Snopes was in Miami, attending a three-day workshop on "How to Manage a Successful Campaign for Public Office." To his acquaintances, his supporters, his lover, he said it would be a valuable experience and help him solidify his strategy for taking a seat on the Atlanta City Council in the 2002 election.

It was all bullshit, of course. The seminar was led by former campaign managers, press secretaries and fund-raisers; the star speaker, a former Texas congressman from years back, was voted out of office after being investigated for improper handling of campaign funds (i.e., he siphoned funds toward the purchase of a yacht), though the seminar's literature was careful to omit this one detail. Perry had been a successful businessman for twenty-five years, owned two upscale antique stores in Metro Atlanta, and knew without attending a single workshop or reading a single book that running a winning campaign was the same as running a profitable business. If he could convince an interior design firm that they were buying an authentic armoire from the eighteenth century and not some 1960s replica barely worth $30 at a yard sale, he could sell the public on Perry Snopes as a city councilman.

No, the seminar on "How to Manage a Successful Campaign for Public Office" was not necessary. And were it not held at a three-and-a-half star resort in Miami's South Beach, Perry might have considered the workshop's $2,500 registration fee a total waste.

That money certainly wasn't wasted this evening. After a few rounds of cocktails with fellow workshop attendees — most of them sharing Snopes' view that the affair was just a good way to use campaign funds for a long weekend in Miami — Perry begged off from several dinner invitations, claiming he felt a little under the weather. He hid out in his room for a couple hours, ordering room service and calling his lover, Winston, back in Atlanta, telling him how much he was missed.

Around 11:00 p.m., Perry sneaked down the hotel's back stairs, slipped into a cab and went club hopping.

He went to a club called Hedonism. Lots of flashing lights and music mixed in such a way that a hundred different songs sounded like the same song playing continuously. Perry was not impressed. Hedonism wasn't any better than the clubs in Atlanta, just more expensive. The only thing that kept Perry at his table, sipping a $15 martini, was the crowd. Every third person in this club had the glossy beauty of a TV star, the rugged athleticism of a sports hero, the palpable sexuality of a porn star.

And two of those beauties asked if they could join Perry at his table.

Introductions were made, but nothing was heard over the relentless disco. Perry doubted their names would've registered, anyway. He was too distracted by the young men's beautiful faces, and he was slightly drunk, besides. Perry dubbed the pair "Goatee Guy" and "Boy Band Singer."

Conversation, what little of it was heard, was shallow and brief. All that registered in Perry's mind was Goatee Guy telling him he liked Perry's mustache, and Boy Band Singer running his hand up the inside of Perry's thigh, making Perry's cock squirm. Perry just remembered telling his new friends they were "so totally cute," sounding like a 14-year-old girl experiencing her first crush rather than a 52-year-old businessman running for public office.

Perry remembered his station in life when the two hotties suggested going someplace more intimate. His hotel was definitely out. Many of the seminar's enrollees were booked on the same floor of the hotel, and Perry couldn't chance one of them seeing him stumble off the elevator with these two young hunks. Not that it was any secret that Perry was gay. In fact, back in Atlanta, he played up this fact (the incumbent was a lesbian). However, Perry took great pains to distance himself from the common perception that gay men were just cock-hungry meth heads who slinked from one circuit party to the next until they overdosed or died of AIDS. Perry frequently and publicly lambasted this image, citing he and his "husband" Winston — they'd been together for close to eight years — as a truer example of gay ideals. In one speech, Perry went on to accuse gay men of being as guilty of perpetuating this slanderous image of themselves as was the straight media — comments which prompted a snarky editorial in Atlanta's gay newspaper, *Southern Voice*, with the headline: "Snopes gay, not gay friendly."

Yet, Perry wasn't above having a little fun, as long as discretion was maintained. He asked the guys if they knew of any place they could go (he sure as hell wasn't going to invite him back to his room). They did; they were staying at a motel not too far from the club.

It was an older, residential motel, a two-story building dwarfed on either side by giant high-rises, done in that ubiquitous art deco style, which was probably what saved the dowdy little building from being razed years ago. The rooms had exterior entrances. Their room was at the rear of the motel.

Inside wasn't as bad as Perry expected. It was clean at least, and the walls had been freshly painted. The shabby furniture looked like it was from the late '50s, complete with a starburst clock on the wall.

Boy Band Singer's searching tongue and groping fingers quickly diverted Perry's attention to the room's decor. Goatee Guy joined in, swirling his tongue around the outer rim of Perry's ear, his hands pulling at Perry's belt.

The three of them made an awkward slow dance for the king-size bed. Perry's shirt was stripped away, his cock set free and immediately inhaled by Goatee Guy. Before Perry could lose himself in the rising pleasures of that talented mouth, Boy Band Singer presented his hard dick. Perry gasped in admiration of the pulsing rod, then took it down his throat.

Perry's mouth moved from Boy Band Singer's cock to his balls, to his pert butt, pushing his tongue into the young man's shaved asshole. Perry felt a second mouth — Boy Band Singer's — closing over his cockhead while the other mouth moved to Perry's low-hanging balls, then traveled lower, teasing Perry's furry hole.

The sexual possibilities with these two men were endless, and more than a little overwhelming. Perry's mind raced with assorted arrangements — wanting to fuck this one, be fucked by that one, or maybe suck their cocks simultaneously until they both came onto his lapping tongue. He felt like a glutton at a buffet table. Where to begin?

His partners guided him along, Boy Band Singer saying he wanted to feel Perry's "big dick up my ass," saying it with enough relish that Perry felt his excitement ratchet upward, his cock pumping out more pre-cum. Goatee Guy lapped up this additional juice before rolling a condom over Perry's throbbing prick.

Perry fucked Boy Band Singer doggy style, rhythmically pumping his dick between the sculpted globes of the young guy's

Jonathan Asche

buttocks. Goatee Guy lay beneath them, getting his cock sucked by Boy Band Singer while his own tongue alternated between his young friend's dripping dick and Perry's swinging balls.

Now Boy Band Singer had his legs up in the air, ankles resting on Perry's shoulders while the older man rammed his ass. Goatee Guy pulled at his buddy's hard-on. "Want me to make 'im cum on his own face?" he taunted Perry.

Perry barely responded to the suggestion, just looked at Goatee Guy with a dazed expression, his senses overloaded with sexual ecstasy. Goatee Guy moved off Boy Band Singer's face. "You gettin' close, baby?" he asked, jacking his friend's cock faster.

The young man answered the question with a loud, whiny moan. His body convulsed, the walls of his ass squeezing against Perry's thrusting cock. Jism rained down on Boy Band Singer's torso and pooled at his sternum. His load didn't quite reach his face, so Goatee Guy scooped up some cum with his fingers and fed the white, glistening cream to his friend.

Boy Band Singer was still licking the taste of his own goo off his lips when he got a second mouthful, delivered by Goatee Guy. Grunting and gnashing his teeth, Boy Band Singer's tattooed friend leaned over him, firing his load on his cute face.

For Perry, seeing Boy Band Singer get his face splattered and his subsequent pleasure in receiving his friend's load, like he'd just took a spoonful of ice cream, nudged this escapade across the line of hot and into the realm of raunchy abandon. These men were totally uninhibited — total whores. *Like his lover.* The bitter thought was quickly obliterated as Perry crossed the threshold of pleasure into the throes of a body-shaking orgasm. He lunged forward, leaning over his hot bottom boy, sweat dripping off him and mixing with the other fluids glazing Boy Band Singer's face. A sharp, final thrust along with a loud, gasping cry, and Perry was filling the condom with his own jizz, his cock buried in Boy Band Singer's warm chute.

The three of them lay on the bed, breathing heavily. Perry felt woozy, and could fall asleep here if he allowed himself. Boy Band Singer sat up in bed. "I need to take a shower," he announced. Perry pulled the rubber off his dick and handed it to him, saying, "Here, flush this while you're in there." That got a chuckle from Goatee Guy.

After Boy Band Singer trotted off to the bathroom, Goatee Guy climbed off the bed and walked over to the corner of the room, digging through a big black duffle bag sitting on a chair. "Got some 'tina," he said casually, removing a crumpled paper sack from the duffle bag. "Want to do a line? Got some Viagra, too. Could keep goin' all night."

4

"No," Perry said flatly. Except for the occasional toke from a joint or the rare line of blow, Perry abstained from drug use and disapproved of it by others.

"Suit yourself."

Perry propped himself up on his elbows. Goatee Guy was shaking a small pile of crystal from a tiny plastic Baggie out onto a tabletop. Using the edge of his driver's license, he pushed the drug into a line. Goatee Guy rolled up a twenty and Perry looked away, disgusted, as the Goatee Guy inhaled, the sound of his harsh snorting cutting through the air.

Something about the chest of drawers across from the bed caught Perry's eye. The top drawer had a hole it where a pull should've been. The hole was a fairly significant one, Perry noticed, and almost perfectly round, as if someone had cut it with a saw. The room's dull light reflected off something inside the hole, something like glass.

Perry got off the bed. "What's this?" he asked under his breath. He reached for the drawer and pulled it open. He suddenly felt his stomach constricting and his blood seemed to stop flowing through his veins even as his heart increased its pace.

"What — ?" Perry turned to confront the Goatee Guy. But as he turned his head he was stopped by the blunt impact of something hitting his nose, so sudden it took a moment for the pain to register. Perry tasted blood and mucus and felt his legs crumpling beneath him.

He heard voices, but his reeling mind couldn't focus on what was being said. Perry didn't know how much time had passed before he finally struggled to his feet. He staggered toward the Goatee Guy, bringing his hands down on the man's shoulders.

They struggled, Perry making threats that didn't sound intelligible to his own ears.

Perry heard a pop. And then he heard nothing.

ONE

"Remember guys, the more you tip the more they strip!" the DJ reminded the crowd at The Tackle Box as he cued the next song.

On the main stage of Atlanta's newest — and sleaziest — all-male strip club, a dancer with long, blond hair, introduced as "Rock Hard Stone," flexed his muscles and rolled his hips. At the start of his three-song set, he'd strutted out with a black bandanna tied around his head, a billowing white shirt and tight, black satin shorts. Now, on song three, he only wore the bandanna and a red thong.

Martin, sitting at the foot of the stage, lit a cigarette and checked his watch. It was 10:42 p.m.

Martin's friend, Conner, pulled a twenty from his wallet and stood up. "Oh, Stone, I got something for you," he called across the stage in a flirtatious singsong, waving the bill.

"Oh, God," Martin mumbled, looking away.

Slowly, the dancer undulated to their side of the stage, seeing if he could arouse any more cash out of his audience along the way. Once he reached them, he hunkered down, leaning over toward Conner. "What is it, baby?" he purred, tossing his sweaty hair behind his broad shoulders.

Conner held up the bill, making sure Stone saw it. "I thought this would look better on you than that thong you're wearin'." Martin heard this line and wanted to crawl underneath his chair.

Stone was unfazed. "Believe that might be more comfortable," he said, turning so Conner had easier access to the garter encircling his thick bicep. The twenty joined the other bills strapped to Stone's arm. Conner held the dancer's attention just a moment longer, placing a hand on Stone's thigh and leaning in to say something into his ear. Martin couldn't hear what was said, and given Conner's repartee with the dancers so far, he was glad of it. And was it his imagination, or was Conner's hand moving a little further up Stone's thigh than management allowed?

The dancer chuckled, took Conner's face in his hands and kissed him on the forehead before standing abruptly, falling back in time to the music.

"What'cha gonna do," moaned a throaty, female voice as a hypnotic bass line throbbed. Stone moved his body to the beat. Unlike most of the other dancers, he could actually dance, his spectacular physique twisting and writhing erotically to the music.

"What'cha gonna do, what'cha gonna do — *to me!*"

He thrust his hips forward, the pouch of his thong lewdly bulging forward. Conner watched, enrapt, his eyes glazed, his mouth agape. Martin was surprised his friend wasn't drooling. Just looking at him made him blush with embarrassment. Then again, he was usually embarrassed when he went out with Conner. Their friendship was a total mystery to him. The two men were close in age (Conner was two years younger, though he pretended ten years separated them), worked together (Conner started at AdVerb about six months ago, moving to Atlanta from Memphis), went to the same gym, the Muscle Factory, and both were gay. They shared circumstances and proximity, but beyond that they hadn't much in common.

Martin was initially attracted to Connor and supposed that sparked his initial interest in getting to know him. Like most gay men, when Martin met other guys he immediately considered the sexual possibilities. Conner was only pretending to be 29, but at least he tried to look the part. His body was sculpted from a rigorous weight-lifting regime, the end result being a pumped-up chest and arms, narrow waist and a hard little butt. As befitting such a well-maintained physique, Conner was perpetually tan. Just to cinch his surfer stud look, he got his light brown hair streaked a golden blond, which also covered up some of the gray that was starting to creep in. Nature at least met Conner halfway, providing him with impish blue eyes, an upturned nose and mischievous smile that, even at 38 and with deep lines framing his mouth, looked boyish and cute. And having seen Conner in the Muscle Factory showers, he knew he was generously hung as well.

Yes, at one time Martin would have gladly fucked — or been fucked by — Conner. So when Conner, after engaging in small talk with Martin during the early weeks at AdVerb, invited him out for a few drinks at Burkhart's, Martin gladly accepted. After an hour with him in at the bar, during which time Conner downed three vodka tonics, did a toot in the men's room, and made crude passes at every remotely handsome (and young) guy who walked within five feet of their table, Martin was cured of his lust for Conner.

Regardless, a friendship was forged in spite of Martin's resistance. It was hard not to be taken in by Conner's boisterous personality. He just wanted to enjoy life, and he wanted those around him to enjoy it, too. And Martin was in need of a good time, even if it was someone else's definition of one. In many ways, his friendship with Conner was vital. But there were times ...

"Aw, man, c'mon! How do I know I wanna suck your cock if you won't show it to me!"

... when Conner was just too fucking obnoxious.

Stone seemed unperturbed by Conner's behavior. He blew Conner a kiss, swiveled his hips like he was grinding up against a hard bubble butt and threw a playful smile Martin's way. Martin managed to flash back a tense smile before dropping his gaze into his cocktail.

Stone did an abrupt turnaround, giving them a long view of his solid, shapely rear. Hooking his thumbs in his thong, he pulled at the waistband teasingly, flossing his ass with the G-string. Keeping in time with the rhythm of the song, he bent down, pushing his ass toward Martin and Conner. His butt-cheeks parted, just enough to make them want to see more. Then he whirled around, and teased them just a few seconds longer with a front view, pulling the waistband of his G-string down to show some stubbly dark blond pubes, then a little bit of shaft, before pulling it up again, giggling at Conner's growing impatience.

Finally, he pulled the thong down, his cock and balls dangling free for all to see. The move got a raucous cheer from the crowd. Conner looked like he came in his pants. Stone was pretty magnificent, resembling some Southern California Tarzan with his flowing blond hair, his taut, athletic body and thick, cut cock. Even Martin, who'd been numb to the whole experience so far, felt his pulse quicken.

Stone wiggled his dick for Conner, then pranced off to collect all the money being waved in his direction by men willing to part with a couple more dollars for a close-up view of his bare cock.

The song and Stone's set ended. The dancer hastily stepped back into his thong, gathered up the rest of his costume and dashed off the stage. A thin, pale guy, whose main appeal was he barely looked seventeen, replaced him.

"Too skinny," Conner said dismissively, tipping back the rest of his screwdriver. "But Stone. Jesus! Did you see that cock? What I'd do to get a piece of that..."

"I'm sure all you'd have to do is name your price."

"I forgot, you're the expert on that. What's the going rate on blow jobs these days?"

"Fuck you!"

"What the fuck's your problem, anyway?" Conner asked, his annoyance disguised as concern. Martin had been depressed for a few weeks now. Tonight was supposed to cheer Martin up, and Martin was refusing to be cheered.

"There's no problem."

"Bullshit. You look like you've got a turd caught sideways."

Martin sighed heavily, stubbing out his cigarette and reaching for another. "It's nothing," he said, pulling a Marlboro Light from the pack.

"Y'know, for a guy who's quit smoking, you've been lighting up a lot lately."

Martin quit three years ago. He was 37 then and in a relationship with a man he thought was "the one." Three weeks ago, he turned 40, and he was alone. Shortening his life suddenly didn't seem so scary.

"You know what I bought today?" Martin said.

"What?"

"Nose hair clippers." He shook his head in disbelief. "Fucking nose hair clippers."

A smile tugged at Conner's lips. "Glad to hear it. You were beginning to look like you'd snorted a hedgehog."

"Goddammit, Conner, don't you get it? I might as well have gotten some Metamucil while I was at it. I'm fucking old."

"Right, like forty is ancient. But I do think you should get some Metamucil. Might improve your mood."

"How old are you, Conner?" Martin asked.

"I'm 35. You know that."

"Your real age, Conner."

Ignoring the question, Conner pushed back his chair. "I know what you need." He rubbed his nose, a conspiratorial grin coming to his mouth. "Come to the bathroom with me," he said, getting up from his seat.

Martin shook his head. "You know I'm not into that."

"It's just a bump. It'll — *hell-o!*"

Stone was standing at their table. He'd gone from pirate to jungle hunk, with his sun-bleached hair tumbling past his shoulders and his generous charms stuffed into leopard-spotted hot pants. "Hey, guys. Enjoying yourselves?"

"You bet!" said Conner, sinking back into his chair. Martin managed a smile and a nod, then looked away, nervously taking a drag from his cigarette.

"You're a shy one," Stone said to Martin, putting a hand on his shoulder. Martin's heart quickened. *He doesn't want you, he wants your money,* Martin reminded himself. Regardless of motivation, the attention of a hot younger man still provided a slight boost in confidence.

"You, uh, dance very well," Martin said, suddenly wishing he could take the words back before they could reach Stone's ears. Fortunately it was difficult to hear above the loud music. Unfortunately, Conner had ears like a bat and heard the clumsy compliment, finding it hysterically funny.

"Excuse me?" Stone said, bending toward Martin.

"He said he likes how you *dance!*" Conner guffawed. "I do, too, especially the way you swing that big dick of yours."

Stone just smiled and said, "Thank you," giving Martin's shoulder an affectionate squeeze. Then: "If you guys are interested, I could give you an exclusive show."

They were interested.

Martin and Conner followed Stone to the VIP rooms in the back of the club. They were greeted by a brawny, bearded guy wearing a white t-shirt silk screened with the club's logo: a cartoon of a hunky guy in skimpy overalls carrying a fishing pole, from which dangled a phallic-looking fish. Stone moved past him, the two sharing a smile like an inside joke. Conner stopped and slipped some folded up bills into the bouncer's hand.

"You gentlemen have a nice time," the bouncer said, directing them to a curtained doorway on the far left.

They passed through burgundy crushed velvet drapes into a small room. A padded bench hugged three of the room's four walls. Light came from dim, torch-like fixtures on the black-lacquered walls. Just enough illumination so you could see what was going on, just dark enough to keep it interesting.

Stone waited for them in the room's center. Martin immediately sat down. Conner pulled more bills from his wallet (where did all this money come from, Martin wondered). "What kind of show do we get for that?" he asked, presenting the money to Stone.

Stone quickly counted the twenties. "A very special show," he promised with a wink.

Conner took a seat next to his friend. "When's the show start?" he asked with a big grin. He leaned back against the cushions, his legs sprawled, like he was about to watch the Big Game.

"How 'bout right now?" Stone replied, easing into the beat of the music blaring throughout the club, swinging his hips, his cock jiggling in the pouch front of his shorts. Spinning around, he presented his ass to his customers, thrusting it at them as he humped air. He yanked the shorts down without further preamble. There was no need to tease dollars away from his audience. He'd been paid for.

The song changed, and Stone expertly adjusted to the new rhythm — slower, with a grinding bass and an intensely sexual vibe. It suited the moment well.

Gyrating obscenely, his spine twisting like a snake slithering across the grass, Stone backed his way toward Conner. The hard globes of his ass clenched and released, inviting his audience of two to imagine sliding their cocks into the deep cleavage of his buttocks. To help their imaginations along, he bent over, slid a hand up between his legs and pressed two fingers into his ass crack.

Conner shifted his weight. He rested a hand on his crotch, periodically squeezing the pronounced mound there. Martin's eyes went from Stone fingering his ass to his friend toying with his cock through his jeans. The two images managed to produce vague stirrings in his own pants. His dick was willing to have fun even if he wasn't. Rather than follow his cock's lead, however, Martin had to summon harsh memories, the catalysts to his depression.

His ex, Ron, telling Martin he was leaving, that he didn't want to settle down after they lived together for three years. A week after Ron moved out, Martin saw him at Nickiemoto's, his arm around a slender man who barely looked the legal drinking age.

Months later, Martin met a hot young man at Backstreet. The guy was coming on to Martin, insisting they "go somewhere," and only after Martin spent $75 on a motel room did the guy reveal his professional interest. "You didn't expect me to give it to you *for free*, did you?" were the hustler's harsh words, like Martin should've known better. Forty-year-old men with thinning hair and lines around their eyes had to pay for it.

And still, Martin fucked the guy. Hard.

Martin no longer saw Stone playing with his butthole or Conner groping his own crotch. All he saw was his lover pawing a barely-legal twink in a restaurant, a smirking hustler telling Martin he was too old. That he'd have to pay for it if he wanted to play with the pretty ones. Pretty ones like Stone, who was given who-knows-how-much so two middle-aged guys could get their jollies and go home — alone.

Martin's cock went down for the count.

Stone stood upright, turned and pressed the fingers that had been prodding his asshole against Conner's lips. Conner took the fingers into his mouth, holding the dancer tightly by the wrist while sucking his fingers. Conner's other hand gripped his hard-on, now desperate to be let out of his black jeans.

"C'mon, smile," Stone chided Martin. Martin forced the corners of his mouth upward and reached for his cigarettes. He pulled one from the pack, but put it back before lighting it, reminding himself he was supposed to be an ex-smoker. That, and he noticed there were no ashtrays in the little room.

"I know what'll cheer you up," Stone said confidently, moving in front of Martin. Slinking his naked body to the groove of the music, he pinched his hard, brown nipples and tossed his hair over his shoulders, adopting a look of sexual ecstasy. He arched his back, pushing his cock and balls toward Martin's face, and lightly caressed his muscular torso. Stone's fingers glided over the curve of his pecs, the rippling terrain of his abdomen, brushed over his severely trimmed pubes and skidded to a halt on the ample shaft of his cock. Wrapping his fist around his dick (still soft, but starting to swell), he pulled on it while rolling his hips, his balls bouncing against his thighs.

This did bring a smile to Martin's lips, but it wasn't a joyful smile; it was an embarrassed one.

Stone moved in closer – closer than county law allowed. Martin could actually smell the sweat on Stone's nuts. The dancer let go of his rising dick, swinging it toward Martin's surprised face. Had Martin been six inches shorter or leaning forward, Stone's cockhead would surely have hit his chin.

"Ya' wanna taste it?" Stone invited. He resumed pulling at his dick.

It was so tempting. Had he been in a different frame of mind, or had the situation been different — like Stone's come-on wasn't paid for, for instance — Martin might've obliged the stripper. Martin's self-pity was stronger than his desire, though. He just looked up at Stone, forced a pained smile and shook his head as if passing on dessert.

"C'mon," Stone cajoled. "You know you want to."

"If he won't, I will," Conner leered. He'd undone his jeans and pulled his cock out, stroking it nonchalantly, never once taking his eyes away from the hard-bodied dancer.

Stone looked down at Martin one final time, giving him a sympathetic smile. He shrugged, silently telling his unresponsive client, "You snooze, you lose," before undulating over to the salivating Conner.

"Maybe you can tell your friend what he's missing," Stone said, stepping between Conner's open thighs and leaning over him, placing his palms against the wall behind Conner's head.

But Conner wasn't listening. Immediately he dove toward Stone's crotch, rubbing his face against his cock, now three-quarters hard, inhaling the musk perfuming his scant pubic hair and nuzzling his balls. His arms encircled Stone's waist, and he clamped his hands onto the muscular hills of the dancer's buttocks. Stone reached down to grip the base of his cock, holding it steady as Conner's mouth closed over it.

The music drowned out Stone's gasps, but his face made it plain he liked what Conner was doing. He gently pumped his dick in and out of his customer's mouth, his eyes occasionally sliding toward the curtained door to see if the bouncer was watching.

He looked in Martin's direction, too, just long enough to give a see-what-you're-missing grin. Martin saw all right. He saw Stone's ass bobbing as he fucked Conner's mouth. Saw his cock sliding between Conner's lips. Saw his friend, in some other place entirely — a place everyone goes when the sex is so intense reality is forgotten — gulping down the stripper's fat cock, the occasional slurping noise crackling through the blasting music. He moved his eyes down to Conner's freed dick, throbbing with excitement. At one time Martin wanted to suck that dick. He supposed he still did; his own cock tingled a bit as he looked at Conner's rod now, thick with curving ridges of veins raised along the shaft. Martin wondered what Conner's reaction would be if he were to lean over and start sucking him now?

Just as Martin thought it though, Stone had gone and beaten him to the punch. The blond dancer got on his knees between Conner's legs, taking Conner's oozing cock in his hand. He gave it a good squeeze, milking out a crystalline drop of pre-cum. He then dragged the purplish cockhead across his lower lip, glossing it with the sap of Conner's dick. Stone looked up at Conner, forming his pre-cum-glazed lips into a partial smile. He was met with the dazed, stupid smile of his customer.

Stone closed his mouth over Conner's fat dong. A low moan tumbled out of Conner's slackened mouth. He rolled his hips, moving his cock against the moist, velvety pillow of Stone's tongue. Reaching forward, he grabbed a handful of Stone's hair. It was damp with sweat and slightly sticky from whatever grooming product coated it. Still, Conner played with it as if it were strands of silk. "Sooo pretty," he moaned.

The raunchy, slow song that had been playing began to fade, the air quickly being filled with a hyperkinetic tune. It was Stone's cue to hurry. Management would look the other way if dancers turned the occasional trick on the premises, just as long as they were quick about it. "Private shows" weren't supposed to last more than two songs. This show had gone on for a song and a half. Stone stepped up the pace of his blowjob, massaging the trick's shaft as he sucked on the head. His other hand cupped the trick's shaved nut-sack, squeezing it gently.

"Wha — whoa!" Conner said, pushing Stone away. "I don't want to get off that way."

"How do you?" Stone asked.

"Get up and turn around."

The dancer did as he was asked, presenting his ass to Conner's face. Gripping Stone's butt-cheeks in his hands, Conner kneaded the firm globes of muscle. He pulled them apart. "Bend over," he commanded.

Stone bent at the waist, and Conner buried his face in the shadowy divide of his ass. Martin could see his jaw working as he tongued the dancer's hole. A grunt pushed out of Stone's mouth as Conner's tongue pushed its way between his ass-lips and curled its way into his chute.

Conner withdrew his tongue and gripped Stone's narrow waist. He pulled the stripper back toward him, down onto his lap, so his cock was sandwiched between Stone's muscular ass-cheeks. "How 'bout giving me a lap dance," Conner drawled in Stone's ear, reaching around his waist to grab the dancer's quivering dick.

Stone rolled his pelvis, pushing his butt against Conner's prick. "You mean like this?" he asked playfully.

With Conner's spit coating the channel of Stone's ass and Conner's cock pumping out pre-cum, there was enough natural lubricant for the dancer's ass to glide up and down the pulsing shaft. And there was enough friction to make Conner shudder. "Oh, yeah, like that," he sighed, pushing his hard-on against Stone's gyrating butt. "Perrrrfect."

The two seemed oblivious to Martin's presence now, even as he stared at them. Or maybe they were aware and got off on it. Stone was a professional exhibitionist, after all, and Martin would never accuse his friend of being an introvert. It should've been exciting, watching them, more so than watching guys fuck on video.

Should've been, but all that the scene aroused in Martin was an odd mixture of jealousy and disgust — jealous that he wasn't participating and disgust at himself for not having a desire to.

As Stone ground his ass against Conner's cock, Conner pulled at Stone's dick more forcefully. Their pleasure was palpable. Martin could almost smell it over the club's odor of stale smoke and spicy cologne. He watched as their harmonious movements stopped suddenly, as they each lost control, their muscles jerking from the pleasure rocketing through their bodies. Conner inhaled sharply, suddenly, and froze as his cock, cradled in the vice-grip of Stone's ass-crack, spewed its hot load.

After he finished cumming, Conner's hand resumed its stroking of Stone's dick. The dancer's body convulsed, and he rubbed his ass against the Conner's spent rod, making Martin's friend jerk and buck beneath him. Conner bit Stone, his teeth pinching the raised muscle on his shoulder, adding enough intensity to the moment for the dancer to shoot his load. Stone's spunk rained onto the deep red carpet and dripped over Conner's hand. Leaning back against his customer, Stone let out a contented breath. He closed his eyes, only to open them when Conner pushed his spooge-covered fingers between Stone's parted lips.

"Suck them clean," he hissed, leaving the "or else" unspoken. Stone obeyed, licking his own cream off his customer's fingers like it was vanilla frosting.

Neither of them noticed Martin heading for the door.

TWO

It took more effort to get out of The Tackle Box than it did to get in. The club had become more crowded since Martin disappeared into the VIP room. He couldn't take a step without saying, "Excuse me." If oblivious patrons wouldn't let him pass and continued chatting as if he weren't there, he'd push his way through, ignoring their indignant comments. He didn't care if he'd offended a few haughty queens. He had to get out, get some air, and get away.

The entranceway was also the club's main exit, and it was filled with people waiting to get their IDs checked, get their money taken and get their hands stamped. The line's progress was impeded by an argument between a slender young man and the doorman.

"I forgot it," he whined. "I had to take it out to show airport security and forgot it in my... "

"I don't need a story. I need to see an ID," said the doorman. Judging by his impatient tone, it wasn't the first time he'd informed the man of this simple fact.

Taking a deep breath, Martin slipped into the wall of people.

"Hey, no cuts!" shrieked a fag hag with an ass as big as a Hyundai.

"Get to the back of the line," snarled a squat queen whose stubby fingers were adorned with numerous gold rings.

"Watch it!" snapped a bleary-eyed honoree of a bachelorette party, clutching a large inflatable penis.

When Martin made it to the door with the glowing green exit sign above it he felt as if he had just reached the top of Mount Everest. Relief flooded him as he pushed open the door and stepped outside.

The summer air was warm and heavy. It had rained while he was inside The Tackle Box, the sudden shower making everything — including this scraggly patch of land overlooking Cheshire Bridge Road — smell lush and verdant. Martin inhaled the rain-cleansed air, then fished his cigarettes out of his shirt pocket.

He headed around the club, to the back parking lot, puffing on his cigarette as the scene he'd witnessed in the back room played over and over in his mind. Martin was not as immune to its arousing power as he thought; he ended up leaving the room with a pretty insistent boner. Maybe he should've stayed, taken the stripper up on his offer and sucked on his dick — or Conner's. But Martin was not, generally, an impulsive man. Consequences always needed to be weighed. (What if management chose that moment to walk in? How would Conner, who liked his men to be in their early-twenties, react to being blown by his 40-year-old friend?) When he did act instinctively, or just let raw emotion stand in for sober judgment, as he did that night with the hustler, he fretted for weeks, wishing he'd not acted so rashly. "Why does everything have to *mean* something with you," Ron, his ex, complained once. "Why can't things just happen, and that be the end of it?"

And then it "just happened" Ron left him for a guy too young to remember the Reagan presidency or life without MTV.

Martin was nearing the back corner of the building when he heard an insistent male voice, "C'mon, just let me in. I'm a friend of..."

"Don't know who you're talkin' about," another male voice responded flatly.

"I told you, he's the fuckin' owner!"

"Never heard of him."

"So that mean's I'm lying? Ask the manager..."

At the corner of the building Martin stopped walking and listened. He hung back not only to eavesdrop unobserved, but to avoid being brought into the potentially ugly situation.

"Go check," insisted the guy wanting to see the other owner. "Ask the manager, he'll tell you."

"You want me to get John? Fine. Maybe you'll listen to him when he tells you to go fuck yourself." The slamming of the door followed the invective.

Martin kept walking to his car. Around the corner, he saw a scowling young man, couldn't be older than 25, standing at the club's back door. Couldn't tell much about his body other than he wasn't fat; the man's T-shirt and jeans were baggy, concealing the details of his physique, though the toned muscles of his arms suggested an equally fit body. An olive green duffle bag was slung over his shoulder, looking stuffed to capacity. Martin kept walking, eyes cast downward, puffing on his cigarette.

"Hey, 'scuse me. Sir?"

Instinctively Martin stopped. Goddamn Southern manners, he cursed himself. "Yes?" His tone was chilly with suspicion.

The young man loped toward him, the weight of his duffle bag making him list to one side, appearing shorter than he actually was. "Wonderin' if I could bum a cigarette?"

"Oh, yeah. Sure." He pulled his cigarettes from his breast pocket and held the pack out toward the guy.

"Thanks," he said, pulling two from the pack. He slipped one behind his ear and stuck the other between his lips. "Gotta light?"

Martin held out the cigarette he was smoking. "Light it off this. Done with it anyway."

The guy's hand shook slightly as he lit his cigarette off the burning butt. He looked like he just woke up from a three-day bender: His face was covered with dark blond stubble, and the delicate skin under his eyes was puffy and dark. Yet, despite his haggard appearance, Martin had to say the young man was pretty damn cute.

The young stranger drew on his cigarette then dropped the butt used to light it. "Thanks," he said, exhaling a plume of grayish-white smoke.

The club's back door opened. "So where is this kid?" a man barked.

"Maybe the little shit got the..."

The young turned abruptly and strode toward the door. "Hey! You, the manager?"

"Fuck, there he is."

Martin continued to his car, chancing a brief glimpse at the men standing in the doorway. One appeared to be in his late forties, early fifties, face and body softened by booze. Even from across the parking lot Martin could tell the man wore a toupee. Standing behind the older man, towering over him by at least a foot, was a man so brawny his chest and shoulders threatened to rip through his white Tackle Box T-shirt as if he were the Incredible Hulk. Presumably, this was whom the young guy was arguing with before Martin stepped around the corner.

His '92 Acura (Christ, even my car is old, Martin thought) was parked about ten feet past the open doorway where the men gathered, just barely outside the reach of the flood light above the back door. As Martin unlocked his car door, he heard the older man snarl, "Don't know nothin' about this."

"Just let me use your phone to call him," was the young man's whiny reply, the last thing Martin heard clearly before climbing behind the wheel and closing the door.

Martin did not start the car right away but sat there, staring out the windshield at the sickly brush growing in the vacant lot behind The Tackle Box, not sure how to proceed. He did not want to go home, alone; that would be like admitting defeat. Yet, the idea of going someplace else, surrounded by the laughter of others, didn't appeal to him, either. That was his dilemma. He didn't want to be alone, but he didn't want to endure the happiness of strangers.

The voices of the men at the club's back door grew louder, angrier. "...tha' fuck OUT!" roared one man, followed by a higher pitched, "Goddamn motherfucker!" Martin turned his head toward the commotion, in time to see the Hulk push the young intruder away from the door. The young man lost his balance, falling backward onto the pavement. "Get tha' fuck outta here," the Hulk growled, savagely kicking the young guy in the ribs.

Martin reached for the door handle with his left hand while his right fumbled for his cell phone, resting on the car's center console. He'd rather just call the cops, let them handle it, but doubted they'd arrive before the melee got worse.

The back door slammed shut just as Martin set one foot down on the pavement. The young man worked free of the duffle bag's shoulder straps and stiffly got to his feet. "Asshole!" he shouted, banging his fist against gray metal door. "Dana'll fire your ass when I tell him! Shithead motherfucker! Suckin' the wrong boss's dick!" The harshness of his words was deflated by the desperation of his voice. By the time Martin was out of his car, the guy was crying.

"Um, you okay?" Martin asked, walking toward the other man.

The young man spun around, tears streaming down his face. "Do I fuckin' *look okay*?"

Martin held his hands up defensively. "Sorry, stupid question. Just making sure you're not hurt badly."

Martin's concern was ignored in favor of another outburst. "Goddamn motherfucker!" the young guy screamed, kicking the door hard enough to leave a small dent. "Let me in, you 'roided out freak!"

The door did not open, and the man gave up his name-calling, giving the door a final punch with his fist.

"Shit, that hurt," he hissed, spinning away from the door, covering the wounded knuckles of his right hand with the palm of his left.

"You're bleeding," Martin observed, pointing at the guy's left arm.

The young man raised his arm, looking at the raw, bloody patch just below his elbow. "Just a scrape," he observed, gently brushing away tiny black bits of tar and gravel sticking to the wound.

"Just be sure to clean it up," Martin said before heading back to his car. He'd been as much of a Good Samaritan as he planned to be.

But no sooner had Martin settled back behind the wheel than the young guy was tapping on the driver's side window. Martin rolled down the window. "Yes?" he asked pointedly.

"Say, man, I hate to ask this, but could I get a ride? I'd take a cab, but, see, I'm outta cash and..." Tears were creeping into the man's voice. "Those assholes won't let me inside... I just wanted to talk to this guy, the owner..."

Don't get involved, Martin told himself. Whatever this guy's story was, Martin didn't want to become a part of it.

"Please?" he pleaded.

"Look, I'd like to help you, but..."

"Just a ride is all I'm asking."

Martin looked away. "I..."

"Shit, you don't care!" the young man snapped.

Taking a deep breath, Martin turned and faced the guy. Whether it was the man's youth, his tears or his attractiveness that ultimately made up Martin's mind, he couldn't say. Even as he told himself to just roll up the window and get the hell out of there, he hit the button for power door lock, unlocking the passenger side. "Get in," he said.

A moment later the guy was tossing his bag in the back seat. "Thanks!" the young man said gratefully as he settled into the car.

Martin started the engine and put the car into reverse. "So, where am I taking you?" he asked, backing out of the parking space.

"Anywhere but here."

"Figured you'd say that," Martin sighed heavily.

THREE

Dane Kensington looked down at the young man kneeling before his chair, full lips wrapped around his cock.

"That's it," Dane said, the words sounding as if uttered in his sleep. "All the way down your throat."

The young man was Jason Belvedere, one of DanKen Studios' newest discoveries. Despite the crude tattoos decorating his arms and legs, Jason's pleasant, boyish face and slender frame still projected a youthful innocence that appealed to the chicken hawk crowd. His cock was about average size, though that didn't matter: Jason was a voracious bottom (several reviewers compared him to the late Joey Stefano). He was even up for a "Grabby," as the gay adult movie awards were known, for his performance in *Up & Over (& Under)*, in which Michael Brandon and Jason Branch penetrated him simultaneously.

Jason's tongue moved down Dane's turgid shaft, down to his nut-sack. He prodded the plump balls with his tongue, pausing surreptitiously to pluck one of Dane's silvery pubes from between his teeth. Jason's mouth went back up the length of Dane's cock, up to the blunt, purplish head. He closed his lips over the cockhead and dipped his tongue into the piss slit, tasting the salty pre-cum Dane's dick kept pumping out.

"You suck cock so good," groaned the older man, running his hands through Jason's thick brown hair. He leaned back in his chair and thrust his hips forward. "So good."

Jason took more of Dane's dick into his mouth, taking it deep into his throat. His hands gripped Dane's naked thighs as his face sank into the older man's crotch. Dane's breathing was shallow now, his broad chest rising and falling with each wave of pleasure. His muscles twitched, signaling a more forceful spasm was on its way.

Dane pitched forward, his large hands now pulling locks of Jason's hair. Gulping in desperate lungsful of air and shutting his eyes tight, Dane was overtaken by an explosive orgasm. He exhaled, releasing a rumbling groan along with the fleeing breath, as his jism flowed into the young porn star's mouth.

Jason drank Dane's load without a moment's hesitation. Another one of his claims to fame: he swallowed — even on camera, as he did *Slurp n' Burp #4*, one of DanKen Studios biggest sellers. He continued sucking Dane's cock until he'd drawn the last drops of semen from it. Only when Dane relaxed his grip on his skull and let his body fall back into the chair, did Jason pull his mouth away, and even then the porn star couldn't resist lapping up the last bead of cum bubbling out of Dane's prick.

"Slut," Dane chuckled, giving Jason an affectionate smile. Jason responded with a mischievous grin and leaned back on his hands. Jason hadn't gotten off, but neither he nor Dane seemed interested in doing anything with his semi-hard dick. Instead, Dane stood up, knees creaking, telling the young man he had to make a phone call.

Crossing the bedroom that was the size of Jason's entire Silver Lake apartment, Dane snatched his cell phone off the top of his dresser and dialed. As the phone rang on the other end, Dane stepped out onto the terrace. It was dusk, but the Southern California heat still lingered in the air, feeling good against his naked skin. He looked across his backyard, across the still blue waters of his swimming pool to the glow of Los Angeles that reached up into the darkening sky and peeked over the back fence. Seemed to him like no matter how high you built your fences you couldn't escape those lights. Then he wondered: When is he going to pick up the fucking phone?

He was supposed to hear something last night, this morning by the latest. Nothing, so he called, but no one picked up. He called again. And again. And still again.

No answer.

And no answer now. The phone rang eight times before an automated female voice came on: "The caller you are trying to reach is currently unavailable..."

Anger quickly erased the relaxing effects of his recent blowjob. Dane hung up and almost hurled the phone into the pool. "God-*damn*-it!" he shouted, arms swinging at his sides as if trying to shake off the excess rage rising within.

He stepped inside and tossed the phone onto a glass-topped end table. "Shithead should've called by now," Dane grumbled beneath his breath.

"Who you trying to reach?" Jason was on the bed now, packing grass into a small silver pipe.

It was none of the porn star's business, but Dane needed to vent to someone. "Someone who was doing something for me in Miami. 'Sposed to call me this morning and didn't. Been trying all day and can't get in touch."

"Anyone I know?" Jason asked before lighting the bowl and taking a deep hit.

"Doubt it. Guy named Rand, new guy. Discovered him a few weeks ago. Danced at Boner's. Hasn't been in anything yet, but he's going to be. Very hot. Was going to cast him in something after he got back from Miami. But if he doesn't call soon, he can suck dick on the Strip for all I care."

Jason nodded, then made a noise like he was coughing up a hairball. "Boner's?" he coughed up the question with a thin puff of blue smoke. "I've danced there."

"Remember a guy named Rand?"

"Not when I was there," Jason shrugged. "Probably used a different name. Have to see him."

"I have some photos," Dane said, heading for the bedroom door. "I'll show them to you."

Dane hurried down the hall to his office. Once there, he removed a tan, six-by-nine envelope from his top desk drawer. He found Jason reloading his pipe when he returned to the bedroom. "Look at these," Dane commanded, presenting the envelope.

Jason set the pipe aside and took the envelope from Dane's hand. There were four Polaroids inside ("Who the fuck takes Polaroids anymore?" said Jason, who couldn't fathom life before the digital age) showing a man about Jason's age, with curly blond hair and a firm, athletic build. The young man was posing on an orange and brown plaid sofa. In one photo, he sat, legs spread, wearing a pair of shiny gym shorts pulled aside to reveal a nut. Next two shots, he'd lost the shorts and was showing off a hard-on. Last shot was from the rear, his ass-cheeks parted, but not enough to see the hole.

"He is hot," Jason observed, setting the photos down on the bedside table and picking up his pipe. "Don't remember seeing him from anywhere, though. And trust me, I'd remember him."

Rand was very memorable, Dane had to admit, his anger with the young man momentarily eclipsed by memories of the erotic adventures they shared prior to Rand's departure.

Jason lit his pipe and took a hit. When he spoke his voice was strained, "Sorry I couldn't be more help."

Dane was thoughtful for a moment. Sitting down on the bed beside Jason, he said, "You can help me in other ways, like waiting here for me, so I can fuck that cute ass of yours when I get back."

"Where you going?"

"Boner's," Dane said flatly. "Now how 'bout giving me a hit off that pipe?"

FOUR

"It's a three bedroom house, but there's only one bed," Martin announced, flipping the light switch by the kitchen door.

"I don't mind sharing if you don't," said the young man he'd rescued from The Tackle Box. He was behind Martin, so Martin couldn't see his face to tell if he meant the line as a joke or a come on.

"I'll get some sheets for the couch," Martin said.

In the car the guy tried to fill in the blanks. Said his name was Rand, and he was 22. Said he was from California, came out to Atlanta from Los Angeles, though he was vague on the reason. "Know some people out here," was all Rand said. He was very selective about which blanks he filled.

"I know people who live in Kansas City, I don't just get in my car and go see them for no reason," he said.

"Of course not," Rand replied. "It's Kansas City."

"So can I take you to any of these people you know?"

"You could if I could get in touch with them. Lost my cell phone on the way out here. Had all their numbers programmed in it. That's why I was hoping I could talk to the guy who owns that place — not that rug-wearin' asshole that runs it but the owner. Know him from L.A. He could put me up for the night. But those shitheads wouldn't let me in."

Martin saw where this was heading, but asked it anyway: "Again, where am I taking you?"

"Uh, that's the thing. I don't really have a place to go until I get in touch with my friend. I was wonderin' if, well, if you could let me crash at your place."

Of course.

"Just for one night," Rand added quickly. "Next day, I'll go back to the club, try to hook up with my friend, be outta your hair."

All kinds of alarms were sounding in Martin's head. "I don't know..." he said distractedly, his attention focused on exiting from the interstate onto Freedom Parkway.

"C'mon, you can trust me," Rand whined.

"Usually the people who insist you can trust them are the ones you can't. I don't know anything about you, really. Not crazy about bringing a total stranger into my house."

Rand waited a moment, then said: "Bet you wouldn't care if I was a trick." He reached across the Acura's center console and put a hand on Martin's thigh. "I can be, if you want."

He was right. In his past, Martin brought home guys whose names he barely remembered, let alone any other personal details. Just knowing they were willing to fuck was enough. Martin looked down where Rand's hand rested, within two inches of his crotch.

There was the slightest tingle of desire as he considered Rand's offer, obliterated by the stranger's shouting, "Hey, man, look out!"

Directly ahead a car was stopped for the red light at Boulevard. Martin slammed on the brakes, going into a skid on the wet pavement, narrowly coming to a stop before rear-ending the car in front of them.

The near-collision left the two men frozen, staring straight ahead and breathing heavily. Martin gripped the steering wheel with both hands, his knuckles white. Rand had his hands to himself. The Cher CD playing on the car's stereo provided an inappropriate soundtrack to their panic.

"Okay," Martin sighed. "You can stay with me."

The light turned green. Martin proceeded forward slowly.

"But only for one night," he added quickly.

At his house in Decatur, Martin directed Rand to the first floor bathroom, telling him he should clean up the scrape on his elbow. He then went upstairs to get sheets from the linen closet — old, worn out sheets, not the good ones — and grabbed a bottle of peroxide from his medicine cabinet. Rand was still in the bathroom when he returned downstairs. Martin was almost finished making up his living room sofa when he heard the toilet flush and the bathroom door open.

"Brought some peroxide down," Martin said, tucking a corner of the top sheet under a sofa cushion, not looking up when Rand entered the room. "You should put some on your arm."

"You know, I wasn't kidding before, earlier."

Martin looked up then. Rand had stripped off his T-shirt, holding it in his right hand while he slowly dragged the fingers of his left across his flat abdomen. Martin saw that he was right about Rand's body: he was very well put-together, from his hard pecs down to his narrow waist. It took a moment before Martin noticed Rand's suggestive grin.

"Kidding...? About what?"

The grin got bigger. "About sharing a bed."

Martin looked away. "You don't have to do that."

"What? I'm not your type or something?"

You don't know how much of my type you are. "Not that. But you don't have to whore yourself for my hospitality. I'm not going to demand anything in return," he said firmly, though his refusal was more out of concern for his own psyche than preserving his houseguest's self-worth. The idea of paying for sex, be it in cash or a place to crash, wasn't boosting his self-esteem.

Rand dropped his T-shirt on the coffee table and moved closer, his steps slow and deliberate, his smile seductive. "I only whore myself for money. 'Sides, you never pick anyone up from a bar before? Think of it like that, makes you feel better."

He was pulling at the fly of his jeans as he spoke, directing Martin's eyes there, making Martin think about what he'd find underneath those jeans. And Martin wanted to find out, his own cock twitching with curiosity. He could hear Conner telling him: Go for it, the guy's offering himself to you. Opportunities like this don't come around every day.

So tempting, but: "I think you should get some sleep." He looked away, busying himself with fluffing a pillow. "Want anything to eat, help yourself to whatever's in the fridge. Good night," he said, managing a wan smile. He dropped the pillow onto the sofa and headed for the stairs.

"Hey," Rand called out.

Martin stopped and turned.

"Thanks," Rand said.

Upstairs in his bedroom, Martin closed the door behind him and exhaled loudly. What had he just done? Turned down his second sexual opportunity for the night and definitely not making the most of his midlife crisis.

He brushed his teeth and got undressed. Staring into the full-length mirror on his closet door, Martin appraised himself, something he'd been doing a lot lately, but it seemed particularly important now. He thought his face was all right, even better since he grew the goatee and mustache. The facial hair concealed the deepening lines around his mouth. Couldn't do much about the crow's feet developing at his eyes, though, nothing short of surgery. When Martin's hairline began its retreat he didn't fight it, just had it cut real short. The look suited him, although he still wished his hair were thicker.

The body was in good shape — better, actually, than when he was in his early twenties, when he was scrawny and undefined. Abs starting to look a little soft, he thought, patting his stomach, vowing to go to the gym tomorrow. A tattoo of his name done in Chinese characters decorated his right bicep, gotten on his thirty-fifth birthday, part whim, part dare. He still liked it and was tempted to get another. His torso was covered with reddish-brown fur, and he wondered, for the umpteenth time, if he shouldn't get a body wax and try the smooth look. Like most men, Martin thought his cock could be a few inches longer, but he did fill out his designer briefs nicely, if he said so himself.

All in all, not bad... "For a guy your age," Martin finished aloud.

Martin tried to sleep but couldn't. He lay in the darkness, eyes closed, but conscious of each passing moment. The clock on his bedside table kept him apprised on how slowly the night passed: 1:10, 1:12, 1:15, 1:17 the glowing red numbers taunted. Martin rolled over, facing away from the clock. Then he rolled back.

Rand's image filled his mind, particularly as he appeared, just before Martin went upstairs, shirtless and seductive. Drawing on the memory of Rand's tight, muscular torso, Martin imagined the young man nude. Thought of his hands on Rand's smooth skin, cupping the imagined fullness of Rand's ass. Rand would be hard, his beautiful cock pressing against Martin's.

These images swarming in his mind sent Martin groping at his own erection, feeling his hardness beneath his underwear. Pornographic scenes, choppy and disjointed, played in his imagination: Rand kissing him, Rand sucking his cock. Martin saw himself with the young man's dick in his mouth, saw himself prying Rand's butt-cheeks apart and fingering his rosebud (thinking of this, Martin slipped two fingers between his own legs and toyed with his fuzzy asshole, stimulating himself to solidify his fantasy). Martin imagined bringing his face between Rand's firm buttocks, his tongue searching.

Martin had his hand inside his briefs, caressing his cock. Release was what he needed. He needed to just shuck off his underwear and jack off. Sleep would come after he did.

He was reaching to open the drawer in his nightstand and get out his bottle of lube when he stopped himself. Downstairs was the man he fantasized about, who had overtly offered himself, and he was up in his bed alone, about to jerk off.

Martin sat up in bed without turning on the light. Doubt prevented him from heading downstairs immediately. Experience had convinced him a sure thing was never so sure, and he was hesitant to go to Rand lest he be rejected. Several minutes had passed, and his hard-on began to wilt before Martin stood up and left his bedroom.

In the hall, he heard noises and stopped. The TV was on, the volume low. Apparently he wasn't the only one who couldn't sleep. Encouraged, Martin kept moving, but a line of dialog made him stop at the top of the stairs and listen.

"Oh, yeah! Suck that big dick."

Certainly wasn't the Lifetime network, Martin smiled to himself. He took the stairs in careful, soft steps, like a trespasser in his own home. At the second from the last step, he stopped. From there, he could see into the living room. He saw what he hoped for, but it still froze Martin in his tracks.

Rand was sprawled on the sofa, naked, his body illuminated by the bluish glow of the television. Martin couldn't see the porno tape Rand was watching, but it didn't matter. Seeing Rand now, methodically stroking his hard cock, his eyes on the TV screen, was better than any video. Instantly, Martin's dick sprung back to life.

The light from the TV flashed against the ridges and curves of Rand's naked body, shadows accentuating the contours of his tight physique. His lips were parted, shining in the minimal light, and he'd periodically look away from the screen, down at his own stiff dick, as if finding his own body as captivating as the raunchy action on screen.

Martin reached to squeeze his own crotch, feeling his hard prick under the ribbed cotton of his briefs. Heat spread through him, his cock tickly with excitement. Just go in there, he told himself. *You both want the same thing. This is what you came downstairs for.*

But he remained standing on the stairs, watching.

Rand's cock was about seven, maybe seven and a half, inches long, Martin judged, but maybe it would appear bigger close up. He thought it was big enough now, big enough for him to want to suck it. He could replace Rand's hand, now moving up and down the shaft in controlled, even strokes, with his mouth. Martin licked his lips and again squeezed the mound in his underwear. He thought about sucking that beautiful cock, licking his balls, maybe even eating his ass. He could hear Conner whispering in his ear: What are you waiting for? Go in there and get some of that. He wants it so bad, he won't say no.

Yet there was an excitement in watching unobserved, so Martin remained where he was. He'd be a voyeur for a while, then he'd join Rand.

Martin slipped his hand inside his briefs, feeling the warmth and hardness of his cock. It was sticky, too, steadily pumping out pre-cum. Rand's was as well — a glistening strand hanging from his cockhead and swinging down to his stomach. Rand reached down to pull on his ball sack. It was shaved, his balls moving around beneath the delicate skin. He rolled his hips, pushing his cock against the rhythmic stroke of his hand.

Martin had his own cock out now, his underwear around his knees. The shaft throbbed in his hand as he pulled on it, his body trembling with erotic sensation. He only took his hand away to spit into his palm, adding some more natural lubricant to the juice trickling out his rod.

Rand's hand slid lower between his thighs, down into the shadows between his legs. Was he fingering his butthole? Martin wondered excitedly. God, he'd like to put his face where those fingers were now; tongue Rand's hole while he jacked off, feel those balls bouncing on the bridge of his nose while he burrowed in there. Martin wondered if he shaved his asshole, too. *Go find out now*, a voice inside urged him. Funny how that voice sounded like Conner's. *Don't just watch the action, be part of it!*

He hadn't wondered if Rand could see him standing on the stairs, jacking off as he watched him. Martin figured Rand was too engrossed in his own pleasure to notice. The light from the TV surely didn't extend beyond the living room, leaving him hidden in darkness.

31

But then, Rand rolled over, showing off his ass. Why would he bother showing off his ass if he thought he was alone?

Martin's stomach started to cave in on itself as he realized he'd been busted. But embarrassment didn't cause him to retreat to his room. Rand was performing, and that performance was for Martin. Rand raised his butt into the air, two of the most perfectly shaped mounds of flesh Martin had ever seen, humping the sofa cushions. Still couldn't see the treasure hiding in that shadowed crevice, but Martin saw enough to realized that yes, Rand shaved there, too.

Knowing that Rand was doing this for his benefit increased Martin's arousal. It also made that devil on his shoulder urge him to act on his fantasy, to go into the living room and sink his face between those creamy white butt cheeks. Rand wouldn't refuse. He had to go into the living room. Now!

But he waited too long. His dick was pulsing in his hand. Martin's balls were drawn up close to his body, the hair on his scrotum standing out like it was crackling with static electricity. He was getting close. As much as he wanted to delay his orgasm, Martin couldn't take his hand away from his cock.

Rand wiggled his ass and pushed a hand up between his legs, fingering his own hole. He returned that finger to his mouth, put it between his lips and returned it to his asshole, playing with it some more, maybe even slipping a spit-lubed finger inside.

Martin came then, his attempts to stifle his groans only half-way successful. His pent-up desire erupted onto his belly, his hand, and the stairs.

Rand was on his back again. His eyes no longer focused on the TV screen, the porno video relegated to background. Now he was looking toward the stairs, at Martin, a slight smile tugging at his lips as he jacked off. He became more vocal, gasping and moaning as his fist hammered up and down the length of his dick. Rand's whole body moved in a wave as he undulated and writhed against the sofa cushions.

Short breaths and a raspy howl announced Rand's orgasm as he raised his hips off the sofa. Jism shot up the length of his torso. The copiousness of his load seemed even to surprise Rand, who snapped his head back, startled. His gasping mouth soon settled into a satisfied, partial smile. His body relaxed. His fingers dipped into the pool of cum collected at his sternum.

Martin, knowing he'd been observed, waited for Rand to call out to him. The young man said nothing, however. Rand brought his index finger, a drop of jizz clinging to its tip, to his mouth. He sucked on the finger noisily, exaggerating his slurping for Martin's benefit. He then held the finger in place between his top front teeth and lower lip, his mouth stretching into a wide smile. The smile seemed to dare Martin to take a taste himself.

But Martin was suddenly slapped in the face with a feeling of shame — over his own cowardice. He quickly pulled his underwear up over his hips, his jizz soaking into the fabric, and retreated up the stairs to pretend he'd never been seen.

FIVE

The Triangle Palms Resort in Fort Lauderdale was too far from the beach, the rooms weren't all that great, and it was overpriced. But you could get a blowjob while lying naked by the pool, so Nick "Nine" Carpetti loved the place.

He came up here early yesterday morning, after leaving Miami. Came up here to celebrate the easiest $25,000 he ever made.

Nine was staying in the Fire Island Suite. Except for now having a bunch of hot naked men in it, there was nothing about the room — which was about as special as a double at a La Quinta — that reminded Nine of Fire Island.

"Wanna do a line?"

It was some guy named Casey, who had shaggy, straw-colored hair, dark brown, quarter-sized nipples and a nice fat dick. He was on the bed, giggling, reclining next to another guy who was lying face down, broad shoulders shaking with stifled laughter. A thin line of blow went from the small of the guy's back down to cleavage of his butt cheeks.

"It'll be a double hit, you do coke and crack," Casey said, laughing like it was the best damn joke he ever heard.

The two other guys in the room laughed, too. They were over on the sofa, lying down, one against the other. One of the men — Nine thought his name was Brent, Brett, something like that — had his arm over the other guy's chest. The other guy's name was Danny. That, Nine remembered. Brent — *Brent*, Nine was sure that was it — was pinching one of Danny's nipples, pulling on it while his eyes darted from Nine, sprawled out on an overstuffed easy chair next to them, to Casey and the other guy on the bed, and then to the TV, a porno video playing on it. Danny's eyes, his black pupils as big as golf balls, seemed focused on nothing in particular. He just laughed along with the other guys, pulling at his hard cock and slowly grinding his butt against Brent.

All these guys he met at Triangle Palms' pool party, which started at four that afternoon and ended, officially, at ten. Still in a partying mood, Nine invited these select few back to the Fire Island Suite. The men were eager to join him. Not only was Nine generous with the drugs, he was hot in a rough sort of way, and hung to boot. (Some people claimed Nine got his nickname because he preferred using a nine-millimeter, but Nine told tricks he got the name because his dick was nine inches.) He looked over at Casey, gave him a crooked smile. "Sure, I'll do a line," he said, pushing himself up from the chair. For just a moment, he felt a little dizzy. He glanced at the digital clock beside the bed. Jesus Christ — 3:47 in the morning? He did need a bump.

He took a rolled up bill, a fifty, from Casey and leaned down to the other guy's back. Nine vacuumed up the snow into his right nostril, snorting so loud he barely heard the guy lying face down on the bed giggle and say it tickled. He followed the line down to where it ended, at the top of the guy's ass crack. The guy's butt cheeks were round and full, just like Nine liked them. He grabbed each buttock, massaged them roughly, then pulled them apart, getting a look at the pink rosebud in there. Nine massaged the guy's asshole with his thumb, feeling it pulse to his touch. Felt himself sliding off the bed, to his knees. Then, grabbing onto the guy's thighs, Nine dove between his legs, between his butt cheeks, his tongue spearing that twitching hole, making the guy cry out.

Casey said, "All right, man." Nine felt Casey's hands run through his hair, his finger glide over his shoulders. The guys on the sofa were chuckling sporadically. From the TV speakers came instructions to "suck that big dick."

Nine pushed his tongue deeper into the guy's ass — he really wished he were better with names — making him squirm and gasp. God, if only he had a longer tongue, he'd really make this guy squirm. As it was, Nine had stuffed the full length of his tongue up the guy's chute. Nine was grinding his face into the guy's ass crack, his nose filling with the man's scent, his face slick with his own saliva.

"Dude, yeah, eat that ass," Casey said, his voice quieter now. The guys on the sofa were quieter, too. The only sounds in the room were those of guys fucking on the video, the porno's cheesy disco soundtrack, and Nine eating ass like a pig at a trough.

The guy on the bed rolled over suddenly, swinging a leg over Nine's head. Now he was sitting in front of Nine, his stiff, uncut cock in Nine's face. He looked up at the guy, at his grinning, boyish face, his dark eyes shadowed by thick eyebrows, his mop of black hair — definitely Italian. Mario — that was his name, the guy's face triggering Nine's memory. Mario said, "Do you suck cock as good as you eat ass?" Grabbing his boner, pushing it toward Nine's face.

Mario's cock looked good, and Nine wanted to suck it, but first he had to show this guy who was running the show. "Tell ya' what," he said, standing up, grabbing his own turgid prick, "how 'bout you suck my dick first."

And Mario looked up at him, still smiling. "If that's what you want." Then he leaned forward, taking Nine's nine-incher in his hand, stroking it, and then putting his mouth over it. Nine gasped, bending forward and putting his hands on top of Mario's head. Goddamn, it felt good, having that warm, wet mouth wrapped around his cock. He thrust his dick deeper into Mario's mouth. Mario didn't even flinch.

"I'll suck your dick if he won't," Casey said. He burrowed his head between Nine and Mario, lowering his mouth onto Mario's cock.

It didn't interrupt Mario's pace. He kept sucking Nine's cock like nothing else was happening, but Nine felt Mario's body shudder. Mario's moans buzzed against the shaft of Nine's dick like he was playing a kazoo.

Nine felt warm, hard flesh, rubbing against him from behind. He felt the head of a cock and fingers tracing his furry ass-crack. "Gettin' me all hot n' bothered, looking at that nice ass of yours," the guy breathed in Nine's ear. Sounded like Brent, but he couldn't be sure. Lot of guys sounded alike when they whispered.

Wet kisses went down Nine's shoulders, a tongue glided down his spine, down to his butt. His ass was being pried open, warm breath tickling his fur-lined trench.

"Oh, yessss!" Nine groaned, pushing his hips forward as Brent or whoever forced his tongue past his ass-lips. Ordinarily, Nine might've protested, said he'd decide when and who he wanted to rim his ass. But it felt so fucking good, he was just going to let it slide this time.

Casey brought his face up from Mario's crotch, drool smeared across his chin, to help his friend suck Nine's cock. Mario moved to Nine's smooth balls — he'd gotten them shaved just the other day, same time he got his back waxed — his tongue prodding the jizz-heavy orbs while Casey gulped down Nine's rod. All these tongues and mouths, sucking his cock, licking his balls, munching his butt, were bringing Nine's blood to a boil quickly.

It was Casey who sensed it first, pulling his mouth away and said, "Bet you want to fuck this sweet ass here." Meaning Mario's ass, Casey's hands between Mario's legs as he said it, massaging his butthole.

Nine nodded, his jaw slack. His dick, jutting out like a flagpole, vibrated and tingled.

"How ya' want to do it?" Mario asked. "Face-to-face, doggie style, me sitting on your dick?"

"Face-to-face." Nine had an idea, what he wanted the other guys to do while he fucked Mario.

Mario scooted back on the bed, making room for Nine to join him. Nine took a step to the side, looked behind him. It was Brent who was eating his ass, looking up at him now, his goatee damp with his own spit, his eyes glazed by drugs and erotic pleasure. Beside him was Danny, standing and stroking his cock. Brent leaned over and sucked on it, just enough to lap up the pre-cum. Then he pulled his mouth away and looked back at Nine.

Casey, acting like some sort of sexual assistant, handed Nine a sticky bottle of lube and a rubber. "Here ya' go," he said. He had two fingers stuck up Mario's ass, working them in and out. "I'll loosen him up for you while you get ready."

"Just don't make him too loose," Nine said, ripping open the condom packet with his teeth.

Sheathed and lubricated and ready to fuck, Nine climbed onto the bed (it wasn't a waterbed, thank Christ, he hated those things), positioning himself between Mario's spread legs. With one hand clamped onto one of Mario's sinewy thighs and the other holding the base of his cock, Nine slid inside that slick, hot hole. Nine grunted and sighed, grooving on the tightness of Mario's ass ring, the soft warmth of his chute pushing down on his shaft. Nine grunted and sighed, grooving on the multiple sensations — the tightness of Mario's ass ring, the soft warmth of his chute pushing down on his shaft. It wouldn't take him long to shoot his load.

Nine started pumping his dick into Mario, the other guys surrounding the bed, cheering him on as they pulled on their cocks, saying the same lame shit that was being said on the porno video still playing on the TV: "Fuck that ass!"

Then one of them, Brent, said, "Oooh, yeah, can't wait for my turn." But Nine had other plans.

"You three, get on the bed, around his face," he panted. "I wanna see all of you cum in his mouth."

Mario said, "Hey, I don't..."

"Yes, you do." Nine's tone made it clear there wasn't room for debate. None of the others said anything as they got on the mattress, closing in around Mario. Casey and Danny sort of smiled, like they were on the same wavelength as Nine. Even Brent, who wanted to fuck Mario, seemed to be okay with Nine's idea.

Nine fucked Mario's ass in slow thrusts, trying to hold back and not cum first. He wanted to see these other guys blow their loads into Mario's open mouth. That always did it for him.

Casey, Brent and Danny jerked off intently, looking down at Mario, occasionally looking over at Nine. Danny's face was all screwed up, his muscles flexing, like he was about to shoot any second. Then, with a loud groan, Danny came, his spooge splattering onto Mario's face and into his open mouth. Mario gasped and sputtered, like someone just dunked him underwater.

"Least give me some warning," he complained, licking Danny's cream off his lips.

But Danny wasn't really listening. His body was still shaking as he squeezed out the last drops of cum from his dick. He pushed his cock down so his cockhead touched Mario's lower lip, leaving behind a white drop of jizz.

"Open up, I'm next," Casey said, aiming his dick at Mario's parted lips.

"Stick out your tongue," Nine barked. "Want to see it hit your tongue."

Reluctantly, Mario stuck out his tongue, just in time for Casey to shoot his wad. It spurted out his cock in one long stream, looking like mayonnaise pooled on Mario's quivering tongue.

"Ooooh," Nine purred, "swallow that load. Oh, yeah." The sight of Mario pulling his cum-covered tongue back into his mouth and swallowing sent a hot surge through Nine's body. He could feel his ball sack tightening. It wouldn't be long now before he let loose with his own load.

Brent started panting and gasping as his fist hammered up and down his red, throbbing dick. "I'm... I'm... oh, yes..." He had to push Danny out of the way so he could get a better shot at Mario's mouth, barely making it. Most of Brent's cream landed on Mario's chin and slid down his neck.

Nine was really close, looking at Mario's cum-covered face, Mario no longer acting like taking a guys load in his mouth disgusted him. No, Nine could tell he loved it. Mario's cock gave him away, hard as steel and dripping like a leaky faucet.

He rose up on his knees, pushing Mario's body up with him, at almost a 45-degree angle, so all Mario's weight rested on his shoulders.

"C'mon," Nine grunted, slamming his cock deep into Mario's ass, "jerk yourself off. I can tell you're close."

Mario pulled on his dick, his foreskin rolling back and forth over the purplish dome of his cockhead. His body shook, and he was breathing shallow. He made short, whiny grunts that got progressively louder, as if he were about to sneeze. It built up to a strangled cry as Mario popped his load. Gleaming white drops of cum rained down onto his smooth, heaving chest.

What really pushed Nine over the edge, though, was when Casey raked up globs of Mario's jizz and brought it to his mouth, sucking Mario's juice off his fingertips. Seeing that made Nine's cock explode with an orgasm so powerful it gave him goose bumps.

"That was fuckin' hot," Nine said, bringing his weight down on Mario's body. He gave him a deep kiss, tasting the tart residue of all the other men who'd deposited their spunk in Mario's mouth. "Fuckin' hot," he repeated before closing his eyes.

Nine opened his eyes when his cell phone rang. Sunlight peeked around the heavy curtains. The bedside clock read 10:22 a.m. He was alone.

Groaning, he sat up in bed, telling himself he was too old for that all night shit. Every muscle ached, his sinuses seemed to be packed with glass, and he could actually feel brain cells dying slow, agonizing death. Each electronic stutter of the phone detonated a micro-explosion in his skull. He swayed on his feet, trying to locate the brain-damaging sound. It rang again, and he winced. On the floor, by the bed, that's where the ringing was coming from. Nine got on his knees and found his cell phone resting at the base of the nightstand, near a discarded condom.

He meant to disconnect the call and throw the fucking phone across the room. Hoped the piece-of-shit device disintegrated against the wall. But he accidentally hit the "talk" button instead. "Finally," bitched a male voice on the other end. "Beginning to think you were dead, too."

Nine recognized the voice and brought the phone to his ear. "Hi. I was meanin' to call you," he croaked.

"You sound like shit," the man on the other end observed with no apparent sympathy. "Have you seen the *Miami Herald*?"

"I haven't even seen daylight yet," Nine said, easing himself back onto his bed.

"Well, there's a story at the bottom of the local section you should read."

He didn't have to see the paper to know what the story was about. "The job's done."

"That depends."

Nine's stomach lurched. "What do you mean, 'depends'?"

"What did you do with that souvenir you found?"

"Souvenir?"

"The police found the camera but no tape," the man said. "What's your problem? You're usually not this sloppy. Why didn't you just take the whole thing, camera and the tape?"

Camera? Tape? But Nine played along. "Shit, I just wanted to get that tape. Didn't think the camera mattered."

The man on the other end sighed into the phone. "Just lucky that you found it. The detective said the camcorder was hidden in a dresser drawer, hole drilled where the handle would be. Could be easily overlooked. I certainly wouldn't think to look for it." The man chuckled. "Wasn't expecting that little quirk."

"Yeah, I was lucky on that one." Nine's stomach was now starting to digest itself.

"Do you still have it? The tape I mean."

"Huh? Oh, shit no! I destroyed that fucker. Burned it."

A long sigh on the other end. "I suppose that's best, but I would've wanted to see it, see what he was up to before you showed up." Changing subjects abruptly, the man said, "Meet me in Atlanta later in the week? Thursday or Friday? I can call you later with a more definite time."

Nine said, "Yeah, gotta be up there anyway to get the rest of the payment settled." But the man already had hung up.

He took a deep breath and exhaled slowly. That was close; glad he thought to say he destroyed the tape. Nine's feeling of relief was short-lived, however. What if the tape surfaced? If he was on the tape he was up shit's creek if the police found it. Just as bad: What if the tape was discovered and his client found out what *didn't* happen? His easy $25,000 just got complicated.

SIX

Dane pulled his Jaguar XJ to a stop in front of a duplex in Hollywood. Unruly, scraggly hedges surrounded the single story stucco building, the patch of lawn in front in dire need of water and mowing. He double-checked the address scrawled on a cocktail napkin. Yeah, this was the place. He grabbed the envelope containing Rand's photos and got out of the car.

A dim yellow porch light illuminated the cracked red tile steps. The doorbell had been pulled from the wall, hanging loosely by two wires. Dane pressed it anyway, and was surprised that it worked. He stepped back and waited, checking his watch. It was 1:25 a.m., and he was out playing detective.

He'd gone to Boner's earlier to ask about Rand. One dancer there remembered him when Dane showed the photos. Said Rand danced under the name Sebastian. "Thought it sounded exotic," said the dancer, who went by the name Torro. He was a slim Latin guy with a pierced eyebrow and a poorly drawn lion tattooed on his right pectoral. Dane asked Torro if Rand, a.k.a. Sebastian, had any friends at the club.

"Hung out with this one guy a lot, Task," Torro said.

"That his stage name or real name?"

"Both. He used the name Zephyr for awhile. Heard it in a Madonna song and thought it sounded cool, but everyone gave him shit for it, so he dropped it."

"He and Rand were friends?" Dane pressed, not wanting this to take all fucking night.

"They hung out, I know that," Torro said, his eyes darting around the dark club. "Whether they were friends, fuck buddies or what, I couldn't tell you."

"Is Task still here?"

Torro shook his head. "Naw, he took off a few weeks ago. Said he found something where he could make a lot more money."

Dane nodded and asked if he knew where Task lived. "Shit," said Torro, "I look like a phone book to you? Have to ask the manager, Jerry. How 'bout a lap dance?"

Dane gave Torro fifty dollars and went in search of Jerry. Boner's was small, but it took nearly thirty minutes to be granted an audience with the manager, a balding, hook-nosed guy with a steroid-built body. Too much time in a tanning bed and a recent chemical peel made it difficult to place Jerry's age, but Dane suspected whatever he guessed would be ten years older than the strip club manager's actual age. Through the cover of dark, wiry hair covering Jerry's left forearm, Dane saw a blurred, faded tattoo of a chicken impaled on a bloody dagger. Or maybe it was supposed to be a dove — the artwork was shoddy. An amateur job, definitely, the kind of tattoo you get in prison.

Jerry was gruff when Dane first entered his closet-sized office, then turned on his oily brand of charm when Dane handed him his card. After Dane turned down Jerry's offers of a cocktail and some cocaine, he pressed the manager for information on Rand or Task. Not a whole lot on Rand he didn't already know: cute kid, hot, left three weeks ago to pursue a movie career. "Figured they were your kinda movies," Jerry stressed. "I mean, the kid was hot, but it ain't like he's gonna be the next Brad Pitt."

Task was deemed a "dumbass" by Jerry. "He was hot, too, but Christ, he had the I.Q. of a squirrel. Good thing he was pretty. He stopped showing up last week. Told a couple other dancers he had somethin' else, but didn't tell me. Don't matter, he's not working here no more."

Jerry got Task's address out of a dented gray filing cabinet. "Lucky I still have this handy," he told Dane as he scribbled the address on a napkin. "Usually just toss ex-employee folders into a box and forget about them. One guy who danced here a year ago was found stabbed to death not too long ago. Cops had me digging up his info, like a dead cocksucker was worth all the trouble."

Dane wanted to leave the moment Jerry gave him Task's address, but Jerry wanted to talk business. Suggested he could work for Dane as an agent. "Hey, we're pretty much in the same business, anyway, right?" he said. The idea that Jerry considered himself a peer made Dane shudder, but he told the manager of Boner's to give him a call Monday morning, they'd talk then.

And now he was here, standing on the front steps of a dilapidated duplex in Hollywood. Dane rang the bell again; less concerned about waking up the occupant than discovering no one was home. Having to come back here and see this place in the daytime was a depressing thought.

He was about to press the doorbell again when he heard footsteps on the other side of the door. A deadbolt turned, and the door opened as far as a security chain would allow. An attractive man in his mid-twenties peeked out with heavy-lidded eyes.

"Bit late to be selling something," he said, sounding sleepy.

"Sorry for coming here so late," Dane said, trying to sound more apologetic than he felt. "I'm looking for Task."

"Why? You a cop?"

"No. A pornographer."

That got the guy to grin. "Didn't know you guys went door to door."

"Is Task here?" Dane asked impatiently.

The guy shook his head. "No."

"Do you know when he'll be back?"

"Your guess is as good as mine. Last time I saw him was Wednesday afternoon. He said he might be going somewhere with a friend."

"Did he say where?"

"All kinds of questions. Are you sure you're not a cop?"

Dane repeated, "Where?" He was tired of fucking around.

"Hey, lose the attitude," the man snapped. "You woke *me* up." Then, he said, "Miami. Think he said they were going there."

Dane put his hands on his hips, looked away and sighed heavily. "Fucking great," he muttered. Turning his attention back to the man at the door, he asked, "He wouldn't happen to have a cell phone, would he?"

The guy nodded. "Have to get the number. Don't exactly have it memorized." He paused, then said, "A pornographer, huh?"

Dane rolled his eyes and nodded. "Dane Kensington. I run DanKen Studios." He pulled a business card from his wallet and handed it to the man.

After looking at the card, the man said, "Just a sec." The door closed, and Dane heard the rattling of the security chain. A moment later, the door opened wide. "You can come in while I get the number."

Now getting a full view of the man, Dane realized he wasn't just attractive — he was fucking gorgeous. His face was like a Greek statue come to life, with deep-set hazel eyes, a long, narrow nose, a strong jawline, and just the slightest cleft in his chin. Even his short, wavy brown hair reminded Dane of ancient Greek or Roman sculpture. He stood about six feet, his bare torso thick with muscle and nearly free of body hair. A tattooed chain of blue curlicues encircled his left bicep. He hadn't bothered to button his well-worn blue jeans at the waist, Dane noted, his eyes drawn to the bulge pushing against the fly.

He offered his hand as Dane stepped inside. "I'm Alex." The two men shook.

"Want anything to drink?" he asked, closing the door and leading Dane into the living room off the foyer, switching on a pole lamp as they entered. The interior of the duplex wasn't in much better repair than the exterior — walls needing a fresh coat of paint, worn carpeting, water stains on the ceiling — but it was surprisingly neat. And strangely familiar.

"I know that sofa," Dane said when the realization came to him.

"Excuse me?"

He pointed at the second-hand sofa upholstered in orange-and-brown plaid fabric. "That sofa. I have photos of it." He handed the envelope of photos to Alex.

Alex looked through the Polaroids silently, shaking his head slowly. "You know the guy in those photos?" Dane asked.

"Friend of Task's," Alex said, slipping the photos back inside the envelope. "Guy named Rand. Only saw him a few times." He handed the envelope back to Dane. "They must've taken these while I was at work."

"You a dancer, too?"

"No," Alex chuckled, revealing a row of even, white teeth. He headed for the kitchen, which was just off the living room. "Just a waiter-slash-screenwriter."

Dane eased himself down onto the sofa. "Really? The way you look I'd have guessed actor."

Alex snorted loudly, as if the idea was totally preposterous. "I'd rather get my rejection through the mail, thank you." Dane didn't bother asking if any of his scripts ever got produced.

Though Dane never responded to his offer of a drink, Alex got two bottles of beer out of an avocado green refrigerator that clashed nicely with the harvest gold stove and chipped white sink. "What about you? You star in any videos?"

"Yeah, back when they were still movies. Made about nine or ten of them, then realized there was more money in selling porn than starring in it."

Alex returned to the living room and handed a beer to Dane. He remained standing, across from Dane, a scarred coffee table separating them. "So, what you want with Task?" he asked.

Dane started to say it was personal, but decided to twist the truth instead. Bringing his eyes up from Alex's crotch, he said, "The guy in those photos, Rand, I'm trying to get a hold of him. He was supposed to be on set today but never showed. Checked his apartment, he's not there. Some guys at Boner's said Task would know where he is."

Alex nodded and took a pull of his beer. "He might. Like I said, saw Rand over here a few times. Don't know the details of their relationship, though."

"Task didn't say?"

"We didn't exactly sit around chatting. He'd paid for his half of things, and about twice a month we'd argue about who drank the last beer or why he couldn't pick up his goddamn clothes off the bathroom floor."

"Sound like you were married," Dane grinned.

Alex rolled his eyes. "Right," he sneered, but then added, "When he first moved in we messed around a couple times. Out of convenience, really. Didn't have money to hit the clubs, so why not stay home and blow the roomie?"

"That why you're home on a Saturday night? Not enough money to go out?"

He rocked back on his heels and shrugged. "Too tired to put up with the bullshit. Besides, why go out when I got hot guys like you coming to my door?"

Dane took a swallow of beer. There was a mischievous smile on his lips when he pulled the bottle away. "Careful. I'm likely to get the wrong idea, you talking like that."

Alex didn't say anything. He brought his beer to his mouth and drank, raising his eyebrows suggestively. The hand toying with his zipper made Alex's thoughts clearer.

Jason Belvedere, waiting naked in Dane's bed, was quickly forgotten. Probably smoked himself into a stupor, Dane reasoned. He set his beer on an end table and motioned for his sexy host to move closer. Alex stepped in front of him, kicking the coffee table back out of the way. A sly grin played across his face. "So what were these 'wrong ideas'?" he asked.

Dane took the beer bottle from Alex's hand and set it on the table next to his own. Alex's crotch was right in front of him, inspiring all sorts of ideas: wrong, right, good and, especially, bad.

"I like to get started with a kiss," Dane said, reaching forward and taking hold of the tab to the zipper of Alex's jeans. Slowly, he pulled the zipper down, exposing the prize beneath it in small increments. First, a dark thatch of pubic hair came into view, then the root of the shaft. Dane pulled the zipper further, seeing more of Alex's thick shaft, a darker tan than the rest of him. He tugged down on the jeans to free the rest of the cock, and Alex assisted. When his dick was fully exposed, Dane paused to admire it (he'd made a career of admiring penises, after all). Its length was a bit above average, cut, with a pink collar of foreskin beneath the crown. The cock curled over Alex's plump balls, then turned upward, slightly, at the tip. His prick was still soft, but thickening with each second.

Dane leaned forward, took Alex's cock in his hand and lifted it to his lips. Tenderly, he kissed the rosy-tan head.

"I like the way you kiss," Alex chuckled, his laughter abruptly turning into a gasp as his dick slid into Dane's hot mouth. His cock hardened within seconds. Dane's hands slid around his waist, molding to Alex's high, round butt.

Alex's body trembled with pleasure as Dane sucked his cock. The porn mogul dropped his mouth down to the younger man's balls, his tongue playing with the full, pendulous spheres. He took a nut into his mouth, sucking on it just hard enough to make Alex gulp in his breath. "Ahhh, easy now," he warned breathlessly, but when Dane rolled his eyes upward he saw the writer/waiter smiling.

His mouth returned to Alex's stiff, drooling rod. He swallowed it eagerly and slurped on it loudly. While Alex's cock was clamped between his lips, Dane fumbled to free his own hard-on from his jeans.

Hearing Dane's zipper, Alex leaned forward, hooked a hand under Dane's arm and told him to stand up; he wanted to suck Dane's cock now. But Dane ignored him, concentrating on Alex's taut torso, pinching the golden skin between his teeth, making the young man giggle and squirm. His mouth traveled around Alex's waist, and one of his hands rose up between Alex's legs, his fingers deftly sinking into the warm crevice of the other man's ass crack. Soon, Dane had forced Alex to lean forward, bent at the waist and supporting himself on the backrest of the sofa. He moved behind Alex, staring at the smooth globes of his ass, appreciating the view.

A second later, Dane was digging his thumbs into Alex's butt crack, prying his cheeks apart. Alex spread his legs as much as he was able — his jeans were still around his knees — and pushed his ass toward his visitor's face. When Dane's tongue pushed against his sphincter, Alex exhaled loudly, as if he'd been waiting for the right moment to release the air from his lungs. His moans soon filled the duplex as Dane's tongue burrowed deeper into his hole.

Dane curled his tongue inside the young man's chute, loving the sound of Alex's cries, the feel of his trembling body. His cock leaked its juice onto the dingy carpet; a gossamer string of pre-cum hung from Alex's cockhead as well. As Dane ate his ass, he reached for Alex's rod and stroked it, his fingers spreading the natural lubrication all over the pulsing shaft.

Alex hissed and shuddered. Pulling Dane's hand away from his dick. "Hold up," he drawled. "You keep that up, and I'll shoot all over the sofa."

"And that would be a problem because...?"

"Because I want to suck your cock, feel it inside me, before I cum," he replied, turning around and confronting Dane with his glistening boner. The pornographer managed a wrap his lips over the head, get a taste of his sweet pre-cum, before Alex sat down. He grabbed Dane's hands and pulled, urging him to his feet.

The moment Dane was on his feet Alex woofed down his cock. Though Alex was at least twenty-five years Dane's junior, his mouth was equally experienced. Feeling the younger man's tongue pushing against his dick took Dane into a higher realm of ecstasy. He could barely concentrate on unbuttoning his shirt the pleasure was so great.

Dane raked a hand through Alex's wavy dark hair. He guided the other man's mouth down to his balls, delighting in feeling a hot, wet tongue prodding his delicate nuts. As often happened, receiving pleasure made him want to give pleasure, and soon both men were free of all their clothes and in a sixty-nine position on the sofa, Dane on top of Alex, sucking the struggling screenwriter's dick and fingering his hole while Alex rimmed the visiting porn mogul's fur-ringed asshole.

Dane pulled his mouth away from Alex's prick, rasping: "I want to fuck you." He already had two fingers in Alex's butthole and he pushed them deeper into his moist chute, as if to drive home his point.

Alex moaned and squirmed beneath him, his ass-lips squeezing against Dane's fingers. A moment later, he said he'd get the lubricant and condoms. Reluctantly, they disengaged, and Dane reclining on the sofa, stroking his eager cock, watching Alex move quickly across the room, enjoying the sight of his muscles in motion as he walked. Seconds later, the young man returned, supplies in hand, his stiff dick bouncing enticingly as he walked.

Dane took the bottle of lube and two condom packets – "You're an optimist," he said – from Alex's hands, then stood up and ordered the other man on the floor, on all fours. He prepared Alex's ass for fucking quickly. "Shove your dick in me," the young man panted hotly, working his ass against Dane's hand. "Go ahead and fuck me."

It only took a minute for Dane to get his cock sheathed and honor Alex's demand. Steadily, he guided his rod into Alex's puckered sphincter, sinking his prick into the chute an inch at a time. Alex sucked in his breath, as if in pain, but then pushed back against the older man's cock, sighing contentedly when it was all the way inside him, the thin skin of Dane's scrotum sticking to his ass.

Dane pumped his dick into Alex in slow, rhythmic thrusts. Alex urged him to fuck harder, and Dane plowed the beautiful hunk's ass with greater force. Dane bent over Alex, his chest against his bottom's sweaty back, ramming him insistently, grunting foul dialog — "dirty slut," "cock whore," — as he speared Alex's quivering ass. Alex responded in moans, yelps and whimpers, his body quaking beneath Dane's.

When Alex could no longer endure his agonizing arousal, he reached for his cock. It was hot and weeping, and throbbed in his hand. It barely took five strokes before Alex was spewing his load onto the carpet. Dane quickly reached beneath him, cupping a hand over Alex's cock and catching the final spurts of spooge in his palm. He then brought that hand to Alex's face, the younger stud eating his own jism without any prompting. Dane came seconds later, emitting a roar as his balls released their steaming load.

Dane pulled out of Alex's ass, and deposited the filled rubber it on the coffee table. Alex had flopped his butt down on the floor, resting one arm across the sofa seat. His other hand rested in his crotch, his fingers scratching at his balls.

"You don't know how bad I needed that," Alex said dreamily. "That was so hot."

Dane stood, wiping his sticky hand on his thigh. He smiled down at Alex and said, "How about getting me that phone number now?"

SEVEN

It was nearly noon when Martin awoke Sunday. His neck was in knots, and his head felt stuffed with cotton. He groaned as he sat up, vocalizing his muscles' protest. Was he forty or seventy, he wondered, stiffly rising to his feet.

First stop: the bathroom. He peed and splashed cold water on his face. One glance in the mirror to confirm he looked as tired as he felt. Coffee needed to be in his immediate future. He stepped into a pair of gym shorts and headed downstairs.

It wasn't until Martin reached the bottom stair and looked into the living room that he remembered his houseguest.

Rand was lying on the sofa, still sleeping soundly. He pushed the sheet off partially, exposing his torso. The front drapes were drawn, making the living room as dark as a cave, but a few streams of light peeked through, illuminating the enticing contours of his body. The sight took Martin's mind below the sheet, to the memory of Rand stroking his cock, wiggling his ass, cheeks spread. The erotic recollections caused an awakening in Martin's shorts.

Martin looked away, feeling his face flush. Christ, I'm becoming a dirty old man, he thought as he headed into the kitchen. Were gay men just programmed to become chicken hawks the moment they turned forty?

As the coffee brewed, he tiptoed to the front door and opened it, wincing as the hinges creaked, fearing the noise would wake his guest. He picked up the Sunday edition of the *Atlanta Journal-Constitution* off the front step and retreated inside, the door creaking once again as it was closed.

On his way back to the kitchen, Martin glanced into the living room. Rand was still sleeping, though he'd rolled over since Martin last looked at him, his back to the room.

Martin poured himself a cup of coffee and moved to the breakfast nook, settling down at a dinette set for four to look over the paper while sipping his morning dose of caffeine. It was his Sunday routine, one he used to share with Ron. They'd have coffee, divvy up sections of the paper — Martin would take local news, editorials and the arts; Ron would look over the front section, sports and comics — and maybe break their respective diets with an elaborate breakfast of sausage, eggs and biscuits. Sometimes, they'd skip breakfast and take a shower together, soaping each other up, producing hard-ons as well as a thick lather. One of them would drop to his knees, take the other's cock into his mouth. Sometimes they'd settle for a hasty tryst there in the shower, other times they'd continue in the bedroom, barely wasting time to towel off before jumping onto the bed.

These memories didn't arouse any sexy feelings now, only sadness, and Martin fought them back quickly.

He scanned the front page of the paper disinterestedly. Additions to the body count in the "war on terror," a football player charged with rape, the president spouting vacuous optimism about the economy while Democrats begged to differ. The usual. Down the side of the page a headline read: "Atlanta candidate found dead in Miami motel." A subhead added: "Shooting possibly videotaped." The article said Perry Snopes, 52, was found dead Saturday morning in a room at the Tropic View Inn in Miami's South Beach. Cause of death: gunshot to the "upper body," no more detail than that. A police spokeswoman said a video camera was found, but no videotape. There was also no known motive yet, but the spokeswoman said robbery might be possible, given that the wallet was found and there was no cash in it. The credit cards, though, were left behind.

Martin had met Snopes recently, at Gay Bingo, a benefit for Pets Are Loving Support, the guy going around shaking hands. He extended a hand to Martin, and Martin said he lived in Decatur, out of his district. Snopes said it was good to meet him, anyway. Then a week later Snopes was in AdVerb's offices, meeting Conner for lunch. Conner introduced them and Martin said they met. Perry Snopes said it was good to see him again, giving a "fuck you" smile the whole time, adding, "If you'd been nicer to me, my campaign advertising might've been in your hands." Like Martin was going to lose sleep over not having to deal with an asshole.

The article mentioned Perry Snopes was in Miami attending some seminar and that he wasn't registered at the Tropic View Inn. Police were hunting for the guy who was. There was some background about Snopes, about how he was a successful businessman, owning Regency Antique Market, with two locations, one in Atlanta and one in Roswell, but how he was better known for his activism.

"Prior to declaring his candidacy for public office," the article read, "Snopes headed the citizens group Clean Sweep. The group's stated goal was to toughen zoning laws in an effort to restrict where adult businesses could operate. Clean Sweep was formed after The Tackle Box, a gay club, opened near Snopes' Regency Antique Market on Cheshire Bridge Road.

"John Klavern, manager of The Tackle Box, accused, Snopes of 'being more concerned about protecting his image with his wealthy clients than the interests of his own community.'"

There was more stuff about how Snopes was a divisive figure in the gay community, urging gays to "assimilate" into straight society, that the discrimination it received was partly its own fault. "When much of gay culture is mired in drugs and indiscriminate — and unsafe — sex," Snopes had said, "is it really any wonder that gays are shunned by straight society?" That comment was fodder for a month's worth of editorials in the local gay paper, the jist of most of them being that Snopes was betraying the gay community to gain straight votes.

The article ended with a brief mention of Snopes' lover traveling to Miami to meet with investigators there. Martin thought he recalled Snopes' husband being an actor, and had actually been in a few TV shows in the 1980s. The newspaper article didn't bring that up, though.

A publicity shot of Perry Snopes accompanied the story. Given the grim news, it seemed wholly inappropriate, the handsome politician smiling at the camera, his dark blond hair perfectly groomed, his white teeth gleaming beneath his mustache. To Martin, he looked more like a lead in a soap opera than a politician, and he certainly didn't look 52. He was pretty sure Snopes had had plastic surgery.

The phone rang. Martin snatched the cordless off the kitchen counter in the middle of the second ring. "Hello," he whispered.

"So what the fuck happened to you last night? Had to run off to church to pray for our sins?"

The inevitable phone call from Conner.

Martin wished he had a snappy comeback, but wit was too much to ask for after only half a cup of coffee. "Sorry 'bout that," he said. "That guy looked hot and all, but... I don't know. Just had to get out of there."

"Was that part of your midlife drama? Jesus, Marty, so you turned forty. Big fucking deal. Just buy a Corvette, fuck younger guys and lie about your age like everyone else. Goddamn, have some fun."

"Actually, it did turn into a pretty interesting evening."

"What? You got home in time to catch the last of the *Designing Women* marathon on Lifetime?"

"Last night was *The Golden Girls* marathon. And no, smart-ass, that wasn't what made the evening interesting. I actually met a guy in the parking lot."

There was stunned silence on the other end. Martin heard movement in the living room.

"No shit?"

"No shit," Martin confirmed. He heard bare feet plodding on hardwood. "Look, I'll tell you about it later."

"What? He's still there? He is, isn't he? Well, thank God!" Conner chortled. "You're gonna have to tell me all the details at the gym this afternoon."

Martin heard the bathroom door slam shut. "Uh, I don't know if I'll be able to make it this afternoon. I'll call you at three, let you know."

More knowing giggles. "Wanna get a little more use out of your trick before you send him on his way, huh? Don't blame you there."

"Yeah, something like that." Then, remembering the news story about Perry Snopes, he said, "Hey, did you see the paper this morning?"

"No, why?"

"Perry Snopes was murdered in Miami. Weren't you handling the advertising for his campaign?"

"I'll be damned," Conner whistled. "They know who did it?"

"Not yet, but according to the paper they found a camcorder in his motel room."

"God only knows what that prick was up to," Conner mused. Quickly, he added: "Don't get me wrong, I'm sorry he's dead, but the guy was a fuckin' asshole."

"Yeah, I know what you mean. Well, I'll talk to you later."

"Later."

Minutes after Martin hung up the phone, the toilet flushed and the bathroom door opened. Rand came padding into the kitchen, wearing only a pair of black boxer briefs.

"'Morning," Martin said, hoping his smile appeared friendly rather than lascivious. "Want some coffee?"

Rand nodded, still appearing only half awake. Martin poured him a cup and handed the steaming mug to his sexy houseguest. "There's the sugar if you want it," he said, pointing to a blue ceramic sugar bowl on the kitchen counter. "There's milk in the fridge if you take cream."

"Thanks," Rand said, the corner of his mouth tugging upward. He went for the sugar bowl. Martin's eyes fell to his ass and followed him.

"Uh, how 'bout some breakfast? I can make some scrambled eggs and, uh..." *Jesus, he's so fucking hot.* "...And I think I have some bacon. If not I could fix omelets. Omelets and..." Rand was at the refrigerator now. *Should've taken advantage of that ass when I had the chance.* "... and toast?"

"Don't have to go to any trouble," Rand said hoarsely, pouring milk into his coffee. "I'm not that hungry."

"It's no trouble at all. Really."

"Scrambled eggs and toast are fine, then."

Martin was grateful to devote his attention to a task, taking his mind off missing his opportunity with Rand. He also was eager to show off his cooking skills to his houseguest, as if he was a spinster eager to show off to a potential suitor what a good wife she'd make.

Not that Martin focused so intently on beating eggs that he wouldn't let his eyes drift over to Rand from time to time. The young man was now sitting at the kitchen table, in the chair Martin vacated, holding the front section of the paper up, his brow furrowed as he read.

"You know anything about this guy who was murdered?" he asked.

"Not a whole lot," Martin replied, pouring the eggs into a hot frying pan. "Couldn't vote for him — I'm in Decatur, not Atlanta — but if I wouldn't if I could. A friend of mine at the ad firm where I work was handling advertising for his campaign, told me horror stories about what a dick he was. I didn't like a lot of his views, either. Seemed to look down on the gay community as a whole."

"But he was gay."

"Yeah. Doesn't make sense, I know. He thought gays should act like straights. Hated drag queens, the circuit parties, Dykes on Bikes — always had something bitchy to say about the Pride celebration. Even thought it should be canceled, said it gave homophobes a cause instead of celebrating gay power."

Rand nodded and dropped the paper onto the table. "He's kind of cute, though, for an ol — for a politician."

"Nice save," Martin chuckled, turning off the stove.

A few minutes later Martin set a plate of scrambled eggs and two buttered slices of whole-wheat toast in front of Rand. Despite Rand's claims that he wasn't hungry, he dug into the meal immediately and with gusto.

Martin prepared a plate for himself and joined Rand at the table. "So, sleep well?"

Rand had a mouthful of food, but nodded an affirmative. After swallowing he asked, "Did you?" Giving the question the slightest twist of innuendo, his eyes glimmering.

"Um, yes," he replied quickly, turning away and pretending to be engrossed in spreading raspberry preserves on his toast. Martin could feel his face flush, and he wondered if Rand was going to make any more explicit references to last night. And what he'd do if he did.

But all Rand said was, "These are good," as he shoveled a forkful of eggs into his mouth.

"So, do you want to try getting in touch with your friends? You're welcome to use the phone."

Rand said, "Trying to get rid of me?" Winking after he said it.

"No, I — no. Just, last night you said you had a friend you needed to call. Said he'd help you out."

"Yeah," Rand bit into his toast and added, while chewing: "Maybe try him in an hour. He's not an early riser."

Martin nodded, then said, "But it's nearly one o'clock."

"This guy's not up before three, usually."

Martin nodded again, though he had suspicions about the existence of this friend. Or perhaps the person existed, but wasn't much of a friend at all — just some trick who'd just as soon not see Rand ever again. Would probably give Rand enough money to get him out of his life.

Maybe that's what I should do, Martin thought. Give him $50, take him to the nearest train station and wish him luck.

But not yet.

He put his fork down on his plate and stood up from the table. "Going upstairs to take a shower. Just put your plate in the sink when you're done," Martin instructed. "I'll load the dishwasher later."

Leaving his guest alone to finish his breakfast, Martin went upstairs. In his bedroom he stepped out of his gym shorts and laid them over the footboard of his bed. Moving to the master bathroom he started the water running and peeled off his briefs, stiff with dried cum from the night before. He tested the water, adjusted the temperature a bit more, pulled up the knob for the shower and stepped in beneath the spray.

The hot water pelting his flesh was at once invigorating and relaxing. Martin luxuriated beneath the shower for several minutes, letting the water pour over his head and stream down his naked body. The small bathroom was quickly transformed into a steam bath, the thick, sultry air easing Martin into a dreamy state.

He was rinsing shampoo out of his hair when the shower curtain was pulled aside. Martin felt hands slipping around his waist before he could spin around to face his guest.

"Thought I'd help conserve water and join you," Rand said in Martin's ear.

Martin could feel the head of Rand's cock brushing against his ass. The temperature of the shower seemed to shoot up ten degrees. His heart beat faster, pumping most of his blood to his dick. "Uh, you did, did you?" Martin replied with a nervous chuckle. *I sound like a goddamn idiot!*

Rand's fingertips were moving up and down Martin's abdomen, leaving a tingling sensation in their wake. "I did," he confirmed. His voice was soft, with a lilting, playful quality. "You're not going to push me away, are you?"

Martin said nothing. He was beginning to breathe heavily. His semi-hard cock became a full-fledged boner the moment Rand curled his hand around it.

"You feel interested," Rand teased, his hand gently stroking Martin's prick. "You looked interested last night. Thought you'd be on top of me the moment you saw me there, playing with my dick. But you just stood there. You only like to watch?"

"I... I wasn't sure... I haven't had..." Martin's throat felt tight. Now wasn't the time to go into his past bad experiences.

Rand was getting hard, too. Martin could feel the young man's cock pushing up against his ass crack. Feeling it there made his own pulse.

His houseguest took his hand off Martin's cock. With both hands on Martin's waist, Rand steered him around so they faced each other. A sexy half-smile played across Rand's lips, and his eyes brimmed with mischief. "You don't have any reason to be shy," he said.

He moved in, pressing his body against Martin's. His hands were resting on the shelf of Martin's ass. Martin reciprocated, enveloping the young man in his arms, holding Rand's smooth body against his own hirsute frame. His stiff cock pushed against Rand's pelvis.

Rand's lips touched the side of Martin's neck, moist and warm. When he spoke, his voice was a ghostly whisper "What do you want to do to me?"

It felt so good, holding Rand in his arms, Martin could only grunt a reply. *Christ, I'm acting like a 16-year-old virgin.*

Rand began his descent, kissing Martin's neck, nuzzling his face into the thatch of hair covering Martin's chest, biting a nipple, kissing his stomach. Martin closed his eyes, caressing the top of Rand's head, liking the feel of his short, damp hair. Liking the feel of all of him.

Once on his knees, face-level with Martin's dick, Rand purred, "So big." Whether he meant it or not, the compliment fired Martin's ego as well as his libido. Rand made a more profound compliment when he took Martin's dick into his mouth.

The breath pushed out of Martin's lips as if he'd just been slugged in the gut. The hot, wet depths of Rand's mouth closing around his cock certainly hit him with as much force as a right hook — but it felt much, much better.

Gasping, Martin thrust his cock deep into Rand's throat, and the young man swallowed it without hesitation. Rand sucked his dick in full, luxuriant gulps. He grabbed hold of Martin's scrotum, cuffing the furry sack and strangling his balls, heightening his pleasure.

Martin's ecstasy was rising a bit too fast, quickly crossing into the threshold of pre-orgasmic. If Rand kept doing what he was doing, he'd have a mouth full of cum in a couple minutes. Though the idea intrigued him — just imagining his load spilling out Rand's lips brought Martin dangerously close to making such a scene a reality — he did not want this to end so quickly.

"W-wait," he panted, gently pushing Rand away. "Let's continue this in the bedroom. My fingers are turning into prunes and I don't know how much longer the hot water will hold out."

Taking Rand's hand, he helped his young guest to his feet. His cock was hard as steel and vibrating visibly. An excited smile played on Rand's lips. Quickly, Martin turned off the water, and the two men hopped out of the bathtub. They shared a towel, drying off one another. Rand kissed the head of Martin's cock as he toweled off Martin's legs. It was something Martin's ex used to do when they took showers together, but he fought back the memory. This moment had nothing to do with Ron.

Still damp — they'd done little more than blot the excess moisture off their bodies — they nearly galloped toward the bed and flopped onto the mattress. Roughly, Martin took Rand into his arms and kissed him. It was a slow, probing, sensual kiss, and to Martin it felt almost as good as Rand sucking his cock. He hugged Rand tighter, as if trying to meld their bodies together, only easing his embrace when he feared he might be causing pain. Rand, however, made no complaint.

No longer reluctant to show his desire, Martin rolled over on top of Rand and feasted hungrily on his body. He felt Rand squirm and shudder beneath him as he bit his hard, pink nipples and traced the valleys between Rand's raised muscles with his tongue. His hands grabbed indiscriminately — kneading a pectoral, sliding down his arms, squeezing a thigh. In no time he was at Rand's cock, stiff and drooling before him. For a moment, he could only admire it, taking in details he didn't see the night before. He saw now how Rand's dick bowed slightly, curving toward his stomach. He saw how his cockhead leveled off, almost flat, on the tip. He revised his assessment of its length, sure Rand had a good eight inches. He closed a hand over Rand's prick and slowly moved his hands down the shaft, feeling the turgid network of veins that throbbed beneath the skin.

"Just suck it," Rand hissed impatiently, cupping a hand behind Martin's head and bringing him forward.

As eager as he was to have the full length of Rand's cock down his throat, Martin took his time, wanting to savor each delicious inch as it slid across his tongue. Rand moaned and stroked his fingers through Martin's hair, telling Martin it felt so good. Martin massaged the rigid shaft with his tongue and sucked the salty nectar from the cockhead. Though he wanted to take his time, his all-consuming lust quickened his pace, making him devour Rand's dick whole. It had been months since Martin had sucked a cock. Even the hustler of a few weeks ago he'd only fucked, and that had seemed more out of anger than real desire. Nothing like this, when he wanted to please another man more than please himself and, in turn, increasing his own arousal as he succeeded.

And he was succeeding with Rand, who twitched and shook, moaned and grunted, as Martin woofed down his cock and fondled his nuts. He brought his mouth to Rand's smooth ball sack, suckling the soft skin and prodding the weighty spheres beneath. He pressed his face into Rand's crotch, inhaling the rich smells of clean skin and ripe sex. His mouth traveled beneath the balls, licking the sensitive area where the scrotum met the groin. Rand cried out, and his joyous cries urged Martin to go further.

Martin pulled Rand's legs upward, so he could get at his asshole. This, too, Martin paused to admire. The tightly drawn, pinkish-tan ass-lips had tiny grooves radiating out from a central point, looking like an obscene flower at the bottom of a valley of flesh. He brought his face to it, placing teasing kisses around the puckered sphincter, the coarse hairs of his goatee tickling the sensitive skin, his breath making it hot.

Once Martin's tongue connected with Rand's hole, the young man cried out. "Oh, fuck, goddamn, YES!" He trembled as Martin's tongue slithered inside his butthole and tickled the inside of his chute. "Oh, shit, yeah, eat my ass!" Rand moaned, clutching at the bed sheets, as if trying to keep himself from sinking entirely into Martin's ravenous maw.

Savagely, he pushed his tongue into Rand's hole, feeling the shaved ass lips fight his entry. He nipped the throbbing sphincter with his teeth, then soothed it with the warm lashings of his tongue. And then he speared Rand's asshole again, eliciting louder cries.

He pulled his face away and slipped two fingers between Rand's buttcheeks, rubbing his spit around the engorged hole.

"I want to fuck you so bad," Martin panted, applying added pressure to Rand's asshole.

Rand pushed against Martin's fingers in reply.

Martin sat up on his knees. His cock ached, and a clear string of pre-cum hung from the head of his dick. "Turn over," he said.

As Rand got into position, Martin climbed off the bed and went to his nightstand. From the top drawer, he pulled out a bottle of lube and a condom.

"Get on your hands and knees," Martin said as he drizzled lube on his fingers.

Once Rand did as he was told, Martin sat on the side of the bed and brought his lubricated fingers to his ass, now splayed in front of him. His fingers slid down the crack, lightly greasing the channel before stopping at the rosebud. He circled the orifice gingerly with his index finger, making it pucker outward, kissing his fingertip. Martin worked the finger inside Rand's hole. He kept it there, buried deep inside the damp tunnel, feeling Rand shudder inside and out. Martin added his middle finger, moving the two fingers in a circular motion inside Rand's ass, coaxing his butthole to open wide.

"I wanna sit on your cock," Rand sputtered, his body twisting against Martin's fingers. "Fuck me now."

Martin withdrew his fingers and the men changed positions, Rand turning over onto his side as Martin stretched out on his back. Picking up the bottle of lubricant and a condom packet from the nightstand, he handed them to Rand, telling him to do the honors. Lying back against the pillows, Martin let the young man get to work.

Rand lay the lube and rubber on the bed, and then took Martin's cock in his hand. In seconds he was hunched over Martin's crotch, licking the pre-cum off his prick and lubricating it with his own saliva. Martin was just about to push him away, about to say he'd cum before he could fuck him if Rand kept that up, when Rand sat upright, an impish grin on his cute face.

Next came the lube, squirted on the length of Martin's cock like mustard on a hotdog, and then smeared around so his dick was coated. Again, Martin had to fight back the rising tides of pleasure as Rand's hand caressed his prick.

The rubber was rolled on quickly.

Rand straddled his hips, slowly easing himself down on Martin's pole. There was a moment's resistance as Rand's ass ring fought the invasion of Martin's cock, then the cockhead popped inside. Rand gasped and smiled simultaneously.

Martin's gaze alternated from Rand's blissful expression, to his bouncing cock, to his own dick, barely visible beneath Rand's balls, being swallowed by Rand's ass until it disappeared. For a moment they were still, Rand acclimating himself to the thick rod embedded in his butt, Martin appreciating the warmth and tightness pressing against his shaft.

Then Rand began to gently rock his hips and squeeze his ass muscles against Martin's cock. Holding onto Rand's hips, Martin thrust upward. His movements were measured, controlled. For once, he was grateful to be wearing a condom. If he hadn't, he'd definitely be cumming by now.

Gradually, their movements became faster and harder until they were truly fucking. Rand leaned over him, his ass bouncing against Martin's upward ramming. Martin almost wished the opposite wall were mirrored so he could admire the beauty of Rand's butt while watching his dick slide into it. He was just as entranced by what he saw now: this gorgeous young man riding him, a dreamy expression on his face as his pretty lips burbled coarse phrases like "Fuck me harder" and "Your dick feels so good in my ass."

The only thing Martin said was, "Oh, God, I'm gonna shoot!"

His orgasm exploded throughout his whole body, paralyzing his muscles, draining his balls and his energy. For a second, Martin lost all connection with his waking life, feeling more like a spirit than a man.

It was Rand who brought him back to earth. He was grinding his ass against Martin's cock. Rand's movements against the hyper-sensitive organ made Martin squirm and buck beneath him.

"Yeah, man," Rand panted, his fist hammering up and down his own dick. "I'm gettin' close. So close..."

He arched his back, his body jerking atop Martin's as he fired his pearl-white load onto Martin's chest and abdomen. Martin made admiring noises as he looked at the gooey puddles frosting his torso, then looked up at Rand, the corners of his mouth tugging upward.

Rand rubbed his fingers through one of the glistening pools of semen. Next thing Martin knew, those fingers were between his lips. "Taste me," Rand ordered. It was not a command he was inclined to disobey, and he sucked the fingers clean.

The taste of Rand's fingers was followed by the taste of his lips as the young man leaned forward to kiss him. Martin held Rand's face in his hands, holding him in place lest he pull his lips away too soon. His hands then moved down the smooth slope of Rand's back as the weight of the young man's body fell against his chest.

Martin never made it to the gym that afternoon.

EIGHT

This was the deal Task negotiated: twenty-five bucks for sex — "Whatever you want" — plus letting him keep the motel room overnight.

The trick agreed, but he chose the motel, someplace that was okay with cash payment. "Wouldn't want to open my credit card statement and find you'd been living in the room a month," the trick said with a goofy laugh. Not any danger of Task doing that at the Gateway Inn. The room was decorated with torn, stained wallpaper and a greasy, whorehouse red carpet covered with enough cigarette burns to form a pattern. It smelled vaguely of a men's room at a porno theater. He wouldn't stay in this shithole for more than twelve hours, and for Task, who'd lived in his share of slum apartments, that was saying something.

"Want another beer?" the john asked, holding up the six-pack of Michelob Lite he bought at a convenience store on the way over to the motel. It was already minus two bottles.

"Uh, okay," Task said, his eyes on room's sagging king-size bed. He felt bloated from the two beers he killed on the way over to the motel. Getting the guy off and out of his life was a greater priority than drinking, but it wasn't like Task to turn down free alcohol.

"Here ya' go," the trick said cheerfully, twisting the cap off the bottle and handing it to him. The trick's name was Kirby. "You know, like the vacuum cleaner," he said, chuckling like it was a joke. Task said he'd never heard of a vacuum cleaner named Kirby, and the trick stopped chuckling.

Task met Kirby at a rest area in Alabama. Hitching his way out of Miami was slow going. A group of giggling Latinas in a tiny Mazda picked him up first, but only took him as far as Boca Raton. After that, a middle-aged couple in a pickup stopped for him, making him ride in back until they got to Orlando, where Task spent the night in the woods bordering the interstate, smoking his last joint, so he could sleep. The next morning he hitched a ride on a tractor-trailer driven by a stern looking man with a beer gut and wearing a dirty NAPA cap. As they traveled up through the Florida panhandle, the trucker went on about how George W. Bush was the best thing to ever happen to America while treating Task to the works of Tanya Tucker. Stopping at the rest area outside Mobile, the trucker demanded Task give him head. Afterwards, he pushed Task out of his truck. "Get outta my sight, faggot."

At the rest stop's snack machines, Task got himself a meal of Coca-Cola and Doritos, then splurged and got a pack of Zingers for dessert. It was just after nine, and he had no place to sleep.

In the men's room Task took off his T-shirt and washed up at the sinks as best he could. Some of the men in the restroom looked at him admiringly, but most ignored him. One man, guiding his 4-year-old son out of one of the toilet stalls, steered him away from the sinks where Task was bathing. "But Mom says your s'posed to wash y'hands," the boy whined. "You can wash them in the drinking fountain outside," his father said, glaring at Task.

Stuffing his T-shirt in the back pocket of his jeans and slinging his black duffle bag over his bare shoulder, Task left the men's room, the heavy, humid afternoon heat covering him like syrup. He headed toward the rear parking area, where the trucks were. Maybe one of the drivers would give him a ride.

A rent-a-cop stepped in his path. "'Scuse me, young man, are you lost?"

The security guard was a foot shorter than Task and at least forty years older. He had the face of a bulldog and liver spots shone through the wisps of white hair slicked back over his flat skull.

"No, I know my way 'round." Task tried to step past him, but the security guard blocked him. Pretty agile for an old dude, Task thought.

"We don't allow no loit'ring here," the guard barked. "'Specially your kind."

"My kind?" He was about to challenge the old fart, press him for what exactly "kind" he thought Task was, not really caring that tangling with the law — even with a rest stop rent-a-cop — was not in his best interest.

But then a hand circled Task's bicep. "Jimmy, Mama's worried sick about you."

Task turned to the man who grasped his arm, a guy in his mid-forties, wearing a magenta-striped golf shirt and a wedding band. "Huh? My name's not..."

"Don't worry officer, he's with me."

"Oh," Task said dumbly.

And that was how he met Kirby. He had silver-streaked hair, a narrow face, and a trim body — all right looking, Task judged as he was led to Kirby's minivan. Not as good looking as the guy from the other night, but he quickly dismissed that memory. For a place to crash and a few bucks, Kirby would do.

Now in their room at the Gateway Inn, Task took a pull of his third beer and asked: "So, whatta you want me to do?"

Kirby sat down on the bed, looking prim with his knees pressed together and his hands clasped in his lap. "Aren't you the romantic," he trilled, like they were on their honeymoon.

"Want me to start by blowing you? I give pretty good head."

"Hmmm, how about you just get comfortable. Get out of those pants."

Task shrugged and said okay. He set his beer down on a nightstand that looked like it had been salvaged from the curb, kicked off his shoes and stepped out of his jeans. He let the john get a look at him in his briefs, then turned around. He removed his underwear slowly, exposing a little bit of his ass at a time, just to tease the guy. When Task dropped his drawers to his feet he bent over. Kirby didn't say anything, but his breathing became loud enough to be heard over the room's clanking air conditioner.

He turned around. "You want to play with it, get it hard?" Task asked, fondling his limp cock.

Kirby flashed him a tight smile. "Not yet. You going to finish your beer?"

What was with this guy and drinking beer? "Thought we could move on to other things," Task suggested.

"No hurry. Just drink up."

Task shrugged and picked up his bottle. Kirby may not have been in a hurry, but he was. Remaining standing, he chugged the beer. "Done," he said, belching loudly.

"Have another," Kirby said, twisting the cap off another bottle.

"Dude, I'm starting to feel like I just ate a loaf of bread. How 'bout we get just get started already?"

"C'mon, just one more beer," the john encouraged, pressing the sweaty bottle into Task's hand.

"Whatever." Task took the warming beer and sat down in an armchair upholstered in vinyl the color of split-pea soup.

As Task pulled on his beer Kirby got undressed. Though his frame was thin it was covered with firm, sinewy muscle. He was also very pale. "So, you live here — in Alabama, I mean?" Task asked.

"Yes," he replied, removing his glasses. "Why?"

Must not go out in the sun. "Just wonderin', is all."

Kirby pulled off his plaid boxers. His cock was soft, but working its way into a semi. Length was about average, though it was pretty thick. Kirby's balls hung low, their weight stretching his scrotum.

Task set his beer bottle on the floor and stood up. "Gotta go pee, but after that I'll see 'bout taking care of you."

"Do you have to go bad?" Kirby asked expectantly.

"Uh, I just gotta go."

"Wait. Hold it for awhile. Start taking care of me now."

"Dude, it'll just take a second..."

"I said now."

He was taken aback by the firmness of Kirby's tone. "Uh, okay. I'll wait, then."

Kirby sat back down on the bed. He spread his legs and Task knelt between them. The trick hooked a hand around Task's head and pulled him forward, into his crotch. Using his tongue, Task maneuvered Kirby's cock into his mouth. "Oh, yes," Kirby breathed as Task's tongue circled around his rod. "Make me hard."

Task felt the older man's dick grow inside his mouth. He pulled his mouth away to take a breath, stroking Kirby's hard-on appreciatively. "So big," he sighed, looking up at the john. You always told tricks they had the biggest cocks you ever saw even if they had dicks the size of Vienna sausages, but Kirby did have a fairly impressive boner.

"Keep sucking it," he whispered, pushing Task's head back into his lap.

Task sucked and licked Kirby's prick, then tongued his balls. His own dick had swollen little, and he reached down to play with it. But an urge other than sex dominated his thoughts.

"Look, I really have to take that leak now," he said, wiping his own spit off his face with the back of his hand.

"Real bad?" Kirby almost panted.

"Like I'll piss all over the goddamn floor if I don't go this minute."

Kirby pushed himself off the bed. "Then let's go."

Let's?

The trick followed him to the bathroom. Task was positioning himself before the rust-stained toilet, but Kirby pushed him away. "No! Not there!"

Task spun around to confront Kirby. "Where the fuck else?"

The john was stepping into the scarred bathtub. "On me," he said breathlessly.

Shit, if I knew this was what he was into I would've upped my price, Task thought. Least he doesn't want to piss on *me*.

Kirby lay down in the tub. He spit in his palm and started stroking his dick. "Go ahead," he commanded.

Task took hold of his cock. "So where you want me to hit? Your chest? Your dick?"

"All over me."

"Like, even your face?"

Kirby closed his eyes and nodded.

Task leaned forward, pressing one hand against the grimy, vinyl-covered wall on the far side of the tub for support. His other hand held his prick, aiming it at Kirby's chest. Though the urge to pee was great, the urine didn't flow.

Kirby got impatient. "Hurry!"

"I'm tryin'! Just a bit pee-shy, is all."

"Great," the trick sniped.

Task closed his eyes and concentrated. Then, "Here it comes."

A pale yellow stream splattered Kirby's chest. "Oh, yes," he sighed, pulling on his stiff dick excitedly. Task directed the flow toward Kirby's crotch, showering his hard-on with piss. That got an ecstatic moan out of Kirby. When Task aimed the stream at Kirby's face, the john was near orgasmic.

"Yes! Oh, God, yes!" Kirby sputtered, moving his head beneath the yellow rain. Task wished he'd close his mouth, but Kirby wanted to taste his piss as well as feel it. As the stream of urine hit his outstretched tongue, Kirby began to shudder. Sputtering exclamations of pleasure, the trick shot his load as the last drops of piss drained from Task's cock.

"Ooooh, that was so good," he sighed contentedly, rubbing his hand over his abdomen, mixing his spooge with the urine covering his body.

The musical tones of Task's cell phone sounded from the next room. "Better get that," he said, backing out of the bathroom. It might be Rand, returning one of the eight messages he'd left throughout the past two days.

Kirby sat up in the tub. "What!? You've got to be kidding?"

But Task was already out of the bathroom, pulling his cell phone from the pocket of his jeans, piled on the floor. The caller I.D. read "Unknown Caller." He picked up by the fourth ring. "'Lo."

"Is this Task?" It was a man's voice.

"Yeah. It's my phone, who else would it be?"

The man chuckled coldly. "I heard you were a quick one. Tell me, Task, is our friend Rand there with you?"

Task felt his chest constrict. "Rand? No, haven't seen him since Friday night. Who's this?"

The man ignored Task's question. "Where is he?"

"Dunno," he answered truthfully. In the bathroom he heard water running. "Was gone when I woke up Saturday. Been trying to call him for almost two days now. Who's this again?"

"I'm Dane, the guy Rand was working for. Maybe he mentioned me?"

As Task searched his memory for the name Dane, the bathroom pipes groaned their protest as Kirby switched on the shower. Thank God he's taking a real shower, Task thought.

"Hello, still there?" Dane prompted, impatient.

"Oh, sorry. Now I remember. You're that porno dude, right?"

Another chuckle. "Yes, the 'porno dude.' Don't believe we've met."

"No, we haven't. Say, since Rand skipped out could you just pay me the whole amount? I mean, me and him were gonna split what you paid him, but he took off, so it's only fair."

The shower stopped, and Task heard Kirby pull back the curtain. Dane said, "If you did what you were hired to do, you'll get paid. So, did you do it?"

"Yeah."

Kirby had stepped into the room now, barely dried off from his shower. His expression was dour.

"Did he suspect anything?"

"Who?"

"Goddammit, you know who!"

"Don't have to yell. Jesus!" Task shot back. "He almost found out, but we handled it."

Dane didn't try to mask his panic. "What! Whatta you mean? Handled it how?"

Kirby was rushing around the room, getting dressed, and Task didn't want him to overhear. So he whispered into the phone: "He's ead-ay."

"Eddie? Who's Eddie? What the fuck you talking about?" Dane sounded frantic.

Task tried again, louder. "No, ead-ay." He looked at Kirby to see if he was listening, but the trick was sitting on the bed, putting on his shoes, intent on ignoring Task.

"Jesus fucking Christ, I don't understand what the fuck you're talking about! Who's this Eddie?"

"You ever hear of Pig Latin?" Task dropped his voice to a whisper. "He's dead."

There was silence on the other end. "Did you say 'dead'?"

Task nodded, then remembered he was on the phone. "Yeah."

"And how did that happen?"

Kirby was heading for the door. "Look, can't really go into right now. Can I call you back?"

"Call me back? Look, you fuckin' shithead, I'm not gettin' off the phone until you tell me what happened!"

Kirby was opening the door. Task called to him, "Hey! Wait!" Into the phone he told Dane, "Just give me ten minutes," and hung up. Dropping the cell phone on the bed, he chased after Kirby.

Outside Kirby was getting into his minivan. "Hey! Wait up! You still owe me money!" Task shouted.

Kirby slammed the van door shut and started the engine. Task ran toward the van, but the john was faster, jerking the vehicle into reverse, whipping it out of its parking spot in front of the motel room.

"Hey, fucker! What about my twenty-five bucks!" Task screamed as Kirby sped out of the parking lot.

He'd forgotten he was naked until he noticed several of the motel's other patrons had come to their doors and windows to witness the drama that erupted outside.

Task pointed toward the parking lot's exit, as if Kirby's van was still there. "Dickhead owes me money!" he told his audience, before storming back into his motel room and slamming the door.

NINE

"How long were you and Per … Mr. Snopes … together?"

The reporter with the Atlanta gay newspaper, *Southern Voice*, had gotten Winston LaGrabe's cell phone number. Probably got it from the arts editor, who'd interviewed Winston earlier in the year when he directed and starred in a local stage production of *The Sum of Us*. The play opened to tepid reviews and worse attendance, closing after two weeks.

Not that Winston minded the intrusion. The Miami papers weren't too interested in talking with him, beyond getting a couple quotes, referring to him simply as "the victim's lover," and the Atlanta press hadn't been putting forth much effort to get in touch with him. He waited a beat before answering the *Southern Voice* reporter's question. "Nearly, let's see… we met in 1994, about two years after I moved back to Atlanta, after my last acting job in L.A…"

Couldn't let the papers forget the TV career, though he was careful not to mention why he abandoned television for his home state of Georgia. A videotape from a party he attended in San Francisco surfaced, the tape showing a naked and very high Winston LaGrabe getting gang-banged by eight men. This was before Pamela Anderson made sex tapes fashionable, and even in today's Hollywood a gay sex tape could end a career. Although the video never got into the public's hands, it did get into the hands of the producer of Winston's upcoming series, *Uncovered*, in which he was to play one of the members of a male modeling/private detective agency. "Don't worry," the producer had told a white-faced Winston. "We've bought up all the known copies. Consider it our farewell present to you."

"Nearly eight years," Winston said definitively. He thought he heard the reporter say "wow" under his breath. Winston himself couldn't believe he'd put up with Perry's shit for that long.

The reporter, a young man who seemed to cringe each time he spoke, asked: "Do you plan to, uh, run in your partner's place. Run for city council, I mean," adding it as if Winston didn't know.

"Oh, no, certainly not," Winston said, almost laughing at the idea. He got up from the bed he was sitting on and walked over to the sliding glass door at the far end of his hotel room. The door opened up to a small balcony overlooking South Beach, but Winston remained inside. "Perry was the politician. I'm just an actor." He almost added that the two were one of the same anymore, but didn't.

"Uh, forgive me for asking this, but, um, well…" the reporter faltered. "This is tough, but my editor wanted me to ask: any speculation why your partner was in that motel room."

Winston was grateful it was a phone interview, giving him the luxury of smirking openly. *Why do you think*, he wanted to say. He spoke into the phone in a measured tone. "The police have their theories, of course. I... I don't... want to believe them, but the facts point to..." Winston sniffled a little for the reporter's benefit before continuing. "Well, I knew Perry wasn't a perfect man, and while the reasons for his being in that room hurt, it's nothing compared to the pain of his senseless" — a choked sob — "murder."

When asked if he had "anything else" he wanted to share about his slain lover, Winston was ready. "Perry is...was... one of the most caring, courageous men I had the privilege of knowing. Certainly more courageous than I. As you know, many actors only feel free when hiding behind a character. But Perry wasn't afraid to be himself, no matter what others thought. I know his views weren't always popular, yet I hope people will admire his courage in voicing them as much as I do. I only hope I have half as much strength to go ...to go on...without him."

The interview ended with Winston weeping and the reporter alternately expressing sympathies and apologizing for bothering him. Winston thanked him for his condolences, assuring the reporter he'd be fine.

Getting off the phone, he went into the bathroom to get a few tissues. Real tears for a telephone interview, Winston noted as he dabbed the moisture from his eyes. And *TV Guide* wrote he had the emotional range of a tree stump!

What to do next, he wondered as he stepped out of the bathroom. According to the digital clock on the night table it was just after eleven, and he was still in his bathrobe. The autopsy would be performed this afternoon, the detectives said, though who knew when he'd learn about the medical examiner's findings. The press will know before I will, Winston thought cynically. Perry's mother and his younger sister — hateful bitches, both — would certainly be notified before anyone thought of calling Perry's male lover.

He looked out the glass door at the Miami skyline, at monolithic high-rises reaching up into the bright, cloudless sky, and let out an exasperated sigh. This had to happen in Miami. The beaches, the nightclubs, even the hotel's swimming pool were all off limits to him. Wouldn't be appropriate for the grieving husband to be caught having fun.

Winston decided he'd go to the hotel gym. Just because I'm grieving is no reason to let my body go to hell, he reasoned, untying the sash to his white terrycloth bathrobe and letting it slide off his broad shoulders and onto the floor.

He dressed for his workout quickly, stuffing his cock and balls into a jock, then stepping into a pair of blue shorts. Next, he slipped on a yellow tank that barely covered his quarter-sized nipples. After lacing up his shoes, Winston shoved his shaving kit and a change of clothes into a small gym bag and left the room.

A few heads, male and female, turned as he stepped off the elevator on the ground floor. Winston doubted any of them recognized him — few people did, anymore — but appreciated the attention, smiling and nodding hello at a particularly cute Latino bellboy as he headed for the hotel's gym.

In the 1980s Winston LaGrabe was a familiar face, if not a familiar name, on television. He appeared in ads, hawking anything from toothpaste to laxatives. Bit parts in daytime soap operas, second-rate sitcoms and fourth-rate movies followed. A supporting role in the prime time soap *Vale's Canyon* nudged Winston into the limelight's outermost edges. The series was summarily panned, and his talent questioned, but the episode in which Winston climbed out of a pool wearing a bikini swimsuit garnered the show's highest ratings. As *Vale's Canyon* limped through its thirteen episodes on the air, Winston basked in the glory of being "The Hottest Star in TV's Least-Watched Show," as *People* magazine declared in 1986. Posters of Winston posing shirtless were big sellers. After the show's cancellation, he was cast in the second lead of a police drama, *Iron Justice*, which lasted six episodes. His biggest success, the syndicated sci-fi series *Mission Omega*, had a year-and-a-half run.

After his firing from *Uncovered*, Winston's TV career was essentially over. His last appearance on camera was in a supporting role in a straight-to-video "erotic thriller," *Deadly Passions*, its release in 1991 barely noticed. He returned to Atlanta in 1992, where he grew up as Lonnie Winston Graber. Instead of coming back the Hollywood success story, he was broke, depressed and addicted to cocaine. Even more distressing to Winston, he was losing his hair.

Winston LaGrabe may have slipped to the Z-list in Hollywood, but he was much sought after by Atlanta's A-list gays. Whether it was a semi-formal dinner party in Buckhead or sleazy, drug-fueled orgy in the bowels of Midtown, Winston could count on being the host's star attraction. With no public image to protect, he staggered out of the closet and dropped to his knees in front of the nearest cock. Coming out got him noticed by the media, briefly — a cover story in the *Advocate* and one-page articles in *Us* and *People* magazines. Winston told reporters he was writing his autobiography, which sounded much better than the truth: that he was living with Shelby Troupe, the owner of a popular Midtown health club, earning his keep as the club's "marketing representative" — meaning he posed for the ads — and by being generous with his sexual favors. As for his biography, he'd managed to scribble down eight pages before deciding writing was too much like work and quit.

Jonathan Asche

It was at Regency Antique Market on Cheshire Bridge that Winston met Perry. Winston was sent there by Shelby (he'd become Shelby's go-fer as well) on a quest for a set of sconces to go on either side of the living room fireplace. Perry projected a strength and self-assurance Winston always found appealing, especially at that particular point in his life, when he felt weak and insecure. Plus, Perry Snopes was hot, and not just for a man of his age. No, Perry was just plain sexy, a face that was leading-man handsome and a body that was made for nude scenes. The moment Perry asked if he could help, Winston knew he wouldn't be with Shelby much longer.

Seems like centuries ago, Winston ruminated as he entered the hotel's small gym. He strode back to the locker room, tossed his gym bag in a locker and headed back into the gym, nearly empty except for one wizened old man on a Stairmaster. Winston did a few stretches first before climbing onto a bench to work on his arms.

While his body did preacher curls, his mind slipped back to the past, when he had left Shelby for Perry. When he was in love — or thought he was. Past experience had made Winston suspicious of the emotion, especially while in Hollywood, where "I love you" was just another line people tried to say with feeling. Yet with Perry, the emotion seemed real. He wasn't like other men he'd encountered. Perry didn't concern himself with the gay scene and, in fact, held it in contempt. "Bunch of drug-addicted fairies," he'd sneer while flipping through the pages of *Etc.*, a local gay rag. "Think life's only about getting high and getting fucked." Winston would look away, guiltily.

But Perry seemed just as taken with his ex-actor and now-recovering party slut boyfriend, romancing Winston as if he were truly a prized catch. They'd go to plays and movies, dinners at expensive restaurants, weekends in Charleston, Asheville or Savannah. Of course, the sex was hot and frequent. Though rigid in his views on how gay men should conduct themselves publicly, Perry was no prude in the bedroom. Even now, the memory of his late partner's marathon rim jobs or forceful fucking caused Winston's cock to twitch.

Another man entered the gym, a creamy-skinned African-American — there was some European blood in there, too, judging by his angular facial features — who couldn't be any older than 30. Nice, cut body, stuffed into a pair of shiny red Spandex shorts. Winston let his eyes slide down to the man's crotch. Well-built there, too, he noted. The man nodded at Winston, giving him a partial smile before climbing into one of the two weight machines. Now Winston's dick was getting hard.

There were darker memories to quell Winston's arousal, memories his mind moved to as Winston moved on to doing leg presses. As he pushed against the weights with his legs, he thought of how Perry insisted Winston help out at one of his antiques shops. The

74

experience soon proved frustrating for Winston, who couldn't tell a sixteenth century French side table from a nineteenth century English dining table. Working in retail was like waiting tables, only without the tips. And while he was an exhilarating lover, Perry was a bitch to work with, frequently criticizing Winston's manners, grammar and overall ability, often in front of customers. Two weeks of working at Regency Antique Market left Winston questioning their relationship.

But he stayed with Perry. He had nowhere else to go.

In 1996, he returned to acting, in a local stage production of *Love! Valor! Compassion!* It was his first time performing in theater since high school, and he, like other members of the cast, would have to do a few scenes nude. Although reviews declared Winston the weakest actor of the cast (the term "wooden" was the most common adjective used to describe his performance), his body drew high praise, with one critic even noting that Winston had one of the nicest asses she'd ever seen. The show was a big success.

Perry, however, was furious. He didn't have a high regard for acting in general, but that his lover would parade naked in front of an audience was unconscionable. What would his clients think? He demanded Winston leave the show. Winston refused, wavering when Perry made an ultimatum: the play or us. Frightened of being left alone, Winston chose, resentfully, Perry.

Their relationship continued, though on much chillier terms. Sex was less and less frequent, and Winston, who'd remained faithful since he and Perry became a couple, became less resolute in his fidelity. In early 1997, while performing in a small production of a nearly unwatchable play by a local playwright, Winston became involved with one of his fellow actors, a young man named Christopher Fiedler. Christopher had been in love with Winston long before they ever met, confessing that when he was 14 years old he'd shoplifted a poster of Winston and masturbated to it frequently. "I even came on your chest," Christopher giggled, giddy that he now had the privilege of cumming on his fantasy man's *real* chest — and face, and dick, and ass, or any other place on Winston's body he cared to — for real. Perry seemed oblivious to his lover's cheating, never commenting on how often Winston was at rehearsals that lasted until two or three o'clock in the morning. He did, however, mention that Winston seemed to be in much brighter spirits.

When the play ended, so did the affair. Winston thought he'd gotten away with it, stealing a few months worth of happiness. Even his relationship with Perry seemed to improve, his partner becoming more attentive, his lust for Winston rekindled and raging hot.

Then Winston returned home from shopping one day...

His legs pushed against the weights with greater force, the same force he used to push away the ugly memories. The sweat dripping down his face camouflaged his tears. His reddened face and quivering lips could easily be mistaken for exertion, not crying. The intensity of his workout would appear to be a dedication to fitness, not rage.

But appearances didn't really matter. By the time Winston ended his workout, he realized he was alone in the gym.

Spent, he headed for the locker room, where he encountered the beautiful black man he'd seen earlier in the gym. His back was turned while he rummaged around in his locker. The Spandex shorts were off. Winston's eyes dropped below the dark stranger's waist, taking in the magnificence of the hard, muscled buttocks. The man turned around, and Winston looked away quickly, though not before getting an eyeful.

He risked a glimpse at the man's face. "Howzit goin'?" Winston said, hoping he sounded casual. The black man responded with a tilt of his head and a smile that let Winston know the admiration was mutual. The man then headed for the showers, tugging at the head of his thick cock as he strolled past.

Winston quickly stripped off his sweaty clothes. Excitement caused his heart to quicken and goose bumps to rise on his skin. His cock pulsed and stretched.

Too soon, he told himself as he walked to the showers. Perry's not even in the ground yet!

It was a communal shower, a white-tiled room with a concrete floor, from the center of which sprung a thick stainless steel post with four nozzles extending from the top like blades on a fan. The black man stood there, his eyes closed, face upturned into the spray of hot water. He was seemingly indifferent to Winston's arrival, but one look at the man's semi-erect prick told him he'd been expected.

Winston took the shower across from the muscular stranger, turning on the water and adjusting the temperature, never taking his eyes off the man. He stepped beneath the warm, needle-fine spray, turning beneath it to rinse the sweat from his body, feeling the man's admiring stare. Winston faced him, and their eyes met as Winston lathered up his hairy chest. A hint of a smile played across the man's full lips. Winston's face remained impassive, though his stare was intense. His dick stiffened.

Winston chastised himself: *I can't believe I'm even considering a locker room tryst.* Yet seeing the coffee-skinned man soaping himself up made it difficult for Winston to fortify his already weak resolve. He stared openly as the man across from him turned around, bent over and slid a soapy hand between his parted legs, lathering up his fur-ringed asshole.

Winston's cock was like granite now, throbbing and pumping out pre-cum. It wouldn't be right, he lamely reminded himself, running his tongue across his lips as he watched rivulets of soapy water wash over the curve of the man's ass and down his sturdy thighs.

Then, the memory he'd fought back surfaced in his mind: Returning home, finding Perry in the living room, fucking another man. Not just any man, but Christopher Fiedler. Didn't even bother to stop what they were doing when Winston caught them. "Your ass feels soooo good," Perry groaned, slamming his dick into Christopher's petite, upturned butt, his eyes concentrating on Winton's shocked face. A malicious smile was on his face. "What's wrong, baby?" he taunted. "We're a couple. We share everything, don't we?"

The voice of the stranger brought Winston back to the present.

"Excuse me?"

"Going to the steam room," the man repeated, his voice having the same chocolaty-creaminess of his skin. He'd turned his shower off and was now standing inches away, close enough that the heads of their erect dicks nearly touched.

Winston nodded. The man left the showers. Winston rinsed quickly and then followed.

The steam room was not much bigger than a walk-in closet. Steam was filling the room when Winston entered, the African-American stud in the corner, sitting on a tiled L-shaped bench, legs spread, hard cock beckoning. Winston walked up to him, and they admired each other's bodies for a few more fleeting moments, before they became enveloped in hot, white clouds. The black man reached forward, gripped Winston's quivering rod.

"You're very hot," he whispered.

Winston smiled confidently. Over the years he'd endured all sorts of savage criticism about his limited acting skill — the most biting comments coming from his late lover — but his physical appearance consistently won him rave reviews. Even going bald didn't seem to diminish his appeal; buzzing the hair he had down to a Velcro-like stubble gave him a butch edge, enabling him to wear age 42 a lot more comfortably. A TV pretty boy transformed into an action star, he thought.

"You're very nice, too," Winston sighed, his body trembling as this man stroked his dick. He started to ask the stranger's name, but then the man took Winston's cock into his mouth, and the question evaporated.

The man's tongue was insistent, swirling around Winston's cockhead and prodding the swollen shaft. Winston circled his hands around the man's skull, liking the feel of the tight curls covering his head. The stranger's hands sought out Winston's ass, squeezing the solid globes in his smooth hands. His fingers crawled into Winston's ass crack and pressed against his puckered butthole.

Winston sank to his knees, leaning forward to kiss the man, their lips meeting and tongues entwining briefly before Winston's mouth was urged lower down. He paused to circle his tongue around one of the man's stiff nipples, and then dragged his tongue down his smooth, hard abs. There was heat rising between their bodies, and it wasn't just from the steam. Winston could feel the man's cock, fat and firm, brushing against his chest as he settled onto his haunches.

His pubes were damp, smelling richly of his musk. His scent filled Winston's nostrils as he lowered his mouth over that thick, dark dick. Winston gripped the base of the shaft with one hand, played with the man's balls with the other.

"That's it," the stranger purred, his voice echoing off the steam room's tiled walls. "All the way down."

Winston moved his mouth down to the man's nut sack, jostling the balls inside with his tongue. He sucked one of those big nuts into his mouth, pulling on it just enough to create a delicious tension — pleasure that toed the edges of pain. Then he brought his mouth back up to his trick's cock, swallowing it in one gulp and getting a loud groan in response.

The dark-hued man stood up abruptly, almost sending Winston backwards on his butt. "Eat my hole," he commanded, his voice as thick as the steam enveloping them.

Winston flipped over, so he was sitting with his back resting against the bench, the man standing over him, ass directly above his face. He pried the man's ass cheeks apart and dove between them, his tongue unrolling into its depths.

The stranger grunted loudly, bending at the waist and pushing his ass against Winston's wiggling tongue. Winston forced his tongue deep into the stranger's chute. *The way Perry used to do to me*, he thought while gnawing at the anonymous man's pulsing hole.

Both men jacked off, the stranger brought closer to orgasm by Winston's stabbing tongue. His quickened breath grew louder, cutting through the hissing steam. As suddenly as he'd demanded a rim job, the man spun back around, confronting Winston with his drooling prick. The actor stuffed it into his mouth. With one hand gripping the stranger's shaft and the other stroking his own, Winston sucked the stranger vigorously, until he was rewarded with a mouthful of tangy-tasting jism.

He came as he gulped down his gym trick's load, his cries muffled by the man's big, black cock. Only when his prick had spurted its last drops of cum did the lover of the late Perry Snopes pull his lips from the stranger's pole.

The steam started to dissipate, making the men appear to each other like washed out images on grainy film. "Man, that was good," the stranger said breathlessly, smiling.

Winston forced himself to return the smile. "Yeah," he agreed. "You're hot."

The man backed toward the door. "Better get going. How long you staying here?"

"Two more days, at least."

"Maybe I'll see you around," he said, flashing a smile that was friendly but made no promises. He then stepped out of the steam room, making his getaway without telling Winston his name.

Winston remained sitting on the steam room's wet floor, his cock now flaccid, his flat belly stippled with his own spunk. Did you see that, Perry? Were you watching from above or below? He thought acidly. Too bad I can't "share" anymore.

And then Winston LaGrabe began to weep.

TEN

Monday afternoon Dane sat in his office at DanKen Studios, staring at the computer screen. He was on the *Miami Herald's* Web site, reading over the update on Perry Snopes' murder — "fatal shooting," the paper called it. No new revelations beyond Snopes being seen at Hedonism, "a popular gay nightspot in South Beach." Police still searching for the man who registered the room at the Tropic View Inn, described as Hispanic, roughly five-and-a-half feet tall, mid-thirties, hair worn long in back, a tattoo of a flaming skeleton riding a motorcycle on his right forearm. Signed in as "Juan Valdez." The article also mentioned a witness — no name given, but it was noted the witness was a male prostitute — saw a man wearing a dark suit, possibly in his early- to mid-thirties, leave the room where Snopes' body was found, around 2:00 a.m.

Dane knew the details about "Juan Valdez": some guy off the street, given a few hundred to register the room, preferably under a fake name, paying cash, free to keep the change and bolt. The man in the dark suit was a mystery to him, though.

But there were no real suspects in custody. Yet.

He'd found one of those suspects. Task. Just thinking of his name caused Dane to roll his eyes and exhale a defeated breath.

When Dane talked to him late yesterday afternoon — a second time, after the little shit hung up on him — Task filled in a few blanks, telling him "they" shot Snopes, but wouldn't say who, Rand or he, pulled the trigger. "Better not, over a cell phone," he warned. "Heard they can pick these things up on police scanners."

Seething, Dane instructed him to get to Atlanta. "Be there by Friday," he said. "I have a club there called The Tackle Box. You go there, ask for John Klavern. He can set you up with a place to stay until I get there. Understand?"

"Just a sec, let me find a pen and something to write on."

"What? You can't remember this? Atlanta. The Tackle Box. John Klavern. That's all."

"So where is this place, The Cracker Box?"

"Tackle! The Tackle Box, you moron. It's on Cheshire Bridge Road. Ask directions when you get to Atlanta."

"How am I s'posed to get there? Don't have a car."

"The same fucking way you got to wherever you are now! Just get your ass up to Atlanta!" Dane had hung up then, fearing if he talked to Task too much longer he'd suffer a seizure.

Next, he placed a call to John. "Yeah," he answered.

"This The Tackle Box?" Dane asked.

"Uh-huh." There was a loud snorting sound on the other end.

"So, is this the manager or some brain-dead barback, doesn't know better than to answer a business phone by stating the business name, something like 'Thank you for calling The Tackle Box' would be nice."

Some sniffling, then: "Who the fuck's this? Lecturing me on how to answer my goddamned phone." More sniffling.

"Dane Kensington. Maybe you've heard of me. I'm the fucking owner!"

"Oh! Sorry, Dane, didn't know it was you! Thought it was one of them smart-ass dancers. You know how they can be." John forced a chuckle, like it was kinda' funny when you thought about it.

Dane didn't think so. "Never mind. Just wanted to give you a heads up. I'm expecting a guy to show up there, name of Task."

"Task?"

"Yeah, that's his name. Should be there next couple days. I told him to go to the club and ask for you. I want you to put him up in that motel near there, what's it called?"

"The Swisher Suites?"

"Really?"

"We just call it that, account of all the hustlers take their tricks there. It's the Cheshire Suites. Kind of a shithole. Sure you want him there?"

"Trust me, he won't complain as long as I'm paying. Call me when he gets there."

"What's he look like?" John asked, ending the question with a sharp, loud snort.

"Dunno, only talked to him on the phone. But how many guys you know named Task?"

"True. Just curious, 'cause the other night — last night — some guy, a kid practically, was here, asking for you. Buggin' us to let him in to give you a call. Causin' a real nuisance, thought we'd have to call the cops."

Dane felt his temper rise. "And what did he look like?"

"Uh, let's see, he was cute, I'll tell you that — pain in the ass, but cute. Kinda' looked like, what's that singer's name, with the boy band, Jason, Justin..."

"And you didn't fucking call me?" Dane asked hotly.

"What? So some kid knows you got a stake in the club, dropping your name like you're pals. I'm supposed to believe him? You won't believe shit people pull to get out of paying cover."

"He shows up again, you let him in and call me on my cell — immediately!"

"Awright, awright. Shit, how's I supposed to know he's special?"

Dane heard the club manager snort again and asked, "You got a cold or something? You keep sniffling."

"What? Oh, no. It's just my... allergies."

Dane knew John Klavern had a coke habit that could subsidize a Peruvian village. He said: "Allergies. Right." Then hung up.

So Rand was in Atlanta. Somewhere. He wondered why, if Rand wanted to get in touch with him, he didn't return the umpteen messages Dane left on his cell phone. Wondered why he headed for Atlanta instead of flying back to L.A., as was planned. Wondered if Rand would try calling again.

His assistant Jamahl walked into his office, rapping on the door as he opened it. "Hey, sweetie," he trilled as he flounced into the room. "What'cha doing in here, hiding out from everyone." A white Southern belle trapped in the body of a black man.

Dane closed out the *Miami Herald* Web page, hurriedly, the way employees at "legitimate" businesses hid evidence they were looking at porn sites while on the job. "Busy," he said tersely.

Undaunted by his boss's sullen mood, Jamahl continued forward. "Honey, you must be. I thought you were 'auditioning'" — he giggled at that — "but I see you're in here alone." He waved a handful of pink message slips. "Got these off voice mail for you."

Dane started to ask if any were from Rand, but realized now he'd better not let on to others he'd ever heard of Rand. "Anything interesting?" he asked, taking the messages from the assistant's hands.

"Not really. A couple aspiring directors, some guy from one of the square states says he'll be in L.A. next week and wants to know if you got his pictures. Some guy named Jerry, says he knows you, talked Saturday night, left about three messages. Could tell he had a hairy back just hearing his voice on the phone."

"Jerry, Jerry..." Dane couldn't place the name. Oh, right, the goombah from Boner's. That's what he got for giving his card out indiscriminately. He shuffled through the rest of the messages. None of them were from Rand.

"Anything else?"

Jamahl said, "Chi Chi wants to move tomorrow's meeting to Wednesday, one o'clock, if that's okay — I said it was — and Chase said he'll be by tomorrow at three, go over the paperwork for acquiring DVD rights to... Genix Pictures? Never heard of them."

"Before your time, baby. Back when you could fuck without a rubber and use Crisco for lube."

Jamahl pursed his lips. "Bet that was before butter flavored, too, huh?"

"You know it." Smiling against his will.

The phone rang and the assistant asked if he should get it, but Dane waved him off, reaching for the phone, saying he'd take it. He picked up as Jamahl was closing the door behind him.

The voice of a young man said, "Hey, Dane. Bet you're wondering what happened to me."

Rand, calling like he was an old friend who'd fallen out of touch.

Dane almost jumped out of his chair. "You're goddamned right, I am!" He looked at the caller ID on the phone. A 404 area code, no name, just said Atlanta, Ga. "What the fuck happened!"

"So you know?"

"Know what? That he's dead? Yeah, your friend Task told me."

"You talked to Task?" Concern creeping into his voice.

"Last night, he filled me in, sort of. Guy's got all the brains God gave cabbage."

Rand giggled. "Too bad for you the smart one's got the tape."

"What the fuck you mean, 'too bad for me?'" Dane asked, trying to keep his voice down. "You got the tape? Good! You're in Atlanta, right? I'm going to be flying in there Thursday. You can give it to me then. I'll destroy it."

In the silence that followed, Dane thought he heard the clinking of silverware against glass in the background, figured Rand was calling from a pay phone in a restaurant.

Rand said, "How bad you want the tape?"

"Huh? What — oh, Jesus fucking Christ! You're *extorting* me?"

Again: "You want the tape? How much is it worth to you?"

Dane took in a big gulp of air, and then another. This couldn't be happening. Last week, Rand was licking his balls. Now he was trying to break them.

But Dane wasn't going to cave in to the little shit. "Nah-uh, you little bastard. I'm not going to play that game. Besides, you got more to lose. You're *on* the tape."

"And what'll I lose? I got nothing. You, you've got, what, a studio, a few clubs, more cock than you'll ever live long enough to suck. Cops get me, I'm going to invite you to join the party. Say you masterminded the whole thing. And you did, didn't you?"

"No one was supposed to die!" He wanted to reach through the phone line, grab Rand by the hair and ram his face into a wall, hard, repeatedly, until that beautiful face looked like ground round.

"Tell you what, I'll just name my price: one million."

"Are you out of your fuckin' mind?"

"Talk to you later." Rand hung up.

Jamahl tapped on the door again but didn't enter. "Everything okay in there?"

Dane melted back into his chair. "Nothing to worry about," he called out. "Just an argument with one of our dick divas."

"Shoulda' let me handle him," Jamahl scolded through the door. "Takes a queen to put a bitch in her place."

He sat, body shaking with rage, white-knuckling the armrests of his chair, wondering how his plan could get so colossally fucked up.

Twenty minutes later, when Dane thought he'd regained some semblance of composure, he picked up the stack of messages Jamahl delivered, flipped through them until he found the number he wanted.

The phone picked up on the second ring. "Hello?"

"Hi, Jerry, this is Dane Kensington, finally getting around to returning your call. Sorry it took awhile, been pretty busy." Jerry started to say that was okay, but Dane cut him off, eager to set things in motion. "Look, I had something I wanted to discuss with you. Thought maybe we could meet someplace for coffee or something and talk about it."

* * * * *

Martin sat at a patio table at Cristoforo, smoking his post-meal cigarette and watching the traffic on East Ponce de Leon as he waited for the check and for Rand to get out of the restroom. Intermittently, he'd smile, seemingly at nothing at all. He just couldn't help himself. He was that happy.

Martin intended to go to work today, got up at 6:30 and took his shower. Wasn't too crazy about leaving Rand alone in his house — Rand hadn't had much luck contacting his friend — while he was at work, but became more trusting when he thought of the previous day, spent caressing Rand's beautiful body, sucking his meaty cock, fucking his pert ass. He was semi-hard by the time he stepped out of the shower.

Rand was awake and sitting up in bed when Martin walked naked into the bedroom. "I can take care of that for you," he said, nodding toward Martin's half-hard dick, his voice gravelly with sleep.

"You don't know how tempted I am," Martin chuckled, opening the top drawer of his dresser, pulling out a pair of briefs. "But I need to get to work."

"Bet you got plenty of sick days. Why don't you use one of them?"

"I will when I'm sick. What makes you so sure I have plenty of sick days, anyway?"

Rand was getting out of bed now, his expression becoming mischievous. "You confirmed it when you said you'd call in when you're sick. A responsible guy."

Martin was going to continue getting dressed, but he just stood in front of the dresser, underwear in hand, watching Rand move toward him. *Jesus, I can't take my eyes off him,* he thought, his cock inching up another notch toward a full erection.

The decision was made just before Martin shot his load down Rand's throat. He wasn't going in to work today. He did, in fact, have plenty of sick days.

They spent the day nude, seeing no need to get dressed when they'd just want to get undressed again. The two men lounged on the sofa, watching loud daytime talk shows and less hysterical home decorating shows. Martin would look over at Rand, melted against the cushions, legs spread, and reach for his flaccid cock. Minutes later, they were both hard, fingering and sucking each other, fucking while on TV a perpetually smiling hostess introduced a couple to their newly remodeled den.

"Used to have days like this when I was in L.A.," the young man said. They were in the kitchen now, Martin arranging apple slices, Brie and crackers on a platter for them to snack on. Rand was sitting at the table in the breakfast nook, smoking one of Martin's cigarettes. His balls were sticking to the chair. "Me an my boyfriend, we'd just hang out together, naked, smoking pot, fucking, eating, watching TV... it was nice."

"We ... my ex and I ... usually could only manage a half day like this," Martin said, bringing the platter of fruit, cheese and crackers to the table. "Guess when you're older you don't want to waste an entire day."

Rand grabbed an apple slice off the plate and bit into it. "Who says spending the day fucking and eating and lyin' around is a wasted day?" he asked while he chewed. "Shit, isn't that what people work their asses off for, so they'll have enough money to do nothing?"

"Yuppie conditioning, I guess," Martin conceded, spreading Brie on a cracker. "If you're not getting something accomplished, particularly a something that makes money, you're wasting your life. But you're right, we all wish we could be slackers. Lot more fun."

"So why'd you and your boyfriend split up?" Rand asked, stubbing out his cigarette.

Martin wasn't prepared for the question to strike him like it did, causing his stomach to constrict slightly, his cheeks to redden. "He found another guy. About your age. What you said this morning? That I'm a responsible guy? He thought I was too responsible." And too old, but Martin didn't say that.

"Shoulda' wasted more days."

"Maybe. But I'm better off without him. What about you and your boyfriend?"

Martin wasn't surprised when Rand said, "Which one?"

For dinner they got dressed. Martin wanted to show Rand off. The best place to display his conquest would be one of the popular midtown bistros, Einstein's or Joe's. Let all of Atlanta's gays see the hot young man decorating his table. Even if the queens assumed Martin was just a sugar daddy, their bitchery would only reveal their envy. But Midtown was too close to where Martin worked. He didn't want to risk his boss driving down Juniper on her way home and see Martin and his boy toy sitting on the patio at Einstein's, sipping cocktails, when Martin called in that morning and said he had "some sort of virus." So Martin took Rand to Cristoforo, a high-priced Italian place, just outside downtown Decatur. More of a mixed crowd here — straight couples and lesbian professionals, mostly, though there was a smattering of men who watched as Rand stood up from their table outside and made his way inside, to the restroom.

It was a beautiful day. Nothing could ruin it, not even the appearance of Martin's ex, Ron, now coming up the front walk and into the patio.

"Marty! Hi," Ron said, walking over, wearing a tight smile on his face. When they split, they agreed to remain friends, which translated into they'd be civil when encountering each other in public.

Martin returned a tight smile of his own. "Hey, Ron. How's it going?" Wishing Ron had gained fifteen pounds or aged rapidly or started going bald, but no, he still looked good, in his crisp white button-down shirt, fashionable jeans that were just tight enough to do his ass justice, and black leather belt with a silver buckle big enough to draw focus toward his crotch.

"I thought you quit smoking."

"Well, a lot's changed," Martin said off-handedly, stubbing out his cigarette in an ashtray roughly the size of a bottle cap. Where the hell was Rand? "What brings you here? Thought Midtown was your stomping ground."

"It's *all* my stomping ground, baby," Ron chuckled. He told Martin he got a new job, in the marketing department for a restaurant chain that had corporate headquarters "just down the road." Stopped at Cristoforo for take out. He startled Martin by saying, "Maybe you could join me at Blake's later."

"You're inviting me? What about... your new boyfriend?"

A shrug. "Over. It, ah, well, let's just say it was fun while it lasted." Then his tone turned serious. "You know, I was thinking about giving you a call. See if we could get together."

Martin began reaching for another cigarette. "Uh, Ron, I don't..."

But Ron stopped talking suddenly, his eyes sliding toward the entrance to the restaurant. Martin followed his gaze, and saw the distraction: Rand stepping out into the patio, squinting in the setting sun. He walked with the easy swagger of someone so aware of his attractiveness he never gave it a second thought.

"Hey," Ron, now in flirt mode, greeted Rand.

Rand nodded and Martin said, "This is Ron. My ex." Rand said nice to meet you to Ron, then slid into the chair next to Martin and draped an arm over his shoulder.

"So, you're together?" Ron said, his disappointment plain.

"I tried to join a monastery, but they were only taking Catholics. So I thought I'd try dating again."

"Fucking, you mean," Rand chuckled, fingers toying with Martin's earlobe. He leaned in and gave Martin a kiss on the lips, making sure Ron saw there was tongue involved. "Guy's horny as a rhino."

Ron responded with a lip-less smile before looking away. He was shifting his weight from foot to foot, uncomfortable. "Glad to see you're having fun," he said, not meaning it.

"You bet he is," Rand said, letting a hand travel up Martin's thigh until it made contact with his crotch.

Rand was laying it on thick, but Martin didn't care. His face was beet red, but the smile Martin shot Ron revealed his vengeful delight. "Yeah, I'm having fun," he agreed.

"How convenient you live close by. Saves you from having to get a room," Ron said pointedly, keeping the smile on his face, so his bitchiness might be mistaken for wit. "Well, it was good to see you again, Marty. Nice meeting you, Ram."

"Rand," Martin corrected, but Ron was already backing away.

Five minutes later, after he paid the check, Martin was still giggling about the encounter with his ex. "You know if you hadn't sat down next to me, he'd have come on to you," Martin said, his hand on the center of Rand's back as walked through the restaurant's small parking lot.

"So you said," Rand muttered. The incident had been rehashed twice already, and Martin was trying for a third time.

"You were perfect," Martin gushed, his hand dropping lower, to the curve of Rand's ass. He drew the young man close and gave him an affectionate smooch on the side of his face. "Now he knows how I felt." Saying those words aloud, he realized he sounded petty and immature, like a jealous high school girl wanting to get even with the lead cheerleader. And then he thought: *So fucking what!*

At the car, Martin opened the passenger door for Rand. "Such a gentleman," Rand said, rolling his eyes, though Martin was sure he loved the attention.

"Sometimes." Martin pushed Rand against the car, pressed his body against Rand's, and kissed him hotly. Immediately, his cock responded to the kiss.

But when he pulled his mouth away, lips wet with Rand's saliva, he asked. "Wanna go get some ice cream?"

Rand laughed. "I don't think that's the kinda' cream you want." He gave the bulge in Martin's blue jeans a gentle squeeze.

The comment made Martin's face redden. Even now he blushed when someone called him on his randiness. "You're right. Let's go home."

In the car, they shared a few more deep, sloppy kisses before Martin turned the ignition. As Martin waited to pull out into traffic, he cupped Rand's face in his hand and stole another kiss. He couldn't keep his hands to himself, just one glace over at the hot young man in the passenger seat and Martin wanted to touch him. Driving down East Ponce de Leon, he kept one hand on Rand's knee.

He thought: I haven't felt this way since I was in... Quickly, he dismissed the thought before he could finish it. This isn't love, he cautioned himself. It's infatuation. Hell, Rand was still pretty much a mystery, keeping many of the details of his life to himself, silencing Martin's questions with his perpetually hard dick.

At a red light at an intersection, waiting to make a left onto Commerce, Martin leaned over for another kiss, slipping a hand between Rand's thighs. A horn blared behind them. The light was green. "God, I can't wait to get you home," Martin breathed lustily, his gaze still on Rand as he hit the gas.

"So don't," Rand said.

"Don't what?"

"Wait."

Rand was playing with the zipper of his fly. His other hand rested in the V of his crotch, pushing against basket. Martin grinned, tried to keep one eye on the road, one eye on Rand. When Rand started unzipping his jeans Martin almost swerved into oncoming traffic.

"Got to stop that, now. I'm going to get us killed if you keep distracting me," he scolded half-heartedly. He dug at his own crotch, adjusting his swelling prick in his pants.

Less than a quarter mile further, stopped at the signal at Clairemont, Rand had his jeans open. He wasn't wearing any underwear and Martin could see a patch of golden pubes and a pink tease of his shaft. "Why don't you find someplace more private," Rand suggested.

"But the house isn't even two miles away."

Rand pulled his dick out of his jeans, semi-hard and getting harder as he fondled the cockhead. "We've done it at the house. Let's try someplace new."

A block later, Martin was pulling into an old parking garage off Church Street, in the heart of downtown Decatur. During the day, the garage provided parking for employees at two nearby office towers, as well as a couple banks in the area. It was nearly 7:00 p.m. now, and the garage was all but vacant. Martin drove up to the second level and headed for a spot at the back of the garage. Rand said no, a spot up front, overlooking the street below.

Martin brought his Acura to a halt across two parking spaces and cut the engine. He started to lean over, eager to get at Rand's cock, but the mischievous man had opened his door and was getting out of the car.

"What...?"

"Too cramped in there," Rand said playfully, holding his pants up with one hand. He motioned for Martin to join him.

"I don't know," Martin said doubtfully, even as he opened the car door. Stepping toward Rand he wondered if the garage was patrolled by a security guard, worried about being caught. At best, they'd be shooed away, like crows in the garden. Worst-case scenario, cops would be called, arrests made, and if it were a slow news day, mention made in the papers. Arrested for lewd acts in public, on a day he called in sick — he'd be fired for sure.

His fears evaporated the moment he made contact with Rand, circling his arms around him, his tongue probing his young friend's mouth. Rand let go of his jeans, letting them slide down his thighs, and set to work unbuckling Martin's belt and unbuttoning his jeans. Feeling Rand's fingers squeezing his boner through his briefs made Martin shiver and suck in his breath sharply.

Rand's mouth was at the side of Martin's neck, his breath warm. Gingerly, he bit Martin's earlobe, then got down on his knees. He didn't free Martin's cock right away, preferring to stroke the pulsing mound in his underwear. A wet spot was forming near the waistband, where the head of Martin's dick struggled for freedom; Rand put his lips on the moist spot and sucked Martin's pre-cum out of the fabric.

Martin groaned loudly, his voice bouncing off the cement walls. Hearing his echo made him self-conscious, and he looked over his shoulder, making sure no one else lurked in the shadows of the cavernous garage.

"Relax," Rand chortled, hooking his hands in the waistband of Martin's drawers. "No one's here."

He yanked the underwear down, Martin's cock jumping forward. Rand took hold of it, squeezing the shaft, milking out another dewy drop of pre-cum, his tongue darting out to lap it up. An instant later, he closed his mouth over Martin's dick. This time, Martin didn't care if anyone else heard him moan. Rand's mouth on his prick felt so good, people could gather round and watch.

Martin watched Rand swallow his cock. He closed his eyes and kept the image with him, tilting his head back and grooving on the sensation of Rand's wet tongue massaging his dick. Martin placed a hand on Rand's head and gently guided him to take more of his cock, Rand's gullet opening and accepting the invasion. He thrust his hips forward, fucking Rand's mouth. His breathing was rapid and ragged, the pleasure rising in him rapidly. Whether it was the novelty of the setting or fear of getting caught or Rand just got him that fucking hot, Martin didn't know, but he was close to losing control.

"You're about to get a mouthful of cum," Martin gasped, his body shaking.

Rand pulled his mouth away then, and suddenly all Martin felt on his cock was the still, stagnant summer air.

"What..."

"Over here." Rand moved with his back against the cement rail. Voices from a few pedestrians on the street below drifted up to them. Rand beckoned, and Martin went to him, surprised that the first thing the young man demanded was a kiss.

"You wanna suck my cock, baby?" Rand whispered when they pulled their lips apart, threads of saliva suspended between them.

"Yes," Martin panted, his prick aching for release.

"Still close?" he teased, circling a hand around Martin's pulsing cock. "Wanna shoot your load on me."

He shivered, gulped in another mouthful of air, panting in the affirmative.

"Go ahead," Rand coaxed, his voice no louder than a breath. "Cum all over my dick."

Martin nodded, took a step backward. His cock drooled profusely, supplying him with ample amounts of its natural lubricant. When Martin took hold of his dick he could feel it pulse in his hand. Rand watched him, his mouth partially open, lips twitching into a smile. Rand held his own cock at the base, pushing it forward to catch Martin's load. "Go ahead," he repeated. "All over me."

Less than a minute later, Martin was shuddering and gasping, his mouth moving wordlessly as he came. His cock spit out his load in short, bullet-like blasts, first splat landing in Rand's pubes, the next three hitting his dick. "Oh, baby," Rand sighed as his cock got splattered. "So hot..." After that, Martin's prick only dribbled. Nevertheless, Martin was impressed with his cumshot. He thought Rand had drained him dry by now.

Breathing heavily, Martin met Rand's eyes, waiting for further instructions from the younger man. Wanting to know: what now?

"Now suck it," Rand commanded, waving his cum-frosted dong at Martin. "You wanted cream, now come and get it."

Martin eased himself onto one knee in front of Rand and wrapped his fingers around his cock. No longer delirious from his own pleasure, he was once again self-conscious and checked over his shoulder, making sure they were still unobserved. As he guided Rand's dick into his mouth, Martin got a whiff of his own semen — a sharp, almost chemical scent. It tasted the same way.

"Lick it off," Rand sighed, hooking a hand behind Martin's head. "Clean your cum off my cock."

He swallowed Rand's dick whole, until the tip of his nose was nuzzling the curly brush of his pubes. Rand rolled his hips, grunting and gulping in air. His movements became jerky, his body getting a jolt each time Martin's tongue curled around his cockhead. Then he froze, cried out, and Martin was rewarded with a mouth full of jism.

"That's it, swallow it all," Rand mewed, holding the older man's head firmly in place, not wanting him to pull his head away — wanting him to get every drop of cum his cock pumped out.

A few minutes later, Rand took his hand away and Martin released his cock from his lips. The two men looked around the garage and then at each other, their cocks — drained and softening — out in the fetid air. They both began to laugh, their guffaws echoing within the concrete cavern.

ELEVEN

There was no calling in sick Tuesday morning — Martin couldn't allow himself to be *that* irresponsible. He left Rand alone in the house. Even though he was still pretty much a stranger, sex had made Martin trusting. He told his guest he could help himself to whatever food was in the refrigerator. Said he'd try to get off work early, but he was already running late.

If Martin's boss had any suspicions about the veracity of his illness, his reputation as a reliable and trustworthy employee pushed such doubts aside. Conner, however, was not so sympathetic. When Martin poked his head into his friend's office to say good morning, Conner took one look at him and said, "You shithead. You were home all day yesterday fucking your brains out, weren't you?"

* * * * *

Rand lounged on the sofa until mid-morning, channel surfing as he had a breakfast of two Diet Cokes and a Power Bar. After watching *Maury* (the topic was children who steal from their parents, something he could relate to), he turned the TV off, grabbed a beer from the fridge and started snooping, seeing if he could find anything interesting – or useful.

He headed back upstairs, figuring Martin's more personal belongings would be in his bedroom. Maybe he'd have more current porn titles in there, Rand thought. All he found downstairs were a couple Falcon tapes from the 1980s.

Rand set his beer down on top of a black lacquered bookcase filled with self-help books, pulp thrillers and a few selections from the mandatory gay reading list, books by Amistead Maupin, Edmund White, Felice Picano and David Sedaris. On the bottom shelf were larger books, most about European countries, filled with lush photographs of Italy, Greece and France. Next best thing to being there. There were a few books of artistic nude photos, too — books that escaped the label of pornography because the pictures were black and white. Rand flipped through a couple of them, pausing to admire a few of the models, then moved on to Martin's chest of drawers.

Nothing surprising in the dresser other than a few pairs of sheer bikini underwear and a bright red thong made out of some rubberized fabric. Rand wondered if these were gifts from the ex-boyfriend. He couldn't see Martin buying them for himself, but what did he know? He hadn't even been with the guy for three full days.

He found more interesting things in the drawers of one of the nightstands. Rand already knew he kept a box of rubbers and bottle of lube in the top drawer of the table on the right side of the bed. He also found some massage oils, raspberry and cherry-almond flavored. The bottom drawer had the sex toys, a rubber replica of some porn star's dick, a big black dildo and a small purple gel butt plug. There were a few skin mags in there, too, the most recent issue published a year ago.

Martin's closet revealed a weakness for shoes and ties, as well as conservative taste in fashion — lots of khaki pants and pale-colored Oxfords. On a shelf above the hanging clothes Rand found a stack of porn DVDs, all more recent releases, most featuring young, muscular men with smooth chests and airbrushed tans. Also on the shelf was a square metal box, painted a muddy gray. The latch on the lid had a tiny keyhole, the kind of lock that could be picked easily.

Intrigued, Rand brought the box down off the shelf, surprised by its weight. He moved over to the bed and sat down. He tried the latch. It was unlocked and Rand flipped the lid open, his eyes widening when he saw what was inside: a Smith & Wesson revolver and a box of bullets.

He picked up the gun, needing to feel it in his hand to convince himself it was real. Holding the pistol up, he aimed it across the room, smiling as he did so.

* * * * *

Nine never thought he'd see the day he had any kind of respect for policemen, but he was at least developing an appreciation for what they went through, tracking people down. Damn, it was hard work.

He'd returned to Miami Sunday, seeing if he could find the shooting suspects before the cops did. Nine was already ahead of the investigators there, remembering that night, waiting outside the Tropic View in his rented Taurus, waiting for Snopes and the two guys he picked up at Hedonism to finish up, wondering if they'd all leave together or separately. Thought he heard a pop, like a firecracker or car backfiring, but who knew. He didn't think it was gunfire. The two guys Snopes was with — young, and he could tell they were cute, even from a distance — left, walking quickly. Nine had watched them walk down the street, both carrying duffle bags. His eyes returned to the door they exited, on the second floor. He waited for Snopes to leave, but after about thirty minutes, it was clear he wasn't in a hurry. That's when Nine went up there and found Snopes dead. Job done.

Nine's mission was altered Monday when he saw an article in the Herald reporting "a witness" said he saw a man in a dark suit leaving the scene at the Tropic View Inn. That man he saw would be Nine. The article also noted the witness was a male prostitute. Yeah, Nine thought, *that* narrows it down. There were how many hustlers in Miami?

The rest of the day was spent asking around, posing as a private dick to find out from the motel clerk at the Tropic View what room the witness was checked into, getting three possible names, none of whom were the hustler. One was, however, the hustler's trick, a chubby, middle-aged guy, lived over in Hollywood. The man claimed he knew nothing about a hustler or a motel in South Beach when Nine showed up on his doorstep, the guy telling him to go away, he was about to sit down to dinner with his wife and daughter. The man was more forthcoming when Nine opened his suit coat, made sure the guy got a good look at the handle of his nine-millimeter tucked in the waist of his pants.

The hustler went by the name of Carter, was a young, white guy who had a tattoo of Jesus on the cross on his left bicep, trolled an area about three blocks away from the Tropic View. Nine spent most of that evening asking every cocksucker he saw if they knew a Carter, had a Jesus tattoo. There were some really pathetic looking guys working the streets these days, and Nine talked to all of them. No luck — until the next morning.

He was having breakfast at a little diner off Lincoln Avenue. The place was crowded with tourists, mostly, and Nine had to take a seat at the counter, on a stool between a hump-backed old man and a portly black woman with blond hair extensions. He had almost polished off his cranberry muffin when he noticed the black woman was gone and in her place was a young guy, looked like he was in his early twenties, with wavy hair the color of coffee with cream. Fairly attractive, but underweight; his cheekbones stuck out like arrowheads and his navy tank top hung loosely off his coat hanger shoulders. The guy's eyes were hidden behind a pair of sunglasses, but Nine suspected they were sunken deep in the shadows of his skull.

The guy also was jittery as hell, drumming his fingers on the counter, swiveling on his stool, his head moving jerkily about. Speed freak, Nine thought.

The servers at the café were actively ignoring the guy. "Hey, can I get a Dr Pepper?" the skeletal customer called out through shredded vocal chords.

"Would you like more coffee, sir?" the Latina waitress asked Nine.

"No, thanks. But could you get that guy his Dr Pepper. And a muffin, too. Kid needs some meat on his bones."

The waitress made a face and said something in Spanish that, judging by the tone, was not positive. In English she said, "Sure thing."

"Thanks, dude," said the jittery guy. He smiled, and Nine winced at the condition of his remaining teeth. "These spics try to act all high an' mighty 'cause they got a fucking job indoors."

Nine nodded. "And you're, what, a CEO?"

"Shee-it, I do what I hafta' do, y'know? Have been, since I was 15."

"Doing what?"

The guy chuckled and shook his head. "Like you don't know." He leaned over then, and Nine got a whiff. He smelled stale, and Nine wondered when was his last bath. "Bet that's why you bought me breakfast? You interested? There's a porno shop around the corner. People work there don't patrol the video booths in back. I'd still charge you, but maybe give you a discount 'cause you were nice an' all."

The idea of doing anything physical with this loser was enough to turn Nine off sex forever. "Thanks, but no. I am looking for some action, but with someone specific. Maybe you know him? Goes by the name Carter? Has a Jesus tattoo."

The guy sat up straight. "You a cop?"

"Fuck no," Nine chuckled. "Just a friend of mine recommended him. Said he worked around here. Know him?"

The waitress set a soda and a blueberry muffin in front of the twitchy hustler, an expression of revulsion frozen on her face. The hustler snatched up the soda and started slurping it up through a straw, not bothering to answer Nine.

"Look, you know where he is, I'll give you twenty bucks. Sound fair?" Guy probably charged half that for a hand-job.

The hustler answered then.

An hour later, he was knocking on the door of a seedy looking two-story building, covered in cracked, baby blue stucco. A sign over the front door advertised furnished apartments, weekly and monthly rates. On the wall next to Carter's door, there was a patch of fresh paint, covering up some graffiti, but not very successfully. The door opened the fourth time Nine pounded on it, a young guy greeted him with, "What the hell do you want?" Trying to snarl, but it sounded more like a whine.

The guy wore a pair of red sweat pants, cut off at the knee. His height was average, his body above-average, all sinewy muscle, decorated with lots of ink: a heart dripping blood on his right pec, a starburst around his navel — an outtie — and a tattoo of Jesus on the cross on his left bicep.

Nine was all smiles. "You Carter? You sure are a whole lot nicer looking than those other guys. Don't see how they make enough to afford to eat."

"Who're you?" he asked, tossing his head back to get the hair out of his eyes, still irritable but warming.

"Nick," Nine said, still smiling. He pointed to the spot of fresh paint by the door and said, "Looks like this could use another coat. You can still make out the 'fucking fag.'"

"You got a reason for waking me up?"

"Uh, yeah." Nine stuck his hands in his tan shorts, rocked back on his heels and looked down toward the floor. "A friend of mine, he, um, recommended you."

Carter almost smiled then. "Recommended me for what?"

Nine said, "Could we talk about this inside?"

"Depends. You a cop? I ask, you gotta tell me."

"Me? Christ, no! I'm just here on a business trip. Thought I'd have some fun. You know?"

Carter's eyes were still narrowed with suspicion, but he motioned Nine into his apartment anyway.

Seeing the interior of Carter's apartment, Nine could understand why he took tricks to the Tropic View. The apartment wasn't any bigger than a motel room, furnished with thrift store rejects. The once-white walls were now gray with age, smoke and mildew. That Carter wasn't much of a housekeeper didn't help matters.

Carter went over to his nightstand — a square of glass balanced atop two milk crates — and picked up a pack of Camels. "So, who was you're friend. The one who recommended me."

"Uh, Barry. Was here a couple months ago. Remember him? Older guy, kind of skinny, wears glasses."

"Half the guys I deal with are older and wear glasses," Carter snorted, lighting a cigarette blowing out a cloud of blue smoke. "Don't matter, anyway. Just making conversation. Your friend tell you the deal?"

"Deal?"

Carter rubbed his thumb across his fingers.

"Oh, the money. I think he said — I brought a hundred. That enough?"

Finally, Carter managed a smile. "Perfect," he said.

Nine removed the hundred from his billfold and set it on top of a sagging dresser. Carter was sitting on his bed now, stubbing out his cigarette in the overflowing ashtray, smoke trailing out his nose. Then he picked up a roach, so small Nine doubted there were even two tokes left, stuck it on the end of a paper clip he'd bent out of shape, and lit it. "Wanna hit?" he asked, his voice strained as he struggled to keep the smoke inside his lungs and speak simultaneously.

"No thanks." Nine, deciding how to proceed, wondered if the hustler did anything harder. He didn't see any track marks, but you never know. "That why you do this? For drugs?"

"No, I got a wife and kids to feed," Carter sneered. "What're you, a social worker? I don't shoot up, if that's what you're asking, worried about unclean needles an' shit." Another toke and the roach was dead, left to burn out in the ashtray. He exhaled and stood up. "Just a second and we'll get started."

In the apartment's closet-sized bathroom, Carter took a swig of mouthwash, gargled and spit. He stepped back out after splashing cold water on his face. "A few rules. You wanna fuck, you have to wear a rubber, don't care how much you paid. You can cum in my mouth, but I don't swallow. You want me to eat your ass, wash up first. You can spank me, you into that, but I don't do golden showers, fisting or scat. Clear on that? Good. Go ahead and get comfortable. You can use the facilities first, if you like."

Nine went into the bathroom and closed the door. A couple minutes later he stepped out, holding his neatly folded tourist garb — shorts and a Dolphins T-shirt — but still wearing his underwear, a pair of red bikini briefs. Carter, sitting back on his bed, whistled. "Nice undies," he said. "Nice body, too. Why're you paying for it? In the closet, married or something?"

"Something like that," Nine said, trying to give a sheepish smile. He set his clothes down on top of a rickety round table across the room, wondering when the last time the table's surface had been wiped off. Nine considered kicking off his sandals but thought better of it. No telling what he'd get if his bare feet touched the puke-green carpet.

Carter stood up, untied the drawstring to his sweats and let them fall to his feet. He wasn't wearing any underwear. Nine raised his eyebrows, impressed. Even flaccid, Carter had a good-sized dick. Cut, with a nice, fat shaft. His thick, black thatch of pubic hair was left un-groomed; his balls, likewise, were unshaven.

"Why don't you lose the panties and we'll get to it," he said, pulling at his nut-sack. "What do you want?"

"Ah, I thought, um..." Nine was struggling to act shy — "how about... I suck you first?"

Carter consented with a shrug and sat back down on the bed, waiting for Nine. Nine turned his back, pulled off his underwear. After a moment's hesitation, he turned back around, letting Carter get a good look, see that Nine was already starting to pop a boner, before he joined him on the bed.

The mattress groaned louder than Carter did when Nine buried his head between his thighs, taking his limp dick into his mouth. Though Carter was slow to vocalize his excitement, his cock let Nine know his oral attention was appreciated: Carter got hard in seconds. A few minutes later, the hustler even managed a few genuine gasps of pleasure, muttering, "You suck cock pretty good, dude."

Nine raised his face from Carter's crotch and said, "Let's see how good you are."

He sat up on his haunches and leaned back on his hands, his cock erect, throbbing against his belly. Carter put his head in Nine's crotch, closing his mouth over Nine's prick. His blowjob was adequate, nothing special, but better than Nine expected from a hustler. He combed Carter's dark hair back from his face. No longer caring he was supposed to be a shy tourist, Nine told him he was a hot little cock whore, thrusting his dick into Carter's mouth.

Nine told Carter to roll over onto his back. When the hustler did so, Nine positioned himself over the tattooed man's face. "Eat my hole," he ordered. Carter flicked his tongue around his trick's butthole, barely grazing the sphincter.

"I said eat it, not lick it," Nine growled, grinding his ass against the hustler's face. "Work your tongue up my hole."

Carter did as instructed, though his movements were still hesitant, rimming obviously not his specialty. Nine felt the tip of the guy's tongue pierce his ass-lips, wiggle around briefly, and do a quick retreat. More licking would follow, then Carter's tongue would push into his chute, followed by a hasty retreat. Like he had to steal up the nerve each time, Nine thought.

"Maybe you'd like getting fucked more," Nine said. He stuck his index and middle fingers in his mouth, got them covered with spit and pulled them out. Leaning forward, he reached between Carter's legs, pushed his lubricated fingers against his hole. "Bet you love feeling a big dick up your ass, don't you Carter?"

The hustler grunted in response, busy poking his tongue through his trick's contracting sphincter. His response was louder and more urgent when Nine's fingers roughly penetrated his own hole.

"Yeah, I thought so. You love it," Nine chuckled, sliding his fingers in deep. "Can't wait to get my cock in there. Your ass is still pretty tight, 'specially for a whore. Must not been in the business too long, huh?" He had his fingers in all the way to the base, pushing against Carter's prostate. Pre-cum oozed from the hustler's fat cock, belying his arousal.

He climbed off Carter's face. The hustler coughed and wiped saliva off his face with his hand. Nine reached over to the improvised nightstand, picking up a sticky bottle of lubricant and a condom packet.

"Want to stay on your back," Nine said, ripping open the condom wrapper with his teeth. "I want to see your face as I fuck you." He didn't turn around to see Carter's glare, but he felt the daggers from the hooker's eyes hitting his back.

His cock covered and lubed, Nine positioned himself between Carter's legs. Carter lay there, his stiff, drooling dick the only part of him showing any excitement. His expression was insolent, challenging. You're making this way too easy for me kid, Nine thought.

Roughly, Nine grabbed Carter's thighs and forced his legs back, making the hustler bring his ass up in the air. The guy's hole was a dark tan, a prominent ring pushing up around the ass-lips. A ring of dark hair surrounded his butthole like a beard. When Nine squirted lubricant on it Carter's sphincter contracted like a sea anemone.

"Hey, try not to get that all over the sheets," Carter snapped. "I gotta sleep in this bed, y'know."

"I know," Nine replied, tossing the bottle of lube onto the mattress, not bothering to close its snap-top lid.

Holding his cock at the base, Nine pushed it into the hustler's puckered hole. The hustler cried out as the whole nine inches filled his gut. "Easy," he said through clenched teeth, but said nothing more, experience having taught him loud protests only made it worse.

"Like that? Huh? Ya' like that, you little whore?" Nine spat, savagely thrusting his cock into Carter's hole, his balls slapping against his butt. "Want me to fuck you harder?"

Carter was biting his lower lip, thrashing his head from side to side. His dick was softening.

Nine eased his pace, fucking the hustler in more cadenced strokes. "This a bit better, baby?" he asked Carter mockingly, reaching between his legs to play with his cock, trying to restore his hard-on. "Prefer it slow and gentle?"

Carter remained silent, though he'd relaxed his mouth. He closed his eyes, and Nine brought his hand down across his face — not real hard, but hard enough to make Carter open his eyes.

"I asked you a question. You like it slow and gentle?"

"It's... yeah, it's good," Carter faltered, not sure what the trick wanted to hear.

"Your cock seems to think so, too. It's getting hard again."

Nine leaned down and kissed him, further confusing the young man. As the trick pulled his mouth away, his lips bowed into a smile. But it was a smile without warmth, and in a split second it was gone, disappearing as Nine spit into his face.

"What? You think I'm in love or something? Fuckin' whore."

The relentless ass pounding resumed. A cacophony of squeaking of bedsprings, Carter's whimpering and Nine's grunts filled the room. Though Nine was fucking him just as brutally as before, Carter remained hard this time, pre-cum streaking down his belly in a thin, slimy trail.

"Thought you'd like it rough," Nine sneered, wrapping his fingers around Carter's cock, jacking it off in hard, fast pulls. "Look at that, your cock's dripping all over the place. You about to cum, whore?"

Gasping and grimacing, Carter managed a weak nod.

"What's that? I didn't hear you?"

"I'm... oh, God...oh, shit."

Carter's body bucked and shook, his load spitting out of his cock. Not an impressive load, Nine noted, but he figured in Carter's line of work his balls didn't get much chance to build up a reserve of jizz.

"Ooooh, yeah," Nine moaned, squeezing his fist around Carter's shaft, forcing a final bead of cum to ooze out the slit. Satisfied he'd gotten the last drop, he scooped up the meager puddles of spooge with his fingers, delivering the viscous cream to the younger man's face. "Maybe you don't swallow other guys' cum, but you're gonna eat your own." At that, Nine forced his cum-dripping fingers between Carter's lips, ordering him to suck them clean. The hustler made a face, but did as he was told, his obvious discomfort heightening Nine's arousal.

Hunching his body over Carter's, Nine slammed his dick into the other man's hole with the force of a Pyle driver. A minute later he was cumming, his body trembling as his cock erupted. He withdrew his dick and pulled off the rubber.

"Open your mouth and close your eyes, you're gonna get a big surprise."

Nine upended the condom over the hustler's face, squeezing out its warm and milky contents, an ugly smile on his face all the while.

"Goddamn motherfucker," Carter spluttered, trying to slap the trick away. Nine threw the sticky rubber in the whore's face, chuckling malevolently as he watched Carter swatting it away, disgusted.

"Poor baby," he teased, patting Carter's moist cheek. He got off the bed and went to the bathroom to wash up. When he stepped back out, Carter was sitting on the edge of his bed, smoking a cigarette. His expression was sullen.

Nine crossed the room, over to the table where he left his clothes. Outside on the street he could hear voices, people talking rapidly in Spanish. A loud truck went by, gears grinding as it went around the corner. Inside the apartment, a tense silence hung in the dank air.

Carter said, "Shit, dude, why didn't you warn me you like it rough?"

"Wouldn't be as much fun that way," Nine said, snapping his red briefs up around his waist. "You want your customers to have fun, don't you? Barry said you did. Said he had a blast when he was with you at the Topic View the other night."

The hustler whipped his head toward Nine. "What're you talking about?"

"Is that where you take your tricks, to the Tropic View? Isn't that where that guy was found murdered?"

Carter shrugged. "Maybe."

"Heard you saw the guy who did it."

The hustler's face turned ashen. "W-what...?"

"Read it in the paper. You saw a guy in a dark suit, leaving a room at the Tropic View early Saturday morning. Ring a bell? " Nine asked, sliding a hand beneath his clothes stacked on the table.

"The papers? What the fuck you talking about?"

Nine pulled his nine-millimeter from underneath his folded shirt and drew it on Carter. "I'm talkin' about this."

He fired twice, one bullet hitting Carter in the center of his forehead, the other landing right between his hard pecs. The cigarette he was smoking fell from his lifeless fingers and smoldered on the dirty carpet.

Nine was dressed in thirty seconds. On his way out, he snatched his hundred-dollar bill off the dresser. Five minutes later, he was exiting an alley a block away and getting into his rented sedan. He pulled his cell phone from the glove compartment and checked his messages. No one left any — in Nine's business, people were skittish about voice mail. But the phone's caller I.D. kept a record of calls received, and someone with a Los Angeles area code had tried Nine twice in the past 45 minutes. He was on I-95 when he got his third call from the L.A. number.

"This Nick?" asked a man's voice.

"Who wants to know?"

"A former associate of yours recommended you. Said you could take care of a problem for me?"

"Maybe. How big's the problem?"

It took a moment before the man spoke again. "I told your friend, and he said it's probably a fifty-thousand-dollar problem."

"When and where can we meet? Discuss it in person?"

"I'll be in Atlanta Thursday. Can you be there then?"

Nine changed lanes, flipped off the old bitch who blew her horn when he cut in front of her, smiling the whole time. To his caller he said, "Just so happens Atlanta's on my itinerary."

TWELVE

Task asked the bartender at The Tackle Box for another rum and Coke, but the rug-wearing manager, John, intervened. "Water," the manager instructed the bartender. Looking at Task, he said, "Unless you're planning on paying, Woody."

Trying to remain incognito, Task shaved his face and dyed his hair that afternoon. The dye job didn't turn out right; it was supposed to be brown ("Warm Mahogany" the box read), but came out red-orange on top. John saw him and said he looked like fuckin' Woody Woodpecker. It was the first time Task saw the club manager smile.

"Thought you were s'posed to be takin' care of me," Task said.

"Listen to you, like you've sucked my dick or something. All I was told was to make sure you had a place to stay, not cover your fuckin' bar tab. Even the people who work here are only allowed two free drinks a night."

Task jerked his head toward the center stage, where a thickly muscled dancer swayed uneasily on his feet. "Looks like he's over his limit by four drinks."

The manager said, "I didn't know woodpeckers could count."

Task took his plastic cup of ice water — handed to him by a smirking bartender — and skulked off to table in the corner of the club.

Wasn't much going on yet. It was a little after six and the after work crowd was just beginning to filter in. The club was more upscale than Boner's. Here they actually had someone clean the restrooms from time to time. The place was bigger, too. The manager was an asshole, though that seemed to come with the territory. Jerry at Boner's was a prick, too.

He got into town about one o'clock this morning. Traveled most of the way with a vanload of evangelists who dropped him off in Montgomery, Alabama, when they realized they weren't going to convert him. A guy in his mid-thirties with cast-in-one-piece hair, driving a Buick, got him as far as LaGrange, and all Task had to do was give him a hand-job behind a Stop n' Shop. A trucker in his fifties took him the rest of the way to Atlanta, and for that Task only had to endure a diatribe against blacks, Jews and homosexuals.

John at The Tackle Box got him a room at this dump called The Cheshire Suites. Better than the Gateway Inn, but not by much. Seemed to him he should be entitled to more than two free drinks, given the fleabag where they put him up.

A few more people were coming in — older, lumpy-looking guys mostly, a few fag hags. He wondered if Rand would stop back by. John told him when he arrived, "Your friend came by here Saturday night, trying to start some shit, coming in the back way. Was told I should look out for him. You heard from him?" He hadn't, but it was good to know he was in town. Task devoted a lot of time thinking about what he'd say and do should their paths cross. Meantime, he had to see about getting some cash, enough to tide him over until that Dane guy got into town and paid him.

Task scoped the room for prospects. A few guys were looking in his direction, all late-forties, overweight and haggard looking, nursing their cocktails until they felt as loose as their ties. They looked away when Task caught their stares. Two of them looked like they'd be good for a couple drinks plus forty bucks if he blew them, something he'd keep in mind if someone more attractive didn't show up soon. Given some of the tricks he'd turned in the past couple days, was it too much to ask to have someone whose dick he *wanted* to suck?

Twenty minutes later he got his wish. A guy entered that looked ten years younger than his other prospects and twenty times cuter. The way he filled out his blue-striped Oxford you could tell he worked out. His skin was tan, and he had a shit-eating grin frozen on his face, like a kid who just walked through the front gates of Disneyland. Task watched the guy swagger up to the bar, saw he had a cute ass, too, and decided it was time for a refill.

He went to the far end of the bar, in sight of the guy who just walked in, standing about five feet away. He watched the guy place his drink order and turn around to check out the dancers. Task kept staring at the guy, waiting to catch his attention. The man turned back around when the bartender placed a drink in front of him. He said something to the bartender; Task couldn't hear what it was over the music, but the guy laughed real loud. The bartender forced a chuckle, and Task saw him roll his eyes as he turned back to the cash register. He also saw the guy check out the bartender's ass. He did not, however, look over in Task's direction.

Task decided to expedite things. "Hey, could I get a refill," he called to the bartender, shaking the ice in his cup. "'Scuse me, bartender. Hey, talkin' to you!"

The bartender slid his eyes over in Task's direction, an expression on his face like he'd just stepped in dog shit. Task didn't notice. He was too busy smiling at the guy in the blue-striped shirt, looking his direction at last, returning Task's smile. Task cocked his head, showed a little more teeth. The guy in the blue-striped Oxford had a big grin now. He looked down at his drink and shook his head, not signaling a negative but like he just couldn't believe Task was flirting with him.

Giving up on ever getting a refill, Task left his cup on the bar and sauntered toward one of the tables, looking over his shoulder a couple times to make sure the guy was watching. He took a seat at a table just outside the glare of the center stage lights. Five minutes later, the guy in the blue striped shirt was walking toward him, two plastic cups in hand.

"Brought you something to drink," the guy said, handing a cup to Task. "The bartender said you were only drinking water."

"Uh, yeah. Thanks," Task said, managing a smile but thinking: I got to find out what car that asshole bartender drives and slash the tires.

"Mind if I join you?"

Task motioned toward the empty chair next to him. "I insist," he said, liking the way that sounded. He heard someone say that in a movie or on a TV show, but couldn't remember which one.

The guy sat down, chuckling. "Well, if you insist. My name's Conner, by the way."

Task nodded, took a sip of his water, then held out his hand and introduced himself, having to repeat himself, as usual.

"Task? Why're you called that?"

"It's my name."

* * * * *

Rand placed a hand on Martin's bare thigh. "Thanks for making dinner," he said, his fingers traveling upward. "You're a good cook."

Martin's cock responded to Rand's touch immediately. "Uh, thanks." He shifted on the sofa, took a gulp of his wine. "Say, you ever get in touch with any of your friends? The ones you planned on seeing when you got here?" trying to make it sound casual, like it just popped into his head even though he had wanted to ask since lunch.

"Finally got through to one of them today," Rand said, taking a final drag off his cigarette and then leaning forward to crush it out in the ashtray on the coffee table. Martin placed a hand on the young man's back, almost instinctually. "But he's traveling for work. Got one of those call-forwarding deals, you know? He said — get this — he's in L.A. now. He's one of the people in Atlanta I want to see, and he's in fucking L.A."

Martin forced himself to chuckle along. "What sort of business does your friend do?"

"Entertainment. Promotions, shit like that," he said, leaning back against the sofa, Martin moving his hand up to Rand's shoulder. "But he'll be back Friday. That cool? I can even take the bus there if you like."

"Yeah, sure." Martin took another gulp of wine, fortifying himself to ask another question. He had a whole list of questions that needed to be asked; that had to be answered. He'd had lunch with Conner, shared details, juicy and otherwise. His friend told him he was being a total schmuck.

"All you know about this guy is he's hot and a great fuck and you let him stay at your house — alone?" Conner said, incredulous. "Jesus Christ, Martin, for all you know he and one of his 'friends' are loading all your stuff up in a truck as we speak."

Martin tried to argue that Conner never met Rand, Martin saying he just had a feeling he could trust him. And Conner said, "You mean like you had a 'feeling' about that hustler you met at Backstreet?"

Martin had meant to hash this all out with Rand as soon as he got home, even before changing out of his business clothes. Scenarios born of paranoia played in his mind as he drove home from work. At best Rand would've only made off with a few valuables, whatever he could stuff in his bag; at worst, Martin would return to an empty house. In reality, neither scenario was the case. The house was as he left it. Rand even said he did a couple loads of laundry.

All he knew about his guest's life in Los Angeles was he attended a few semesters of film school and supported himself waiting tables and "dancing a little." Was the friend in Los Angeles on business someone Rand met while "dancing a little"? One of Rand's ex-boyfriends, maybe?

Rand's hand was moving further up Martin's leg, his fingers underneath the hem of Martin's gym shorts.

"What?" Rand said.

"Huh?"

"You looked like you were about to say something."

Martin's dick was like granite. "Um, I forgot. Lost my train of thought."

* * * * *

"Oh, shit, that feels so fuckin' good," Task groaned, pushing his ass back into Conner's face. He was going to return his mouth to Conner's dick, but then Task felt that tongue dig deeper into his butt, and he had to groan again.

He bent his head down, licked the pre-cum off the tip of Conner's cock, feeling the shaft throb beneath his grip. Conner grunted into his splayed ass, pushed his dick upward. Task took it between his lips then, swallowing Conner's prick to the hilt.

Task couldn't believe his luck, getting picked up by this guy. After ten minutes of small talk at The Tackle Box, Conner asked Task if he wanted to join him in the men's room, asking the question while rubbing the tip of his nose. In a stall they did a couple snorts each. Conner put a hand between Task's legs and squeezed his package. "Let me see it," he said. Task unzipped and displayed himself. He didn't think he looked all that impressive, his cock in its dormant state, but Conner took care of that. He took Task's prick in his hands and played with it until Task was semi-hard. Conner kissed him then, and said, "Let's go."

Task sucked it during the drive to Conner's apartment. Conner had a well-proportioned cock — nice and thick. Sucking it didn't even seem like work. Task didn't raise his head up from Conner's lap until the car was pulling into the parking area behind his condominium, ten minutes later.

They didn't waste time getting naked and getting to the bedroom. They fell onto Conner's low platform bed, kissing and groping, Conner kneading Task's ass; Task pulling on his trick's hard-on. The guy was definitely an ass man, only giving Task's cock cursory attention as they fell into a sixty-nine position. Conner's tongue had remained buried in the younger man's chute for the past ten minutes.

"Ya' like that tongue up your ass, baby," Conner gasped, finally coming up for air. He rubbed two fingers against Task's wet, winking butthole. "You got a hot ass," he added, slipping the tip of his index finger past the furrowed ass-lips.

Task shuddered and rolled his hips, rubbing his stiff cock against Conner's chest, a pool of his pre-cum enabling his dick to slide easily, pleasurably, against the other man's skin. Another breathless "oh yeah" pushed its way out of Task's throat as he stroked Conner's rod with one hand, played with his balls with the other.

Another finger went inside his asshole, sliding into him, pressing against his prostate and making Task's dick quiver. Conner murmured approvingly, moving his fingers around Task's moist interior in a gentle, circular motion. "Can't wait to get my dick inside this tight hole," he rasped.

Stroking Conner's prick, Task imagined he wanted to feel it in his hole, too. He closed his eyes, pressed his ass back against the probing fingers.

The fingers slipped out, and the tongue slipped back in — forced its way in, more like it. Task groaned loudly, "GOD-*damn*, man, you're killing me!" Thinking: But in a good way.

Conner pulled his mouth away. "Hell, this is just the torture. I haven't even started killing yet."

* * * * *

Rand hopped up suddenly and said, "I've got an idea!"

Martin raised his head up from where it had been resting against the sofa cushions, staring up at the ceiling while Rand polished his knob. "I hope it's sexual, because I went out with a guy one time, years ago, who'd make out with me, and when I thought we should getting out of our clothes he'd jump up and say he wanted to go walk in the park."

"I hope you dumped him."

"I did after our second date, when he stopped everything because he wanted to catch some show on TV."

"We're not stopping," Rand assured him. "Just wait right there."

Martin promised he would, remaining on the living room sofa, admiring the rise and fall of Rand's pert ass as he walked out of the room, then bounded up the stairs.

A minute later, Rand was back in the living room, a bottle of lubricant and a couple condom packets in one hand, a plastic replica of a large, cut cock in the other.

"You've been snooping," Martin scolded, feeling a small spark of irritation, thinking about Conner's warnings during lunch and wondering if Rand spent the day going through his stuff, maybe looking for something to steal. His eyes dropped to Rand's prick, sticking out enticingly, and arousal quickly eclipsed his annoyance.

"Stumbled across this while putting away clothes," Rand said, his grin belying that even he didn't buy his excuse. Wiggling the fake cock in his hand he asked, "Whose dick is this?"

"Uh, Eric Hanson's, I think," he said. "This your idea, you want to be fucked by Eric Hanson instead of me?"

"Noooo, I want *you* to get fucked by Eric while you're fucking me."

"Uh, okay," he said, a partial smile coming to his face. "Never done that before."

"You never used this?"

"It was a gift — I gave it to Ron, my ex. Kind of a smartass Valentine's gift. He was obsessed with Eric Hanson at the time, so I got him Eric's dick. He must've figured he wouldn't need it when he moved out. That, and I hid it from him."

Rand giggled and stepped forward. "But you never tried Eric's dick?"

"Um, once," Martin admitted. "I was more comfortable with the butt plug. You probably found that, too."

"So you *are* versatile," saying it as if he had just won a bet.

"I can be, yes." He'd never been overly hung up on categories like "top" and "bottom," never announcing it like so many Midtown homos, like it was something pertinent to him as a person. Usually he was a top — he had been with Ron — but he'd bottom when the mood struck, or if his partner desired him to be.

Rand stood directly in front of him now, his cock right at mouth level, bouncing as the young man moved. Martin leaned forward and steadied the shaking dong between his lips. There was a sharp intake of breath, an exhaled moan, and Rand dropped the rubbers and bottle of lube onto the floor, freeing his hand to place it on Martin's shoulder. He still held the dildo in his other hand, though,

Martin feeling the head of the rubberized cock brushing against his bicep.

"No more stalling," Rand said, saying the words with great effort as he pulled away, his cock dripping with Martin's spit. "I want to watch you take this up your ass," he commanded, thrusting the dildo in Martin's face.

Martin gripped Eric's replicated cock around the base, wondering if his ass would be accommodating to its girth. He set the dildo down beside him on the sofa and scooted his ass forward on the seat cushion. Spreading his thighs, exposing his hairy hole to his guest, Martin said, "Why don't you get me ready, first."

Something between a smirk and a grin pulled across Rand's lips. Tugging at his ball-sack, he knelt down between Martin's legs, brought his face down between the older man's spread thighs. First, he teased him by swabbing his tongue over Martin's tightened scrotum, prodding his balls beneath their velvety sack. Then his mouth moved lower between Martin's legs, Rand's tongue caressing Martin's groin, moving lower until...

"Oooh!" Martin arched his back, his body trembling as the younger man's tongue pushed its way inside him. His asshole pulsed against the invading tongue. Martin gripped a sofa cushion with one hand, his cock with the other. "Feels so good..." he hissed.

Rand's fingers were next to invade Martin's ass, starting with an index finger. The middle finger was added, increasing the pressure against his tight sphincter, but Martin made no noises of discomfort until a third finger — Rand's forefinger — joined the other two.

"Careful," he grunted. "My ass hasn't been stretched this wide in a while."

His warnings went unheeded, Rand's fingers tunneling deeper, Martin's ass-lips contracting against the digits. The pads of Rand's fingers pressed against the damp walls of his anus, blindly finding his prostate, the tension eased by rush of pleasure.

"Ready now?" Rand asked impishly, responding to Martin's ecstatic gasps. Martin gurgled something unintelligible, but managed a nod. Rand picked the dildo off the sofa cushion and the bottle of lube up from the floor, handing both to Martin.

Martin squirted a generous amount of lubricant into his palm, not caring that he spilled some on the floor and on the sofa's upholstery. He made sure the dildo was well coated and slick, then pushed two of his slimy fingers into his asshole. A deep breath later, he had the head of the dildo knocking at his ass-lips, which met the plastic phallus with suspicion, tightening as Martin pushed the dildo against them.

Rand said nothing, just watched intently. When the dildo's first inch made its way past Martin's resolute sphincter, Rand let out a breathy "oh, yeah." Martin's exclamation was louder and more forceful — mirroring his physical sensations. The dildo felt as if it had punctured its way inside rather than slid. His cock sagged. It had been awhile since he'd had anything larger than a finger up his ass, and he had to pause a minute, wait for the sharp stinging to subside before he pushed the dildo any further.

Another intake of breath, and Martin was ready to push the dildo deeper into his ass. It was easier now, now that the initial shock of entry was behind him (so to speak). There was still the slight tinge of discomfort buzzing at his ass-ring, but the sensation of the porn star's plastic cock filling his chute offset the pain.

"Let me do that," Rand said, brushing Martin's hand away as he took hold of the dildo's plastic scrotum. Gently, he worked the fake dick back and forth. Martin curled a lubricated hand around his cock, stroking it back to a full hard-on.

Rand stood up and turned around, presenting his ass to Martin. "Now get me ready."

Martin brought one hand up to the young man's butt, palming open his cheeks and rubbing the tip of his thumb over Rand's smooth asshole. His other hand reached for the bottle of lube, lying on the sofa next to him. Upending the bottle just above the split channel of Rand's buttocks, Martin squirted lubricant over Rand's butthole and over his own prodding fingers. His thumb poked its way inside, making Rand gasp. Rand rotated his hips against the curious digit, reached between his legs and played with his stiff, seeping cock.

"It's about time you put on one of those rubbers," Rand panted.

Martin had his dick sheathed and lubed within seconds. Moments later, he was watching his cock get swallowed up by Rand's ass.

A hot ecstasy seethed through Martin's body, the dual sensations of fucking Rand's ass and his own ass stuffed with a dildo heightening his pleasure beyond his imaginings. He wondered why he never tried this before and couldn't wait to try it again.

Rand leaned back against him, the smooth skin of his back resting against Martin's hard, hairy chest and torso. "Hard as you want to," he purred, reaching behind to give Martin's face a clumsy caress. "Fuck me as hard as you want to."

Martin pumped his cock deep into Rand's ass. Reaching around the young man's waist, grabbing his dick and stroking it in time to his forceful thrusts. He could feel Rand's body tremble, feel the walls of Rand's ass squeeze his shaft, feel the Eric Hanson dildo push against his prostate. Their bodies, lubricated by sweat, moved easily against each other.

Arching his back and crying out, Rand shot his load onto his belly. It wasn't a copious load — they'd gotten off more times in three days than many people did in a month, so it was a wonder the two men weren't drained completely dry — but Martin admired it all the same, rubbing his hands through the lumpy droplets of warm, sticky jism.

Rand grabbed Martin's wrist and raised his hand, kissing his fingers and tasting his own load. "Mmmmm," he moaned, his face the portrait of contentment.

Martin's body jerked spastically beneath Rand. A groan fought its way out of Martin's mouth but got stuck in his throat, his body paralyzed in orgasm. For a millisecond only his cock and balls seemed able to function. His nut sack drew up tight, and his dick pulsed inside Rand. Martin felt his sphincter squeeze the plastic shaft of Eric's dong.

His muscles relaxed, and he seemed to melt against the sofa cushions, taking Rand with him. They lay like that for several minutes, with Rand still impaled on Martin's cock, their eyes closed, not saying anything. Just breathing.

* * * * *

Grunts, groans, shallow breathing and whispered obscenities filled the bedroom as Task bounced astride Conner's cock. Task clawed at Conner's sweaty back, his body trembling with each violent stabbing of the other man's dick up his chute. Conner's fingernails dug into the taut flesh of Task's butt cheeks.

"So fuckin' hot," he hissed into Task's ear, looking over the younger man's shoulder. He was staring at the image reflected in the mirrored doors of the closet, the image of them, perched on the edge of the bed with Conner's dick sliding up Task's asshole. The sight made him thrust his cock upward, hard, making Task moan loudly, making his ass-muscles contract and squeeze against Conner's shaft.

"I'm so close," Task sighed in Conner's ear, grinding his drooling dick against Conner's hard abdomen, the sensation making his entire body shiver.

Conner dug his fingernails in deeper, fucked Task's ass harder, in quick, mean thrusts. He bit Task's shoulder, making him yelp in pain. Conner kept ramming, hot breath hissing between his clenched teeth, eyes wild with an expression that could just as easily be fury as it was ecstasy. A hand went from Task's left buttock up to his head, gabbing a tuft of his red-orange hair and yanking on it savagely. Task responded by hooking his fingers into the tensed muscles of Conner's shoulders.

The noise level of the room increased as they unleashed their white-hot loads, almost simultaneously. Task moaned through halting, gasping breaths; sounding like a seal suffering an asthma attack. Conner snarled, a wolf tearing into its prey.

Their muscles tensed. Task could feel Conner's dick pulsating within his ass. He could feel the stickiness of his own load, cementing their torsos together. Conner's harsh breathing buzzed in Task's ear. Task's trick spent an extra minute staring over his shoulder at their reflection in the mirrored doors, getting one final look at his fat dick buried in Task's butt. Then he fell backwards, exhaling loudly.

"Gosh-almighty-damn, that was fun," Conner drawled, his fingers caressing the curve of his own pecs.

Task started to say it beat the hell out of blowing truckers, but decided that might wreck the mood. Instead, he just smiled in agreement before carefully extricating himself from Conner's dick.

They relaxed on the bed a moment, sharing half a joint. Conner said, "So, you said you're from L.A., right?"

"Yeah," Task nodded, taking the burning doobie from between Conner's fingers. He was surprised Conner remembered, seeing how that tidbit of information was given in their pre-fuck small talk. It had been Task's experience that men generally didn't remember little details about their tricks after they got off. Hell, Task didn't, so why should they?

Conner nodded. "Funny, this friend I work with, Martin, he hooked up with some guy from L.A. over the weekend. Met him at the same place, The Tackle Box. Only in the parking lot." Conner chuckled at that.

Task took a long drag off the joint and slid his eyes over at Conner. Handing the joint back to the other man, he exhaled and said, "Is that right?"

"Yeah, isn't that a coincidence." Shaking his head, Conner added, "The kid told him some story about having no place to stay and now the dumb bastard's letting him stay at his house. They're fucking their brains out, but still..." He paused to take a hit off the joint.

"What's the guy's name?"

"Martin."

"No, the guy from L.A."

"Oh, right, L.A.'s such a small town you guys prob'ly know each other, right? Shit, I don't know the guy's name. I don't have to — I'm not fuckin' him." It was doubtful Conner remembered Task's name.

Conner had one more toke off the joint and extinguished it in a clear glass ashtray on the bedside table, not bothering to ask Task if he wanted another hit. "Gonna take a quick shower," he announced, standing up and stretching his arms over his head. "You can join me if you want."

Task's eyes glided down Conner's naked body, considering the firm muscles flexing beneath the tan skin, that thick cock, now limp and the head glazed with dried cum. Though tempted, he shook his head. "No, I'm good."

Unfazed, Conner shrugged and went into the bathroom, scratching his balls as he walked.

Task waited until the water started running before getting dressed, hurriedly slipping into his jeans and T-shirt but waiting to put on his socks and shoes.

Martin, Martin ... he repeated the name in his mind, looking around the sparsely furnished bedroom. On the nightstand, besides the ashtray, was a bottle of lube, box of condoms and a phone, none of which Task was looking for. He looked on the dresser across the room, saw a couple books — *Excel for Dummies, The New Joy of Gay Sex* — some loose change, a few receipts, a quart-sized souvenir glass from New Orleans filled with Mardi Gras beads and little rubber cocks. Draped over the top of the glass was a spangled G-string. Task was sure there was a story behind that, but he didn't care enough to want to ask. His eyes moved to the clothes Conner had been wearing, now on the floor where they'd been hastily discarded. He hadn't bothered to empty his pants pockets, and for a moment, Task considered going through them, maybe riffle through the wallet and snag a few bills.

Maybe later, he told himself, leaving the bedroom. After he found what he was looking for.

He made cursory searches of the living room and dining room, both as sparingly furnished as the bedroom. In the living room, he only found a few issues of *Details* and a pathetic CD collection (way too much Celine); in the dining room, he only found a thin layer of dust covering the glassed-topped dining table.

Martin, Martin, Martin. Mentally he chanted the name as he moved into the kitchen.

"Hey, where did you go?" Conner called out.

"Uh... just in the kitchen. Getting a glass of water."

His eyes moved around the kitchen, zeroing in on the cordless phone sitting at the end of the faux-marble countertop. Beside it was a small address book. The word "Tricks" was printed in white on the glossy black cover.

"Get a glass for me, too," Conner said, his voice sounding closer. "Fucking dehydrates me."

Task grabbed the address book. "Sure thing," he said, stuffing the book down the front of his pants. He was adjusting the hem of his T-shirt over the waist of his jeans when Conner entered, wearing a pair of designer bikini briefs.

"Where's my water?"

"Uh, where do you keep the glasses?"

Conner rolled his eyes and pushed past him. "Gee, I don't know. Maybe try the cabinets?"

Task nodded. "Oh, yeah. Right." He chuckled, like he couldn't believe his own stupidity, watching as Conner pulled two glasses down from the cupboard by the sink. In the back of his mind, he continued to chant the name: Martin. So intent that the name not leave his memory that he didn't even bother to appreciate how nice Conner's ass looked in his form-fitting undies.

THIRTEEN

Rand slept deep into Wednesday morning, not waking until nearly eleven. It had been a heavy, dreamless sleep. He barely recalled the goodbye kiss Martin placed on his forehead before leaving for work. Like we're lovers or something, Rand thought with a smirk, not allowing himself to be touched by the sweetness of the gesture. Be just his luck Martin would become attached, even if that attachment made him trusting.

Bullshit, Rand corrected himself. Ball-draining sex two, three times a day made Martin trusting. And less inquisitive.

Not that he was really trying to hide that much from Martin. If he wanted, he could share a lot more details of his life, tell him about growing up in Clovis, California, he and his siblings — an older brother, a younger sister — being herded from one shitty apartment to an even shittier apartment by their alcoholic mother, sometimes joined by one of a string of new daddies.

He could tell Martin about the summer when he was 14, when he and his brother went swimming.

Rand was sitting on his towel, laid out in a spot behind the diving board, the sun drying his skin almost instantly. He stole a few glances at some of the other people around the pool: A couple of women in their early twenties, wearing string bikinis, lying face down on their chaise lounges, trying to get their tans a shade darker; another woman, in her thirties, fifteen pounds overweight, smearing sunscreen on her two little children; and a man, also in his thirties, a bit of a spare tire developing around his otherwise average physique, wearing a pair of yellow swim trunks, seemingly asleep behind his Wayfarers. He didn't look at any of these people for very long, fearing they'd make eye contact and tell him to get out, tell him he didn't belong there. Rand then turned his eyes to his brother, J.T., still in the water, kicking his way across the length of the small, kidney-shaped pool.

The pool was at the Willow Hill Apartments, two blocks up the street and a world away from where they lived, at the Harvard Court apartments. Harvard Court had a pool of its own, but the only water in it was a scummy three-inch puddle in the deep end, collected from infrequent rains. Still, when temperatures reached the upper nineties, a few of the Harvard Court's four-year-olds could be found splashing around in that murky green puddle, getting more relief from the heat in the rancid water than they would in their apartments, where a box fan in the window passed for air conditioning.

J.T. suggested going to the Willow Hill Apartments. No one would know they didn't live there, he said, his confidence convincing Rand to go along. Their sister Kayla wasn't around — probably hanging out with her friend, Tammy, a skinny, stringy-haired girl with a serious Bubble Yum habit — but the brothers wouldn't have included her, anyway. Of the three kids, she was the snitch. And a blackmailer: If Kayla went with them, she'd demand a few dollars from her brothers to keep their excursion a secret, even though she was a participant. But if Kayla got pissed off at J.T. or Rand, she'd tell anyway.

Once the brothers got to the Willow Hill's swimming pool and Rand saw a few of its residents sitting around it, he began to have second thoughts. No one was going to mistake him and his brother for residents at Willow Hill, not when they wore ill-fitting gym shorts instead of swim trunks and carried threadbare towels that these people wouldn't use to dry off their dogs. But J.T. pushed Rand through the gate to the pool, telling him not to worry about it.

J.T. certainly wasn't worried, not even noticing the dirty look he got from the fat mom when he inadvertently splashed her as he swam to the deep-end. Reaching the ladder at the lip of the pool, J.T. hoisted himself out of the water, his muscles flexing, his wet skin shimmering under the sun's harsh spotlight. The navy blue, polyester shorts he wore, part of his high school gym uniform, were a size too small — their mother said she wasn't going to pay no goddamn $35 every school year — and hugged his brother's body, a body that Rand found increasingly fascinating.

At 17, his brother already had a man's physique, solidly built, the rigid muscles of his torso accentuated by dark hair. A line of that hair led Rand's eyes from J.T.'s navel to the elastic waistband of his shorts, down to the full, heavy bulge in his crotch. He could make out the outline of his brother's cock, the subtle indentation between the head and shaft advertising to one and all that he was circumcised. Rand had seen J.T. naked on a few occasions (there wasn't much privacy in his family's two-bedroom apartment at Harvard Court). One time, a month before school let out for the summer, he barged into the bathroom one harried morning as his brother was finishing his shower, J.T. yelling at him to get the fuck out, but their mother — hung over, meaner and louder — countered that Rand was already running late for school and didn't have time to wait for his brother to finish "primping like a girl" Besides, she said, it wasn't like J.T. had anything Rand didn't. But in Rand's eyes, his brother did: A man-sized dick, longer, thicker and more interesting than his own. A fluffy bush of dark pubic hair bloomed above his prick; his balls hung low and full beneath. Rand didn't realize he was staring at his brother's cock until J.T. chided, "Watcha' starin' at, queerbait," and threw his damp towel into his brother's face.

Rand was staring now as his brother walked toward him, feeling a tingle between his legs that was both exciting and frightening. He's your brother, he reminded himself. And, more importantly, *he's a guy.*

"You just workin' on your suntan today?" J.T. asked, swatting at Rand's forehead, Rand whining for him to cut it out.

Both boys felt someone else's eyes on them and turned. The man in the yellow swim trunks was walking toward them. "Like living in an oven, isn't it?" he called out.

J.T. shrugged. "S'pose so."

"Guess I can't complain too much," said the man, coming to a stop beside J.T. Up close he looked closer to forty, with two days growth of dark stubble highlighting rather than camouflaging the deep lines around his mouth. Rand's eyes dropped to the man's crotch (he'd been checking out men's crotches more and more lately). The bulge there was significant.

"From Michigan myself," the man continued. "Gladly live in an oven than that freezer. A winter here is like a summer vacation up there. You boys from this area?"

The brothers nodded. "I see. Natives," said the man, rubbing his forefinger along his chin, like a scientist considering a rather interesting specimen. "You guys live in the complex? Don't remember seeing you two around."

Rand felt the color drain from his face. J.T. told the man they'd just moved in, but the man only chuckled and said, "Don't worry, your secret's safe with me. No harm done, getting a little break from the heat."

Rand looked away. Something about the man made him uneasy, but he shook his hand anyway when it was offered, the man telling Rand to call him Bob.

"You guys bring any sunscreen?" Bob asked. When the brothers shook their heads, he scolded them. "You'll fry to a crisp out here without it. This little guy" — he pointed down at Rand — "is already looking a little pink."

Bob said they could use some of his sunscreen, but he'd left the bottle at his apartment. "Why don't you boys just come on over and you can get a layer of sunscreen on, maybe have a bottle of pop, too."

The offer set off alarms in Rand's brain, but J.T. nodded and said, sure, okay. Rand didn't protest — he couldn't, not with Bob standing right there.

The Willow Hill Apartments were a maze of one-story units, and Bob's apartment was somewhere in the middle of the maze. Conversation on the walk there was mundane, Bob asking the usual adult questions: How old are you? What grade are you in? Rand and J.T. didn't ask Bob anything until they were at the front walkway of his apartment and saw another swimming pool, less than one hundred feet from Bob's apartment. "How come you don't go to that pool?" Rand asked.

Bob, working his key into the front door lock, looked over his shoulder. "Hmmm? Oh. Usually too many people go to that one."

Inside his apartment was dark. A large bamboo shade was rolled down over the living room's picture window, but Bob turned on a lamp rather than raise the shade. The place was clean, the decor basic and impersonal, with only a couple framed old movie posters — one for *Casablanca*, another for *Giant* — giving the apartment any personality. Compared to Rand and J.T.'s apartment at the Harvard Court, though, Bob's was a palace. Bob told the boys to sit down, make themselves at home while he went into the kitchen to get them sodas.

Tossed casually on the coffee table, alongside issues of *People* and *Newsweek*, were titles like *Cock Slut* and *Butt-fuck Bitch*. The covers featured overly made-up women, nude or almost nude posed with men who were aiming their hard dicks at one of their waiting orifices.

J.T. chuckled and opened one of the magazines, Rand looking over his shoulder. He saw a platinum blonde with silicone tits straddling a man, his cock disappearing into her pussy. J.T. flipped through several more pages, pausing on an image of the blonde cradling an erect cock between her enhanced breasts, cum dripping off her chin. Rand stared at the plump head of the dick sandwiched between the woman's tits, feeling a familiar tingling in his groin and telling himself it was the woman who aroused him.

"Enjoying the reading material, boys?" asked Bob sternly, startling them. J.T. slammed the magazine shut and jumped back against the sofa. Their host chuckled. "Forgot I left those out here," he said, smiling, handing them each an icy glass of cola. "I'm sure it's nothing you haven't seen before. You can keep looking at them if you like. Just don't tell your parents."

J.T. snorted at that. "Yeah. Sure." He picked up *Butt-fuck Bitch* and started to thumb through it. Rand didn't pick up a magazine himself — it seemed weird now that Bob was in the room, watching them — but shared the one J.T. was looking at, marveling at images of the titular bitch working a dildo into her anus while a man who looked like he belonged in a B-grade gangster movie fed his fat dong between her scarlet lips.

Bob took a seat on the sofa, next to Rand. Sitting a little too close, but Rand wasn't going to say anything about it. He continued to look over J.T.'s shoulder while Bob looked at them. From the corner of his eyes Rand saw their host had a hand clamped over his crotch, squeezing the mound there.

"I've got movies, too," said Bob, reaching for a remote on the coffee table. "You guys interested?"

"Dirty ones?" asked J.T., tossing the copy of *Butt-fuck Bitch* onto the coffee table. Bob just grinned, turned on the TV and hit "play."

A man's low, rumbling moan — "Yeah, baby, suck my cock" — was heard over the television speakers before its corresponding image formed on the screen. When the screen brightened, Rand's jaw dropped, and his dick snapped to attention. A man was lying on a queen-sized bed while a woman with light brown hair was giving him head. Rand barely noticed the woman, concentrating on the man instead. Unlike the men in the magazines, who were mildly attractive at best, the man in the video was hot: handsome features, long, dark hair and a well-built body, thick with muscle. The camera, however, remained on the woman sucking his cock. Rand didn't complain; the man's cock was good-looking, too.

The woman in the video reached for something off camera. A long, skinny beige dildo came into view. A close up of the man's face, him groaning, "Oh, yeah, fuck me, baby," and then a tight shot of the woman working the dildo up the man's ass. Rand nearly came in his pants.

J.T. shifted in his seat. Rand looked over at his brother. J.T. was resting a hand between his legs, but couldn't entirely conceal the hard-on straining against his blue shorts. Seeing that just made Rand's arousal that much more intense.

"Pretty hot, isn't it," said Bob, his voice taking on a conspiratorial edge.

Rand was afraid to look in their host's direction, but did so anyway. Bob had a pretty obvious boner, too, making no attempt to hide it — he even squeezed it when he noticed he had his young guest's attention. Despite his wariness toward Bob, Rand was curious about seeing his cock uncovered. The only erect adult penises he'd seen were in photos and videos; he'd never seen one "for real."

"I could just jack off now, watching it," continued Bob. "You boys jack off?"

J.T. shrugged, his response to most questions he didn't want to answer. Rand kept silent, more embarrassed about answering in front of his older brother than admitting to Bob he beat off.

"Nothing to be embarrassed about," Bob said, his voice getting softer. "Everyone does it. Perfectly natural. You guys want to, feel free. I won't mind, and I certainly won't tell anyone."

For a moment the only sound in the room was the two people in the porno video. The woman was riding the hot guy now, simultaneously fucking the guy with the dildo while he fucked her. Rand and J.T. exchanged a look, silently daring each other to be the first to pull his cock out as well as share the unspoken observation: *This is getting really weird.*

Bob stood up and said, "Well, if you guys don't mind, I'm going to indulge." Sounding like he was doing nothing more than ordering extra fries with his lunch.

Then Bob's yellow swim trunks came off.

J.T. chuckled and shook his head. "Shit, I'm not believin' this."

Rand stared at Bob's stiff dick, dumbstruck. Conflicting thoughts and feelings swirled inside him: Fear, apprehension, curiosity, arousal. He felt like he could either vomit or cum at any moment.

Bob returned to his seat next to Rand, sitting with his legs spread. Rand tried to keep his eyes on the TV, pretend that a naked man with a hard-on wasn't sitting next to him, close enough so their knees touched, but he kept stealing glances. He supposed Bob's cock was a pretty good size, seven inches long — eight, maybe — with a short, blunt crown. His balls were large, tumbling onto the sofa cushion in their thin, almost hairless sack of pink skin. Bob's pubes were ash blond.

If he wants you to suck it, will you? Rand asked himself. He told himself no, but only because J.T. was right there, and he didn't want his brother thinking he was a fag.

But Bob didn't ask Rand to suck his dick. Instead, he slid a hand between Rand's thighs, the warmth of Bob's fingers on his own erect cock felt through the cloth of his shorts. "I can take care of that for you if you want," Bob offered. His voice was very low now, his seduction tone. "I can take care of both of you. I give a pretty mean blowjob."

The words hit Rand's ears and burned through his body until he could hear nothing but his own beating heart. Goosebumps rose along his skinny forearms and he felt himself grow pale.

As he'd hoped, J.T. intervened, though not in the manner Rand had expected. "How 'bout you start with me?"

Both Bob and Rand looked over at him, eyes wide with surprise. "Well, uh, I..." Bob stammered. Clearly this wasn't part of his plan.

J.T. stood up from the couch, thumbs hooked in the waistband of his too-small gym shorts, his hard-on plainly outlined. "Suck me first, then you can have my brother. Rand, why don't you go someplace else, maybe wait in the bedroom."

"No!" Bob blurted out, struggling to regain control. "I want him here. I want him to watch."

Rand wanted to watch, too.

J.T. didn't contest the older man, just gave another one of his shrugs and said, "Okay."

When his brother pulled off his shorts, Rand was so awestruck he stopped breathing for a second. He'd seen J.T.'s cock before, but never hard. It was now twice its regular size, the shaft thick and veiny. His nut-sack had drawn up tight, the dark hair covering it standing on end as if full of static electricity.

The brothers were careful to avoid eye contact as J.T. stepped over to where Bob sat and presented his stiff dick to their host. Bob brought his eyes up from J.T.'s hard-on for a moment, as if asking permission, then took hold of the younger man's prick. A moment later, he took J.T.'s cock into his mouth.

Rand watched the scene as if he were not a part of it, like it was just part of the porno video still playing on TV. J.T. and Bob seemed to forget his presence. Bob gulped down J.T.'s cock, reaching around the young man's narrow waist to grip his ass cheeks. J.T. thrust his hips forward and even grabbed a handful of Bob's wavy, sandy-blond hair. Rand looked up at his brother's face. J.T.'s eyes were partially closed, his mouth slack, lips only moving to let out a grunt or exhale a heavy breath.

He slid a hand under his shorts, feeling his own adolescent cock. Rand's hard-on was intense, aching pleasurably. Rubbing his thumb over his cockhead, over the slit, he felt moisture there, the fist time he remembered secreting pre-cum. He was aroused enough to forget his inhibitions, to stroke his dick while he watched J.T. get blown by the stranger. But what if he came before it was his turn? Rand didn't want to cheat himself out of his first blowjob.

J.T.'s breathing became very shallow, and Rand detected a slight tremor in his brother's shoulders. The words "Oh, yeah," came out J.T.'s mouth in a gasp, so soft they were nearly drowned out by the shrieking orgasms on the porno video. Bob was sucking J.T.'s dick harder now, taking it down his throat in quick, desperate gulps. Rand saw his brother's body stiffen, and J.T. forced out a strangled cry as he came, sending his load down the older man's greedy throat.

When J.T. pulled his cock out of Bob's mouth, it was wet with saliva. A lingering drop of jism seeped out the slit. Rand stared at his brother's hard dick a moment longer, then looked over at Bob, who met his gaze with a creepy grin. Without saying anything, Bob moved to the floor, getting on his knees before Rand. Rand took another look at the man's cock. It looked the way his own felt: painfully hard, throbbing and steadily oozing pre-cum.

Bob slipped his fingers beneath the elastic waistband of Rand's shorts and started to pull. "Let's see what you've got for me," Bob whispered excitedly. Rand closed his eyes, imagined it was the sexy man in the video who was pulling his pants off, or J.T. He clenched his fists and waited to discover how it would feel to have his dick sucked.

But J.T. intervened again.

The recollection made Rand hard. He fondled his rigid prick absent-mindedly, contemplating jerking off. He decided against it — he risked getting raw as it was — and rolled out of bed, trudging to the bathroom. Standing beneath the shower, he planned his next move. He needed to get back in touch with Dane before he left for Atlanta, remind the old fart he expected his money. If he still balked, well, Rand would just have to show him he was serious.

The phone was ringing when he stepped out of the shower. The machine was picking up as he walked into the bedroom, rubbing a towel over his damp hair. He heard Martin's recorded voice, sounding very businesslike as he apologized for not being available to take the call. Then the caller spoke, and Rand froze in his tracks.

"Uh, hey there. You don't know me, but I heard a friend of mine might be staying with you, a guy named Rand."

Task.

* * * * *

The house was empty when Martin got home Wednesday evening. He didn't see anything of his stolen or anything of Rand's left behind. Rand hadn't even left a note.

Thursday Martin called in sick.

FOURTEEN

Thursday Dane Kensington boarded his plane at LAX at 8:00 a.m. and touched down in Atlanta at 3:15 p.m., the different time zone robbing him of three hours, making him feel rushed upon arrival. He pushed his way through the crowds at the Hartsfield-Jackson Airport, waited impatiently for his luggage at baggage claim, then hurried outside, slapped in the face by the damp summer heat. A driver, a wiry black man in a black suit, holding a hand-lettered sign reading "D. Kennington," greeted him at the curb, telling Dane his name was Reggie as he took Dane's bags from him. Minutes later, Dane was sitting in the back of an air-conditioned Lincoln Town Car, Reggie expertly threading his way through the clutter of cars and travelers gathered around the terminal.

"So, what brings you to Atlanta, business or pleasure?" Reggie asked.

Great, a talker. "Both," Dane said. "Pleasure is my business."

That got a chuckle and a nod from Reggie. "That right? What sort of business is that?"

"I make and distribute gay fuck films."

Reggie didn't have much to say after that.

An hour later, Dane was in the penthouse suite of the Wilkes Overlook Hotel, a fifteen-story glass tower at the edge of Midtown. Staring out at the hazy, amber-hued sky (Christ, just like L.A., Dane thought), he placed a call.

"Nick?"

"Yeah."

"Are you in Atlanta?"

"Yeah, got here last night."

"Got a car?" Dane continued after another "yeah": "Good. Could you meet me in front of the Wilkes Overlook? Know where that is? Just off Fourteenth Street, in Midtown. I'll wait out front."

An hour later Nick was pulling up in front of the hotel, driving a dark blue Taurus. Dane slid into the front seat and gave Nick a quick once-over. He was an attractive man, in his mid-thirties, tan, with short, wavy black hair and thick eyelashes that made his amber eyes that more intense. Looked like Nick stayed in shape, too, the way he filled out the short-sleeved gray knit shirt he wore.

After quick introductions, Dane said, "Hope you don't mind me saying, but you're not at all like I pictured you."

"You were expecting some fat goombah with a crooked nose and wearing a Hawaiian shirt, right?" Nick said, pulling out into traffic. "Maybe carrying a machine gun in a violin case? Like from the old gangster movies."

"Something like that," Dane admitted.

"So, where to?" Nick asked, heading east on Fourteenth.

"Someplace where we can talk, with few witnesses."

Nick took them to a McDonald's on Ponce de Leon. Dane made a face. "McDonald's?"

"Yeah. No one pays attention to shit in a McDonald's."

They both bought Diet Cokes and took a booth in back. "How you know Jerry?" Nick asked.

"He's an acquaintance, actually. Met him while trying to hunt down one of the guys I want you to take care of."

"He still running that sausage shack off Santa Monica?"

"That's where we met, yes. He said you two did time together?"

Nick nodded. "At Chino. I got three years for aggravated assault. Jerry was in for ... I wanna say extortion, fraud, something like that. We were cellmates."

Dane was curious if Nick was Jerry's bitch, but forced the thought from his mind. He really didn't want to know. Instead he asked, "You give him that tattoo?"

Nick laughed. "That shitty thing? Fuck, no. He did that himself. Got infected after he did it, and he had to go to the infirmary." The sexy hit man shook his head, chuckling, "Dumbass."

The conversation switched gears suddenly, with Nick asking, "So what you need me to do?"

"I'd hired this one guy to do a job for me in Miami, supposed to be simple ... fuck this asshole politician, running for office here in Atlanta, get it on videotape." Dane paused, looked around the room for the hundredth time to make sure no cops were around, and dropped his voice anyway. "But he brings his dumbshit friend along and, long story short, I could be implicated in murder if these two guys continue walking around. Shit, one of the fuckers is already trying to extort money out of me."

Nick leaned back in the white fiberglass bench, looking thoughtful as he took a sip from his Diet Coke. "You say this was in Miami? When?"

"Last weekend. Why?"

The corners of Nick's lips tugged upward. "I was just down there. Think I heard something about this. Guy found shot in a motel down there?"

Dane felt his stomach constrict. "Yeah, that's it."

"You got a plan for how this should be done ... people usually do, when they call me. Let's hear it, and I'll tell you if it'll work in real life or if you watch too much TV."

After yet another quick check around the room, Dane leaned forward and outlined his plan for the hired gun. "I already have one of the guys ... the stupid one ... here, waiting for me. He's expecting to get paid for the original deal..."

"The blackmail plan?"

"Ssssshhh! Not so loud. But yeah, that. The other guy, the one trying to extort me? He's here, but I don't know where. He's been in touch though, and that's how we'll get them. I'm hosting this event tomorrow night, at this club I own, The Tackle Box. My 'Porn Star Search.'"

"You do porn?"

"You didn't know that?"

"You didn't say. What movies you do?"

Dane let out an exasperated sigh. "You ever hear of DanKen Studios? We did *Five-Fingered Fuck*, *Homo High*, *Dickweed & Roy*..."

"*Dickweed & Roy*, I like that," Nick chuckled. "Who's in it?"

"I'll give you the DVD free as part of the deal, okay?" Dane snapped. "Anyway, I'll be having a party afterwards at the hotel. During the contest, we give invites to a select few people in the crowd — guys we think are hot — as well as all the contestants. I'm going to make sure Task and Rand — that's their names — are there. Figure you could get them then, when they're leaving. Maybe make it look like a mugging or something."

Nick was silent, his hands clasped before him on the Formica tabletop as he turned the plan over in his mind. "You said one of these guys was named Task?"

"Yeah, never heard that one before, either, and I live out in L.A. So I take it the plan's okay with you?"

"A few questions: What time are the guys going to leave the party? And how're you gonna make sure they leave together? They're not together now, so what makes you think they'll wanna hook up after a night of fun, especially since it sounds like they both just want to get as much as they can out of you and split."

Dane hadn't thought out the minor details, but tried to cover that fact quickly, offering the suggestion that he'd put the guys in a limo, give them a ride back to wherever they were staying.

"And then you got the limo driver involved," Nick said, shaking his head.

"Get them before they get in the car."

"Right, just drive up and blow 'em away in front of the swanky hotel. No one will notice that."

"Okay, okay, I get your point. So what do you suggest instead?"

"Have me at your party."

"That's your brilliant solution?" Dane laughed aloud. "What, are you going to shoot them *during* the party? That'll make it the social event of the season, bigger than the White Party, even."

"I'm serious. I'm just another guest. You point these guys out to me, I can get them someplace private and do the job. They're basically whores, right? I flash them a little cash, and we all leave together. For all they know, I'm just some rich closet case who wants some fun before he has to go back to the wife and kids."

Dane rubbed his forefinger across his bristly goatee. "Aren't you afraid you could be identified, later, when the bodies are discovered?"

"*If* the bodies are discovered." Nick corrected. "Anyway, these parties of yours, I'm assuming it's not people sipping martinis, eating canapés and discussing world politics. More like guys getting drunk, doing X and sucking each other off, right?"

"Pretty much the scene, yeah," Dane confirmed.

"Then they're not going to notice one more stranger there. Hell, I take my pants off, they'll probably never look at me above the waist. Y'know, my nickname's Nine, that's what people call me. I'll let you guess why."

Dane raised an eyebrow. "Is that so?"

"That mean I'm invited?"

He exhaled slowly. "Sure. We'll do it your way. Just keep your distance from me during the party. I don't want anyone linking us together."

"What? I'm not cute enough for you?" Nick quipped. Dane was grateful when Nick — Nine — checked his watch, made a move to stand. "Hate to cut this short, but I gotta run. There's a friend who lives here I need to see."

* * * * *

"Mmmmm, that feels soooo good," Winston purred, lying nude on a massage table as the pair of strong hands kneaded the tense muscles of his back, working their way down to his ass.

The guy's name was Tom. According to his ad in the back of *Hot Spots*, he specialized in "sensual massage," meaning Winston could, at the very least, expect a hand-job. What Winston hadn't expected was an actual massage, surprised not only to discover Tom was as attractive in person as he was in the photo in his ad, but that he brought a portable massage table.

"You like that?" Tom asked, digging his thumbs into the small of Winston's back.

"Oh, yes," he replied, raising his butt slightly and sliding a hand beneath his body to adjust his growing cock. "You don't know how much I need this."

God, the previous six hours had been utter hell, having to endure the company of Nora, Perry's mother, and Katrina, his sister — the Iron Cunt and Frozen Dyke. Through some cruel coincidence, the bitches were on the same flight to Atlanta as he, and even though the women disliked him as much as he hated them, they shared a cab to Miami International, leaving the hotel at 6:00 a.m. for a 10:00 a.m. flight because Nora didn't want to risk being held up by security. By 7:30, they were at the gate, nothing to do but wait, which they did in each other's company because Southern manners dictated it would be rude for Winston to sit on the opposite end of the waiting area. At least the Frozen Dyke kept her mouth shut, only looking up from her Rita Mae Brown novel to throw a smirk Winston's way whenever he spoke — which was seldom, Nora doing most of the talking. Winston's nerves got so frayed he hid out in a men's room stall for thirty minutes, preferring to endure the fetid stench of piss and shit to the Iron Cunt's snide comments.

In Atlanta, they shared another cab. Winston told the driver to take them to the Sheraton in Midtown. "There's not enough room for us to stay at my son's house?" Nora asked pointedly.

"I just thought you two would be more comfortable in a hotel," Winston said.

The Iron Cunt pursed her lips. "Are you sure it's our comfort that concerns you?"

Nevertheless, the women let Winston put them up in the hotel, no doubt just as eager as he was to part company.

As soon as he returned to the house in Morningside — always *the* house, not *their* house or *his* house — Winston smoked a joint and flipped through the classifieds in *Hot Spots* magazine, calling Tom because he liked his picture and the promise of a "10+ personality." He hated the idea of hiring a whore, but he couldn't exactly go hit the bars, not when he could bump into someone he knew. Or worse, someone Perry knew, one of his Log Cabin Republican pals who'd wonder why Winston was out trawling for dick when his lover wasn't even in the ground yet. A hustler was just more convenient.

"You've got a great ass," Tom said, rubbing the full globes of Winston's buttocks. "I'm not just saying that, either. You're in great shape."

"Thanks. I try to work out at least ... least three times a week," he said dreamily, the stranger's manipulation of his muscles at once arousing and relaxing.

Tom's hands worked their way toward the crack of Winston's ass, the edge of one hand slicing down the cleft between his muscular butt cheeks. His butthole twitched, his cock throbbed. Tom slipped two fingers between Winston's legs and prodded his sphincter, his fingertips moving in a circular motion against Winston's quivering ass-lips.

Winston let out a low, husky moan, and rolled his hips. He felt himself sinking into the blissful feeling, but then a thought or memory would interrupt, pulling him back to the surface. He got a mental flash of the glaring investigator in Miami, going over Winston's alibi for the third time. He saw Perry's body, laid out in the city morgue. He saw Nora's accusing glare.

He tried to push the recent memories back, to slip back into the enjoyably mindless present before his cock went completely limp. Just think about now he told himself.

— Tom inserting a spit-lubed finger into his hole quickly erased the unpleasantness of his immediate past. Winston regained his erection almost instantly as Tom's index finger wiggled inside his chute. The hustler added his middle finger, Winston's pleasure spiraling upward as the two fingers massaged his prostate.

Winston raised his ass into the air to meet Tom's probing fingers, crying out a stream of foul-mouthed gibberish — "OhJesusfuckgoddamnYEAH!" — as his pleasure increased. Tom finger-fucked his hole faster, harder, the way Winston hoped Tom would fuck his ass with his cock. The table wobbled beneath him. If we keep this up, Winston thought, I'll either cum too soon or the fucking table will collapse.

"Let's move over to something more stable," he said, sitting up and swinging his legs over the side of the massage table.

Tom followed him to the full-sized bed that dominated the master bedroom with its ornate headboard, crafted in France during the late Eighteenth century — or was it the early Nineteenth century? Winston neither remembered nor cared, antiques mattering less to him now than ever before. He sat at the foot of the bed and spread his legs, tracing his upper lip with his tongue as his hired cock stepped into the space between his parted thighs.

"Let me get a taste of this ten-plus-inch 'personality' of yours," Winston said playfully, curling a fist around the hefty shaft of Tom's dick. Not quite ten inches in Winston's estimation; more like eight and a half, though that was more than serviceable. Tom smiled down at him, revealing lines on his boyish face that made Winston doubtful the hustler was 24 years old, as his ad claimed. He's in his early thirties at least, Winston surmised, immediately disheartened by the fact that this still made Tom a young man in comparison to him.

Tom's cock, however, was ageless, and Winston took it down his throat ravenously. He sucked the hustler's dick in long, even gulps, taking it to the hilt until Tom's cockhead was tickling his uvula, then slowly pulling back, his tongue massaging the pulsing flesh of the shaft as his mouth made its retreat. Just when the smooth, red crown was about to pop from Winston's wet lips, he took a downward dive, swallowing Tom's prick whole. Tom grunted and pushed forward, and Winston could feel a hand caress the top of his head.

"You want me to suck your cock now?" the hustler rasped.

Like asking a guy if he wants a million dollars, Winston thought. He leaned back, resting his weight on his hands, while Tom knelt on the floor. The hired dick gave the head of his cock a few cursory licks, lapping up the pre-cum oozing out the slit, and then closed his mouth over Winston's dong. He watched the shaft of his cock slide between Tom's lips, enjoying the sight but compelled to close his eyes anyway, losing himself in the sensation as he would a sweet dream.

The whore's mouth moved lower, his warm, wet tongue sweeping over Winston's ball sack before sliding down into the dark crevice between his thighs. Winston eased himself onto his back and raised his legs, resting them on Tom's strong shoulders. He felt the other man's tongue circle his hole, teasing the sensitive flesh of his ass-lips. Tom parted those lips with his fingers, stabbing his tongue through the opening.

Winston's ecstatic cries filled the bedroom. Leveraging his weight against the hustler's shoulders, he raised his hips off the bed, pushing his ass into Tom's face. "Fuck me," Winston moaned. "Fuck me, please."

Tom pulled his face away from Winston's ass. "You bet," he drawled.

* * * * *

Nine parked behind a dinged-up silver Mazda in the driveway and got out of the car. The house stood out from its neighbors in design, its architecture exhibiting a Mediterranean influence rather than Tudor and Colonial styling favored in the area, but it was just as large as the other houses in the neighborhood. Probably just 500 square feet short of qualifying as a mansion, Nine thought, looking up at the old two-story home, wondering what a house like this went for in this neighborhood. Had to be a million, at least, if not more.

He pushed the front doorbell but didn't hear any chimes sound inside. Nine pressed the doorbell again, but it triggered nothing. A million dollar house and the fucking doorbell didn't work. He tried the brass knocker instead, but that didn't bring anyone to the door, either. The door was unlocked, however, and he let himself inside.

Nine peeked into the rooms on either side of the foyer — on his right, a formal dining room; on his left the living room. Lots of antiques, delicate vases and baroque-style oil paintings in gilded frames. Decorated for show, not for living. He was about to call out when he heard voices. Male voices, coming from upstairs. Grunting, groaning, occasionally saying something — nothing that Nine could decipher, but he understood from the tone. These were sounds he usually heard when guys were either bench-pressing fifty more pounds than they could handle or fucking, and he doubted the guys upstairs were lifting weights.

He stepped quickly across the marble floor to the staircase at the end of the foyer. The voices got louder as he neared the top of the stairs. "Fuck my ass, oh, yeah, fuck me," panted one. The other man was letting out a steady stream of grunts, punctuating each thrust. Nine followed the voices to the end of the hall and into a spacious bedroom where he found two men in bed, one sitting on the fat cock of the other.

"Mmmmm-mmmm! I like the way you handle your grief, Winston," Nine said, unbuttoning his shirt as he walked toward the bed.

The men froze, mid-fuck. Winston whirled his head in Nine's direction, his face turning ashen. "What...? How did...? Get out!" he sputtered.

"We have business to discuss," Nine replied calmly, dropping his shirt in a nearby chair as he rounded the bed. He put a foot up on the chair and began to untie his shoe. "But it can wait. Pleasure before business, I always say."

While Winston was still struggling to form a complete sentence, the guy beneath him spoke up. "You his boyfriend or something?"

Nine looked over at the guy. Cute face, tightly built body, his muscular torso shaved smooth, a Yin-Yang symbol tattooed on his left bicep. His light brown hair stuck up at odd angles on top of his head, its dishevelment no doubt carefully arranged to affect a stylish just-rolled-out-of-bed look. "I'm 'or something.'"

"I charge extra for three-ways," said the guy.

Nine removed his nine-millimeter from his ankle holster, made sure the guy saw it. "That right?"

"Why you got that?" The hustler's voice squeaked. Winston looked like he might be ill. "You a cop?"

"Yeah," Nine chuckled, unbuckling his belt. "Wanna see my badge?" He unzipped his black trousers, letting them fall to the floor. After a moment's pause to let the two men get a look at the bulge at the front of his white cotton briefs, he shucked off his underwear. The anxious expressions of his audience transformed into looks of admiration and lust.

"People call me Nine," he said, pulling on his semi-hard dick as he stepped toward the bed. "You got a name, or do you just go by Jizz Whore?"

The hustler scowled. "My name's Tom."

"Nice to meet you, Tom," Nine said, nodding as he climbed onto the bed. "Always like to know a guy's name before I have him eat my ass."

Facing Winston, Nine threw a leg over Tom's torso. As he lowered his ass onto the hustler's face he said, "Just put this on my pal Winston's tab."

Tom rimmed Nine's ass half-heartedly at first, the tip of his tongue barely making contact with the outer lips of the hit man's hole. "Goddamn, does no one teach you whores how to eat ass anymore?" Nine griped. "C'mon, Tom, I know you can do better than that." At that, Tom proved he could, shoving his tongue into Nine's asshole, wagging it inside his chute.

"There you go," Nine sighed, rocking back against the hustler's darting tongue. His cock stiffened in response.

Winston appeared unsure of what to do. His eyes were filled with apprehension, even as he dropped his gaze to Nine's hard-on. Nine put one hand beneath Winston's chin and guided his face upward. With his other hand he grabbed Winston's cock. It had gone soft but was beginning to revive.

"Relax, nothing bad's gonna happen. Just want to have some fun, is all." He gently stroked Winston's prick, feeling it grow in his hand. "Besides, I've never fucked a TV star before."

That comment got a smile out of Winston. Probably got more excited hearing that than by me rubbing his dick, Nine thought. When they first met, three months ago, he was sure to let Nine know about his TV career, even though it had been more than a decade since Winston was in a series. Nevertheless, for a never-quite-was has-been, Winston held up quite well.

Nine leaned forward and kissed him. Whatever trepidation Winston felt evaporated when Nine's tongue slipped inside his mouth. The ex-TV star reached forward and curled his fingers around the hit man's nine-inch dong, pulling on it with his soft hands. A moan rumbled deep in Nine's throat. The dual stimulation of his cock being stroked while a tongue snaked up his chute sent an electric current crackling beneath his skin.

"Ya' wanna suck it, baby?" Nine asked Winston, his voice a hoarse whisper. Without waiting for an answer, he raised his butt off the hustler's face, moving backwards a few inches so his balls dragged across Tom's mouth. Nine brought himself up on his knees and reached for Winston, urging him to lean forward.

He let out a loud, satisfied groan as his cock was engulfed in Winston's hot mouth. Winston swallowed the whole thing easily, as Nine knew he would. Those years in Hollywood probably were more instrumental in helping Winston learn to control his gag reflex than teaching him how to act, Nine was sure. Winston LaGrabe was reputed to be a hundred times better in bed than he was on screen.

"Ooooh, that feels nice," Nine moaned, thrusting his hips forward, fucking Winston's mouth. Tom was thrusting, too, back in the mood now after eating Nine's ass. The firm mattress bounced slightly as the hustler rammed his cock into Winston's hole.

"Need more lube," Winston gasped, rubbing the head of Nine's dick against his face.

"I'll take care of you," Nine volunteered. Though he hated to interrupt the blowjob he was getting, he was eager to get his hands on Winston's ass.

He hopped off the bed and, after locating the bottle of Eros on the floor beside the bed, picked up the lube and moved around to Winston's rear. The guy was hot all over, but in Nine's opinion, Winston's butt was his best feature. A nice round, muscular bubble butt, looking even hotter now with a cock buried in it. Trouble was it wasn't Nine's cock piercing those succulent globes.

I'll fix that, Nine vowed.

"Lift your ass up," he ordered Winston. Winston slowly lifted his butt up off the hustler's body until Tom's sheathed cock popped out and fell against his belly with a wet smack.

A good-sized cock on the whore, Nine observed. He'd have to compliment Winston on his taste.

Nine poured lubricant onto his open hand and brought his wet, slick fingers to Winston's shaved hole, spreading lube around the flushed ass-lips before slipping a finger inside. It went in easy, which was no surprise. Nine had heard Winston was a voracious bottom. Heard there was even a videotape of his beautiful ass getting gang-banged that cost Winston his stardom. Damn, he wished he could get a copy of that tape.

He kept adding fingers, Winston's hole not giving much resistance until Nine had four fingers up there. The actor groaned and Nine could feel the walls of his ass quiver against his touch.

Nine squirted lube down the length of Tom's prick, like he was putting mustard on a hot dog, and dropped the bottle on the floor. He pulled his fingers from Winston's butthole and used both hands to play with the hustler's cock and balls.

"Got him ready for you," he said, squeezing the shaft of Tom's cock. "Can't wait to have this huge dick back up your ass, can you, Winston? Wonder who's the bigger whore, you or Tom here?"

Neither man seemed to take offense at Nine's comment. Tom, he figured, was anesthetized to any slurs toward his profession. Winston was an actor; it was a good bet this wasn't the first time he'd been called a whore.

Gripping the hustler's dong with one hand and pressing down on Winston's ass with the other, he helped the two men rejoin, Winston letting out a satisfied sigh as Tom's large cock slid into his hungry hole.

The mattress creaked softly, rhythmically as Tom thrust his hips upward, regaining the momentum he had before Nine's interruption.

Nine walked around the right side of the bed, to the bedside table where a box of rubbers sat.

"I want — *ohhh!* — I want to suck your cock some more," Winston burbled, his muscular body bouncing atop Tom's.

"I got a better idea," Nine said, pulling out a strip of condom packets from the box and tearing one off. Winston watched as Nine rolled a rubber over his formidable endowment, but his attention was quickly diverted by the hard fucking he was getting from his whore. He wasn't watching when Nine climbed onto the bed, and neither of the men expressed any curiosity in what their uninvited guest was up to, too deep into their own pleasure to really care.

It was only when Nine positioned himself between Tom's legs and began slapping his cockhead against Winston's buttcrack did anyone comment.

"Hey, dude, already occupied," Tom said through clenched teeth.

"So?" Nine said. "You whores have no imagination."

Winston looked back over his shoulder. "What're you...?"

Before he could finish his question Nine was pressing his cock against Tom's engorged shaft, the tip of his dick nuzzling the stretched lips of Winston's hole.

"Just relax," Nine said, placing a hand on Winston's left butt cheek to steady himself. "There's room for one more."

"I've never... I... don't."

"I'll go slow," Nine said, applying more pressure.

Winston sucked in this breath, air hissing against his teeth. The actor's muscles tightened as the head of Nine's cock fought its way into Winston's asshole. Nine pushed a little harder, making Winston cry out, clutching fists-full of the bedspread. He begged Nine to be careful, but not to stop.

Another push, a shrieking cry from Winston, and Nine was inside him. Couldn't work his entire cock up Winston's chute — the guy wasn't *that* loose — but he got enough inside for it to feel nice. Tight as a virgin's, Nine thought, undulating his hips, grooving on the pleasure of his dick rubbing against Tom's, pressed together in the confines of Winston's rectum.

"Oh, *yeah,*" Tom moaned loudly, working his dick against Nine's. He was grooving on the pleasure, too.

Winston's cries settled into a grunt-groan, uttered at a steady rhythm that seemed to match the thrusting of the two cocks stuffed in his ass. Muscles flexed and cocks pumped. Sharp grunts and protracted groans bounced off the walls. The air was thick with the smells of sweat and lube.

Nine curled an arm around Winston's waist, reaching for the actor's cock. As he expected: Hard as steel and dripping. He started stroking it, the extra stimulus causing Winston to vibrate beneath him.

The hustler came first, chanting, "Oh, shit, oh, shit, oh, shit..." like he was about to have a head-on collision with a freight train. He thrashed beneath Winston, raising his head up off the pillow, his teeth bared, his nostrils flared, his eyes wild. Then Tom froze, closed his eyes and exhaled a gasp that popped like a bubble in the air. A calm washed over his face as his head fell back against the pillow.

Nine and Winston came in short succession, one right after the other. Winston, his hips in constant motion, thrusting forward so he was fucking Nine's fist and pushing backward the cocks stuffed inside him. He announced his orgasm with a high-pitched shriek that was within an octave of sounding feminine. Jets of spooge fired across the hustler's torso, creating thick, white puddles on Tom's tan skin.

Nine continued to fuck Winston, pounding him relentlessly like a jackhammer. Each time he stabbed his cock into that crowded chute, Winston let out a deep grunt and Tom would shudder. Even covered with a rubber, his spent dick was extra-sensitive to the continued stimulation.

Snarling and panting like a crazed dog, Nine came, his orgasm so great that it seemed to take all his strength with it. He barely remembered pulling out of Winston's ass and flopping down on the mattress beside Tom.

"Oh, my God," Winston sighed. He was off the bed now, standing, his body hunched slightly. "That was hot. I haven't been fucked that good since..." His voice trailed off, and no one pressed him to finish the sentence.

Nine was next to get off the bed. Pulling the loaded condom from his cock, he said to Tom, "Okay, whore, it's time for you to clock out. Get your money from Winston and get the fuck out. Your client and I need to have a business meeting."

FIFTEEN

Task ran his hand over his skull, still not believing he was now bald. He got it shaved yesterday — couldn't stand that orange shit any longer — at a little barber shop up the street from the Swisher Suites. Paid for it with money he stole from a few of the guys at The Tackle Box. Someone would throw a few dollars down on the bar to tip the bartender, and Task would take it. He had no qualms snatching the afternoon bartender's tips; served the bitchy queen right. He did feel a bit guilty stealing from the dancers, though. After all, he used to be a dancer himself. But when one of the dancers, a guy who went by the stage name Dario, left his gym bag unattended, Task seized the opportunity. He only took twenty bucks and a few tabs of whatever it was Dario had in a baggie, but he still felt guilty about it.

He liked the bald look. Made him look tough, he thought. Liking the look didn't make it any easier getting used to, though, feeling skin instead of hair when you touched your scalp.

Task took his hand away from his head and pressed the doorbell. Again. He knew the guy was home; his car was in the driveway. Task pounded heavily on the door, in case the guy didn't hear the bell. That brought the sound of footsteps from inside, a man calling out, "Coming!" In a lower tone Task heard him grumble, "Jesus Christ…"

The door opened, a man greeting Task with a scowl.

"Yeah?"

"Uh, hi. You Martin Richter?"

"It's pronounced *Rick*-ter. That's me. Whadda you want?" sounding annoyed.

So this was whom Rand was shacked up with. The guy was a butch daddy type. Looked a bit rough today: dark circles beneath red-rimmed, bloodshot eyes; the lower half of the face beyond the goatee was darkened with stubble. The body looked fit, though, solid pecs and beefy arms straining the fabric of his coffee-stained T-shirt commemorating AIDS Walk Atlanta, 1996. A nice basket in Martin's blue cut-off sweat pants, Task noted. Not wearing any underwear, either; the outline of his dick quite plain.

Yeah, Task thought, he wouldn't mind doing Martin *Rick*ter, even if he did look like he was on a four-day bender.

"I was looking for Rand. Heard he was staying here."

Martin's scowl made room for sadness and rejection. "*Was* is right. Got home from work yesterday, and he was gone," sounding defeated now.

"Know where he went?"

A heavy sigh, then, "No. Didn't leave a note saying kiss my ass, good-bye, nothing. Your guess is as good as mine. By the way, you didn't introduce yourself."

"Sorry. I'm Task." He spoke with exaggerated formality, like he was in a job interview. He offered his hand and the two men shook for fraction of a second.

Martin nodded. "Task. Haven't heard that before."

"Rand never said anything about me?"

"He said he was in town to visit friends. Said the guy he planned to stay with was out in L.A., on business. That wouldn't happen to be you, would it?"

Task waited a moment before answering, not sure what tack he should take. He decided a little bit of truth couldn't hurt. "Actually, I live in L.A., too."

Martin raised his eyebrows. "And you came out to Atlanta looking for him because...?"

"I'm his boyfriend. At least I used to be."

The words seemed to age Martin ten more years, his face turning gray. He looked away, shaking his head, taking deep breaths. "Maybe you should come inside," he said, not bothering to look at Task. "Sounds like we got some stories to share."

* * * * *

Back in his suite, in the minutes that followed his meeting with Nine, Dane was plagued with second thoughts.

He was about to hire someone to commit double homicide.

No, he told himself, he was hiring someone to fix a problem.

Same difference. But he wasn't a murderer. He wasn't the one who killed Perry Snopes, or even planned to have him killed. Just wanted to blackmail him was all. Get the asshole to drop his campaign for city council, get him to drop his crusade against The Tackle Box. He didn't want Snopes dead, just wanted him to back off.

Dane didn't kill people. That's why he was hiring a hit man. But, he reminded himself, until he made a payment to Nine — $25,000 tomorrow, $25,000 when the job was completed — the deal wasn't official. There was still time to back out.

If he wanted to.

Dane had emptied the second little bottle of Black Label from the mini bar into his tumbler when his cell phone rang. The caller I.D. showed a local number but no name. Still, he had a good idea who was calling. He picked up on the fourth ring. "This is Dane."

"So, you thought about my offer?"

He heard traffic in the background, horns honking. Rand calling from a pay phone.

Dane didn't answer right away, his mind racing, trying to think how to play this. "Hello? You still there?" Rand prompted, impatient.

"I'm here." Dane's tone was flat, hard. "Yeah, I thought about it."

"And?"

The second thoughts evaporated quickly. Dane took a large swallow of scotch, and then let out a loud sigh. "What choice do I have? You've got me over a barrel, you little bastard. You win."

"So you've got the money?" Sounding like he was the winning contestant on a game show. "You're in Atlanta, now, right? We can make the trade tonight."

"Can't be tonight."

"Why not?" Irritated now.

"What, you think I just got that kind of money in my checking account? Just write a check for one million and cash it? I have to pull the money from different sources, including some business accounts. And since you're a budding young criminal you should know that's embezzling, and it takes time." All this would be the truth, if Dane actually intended to pay the little shit.

"So what're you telling me?"

"I'm telling you you'll get your fuckin' money, but you'll have to wait until tomorrow night. Late."

"Like, how late?"

"Like midnight." Dane's tone suddenly turned friendly. "Look, I'm hosting one of those porn star searches earlier in the evening, and then a party in my suite after that. Why don't you come to the party. Have some fun, get laid — lots of cock n' coke — and then later you and I can settle up."

"Sounds like a set-up."

Well, Dane couldn't argue that, but he was quick with the bullshit. "You afraid I'll have the cops waiting for you? You said yourself I have more to lose. You go down, I go down farther. Or you afraid I'll be waiting with a gun?" He chuckled, as if the idea was too ridiculous to fathom. "I may be a horny sonuvabitch, but I'm no killer. That's *your* department."

Rand exhaled slowly, his breath creating a roar of static in Dane's ear. He knew Rand was thinking: *What to do, what to do...*

"Okay, I'll show up at your party tomorrow," he agreed, reluctantly. "Where's it at?"

He gave him the name of the hotel. "In the penthouse suite, of course. See you around midnight." He hung up before Rand could.

* * * * *

"So, let me get this straight," Martin said, pulling a cigarette — his third since this stranger arrived — from the pack of Marlboro Lights resting on the kitchen table, "Rand left Los Angeles for Atlanta to become a porn star?"

Task, sitting across the table, shook his head. "No, to find Dane Kensington. You saw the ad." He jerked his head toward a digest-sized magazine that sat between them on the table. "He's here this weekend."

The magazine was *David*, and it was opened to a full-page ad. Task had presented the evidentiary ad for Martin's review shortly after he was invited inside. "See, I'm not lying," he'd said. Neon green text reading "Have you ever dreamed of becoming a PORN STAR?" competed with a photo of a buff, dark-haired man in a bulging jock strap, "DanKen Studios Superstar Todd Trulaine." The ad gave the details of DanKen Studios' "Porn Star Search" scheduled for Friday — tomorrow — at The Tackle Box. DanKen founder and president Dane Kensington would host. There was a picture of him, masked within a circular frame: An older man, silver hair buzzed close to the scalp, mustache and goatee surrounding a mischievous grin that revealed bright white teeth. Pretty nice looking, Martin thought, hoping he aged that well himself.

"And Dane Kensington will make him a porn star." Martin flicked a lighter at the tip of his cigarette and exhaled a cloud of blue-gray smoke. "Seems like he's going about it back-asswards, coming out here when he was already living in the porn capital of the country."

"I told you, he and Dane already had a history, and he knew I didn't like it. He found out Dane would be here this weekend and figured he could meet up with him here."

"Away from you."

"Away from me," Task nodded emphatically. "Now you're getting it."

"No, I'm not, because if you say he left you last week, I don't see how he got out here so fast, hitch-hiking all the way from California. I mean, I met him this past Saturday."

"Who said he hitch-hiked? He stole my fuckin' car!"

Martin furrowed his brow. "He didn't have a car when I met him. If he did he'd never need a ride from me. Never said anything about having one."

"It was a piece of shit. Probably broke down in Texas, Oklahoma, someplace. I had to take the goddamn bus out here."

"How'd you track him back to me?" Martin asked, tapping his cigarette in the ashtray.

"I met this friend of yours, at The Tackle Box. When I told him I was from L.A. he said he had a friend who picked up some guy from California, too."

"A 'friend' of mine?" Martin rolled his eyes. "Shit, Conner? You fucked Conner?" Conner was bragging about picking up this guy at The Tackle Box the other night. Told Martin: "Got me some of that California cock just like you." Jesus, this was too weird.

"Who said we fucked?" Task snapped.

"He did. We work together, and Conner isn't known for keeping his private life private. Said he fucked some guy from California. Only he said the guy had red hair."

"I shaved it, okay?"

"So he told you my name but didn't tell you how to pronounce it?"

Task rolled his eyes. "Whatever," he said, dismissing the discrepancy. Continuing, he said, "I checked it out in the phone book. I left a message on your machine yesterday. You didn't get it?"

"No messages," Martin said.

"Rand probably heard it, that's why he bolted. Erased it before he left."

Or you're full of shit, Martin thought. But this explanation made sense, more so than most of what this bald stranger was telling him. He took a drag off his cigarette and shot Task a doubtful look. "This is all sounding a bit far-fetched to me."

Task shrugged. "It's the truth. What did Rand tell you?"

"Um, well..." Martin felt his face flush. "He said he was here from California and... something about how he knew the owner of The Tackle Box, and he also had some friends out here, but..."

He didn't tell me much of anything.

"I tried to ask him more about his past," Martin continued, "but, um, he was pretty good at changing the subject."

Task's lips twisted into a knowing grin. "He let you fuck 'im, didn't he?"

Martin stubbed out his cigarette. "He never said anything about a boyfriend."

"And you never asked."

"Okay, you made your point. So, what, you came out here to win back your boyfriend's heart? Maybe get revenge for him stealing your car? Either way, I don't know what you expect me to do about it. Not sure it's in his best interests to get back together with you, anyway, 'cause, tell you the truth, you don't strike me as all that trustworthy."

"Maybe you'd change your mind if I sucked your cock," Task sneered.

Martin's gaze chilled instantly. "You can go now."

Task raised his hands, surrendering. "Hey, just a joke man, okay? I'm not trying to get the guy back. You can have him, all I care. Just don't want him ending up with this guy Dane. He's bad news."

"What, is he dangerous?"

"He uses people, and when they're all used up he kicks 'em to the side like garbage."

"Sounds like some boyfriends I've had," Martin snorted.

"Yeah, but were they taping you getting fucked and then selling the tapes to get rich? 'Sides, you want Rand becoming a whore? I know he and I used to be dancers, but that ain't the same thing. I told him that, too. Said, 'You do porn, you're nothin' but a whore. Only difference between that and working the street is there's a camera in the room.'" The vehemence with which Task spoke seemed genuine, Martin wondering if this stranger had some real feelings for Rand after all.

"So you want to go to this porn star thing tomorrow night, see if you can get to him before this Dane guy?"

Task nodded. "Yeah, pretty much."

"Why tell me all this?"

"You're not curious? Hell, if nothin' else, figured you'd want to find him, so you can make him explain why he wasn't up-front with you."

Martin sighed, feeling defeated. He turned his gaze to the window behind Task, looking at the late afternoon sun and wondered why this time of day, the final hours of daylight, usually left him feeling forlorn. More so now that he was, once again, alone. Not that he thought he and Rand would ever be lovers, but he had hoped the ride would last a little longer, that it would end less abruptly than it did.

And Task was right. He was curious. He did want to find Rand again, find out his side of things. Find out if Rand was just using him. But if he was, Martin wasn't sure he wanted to know. He also was pretty sure that if he aligned himself with Task he'd just be permitting himself to be used again.

"You got a phone number? I can let you know what I decide tomorrow."

"No prob," Task said. "You got a pen?"

Martin got up from his chair and grabbed a small pad of neon-pink Post-Its and a pen off the kitchen counter, near the phone. Task took the pad and pen from Martin's hands, scribbled down his phone number, and pushed away from the table. "That thing at the club starts at eight, so you call me before then."

"I will." Martin said. "By the way, what club did you two strip at in L.A.?"

"Why, you plannin' on visiting?"

"Just curious," Martin shrugged. "I've taken a few business trips out there. For all I know I've been to the club where you two worked."

"Place called Boner's."

He shook his head, "Boner's? Can't say I've been there."

Martin ushered Task to the door, noting to himself that while he didn't trust this man claiming to be from Rand's past, he did cut a nice figure.

At the door, Task asked, "Hey, I was wondering, would you be able to give me a ride?"

Martin opened the front door. "Sorry, can't. You got here on your own, you can leave on your own."

* * * * *

A soft thud — something hard hitting flesh. A sudden expulsion of breath. "What're you — "

Another soft thud.

Bob crumpled to the floor, producing a louder noise as his head smacked the coffee table.

J.T. remained standing, breathing heavy, a large ashtray made of thick, amber glass clutched in his hand. He was still naked and even though he'd just done something horrible, Rand thought his brother looked incredibly sexy.

Then he saw Bob, on the floor, looking like he was sleeping. Blood stained his forehead and soaked into the pale beige shag carpet.

"Eat my pussy, stud!" The words came out of the TV speakers like a gas leak, but neither J.T. nor Rand turned their attention to the porno that still played. They just kept looking at Bob, wondering if he'd suddenly spring back to life like *The Terminator*, or if he'd never move again.

Rand spoke first. "You think he's...?" He didn't have to finish the question.

"Think I just knocked him out. Here." J.T. thrust the ashtray toward him. "Go wash this. I'm gonna go see if I can find his wallet."

Rand took the ashtray and set it down beside him — he needed both hands to pull up his shorts. J.T. had snatched up his own shorts from the floor and was stepping into them. Rand managed one more peek at his brother's dick before it disappeared behind blue polyester.

The brothers rushed around the apartment like a couple that are late for a flight and can't find the car keys. In the kitchen, Rand held the ashtray under running water, leaving it in the sink when he thought he'd rinsed off all J.T.'s fingerprints and all of Bob's blood. He heard J.T. cussing.

"Bastard only had twelve bucks in his wallet," he said as he walked into the living room, holding up the bills for Rand to see. He quickly tucked the money into the waistband of his shorts. "When I get the ten broke I'll give you your half. Now get your shit and let's get the fuck outta here."

They grabbed their towels and headed out the door, J.T. covering his hand with his towel before turning the doorknob. One of Bob's neighbors across the walkway, an obese woman in her twenties, wearing a purple smock and carrying a large Kenya bag, was stepping out of her apartment the same time the brothers exited Bob's apartment. She looked startled to see them, but then quickly turned her attention back to locking her front door.

Rand wanted to run, run until the Willow Hill Apartments could no longer be seen behind them. But J.T. said that would be too suspicious, so they walked, albeit quickly.

A block later, Rand risked asking: "What if he calls the police?"

"He's a perv. He ain't gonna call no one."

A pause, then Rand asked. "What did it feel like when he was, y'know, sucking you."

"Felt good. Kind of like when you jerk off, only wet and soft." He shrugged. "Dunno. Just felt good. Can't really describe it."

Hesitantly, Rand asked: "J.T., does that make you... queer?"

Another shrug. "Just let a guy suck my dick, is all. Don't mean nothin'."

Rand thought of those words now as the man pushed down on the top of his head and urged him to "take it all."

Don't mean nothin', Rand told himself, the head of the stranger's dick hitting the back of his throat, the man's tangy scent filling his nose, the steering wheel of the man's SUV pressing against Rand's shoulder. Light from a nearby streetlight filtered into the SUV's beige interior, glinted off the guy's gold wedding band.

Rand met him at an adult video store up the street, on Cheshire Bridge. He'd gone there after getting the runaround from Dane, pissed and wanting to get even, but needing cash more. Only sixteen dollars remained of the wad he took with him when he fled Miami, most of that money going to a night at this fleabag near Agnes Scott College in Decatur. Paid way too much to stay in that dump, but he was too desperate to shop around. Besides, he thought he'd be a millionaire by now.

A dumpy woman standing behind the counter at the video store glared at him as he entered. "Can't bring that bag in here," she said, her rusted hacksaw of a voice cutting through the raunchy rap music blaring on the sound system.

"Can I leave it behind the counter, then?"

The woman made a face that brought out her jowls and crows feet. "I guess," she said, sounding put out. Rand handed the duffle up to her. "Jesus, what the hell you got in here, a dead body?" she carped.

Rand smiled at her. "Not yet."

He did a slow stroll through the back room, where all the gay videos and DVDs were kept, more interested in checking out the customers than the titles. A couple of young guys — one pretty cute, the other kind of plain and about ten pounds overweight — were checking out the new titles that lined one wall. There was a black guy with a body-builder's physique and hair chemically coerced into a white guy style, alternately checking out the Kristen Bjorn videos and Rand. The black guy looked to be in his late twenties, early thirties. He remembered his past coaching: Go for the older guys, the married guys; they're more likely to pay for it. Rand looked away from the black guy and continued his perusal around the room.

There was one other man in the room, in the corner by the BDSM videos, the one with the most potential. Had to be in his late sixties, at least, the way his skin sagged on his face, obliterating any lingering traces of how he might've looked as a younger man. He wore a pair of large, plastic framed glasses and a Members Only jacket. Seemed kind of short, too, Rand thought, but maybe the man's stooped posture just made him seem that way. This guy would pay to get blown by a forty-year-old, Rand was sure of that. And he better, because Rand wasn't going to suck the geezer's dick for free.

Rand was heading toward the old man when another man entered the room. This one looked to be in his forties, fairly attractive – a helluva lot more do-able than the geezer checking out bondage tapes, at least – tanned, square jaw, salt-and-pepper naturally curly hair a few weeks past due for a cut. The man wore a pale yellow shirt, top button undone to reveal an undershirt, a few sprigs of chest hair curling over the collar. The guy had a slight paunch around the middle, but otherwise was in decent shape.

The man went for the Falcon DVDs, and Rand moved beside him. The man's eyes went from the DVD he was holding to Rand's face and then to his crotch. Rand saw the wedding band on the man's finger and smiled. The man's face colored, and he turned away, but only for a second. He looked back at Rand and risked returning the smile.

For ten minutes they went on like that. Rand following the man around the room, the two sharing innuendo-laden stares, trading smiles, then looking away. Rand squeezed his crotch a few times to kick things up a few notches. Then he left the room, giving the man one last lingering look over his shoulder.

Rand collected his bag from the bitch behind the counter and left the store. He stood outside and waited. Several minutes later, out came the closet case, clutching a black plastic bag containing his rented DVD. Seeing Rand, he paused, looked away, and then looked back, this time with a partial smile on his face.

"What did ya' rent?" Rand asked.

The question seemed to startle the man. "Uh, it's called, um... *Cock Hunters.*" He dropped his voice, the title barely audible.

Rand nodded. "Sounds good. Want someone to watch it with?"

"What? Oh!" The man rocked on his heels, chuckling. "No, I'm not planning on watching this tonight."

"Waiting 'til the wife's out shopping, you have the place to yourself?"

The man's face reddened.

Rand shrugged his shoulders, looked out toward the traffic on Cheshire Bridge, then back at the man. "That's okay. I like doing better than watching, anyway."

A full minute passed before the man replied. Rand could practically see an angel and a devil perched on either of the man's shoulders as he deliberated his answer. "I'm parked on the side," he finally said.

They exchanged names and promptly forgot them. They got into the man's Ford Explorer, struck a deal, and then the man drove up the street, looking for someplace secluded.

"This'll do," he said, parking behind a camera and video store that faced a side street off Cheshire Bridge.

Rand took out his cock, playing with it while the man watched, his mouth agape. "You want to touch it?" he asked, wiggling his semi-hard dick at the man.

The man reached across to the passenger seat, his hand shaking as he made a grab for Rand's cock. His palm was sweaty and his manipulations clumsy. He spent as much time looking over his shoulder as he did studying Rand's prick. To help his erection along, Rand thought of past experiences...

Jerking off with a junior high friend, Pablo, who had the first uncut dick Rand ever saw.

Getting his first blowjob at age 16, and sucking his first cock soon thereafter.

The weekend in Palm Springs with Dane and a couple of his "stars." "Lick me clean," Dane commanded after the two porn stars shot their loads all over his balls and throbbing dick. He could still recall the taste.

Martin sucking his cock in the parking garage, Rand enjoying the thrill of being in control of their sexual escapades.

Task holding Rand tight against his body, his prick buried deep in Rand's ass, and whispering in his ear...

"Oh, that feels good," Rand sighed, like the trick was the greatest lover he'd encountered. "For an extra ten dollars you can suck it."

The man didn't answer, or lean down to take Rand's stiff cock between his lips. He didn't take his hand away, either.

"Let me see your cock."

The trick withdrew his hand, and Rand thought he caught the traces of a smile pulling at his lips. The man leaned back in his seat, unbuckled his belt, unfastened his pants and unzipped his fly. He wore a pair of tighty-whities underneath, the light from the streetlamp accentuating the significant mound beneath the white cotton. The man jerked the waistband down, exposing a thick slab of man-meat.

"Oh, yeah," Rand sighed, not having to feign his appreciation. The trick was packing.

He leaned over the center console, bringing his face to the man's crotch. Slowly, he dragged his tongue up the shaft, tracing the seam to the cleft at the bottom of the crown. He tasted the light saltiness of pre-cum, closed his mouth over the head and started sucking.

Pleasure soon eased the john's apprehension and nervousness. He became more vocal, repeating dialog he'd picked up from his covert porn viewings. "Suck my cock," he gasped, rising in his seat.

Rand fondled his own dick while he deep-throated the man from the porn store, no longer relying on memories to stay aroused. His professional detachment ebbed as his excitement increased, and he found himself wanting to feel the stranger's mouth on his cock for reasons other than earning an extra ten dollars.

The man's breathing became loud and shallow. He jerked in his seat, causing the vehicle to rock slightly. Rand's mouth was flooded with the acidic taste of the stranger's jism. As agreed, Rand swallowed the man's load. For show, he pulled the john's dick out of his mouth, rubbed the head against his face, smearing a thin trail of spooge across his cheek.

Rand squeezed the man's shaft and lapped up the last pearly drop of jizz. "That's better than any video," he teased.

The man's smile came and went so quickly Rand hardly noticed. He exhaled sharply, looked out the side window, and then checked his watch. "Should probably be getting home."

Rand sat upright. "You want to get me off?" he asked, leaning against the passenger door, his fingers tracing a thick vein zigzagging up his engorged shaft.

The john looked away. "Need to be getting home," he repeated, pulling his underwear up, covering his sagging dick.

"Fine," Rand said, his tone inadvertently snippy. He stuffed his swollen cock back into his shorts. "You can give me my money now."

After zipping up and buckling his belt, the man pulled his wallet out of his back pocket. He handed Rand a twenty-dollar bill.

"It was thirty if I swallowed. Remember?"

The man harumphed and gave Rand another ten.

"Would you be able to drop me off at a motel?" Rand asked, slipping the money into a side pocket of his cargo shorts. "There's one up the street."

The trick shook his head. "I've really got to..."

"I know, I know. Back to the wife." He opened the door. "Thanks, anyway."

The SUV's engine roared to life as Rand hopped down onto the cracked pavement of the parking lot. The man put the vehicle into gear the instant the passenger door slammed shut.

"Goddamned closet cases," Rand muttered in disgust as the trick pulled away, not bothering to look back in his direction. He's probably going to take a shower as soon as he gets home, Rand thought, watching the Ford Explorer peel out of the parking lot.

A sudden realization hit him with the force of a bullet: He didn't have his duffle bag.

It was still sitting on the back seat of the trick's SUV.

Rand felt his insides liquefy. *The tape!*

SIXTEEN

Friday the sky over Atlanta was the color of galvanized steel, making the city appear cold and dreary. Step outside, however, and one was immediately reminded it was summer in the South. The gray clouds blocked the sun's light, but did little to keep the heat in check, the temperature only dropping to the high-eighties.

"On the radio, they said it's gonna rain," remarked the bucktoothed deliveryman as he unloaded flats of bottled water from a dolly.

"Looks like it," Dane agreed, looking through the sliding glass doors that opened to the penthouse's small terrace. "Fortunately it's an indoor party. Only the smokers have to worry about getting wet."

"What's the party for?" the deliveryman asked. He'd finished unloading the bottled water and was now picking up one of the two cases of wine that remained on the dolly.

Dane looked the guy over. Young, but a bit thick around the middle, not to mention he could eat corn on the cob through Venetian blinds with those teeth. More than likely straight, too. "Just some PR thing," he said with a wave of his hand.

"A 'PR thing'? Is that what you call your orgies?"

Nine was walking across the room, big grin on his face, wearing a dark suit and carrying a briefcase. "Door was open," he explained.

"Hi, how're you?" Dane said, masking his irritation with an icy smile, forcing a chuckle. "Wasn't expecting to see you until later."

"Got tired of sitting in my room watching the E! channel. I actually watched one of those *True Hollywood Stories* on the cast of *Facts of Life*. Can you believe that shit? Did you know Lisa Whelchel writes Christian parenting books now?"

"Which one was she?"

"Blair. The rich, bitchy one."

"What show was that?" the deliveryman asked, holding a clipboard and pen out to Dane.

"Stupid sitcom from the early '80s," Dane said, taking the clipboard and pen. "You were probably just learning to walk when it was on."

"Probably. Not ringin' any bells." After Dane signed the receipt the deliveryman said, "Thank you, sir. And enjoy your party."

"Oh, he will," chimed in Nine, his grin broadening.

Once the door closed behind the deliveryman, Dane launched in. "What the fuck do you think you're doing? I said I would call you."

"Like I said, got tired of waiting in my room. You got the money?"

Christ, he was as bad as Rand, Dane thought. "Yes, but if you showed up two hours earlier I wouldn't. That's why I was going to call, let you know. Wait a moment and I'll get it."

Dane crossed the room, going into the bedroom suite. In the closet there was a small safe for guests to keep valuables. Reading the combination off the back of a hotel business card, where the desk clerk scribbled it down, Dane opened the safe and removed the first installment of Nine's payment, surprised how insignificant $25,000 looked. There was a time in his life, back in the mid-'70s when he was slaving away in crappy retail jobs, when he would've killed to have $25,000. Now he had $25,000 as a down payment to have people killed.

He transferred the money into a small shopping bag. Crossing the room to a writing desk, Dane opened his briefcase, selected a Polaroid photo from an envelope and returned to the penthouse's parlor.

"Here you go," he said crisply, handing the shopping bag of cash to Nine.

"In an A&F bag. Cute." Nine went over to the credenza by the front entrance, setting his briefcase on top of it. Dane watched him transfer the cash to the briefcase, noticing there was no gun inside the case. Where did Nine keep his gun, he wondered. He was tempted to ask, then figured he probably shouldn't.

"One more thing," Dane said, walking toward Nine, holding out the Polaroid. "Here's a photo of Rand. Told him to show up here around midnight."

Nine took the photo from Dane's hand. "Damn!" He whistled through a lascivious grin. "Think I'll have some fun with this one."

"Do whatever you want," Dane said, looking away. "Just as long as he's ... you know ... by tomorrow morning."

"What's the matter, Dane? Afraid to say it out loud? Afraid the FBI's got your penthouse bugged."

Dane walked over to the sliding glass doors that opened to the terrace. "I just don't like talking about it," he said, looking out at the foreboding clouds hovering over the city.

* * * * *

"I'm Linda Joffey, I live up the street," the ferret-faced woman at the door introduced herself, her voice a nasal whine. "I was so sorry to hear about what happened to Perry. I wanted to leave this here for you."

She handed Winston a foil-wrapped casserole dish, still warm from the oven. "It's a chicken Alfredo casserole," Linda Joffey informed him.

"Thank you," Winston replied mechanically, lifting the foil wrapping for a peek. A layer of buttery breadcrumbs blanketed a rich, creamy sauce. Christ, was there some sort of *Cooking with Carbohydrates* recipe book circulating among the straight community? The kitchen was filled with deep-fried morsels, artery-clogging casseroles and fattening desserts. Would it have killed any of these people to bring a fucking bottle of Absolut? "That's very thoughtful," Winston said, forcing a gracious smile.

"Are you with the family?" she asked.

"I was his lover."

"Oh!" Linda Joffey brought a hand to her lips, her gaunt face coloring. "I'm sorry. I didn't..."

The Iron Cunt swooped in. "Hello, I'm Nora, Perry's *mother*," she said, making it plain whom she considered the most important person in her son's life. She'd pretty much taken over hosting duties since entering the house an hour ago. No mystery from where Perry got his domineering qualities. "Come inside, won't you? Have some coffee. Winston, be a dear and take that into the kitchen."

"Certainly," he said as he stood back to let Linda Joffey, who he'd never seen before in his life, step into the foyer. She barely glanced in his direction now.

Three of Perry's Log Cabin Republican friends were in the kitchen, sipping cocktails and dishing about some rumored-to-be-gay city official. They scarcely looked in Winston's direction as he entered to deposit the fat-laden casserole on the counter with the others. Perry's death was just another reason to get together and socialize, and like the parties thrown when Perry was alive, Winston remained an outsider. He didn't follow politics, and most of his awareness of current events came from scanning headlines in the local gay weeklies or from fleeting glimpses of TV news. The last book he read was by Jackie Collins. But Winston looked good and was therefore granted a condescending tolerance by Perry's friends. *I've become Andrew Ridgely of Wham!* he winced.

Winston wandered into the living room where people clustered in groups of two or three. Linda Joffey was in the corner talking with the Iron Cunt. The Frozen Dyke, dressed like a WAC, was talking with a young straight couple Winston didn't recognize. In fact, he barely knew any of the people in the room. Most of his friends had only stopped by for a minute or two, for appearances sake. Some sent flowers, others called to say they would see him later, at the visitation or funeral. As for Winston's own family, his mother had died four years ago, and his father and brother weren't too inclined to lend much support over the death of his lover. Like Perry's mother, they were reluctant to acknowledge Winston's relationship to Perry.

He was alone.

He was in trouble.

Tears welled up in his eyes, and he began to sniffle. Even if the emotion was legitimate, Winston's handling of the feeling was calculated, like an actor approaching a scene. Should he remain stoic, or begin to wail out loud? Realizing he'd be playing to a less-than-sympathetic audience, he chose stoicism. Struggling to stifle his tears, Winston backed out of the living room and headed up the stairs. No one called out after him. He went to his bedroom, closing and locking the door behind him, and then headed for the master bathroom. Sitting on the toilet, covering his face with his hands, Winston let the tears flow.

He was grieving. Not for Perry, but for himself.

After sobbing for a steady ten minutes, Winston blew his nose a final time, stood up and went to the sink, where he splashed cold water on his face. Weeping had left his eyes red and puffy. Winston's vanity dictated that he dab some cucumber eye gel on his face to reduce the puffiness, yet it would be to his benefit if people saw evidence he'd been crying. Vanity won out, as always.

Winston took one step out of the bathroom and froze.

Nine was sitting on Winston's bed, leafing through a copy of *Details*, the one with Matt Damon on the cover.

"You know, I used to think if I had a choice between fucking Ben Affleck or fucking Matt Damon, I'd choose Ben. But, I don't know, Matt's starting to grow on me," Nine said.

"How ... how'd you get in?" Winston pushed the question out as if he'd just taken a blow to the gut. "The door was locked."

Nine dropped the magazine on the bed and stood. "Y'know that thing you see guys do on TV, jimmying the lock with a credit card? That actually works."

"Why are you here?" But Winston already knew why.

"See how you were holding up, big guy," Nine said, grinning. "Was expecting to hear from you today, and when it started getting late, figured I'd come check on you. Doesn't seem like any of those people downstairs were going to. Didn't even know where you were. Whose the dyke dressed like she's on leave from the Navy? All she needs to complete her outfit is an officer's hat."

"Perry's sister." Winston felt his heart beating faster. "Look, I can give you the money I have so far. I got most of it, as much as I could without Perry's lawyer asking any questions. The rest I'll have to get through credit card advances, and I couldn't do that today. Not with all these people coming by. Jesus, I'll be glad when this is all over."

"A death of a loved one can be stressful."

Winston rolled his eyes and crossed the room to his dresser. "You're telling me."

From his top dresser drawer Winston removed a plastic grocery bag that swaddled a small stack of bills. He handed the wadded up bag to Nine.

"Nice packaging."

"I was going to put it in an envelope," Winston said.

But Nine was no longer paying attention to him. He'd pulled the cash from the grocery bag, letting the bag float to the floor, and began counting the money.

"A little over four grand short," Nine said, thumbing through the bills. "Four-thousand-two-hundred-seventy-five short, to be exact."

"I said I was going to get the rest from credit card advances." He winced, hearing a whine come into his voice. He felt cornered, as he often had when talking with Perry. "I just couldn't make it to an ATM today." Not to mention all his cards were practically maxed out. He'd be lucky to scrape together $1,000.

Nine advanced toward him "You better," he said, his tone hard. Winston had to fight the urge to step backward. Pretend you're playing a tough guy, Winston told himself, even though his guts were roiling with fear.

When he was a foot away, Nine broke into a wide smile. "Relax," he chuckled, giving Winston's shoulder a playful punch. "I know you're good for it. Just get it to me tomorrow."

Winston forced himself to smile along, but his was a nervous smile. "Well, tomorrow's the funeral, but ..."

Nine shot him a threatening look.

"... I'll see what I can do."

"Gotta take a piss," Nine said, turning on his heels and heading toward the master bathroom. Just before he entered the bathroom, he tossed a glance back at Winston and said, "You can watch, if you want."

His tone was suggestive enough to make Winston want to follow.

Nine was standing at the toilet, unzipping the fly of his black trousers. "Couldn't resist, could you?"

Winston stepped closer, leaning over the rose marble counter top of the sink to get a better view as Nine dug his hand inside his fly and pulled out his cock. Seeing it again sparked an excitement in Winston's own groin. He licked his lips lustfully as he studied the long, thick phallus dangling over the toilet bowl.

"You can move closer if you want," Nine encouraged, sinister grin on his wickedly handsome face.

"Y'know, I really had fun, yesterday," Winston said softly, his eyes never leaving Nine's prick as he moved closer. "If I'd known you had such a huge dick ..."

Jonathan Asche

"Told you when we met I was called Nine for a reason."

"Yeah, but guys always *say* they're hung. And when we met, I wasn't exactly looking to get laid."

He'd thought Nine was attractive when they first met, three months ago at hotel bar in Nashville, during what Perry had termed a "long romantic weekend." It was really a business trip, Winston found out later, Perry wanting to attend an antiques show. They fought upon arrival, and after that spent the weekend apart, only seeing each other at night, in bed. Sleeping. Bored and feeling neglected, Winston passed the time getting drunk in the hotel bar while Winston went in search of a bargain sixteenth century armoire.

He couldn't remember if he tried to pick up Nine or vice-versa. He just remembered being shit-faced drunk when they met, Nine walking up to the booth where he sat drinking his fourth vodka tonic and asking if Winston minded if he joined him. Winston was eager for the company, and bent Nine's ear with tales of his miserable relationship with Perry, that it wasn't even a matter of not loving Perry, but of growing to hate him. Telling Nine the only reason he stayed with Perry was the money.

Not exactly a conversation to entice a potential trick, but Nine stayed. Nine had asked him how much money, and Winston said he didn't know how much, exactly, but assured him Perry was "pretty rich."

"I can help you, if you want," Nine had told him after buying another round of drinks. "Get you out of the relationship, maybe even get you the money, too. Are you in his will?"

"Do you mean...?" Winston broke out laughing, thinking he was joking.

Nine wrote his number down on a cocktail napkin. "Think about it. Give me a call."

A month later, Winston dialed the number and asked if Nine was joking. Nine wasn't.

The sound of piss hitting water brought Winston back to the present. He was never much for water sports, but seeing the pale yellow stream issuing from the plump head of Nine's cock was triggering some daring fantasies, making his own rod pulse.

"You like watching guys piss?" Nine asked.

"I like watching you piss."

"You and Perry ever get into water sports, Win?"

"Uh, um, no. Perry didn't like things too kinky."

"But you do?" Nine asked, raising an eyebrow. He'd finished relieving himself and made a move to shake the last few drops of urine from his dick, but instead he turned on his heels, facing Winston.

152

"Why don'tcha get on your knees and lick off the last few drops. Don't worry, Perry isn't around anymore to tell you no."

"I..." Winston tried to formulate a protest, even as he was sinking onto the floor before Nine's mighty cock.

"That's it," Nine encouraged as Winston gripped his dick, lifting it toward his open mouth. "You've been wanting to taste my cock since I showed up."

Winston closed his lips over the fat, fleshy shaft of Nine's prick, savoring its weight inside his mouth. His tongue pushed against the smooth, round head, picking up the slight taste of piss. His cock was now like iron in his pants as he began to suck Nine in earnest.

A sudden flood of salty liquid filled Winston's mouth. He jumped back, spitting out a mouthful of urine onto the floor. "You sonofabitch!"

"Sorry. Guess I wasn't done yet," Nine chuckled.

Winston scrambled to the sink, turning on the water and bringing handfuls of water to his mouth. "You could've warned me," he whimpered.

"What's the fun in that?"

Nine had zipped up when Winston turned to face him. "It's about time for me to go."

"No, wait." Winston rushed to him, pleading. "Don't go. Not yet. Couldn't we... y'know, have some fun first?"

"We just did."

"You know what I mean." Winston pushed his crotch against Nine's. "At least let me suck your cock."

"Not now," he said, pushing Winston away.

Winston looked as if he'd just been slapped. "Why not? No one will know. You said yourself no one's exactly making a point of checking on me."

"Saving myself for tonight," Nine said, checking his reflection in the mirror, patting his hair down on the sides. "Going to a hot party. Remember?"

"Oh, yeah. That," he pouted.

Nine headed out of the bathroom. "You should come along. I bet you'd be real popular."

Winston followed him to the bedroom door. "I can't go to a party! I've got Perry's visitation tonight."

"Well, I'll be thinking of you, then," Nine smirked. He planted his hands on Winston's shoulders and, raising his voice, he said, "Just hang in there. Allow yourself to grieve. It's good for you." He pulled Winston forward and kissed him on the forehead, and then turned to open the bedroom door. "Take care, big guy."

SEVENTEEN

Rand lay on his back; eyes open, staring up at the water-stained ceiling. Outside rap music blared from a car, and he could hear young men laughing and talking, speaking so rapidly it was difficult to tell if they were speaking English or Spanish. Occasionally, a car backfiring or a gun going off could be heard, distant, but still too close.

Welcome to L.A.

Sleeping beside him, on the mattress on the floor, was his brother J.T., turned on his side, his soft breathing barely audible above the noise outside. The light from a street lamp crept in through a sheet-covered window, casting the room in a pale gray light. Rand studied J.T.'s back, broader than he'd remembered it, and his arms, also thickened with muscle. His biceps were now decorated with tattoos. On his right arm was a picture of a skull engulfed in flames, done in blue-black ink. The other one J.T. got in jail, by a guy who was "pretty good as long as you didn't want anything too hard. Mostly he did names, hearts, knives, shit like that." Of the "shit like that," J.T. got a pair of crossed knives through a bleeding heart.

It was the knives-through-bleeding-heart tattoo that was exposed now, J.T.'s arm resting on top of the sheet, along the length of his body, looking like a dark smear in the near-darkness. Rand wanted to reach out and touch that smear, to feel the hardness of the muscle beneath.

"You've been working out?" Rand asked, when J.T. was showing off his tats.

"Yeah. When you're locked up, you gotta do somethin'."

J.T. was caught at school with two joints, a few tabs of acid and a wad of cash. Initially he was charged with possession with intent to distribute, but that got reduced to possession. He was arrested less than two months past his eighteenth birthday. J.T. was tried as an adult.

"Figures," their mother said.

He moved to L.A. after he got out, and Rand soon joined him. The location was new, but their standard of living remained the same.

Rand's cock ached, keeping him awake. He sneaked a hand down to his crotch, slipped his fingers into the fly of his boxers and felt his hardness, felt the wetness of pre-cum. He wanted to — needed to — get off. Locking himself in the bathroom and jacking off was out; he did that his first night there only to have the mood shattered when a cockroach fell from the ceiling and onto his head.

Maybe now, he dared himself, while J.T.'s asleep.

He pulled his boner out of his underwear. If he looked down toward his feet he could see his dick throb beneath the threadbare sheet. Lightly, he stroked himself, keeping his movements minimal so as not to wake J.T.

His brother made a couple harsh snorts and rolled over abruptly. Rand's breath hung in his throat for a minute, not released until he saw that J.T.'s eyes were still closed. His breathing steadied, a quiet wheezing now heard when J.T. inhaled.

Rand's hard-on pulsed, reminding him it was waiting. He shifted his weight, attempting to scoot away from his brother, an inch or two so the movements of his hands beneath the sheet wouldn't be detected. But in his movements, Rand's hand brushed against J.T.'s body, touching the front of his worn cotton briefs.

Feeling the hardness beneath.

Rand pulled his hand away as if he'd touched an open flame, then, seeing J.T. continued to sleep, he cautiously returned his hand to his brother's crotch.

J.T. didn't wake up.

Emboldened (or crazy), Rand worked a hand beneath the elastic waistband of J.T's briefs. An electric shock went through him when his fingers came in contact with the smooth, hot skin of J.T.'s shaft. There was a catch in his brother's breathing then, making Rand freeze and his stomach constrict.

A second later, J.T. resumed his regular breathing pattern: inhale-wheeze-whine-exhale.

Rand's heart soon became the loudest noise in the room as his fingers caressed J.T.'s thick, hard cock with one hand and stroked his own, clumsily, with the other. He'd felt other dicks before — it became a quest after the brothers' encounter with Bob the Molester — but it was always J.T.'s that fascinated him. Rand wanted to do more than just give his brother a clandestine hand-job. He wanted to suck it, take it all the way down his throat like Bob had done. He imagined J.T. pumping his dick into his mouth, running his hands through his younger brother's hair and telling him he sucked cock better than a girl. And even though he didn't like the taste, he'd let J.T. cum in his mouth, and he'd swallow his load, happily.

His hand pulled more forcefully on J.T.'s prick, his thumb traversing his brother's engorged cockhead, taking away the wetness there. Rand's own dick throbbed painfully, but it was a good pain.

J.T.'s breathing hitched, but Rand didn't stop. He was past caring.

His brother's chest swelled with a held breath, and when he exhaled...

Rand felt a hand slide between his legs. "Look's like someone's havin' a good dream."

He cracked his eyelids open long enough to see it was daylight and closed them again. The hand between his legs was cupping his balls now, fondling them while a man said he could make that dream come true.

Rand opened his eyes again, all the way this time, and saw the guy there, sitting on the side of the bed, playing with his balls. Sometimes his fingers would slip lower between his legs, prod his asshole. The man was too busy staring at Rand's hard-on to notice he'd woken up. Rand let out a soft moan, and the man looked up. Some guys when they got old, you couldn't imagine them any younger; but there were enough clues left on this guy's softening features that Rand got a pretty good idea that he was hot in his day. He wasn't bad now.

The man smiled at him, his hand moving to Rand's cock. Rand smiled back and the guy went down on him, his warm, moist mouth closing in around Rand's hard-on.

The guy's name was George, Rand remembered. Met him last night. After the trick took off with his duffle bag in his back seat, Rand had returned to the porn shop, hoping to get the guy's address and phone number. The same dumpy woman was behind the counter, her mood no better. She told him if his stuff was stolen to call the police, they didn't give out customers' information. He pleaded, begged, made puppy-dog eyes and the woman said *she'd* call the cops if he didn't get the hell out of the store, picking up the phone to show she meant it. He called her a cunt as he stormed out, and she said something back, but the door closed behind him before it reached his ears.

He met George a couple hours later, after getting something to eat at a taco place on the corner of Piedmont and Cheshire Bridge. Rand met him at some hole-in-the-wall bar behind a tire store. Of the bar's eight patrons that night, Rand was the only one under 45. They saw Rand and practically formed a line, offering to buy him drinks. George's was the only offer he accepted, him being the least pushy and most attractive man there. Less than an hour later, George was taking him to his cramped two-bedroom in a complex off Buford Highway.

George's tongue fluttered against his cockhead and Rand closed his eyes, trying not to think about anything but how good the older man's mouth felt on his dick. He thrust his hips upward, gently, moaning as he did it.

"I'd ask what you did last night, but it appears you're still *doing it*."

Rand opened his eyes then, pushing himself up onto his elbows. Standing in the bedroom's doorway was a young black man with a shaved head, lips pursed and hands on his narrow waist, masculine looking but acting like he was Diahann Carroll in *Dynasty*.

George had stopped sucking him, but still held on to his cock. "Hi, Kadin. I didn't expect you this early."

"*Obviously.*"

"Don't be mad. We agreed."

Kadin stepped into the room like he was wearing imaginary pumps. "We *agreed* that if we got ourselves a trick it was *his* place, *not* ours."

"But he didn't have a place," George whined. "He's from out of town."

"And I suppose every hotel in Atlanta's full up?"

Rand started to scoot off the bed. "I'll leave."

"No, baby, you just stay right there," Kadin said, raising a hand. "Not your fault. Just reminding Georgie here of our agreement." He broke into a grin. "'Sides, you stay, maybe all three of us could spend the morning together. What you say?"

Rand said, "I have to piss."

He flushed and exited the bathroom a couple minutes later and found Kadin naked and lying on top of George, George's fingers sinking into the crack of Kadin's full, round butt. Between kisses Kadin said, "I found myself this bodybuilder at Burkhart's, the nig's got himself a *ten-inch* horse dick, baby. *Mmm-mmmm*, I wanted it up my ass so bad."

"He fuck you good?" George gasped, his fingers slipping down a little deeper.

"Didn't fuck me *at all*," Kadin giggled. "Muh'fucker's a *bottom.*"

They became quiet, kissing and writhing on the bed. Rand thought about leaving, his only reason for hesitating was he saw a wallet sitting on the dresser. He wondered if George and Kadin were into to each other enough not to notice him.

"Hey, *bay*-bee. Don't be shy. Come join us."

Kadin had rolled off George, lying on his side now. George was hard and Kadin was getting there, his cock two shades darker than the rest of him. Kadin was looking at Rand now, his grin all teeth.

Rand joined them on the bed.

The moment Rand had his knees on the mattress Kadin leaned over George and took Rand's semi into his mouth, the rush of sensation almost causing Rand to lose his balance. He steadied himself with a hand on Kadin's back, liking the contrast of his white hand on the other man's dark skin. He liked the feel of Kadin's mouth on his cock, too, the way he was gulping down the whole thing and massaging the shaft with his tongue. Fingers traced his butt-crack, Rand not sure if the fingers belonged to George or Kadin.

Rand was stiff and throbbing by the time Kadin pulled his mouth away. "You ever suck a black man?" His voice had dropped to a lower register.

"A few times." Rand almost said he wasn't choosey, long as they were clean and had cash.

"How 'bout sucking one again."

It was Rand's turn to lean across George — George's dick brushing against his shoulder as he moved in to take Kadin's into his mouth. He almost felt bad for the guy, them leaning back and forth across him like he was a coffee table. Things got evened out, though, when George got between Rand's legs and started slurping on his cock.

Kadin said. "I wanna feel the white boy's cock up my ass." Rand was lying on his back, George sucking his cock and licking his balls, and Kadin sitting on his face, when he said it. "Just lick that hole a little more and I'll be ready for you," Kadin panted, his ass pressing against Rand's nose.

They got into a sideways position, George sitting beside them saying he wanted to watch Rand's dick sliding into Kadin's "black hole." Kadin reached between his legs and helped guide Rand's sheathed cock into the dark divide of his ass.

"That's it, baby, slide it in *deep*."

George looked at them like a kid discovering on Christmas morning he got the bike he asked for — except George was naked and jacking off.

Kadin's shoulder got pushed into the pillows each time his butt was rammed. "You want a sandwich, Georgie?" he asked, his voice quavering as Rand drove his cock into him. "Ya' wanna help us make one?"

In less than a minute George had a rubber on his pole and was rubbing lube onto Rand's asshole. Another half minute after that, he was pushing his cock into Rand's hole, slow and easy. The three fell into a rhythm, Rand slamming his dick into Kadin's ass, and George jabbing upward to catch Rand on his backwards thrust. Kadin moaned, Rand panted and George grunted as their naked bodies moved together on the bed, the heat among them growing.

The combined sensation of having his chute stuffed with man-meat while he fucked another guy energized Rand, like getting a hit of speed laced with an aphrodisiac. His hips moved rapidly to and fro. He was the pump in an erotic machine. Jesus, it felt so fucking good. Even in the threesomes he'd been in — and he'd been in many — sandwiches seldom got beyond the fantasy stage. Someone usually came before they could get their cocks and asses into place. And if they did get it together, Rand was usually the end piece of bread, the piece Kadin was now.

Kadin's moans were getting louder. "Oh, baby, yeah, baby, fuck my black ass." Wiggling his body around snakelike, his movements working real well with Rand's probing cock. Worked so well Rand could feel himself getting close, making his skin feel tight as if his excitement was too great to fit inside his body.

He hissed, gasped, panted and cried. And then he came.

"Oh, yeah, baby," Kadin purred, reaching between his legs to squeeze Rand's nuts. He wiggled around a bit more, and Rand's cock pumped out another thick wad of jizz.

Rand reached for Kadin's dick, hard as cement. He stroked Kadin's cock, keeping his own up that warm, dark ass, hardly moving now except from the impact of George ramming him. Kadin would wail and thrash his body each time Rand's hand moved up his shaft. George was fucking him harder now, sounding like he was running the last mile of a marathon. Rand wondered who was going to cum first.

Kadin shot first, his prick spewing a load as thick as a milkshake onto the blue-flowered sheet. Rand squeezed the shaft, pushing out another heavy dollop of jism, pausing to admire the white bead of cum clinging to Kadin's pinkish-brown cockhead. He scooped up the bead onto his index finger and brought it to Kadin's mouth, wiping it off on his lower lip. Kadin's eyes widened, as if to say: *what the fuck?* Before he could say anything aloud, Rand kissed him, Kadin's jizz cementing their lips together.

George came, huffing and puffing and saying a string of "oh yeses," keeping his cock buried in Rand's ass up to the hilt until his balls were completely drained.

"I hope you know I don't do that sorta' thing," Kadin said when Rand pulled his mouth away, his tone in transition from ghetto to diva. "Man, have me tasting *my own cum.* Shit, I don't even *swallow.*"

"While you're busy lying, you going to tell me you're usually a top, too?" Rand said. He smiled and licked his lips. "'Sides, what're you bitching about, sweet as you taste."

Rand took a shower; glad neither George nor Kadin asked to join him. He took his time, relaxing under the hot water and procrastinating having to deal with his hosts and the day ahead.

He stepped out into the bedroom, a towel wrapped around his waist, and Kadin slid past him, saying it was his turn and hoped Rand left some hot water. George wasn't in sight. Rand dressed quickly, his eyes on the wallet sitting on the dresser. Only eleven bucks in the wallet, but that was enough to last him until that evening.

Rand stuffed the money into his front pocket and headed out of the bedroom. A few steps down the hall and he was passing the kitchen, George in there bent over, wearing a pair of shorts that barely covered his ass, his head inside the fridge. Rand paused, wondering whether or not to say goodbye. He decided to keep going.

Six thirty Friday evening, Martin was still undecided: Go with this Task guy to The Tackle Box tonight on a search for Rand, or stay home and feel sorry for himself. He was quite prepared to do the latter. He'd called in sick again today, and though he had a stellar attendance record, his recent spate of absenteeism was clearly annoying Sandra, his boss. "Perhaps you should see a doctor," she coolly suggested.

"I'm sure it'll clear up by the weekend." Martin was a tad hung-over, so it didn't take much acting skill to affect a sickly tone. "I'll be in first thing Monday."

"I hope so. Our clients are getting impatient."

This left the day open to drink. And think: About what he should do tonight, about the sexy-but-suspicious stranger with the shaved head who showed up on his doorstep yesterday, and about Rand. Especially about Rand.

Why did he leave? What was he running from? He had trouble buying Task's story that Rand was trying to get back with this Dane Kensington guy, though some of the details did check out. The fact that Dane Kensington was in town was hardly a secret to anyone who'd picked up a copy of *David* or *Hot Spots*, so that part of the story was easily fabricated, although that was crediting Task — not exactly a Rhodes Scholar — with too much imagination. Then there was the information he'd gotten from the manager at the L.A. strip club where Task said he and Rand worked. Martin dialed 411 right after Task left yesterday. Getting the number, he called Boner's, forgetting the time change. It was early in the afternoon there, and the daytime bartender said he had no idea who Rand and Task were, but the strippers came and went so fast they could've worked there. Martin was told he needed to talk with the manager, Jerry. "Doesn't come in usually until eight." He placed a second call a quarter after eleven, but Jerry wasn't in yet. When he dialed at midnight, he finally got the elusive Jerry on the phone.

"What's this about?" the bar manager growled.

"Jus' wanna check on a couple guys used t'work there," Martin slurred. He had been steadily working his way through a bottle of Jim Beam and was fairly well drunk by the time Jerry came on the line. "Name's of Task and Rand?"

"Oh, yeah? And who wants to know?"

"I'm a ...." Christ, what did he tell him? "I'm Martin. I'm assistant manager at The Tackle Box? A club here in Atlanta. These guys applied as dancers here. Just verifying employment."

"Verifying employment for dick dancers?" Jerry thought that was so funny he didn't question why Martin didn't mention Task and Rand's full names, nor supplied a last name for himself. "Shit, that's a new one. S'long as they look good and don't have any tracks on their arms is enough for me."

"We're a bit more ... formal here, down South an' all. So, these two guys, Task and Rand, they work there?"

"Yeah, they worked here. You need me to tell you if they're good dancers, too? Maybe ask me if they're hot-lookin', or are you Southern boys able to figure that out on your own?" Jerry let out an abrasive laugh, then ruminated aloud, "Weird, second time this week someone's asked about those two guys.

The comment almost startled Martin into sobriety. "Really? Not cops, I hope. We don't need any trouble."

"Nah, nothin' like that. You through with your questions? Got work to do."

"Jus' one more. This Rand guy, he says that he knew this porn guy, Dane Kensington? That true?"

"You shittin' me? Goddamn, that was who was askin' about those guys earlier this week."

The information, rather than calming Martin's suspicions about Task only heightened them. Something hinky was going on, but only Task, Rand and Dane Kensington knew what it was. If he met up with Task at The Tackle Box, would he really get any real closure, or just sink deeper into a pile of shit?

A call from Conner early that afternoon gave him a brief respite from his quandary. "What the fuck is up with you?" he shouted into the phone, his cell phone voice. "You never call in sick, and suddenly you're out three days in one week."

"Don't think my past attendance record affords me any leniency," Martin said. "Sandra was running out of sympathy when I called this morning."

"She's just stressed, is all. You know how ... shit!" Martin heard the blaring of a car horn. "Asshole!" Conner snarled before resuming his conversation. "So, are you really sick?"

"Why is it whenever someone calls in sick, everyone assumes they're faking?"

Conner's tone became conspiratorial. "You're playing hooky aren't you? Having fun with your twink from California?"

"No!"

"Hey, I don't blame you. Get a hot piece like that, why not?"

"He's gone."

"Since when?"

"Wednesday, when I got home from work."

"Oh. Did he steal anything?"

"I knew I could depend on you for a few consoling words. No, didn't take anything that wasn't his."

"So you're, what? Staying home sulking because a trick left without saying goodbye?"

"He wasn't just a trick," Martin bristled. "He was..."

"You two were in love?" Conner snorted. "C'mon, you know better than that. It was nothing more than a one-night-stand that went on for four nights. Don't waste any more time moping about it. You had your fun, now move on."

"Wish it were that easy," Martin sighed. "But it doesn't end there. Yesterday..."

"Hey, Martin, hold on a second." Martin heard Conner shout out his car window: "Yeah, I'd like the broiled chicken salad, with Italian dressing and no croutons. Got that? And..."

"Look, maybe we can talk later."

"...a large un-sweetened tea, but give me a couple packets of Equal. What was that Martin? Wait ... did you say $7.10. Seven? The menu says the salad's only $4.99. How much you charging for tea?"

Martin let out a frustrated sigh, and for the thousandth time questioned his friendship to Conner. "Maybe later would be a better time to talk."

"That's better. Yeah, maybe later would be better idea. What're you doing tonight? No, not you," he shouted at the hapless fast food employee. "I'm on the phone. Girl thought I was asking her out," he chortled.

"Are you talking to me now?"

Conner ignored the question. "You gonna be home later? I've got to go to that visitation for Perry Snopes. Shake hands, say I'm sorry for your loss ... y'know, show the family the firm really cares ... then get my ass out of there. I'll be there fifteen minutes, tops. After that, my evening's free. Maybe I'll stop by after."

"Yeah, do that," Martin said without enthusiasm. Conner wasn't what he needed right now. He needed answers. He needed closure — or maybe, just one more chance.

At seven o'clock Friday evening Martin made his decision, and went into the kitchen to find the Post-It note with Task's number scrawled on it.

* * * * *

In the past week, Nine had seen the same goddamn suspense movie three times in three different motels.

He was in his room at the Fairfield Inn, stretched out on his bed, shoes and shirt off, drinking a beer, channel surfing until it was time to get ready for Dane's party. He clicked over to Showtime and there was that same movie, the one about the two guys terrorized by a truck-driving serial killer. It wasn't a bad movie. Not great, but

Jonathan Asche

entertaining enough. Not worth seeing three fucking times, maybe, but the actors were cute, and they bared their asses in one scene.

Nine left the TV on Showtime.

His cell phone rang. Nine knew who it was even if the phone only identified the caller as "Atlanta, Ga."

He hit the mute button on the remote and then the talk button on the phone. "I'm supposed to call *you*."

The caller didn't bother with hello, either. "Are you in town?"

"Yeah."

"Where're you staying?"

"Better not say."

"I need to see you."

"You will, but not now, not here."

"Later? Tonight?"

"Not tonight. Got plans."

"What kind of plans?"

"Plans that can't involve you, okay?"

"Okay, okay. Shit, you don't have to get bitchy about it. I want to hear a progress report."

"You'll get one," Nine said distractedly, eyes focused on the TV. He saw the movie was almost at the scene where the two guys walk naked across a truck stop parking lot and said to his caller: "Look, I gotta go. I'll call you tomorrow, all right?"

EIGHTEEN

Dane sat in a lumpy, vinyl-upholstered armchair, taking in his dreary surroundings. Cinderblock walls covered in yellowed paint were incongruously decorated with OSHA regulations and signed posters of visiting porn stars, all of whom scrawled "XXX" beneath their signatures. A couple black filing cabinets that looked as if they fell off the back of a truck were pushed in the far corner; a dust-covered silk ficus tree stood in another.

"So, who was the gas station attendant who decorated your office?" he asked.

Dane's sarcasm was met with long, loud snorting. He looked toward the battered, putty-colored desk to see the last of a white line disappear up a straw and into John Klavern's nose.

The bar manager sat up, sniffling and rubbing his nose, his eyes bugging out before focusing on Dane. "Want to do the other one?" he asked, motioning toward the second thin white stripe across his dark Formica desktop.

"No thanks." Dane's nose wrinkled in disgust. "I'm jittery enough." His stomach lurched, as if to second his statement. He always got a touch of stage fright before hosting a big event (he sometimes thought it was easier to fuck on camera than stand up and speak to a hundred strangers), and knowing he'd be responsible, albeit indirectly, for two deaths this evening — shit, he was a fucking wreck.

John shrugged and leaned back down. A sharp, honking snort later, and the second line of powder was gone.

Dane turned away. He couldn't stand to look at this flabby, pig of a man with his suspicious eyes and cheap toupee for more than thirty seconds at a time. Dane checked his watch and asked, "Is Task here yet? I have yet to see him, and we start in twenty minutes."

John sniffed and wiped his nose on the back of his pudgy hand. "This kid got a foot-long dick or something? Relax, I got Steve looking out for him. Guy's been hanging out here every night, hustling for drinks. Think he's been stealing tips, too, case you want to bring that..."

There was a brusque pounding on the door. A hoarse voice shouted from the other side, "It's Steve."

Dane was on his feet and opening the door before John could get out of his chair. Steve, hatchet-faced and barrel-chested, entered the room like he was fully prepared to kick some ass.

"That dickhead you're looking for, he's here now, hanging around up front," the bouncer said.

Dane asked Steve to point Task out, then followed the bouncer out of the office, down a short hall and to a doorway covered by a beaded curtain. Stepping through the curtain, they were then behind the bar and in the path of a harried bartender, a slim man except for a distended belly, who almost bounced off Steve's chest as he rushed to fill the next drink order.

"Watch it!" the bartender shrieked.

Steve sneered, "Hey, Crix, wanna meet Mr. Kensington? He owns the place. Maybe bring up the issues you have with our insurance."

"Sorry," the bartender said meekly, scuttling past them.

"There he is," the bouncer said, pointing across the club. "Guy with the shaved head and red T-shirt, standing up front? That's the dickhead."

It took a moment to isolate the man Steve was pointing to, his near-sightedness and the club's low light making the crowd appear as one indistinguishable blur. Then he saw him, leaning against the cigarette machine, his expression blank as he looked around the club. So this was Task. An attractive man, certainly fuckable. He could easily be a contender in tonight's contest, Dane thought. Too bad he'll be dead.

"I thought he was blond," he remarked.

"He was when he first showed up." John had caught up with them and was now standing on Dane's left. "Then he dyed it red. Looked like Woody-fuckin'-Woodpecker. Looks better with it shaved off."

"Still a dickhead," Steve said.

"Excuse me," Dane said, leaving the men, ducking under the bar's gate and emerging in the packed club, weaving his way through the growing crowd.

"Hey, aren't you...?"

"Your videos are awesome! I jacked off to *Trucker Fuckers* so much I was..."

"I'm a friend of the guy that runs Hot House, and..."

Dane smiled his way past fans, starfuckers and wannabes, entering a door beside the DJ booth that led to the dancers' dressing room (someone had taped a homemade sign on the door reading "The Undressing Room"). Inside, an assortment of men — from 21 to early thirties; gay and straight; white, black and Latino; smooth and hairy; slim, athletic and muscle-bound — milled about, stuffing themselves into G-strings, counting the money from their last set, flexing in front a mirror, sitting around talking (on cell phones, not to each other). Smoke from tobacco and marijuana hung in the air. A drag queen, wigless, concentrated on adjusting her fake tits.

The noise level of the room dropped a few decibels as Dane crossed the room to the corner where Todd Trulaine sat, ears plugged into his iPod, eyes closed, nodding in time to the music. The nodding stopped and the eyes opened, their dilated pupils focusing on Dane.

He grinned, pulling out his earphones. "Hey, man. Come to check out the 'private' dressing room?"

"Come to make sure you can still stand up."

Todd sat up "I'm cool. Just smoked a couple joints earlier, is all."

Dane nodded, not believing a couple joints were all, but not pressing it. "You got the invitations for the after party?"

"In my bag." Todd kicked the Lakers gym bag beneath his chair. "Where they were when you asked thirty minutes ago."

"Come with me."

Todd followed Dane out of the dressing room, taking his gym bag with him. "These fuckers'll rob you blind, you just don't know," he said. They stopped at the door that led out into the club, Dane surveying the crowd, looking for Task.

"Okay, see that guy there, cute, with the shaved head, standing in line at the bar?"

"Think so."

Dane pointed. "Look until you know so. He's wearing a red T-shirt."

"Yeah, I see 'im."

"Make sure he gets an invitation. Stress that I personally asked that he attend."

Todd exposed a row of white teeth. "You gettin' bored with me already," he teased.

"Just..."

Dane saw Task, looking directly at him, pointing at him and pulling on the sleeve of the man next to him — an older, daddy-type, fairly hot except he looked like he'd rather be taking a dump — talking excitedly.

"Do it," Dane whispered as he backed away from the door.

* * * * *

"Thanks, that means a lot," Winston LaGrabe said to a short, boxy woman in her fifties, hoping the words sounded true. Convincing portrayals of sadness and sorrow were never his forte as an actor. That's why he always sought roles that played on his strengths: smiling, scowling and taking off his shirt.

The older woman patted his hand. She said they had met before at a Clean Sweep meeting, but Winston didn't remember and forgot her name seconds after she re-introduced herself. "Just be strong," she assured him, before stepping over to speak to the Iron Cunt.

Winston surreptitiously checked his watch. A few minutes past eight o'clock. The visitation lasted until nine, and then there would likely be more wellwishers stopping by the house for a few more hours after that. Tomorrow afternoon was the funeral, and then more people expressing their deepest sympathy. Why couldn't they just stick Perry in the ground and be done with it?

He started to look toward the casket. It was closed, thankfully — he'd insisted on that, saying he did not care how adept they were at making him up. He didn't want to remember Perry as a mask of pancake makeup and mortician's wax. To Winston's surprise, Nora conceded, saying displaying a photo of her son atop the casket would be sufficient as well as more flattering. But then the Cunt got even by choosing to bury her beloved Perry in the most expensive casket she could find. Christ, it would've been cheaper to bury the bastard in a Mercedes. The Cunt's extravagance compromised Winston's plan to pad the funeral costs and keep the difference to pay off Nine.

Winston was about to force himself toward the casket — he thought it would look good if he frequently stood before it wearing a wistful expression — when a man intercepted him. "Hey! Winston, right?" the man said, pumping Winston's hand. He didn't recognize the man and was sure they hadn't met before. He was about Winston's age, but retained a boyish appeal of someone much younger.

"Um, yeah," Winston answered. Thinking: Does he go to a tanning bed or does he use bronzer?

"I'm Conner Blivett, with AdVerb? I was handling the advertising for your Perry's campaign."

"I see."

Conner put a hand on his shoulder. "A shame what happened. How you holding up?"

"I'm... I'm getting by. It's still pretty overwhelming." He liked feeling the weight of Conner's hand on him, and was crestfallen when Conner took it away.

"I just wanted to stop by, pay my respects," Conner said. The part unspoken: he was here out of a sense of duty, not because he gave two shits about the passing of his client Perry Snopes.

"You're welcome to come by the house later," Winston said, the first time he'd uttered those words to anyone all evening. "There's certainly plenty of food."

Conner flashed a half-smile. "Like to, but I promised to get together with a friend later tonight. But, here, take this." He pulled a sterling silver cardholder from inside his suit jacket, flipped it open and thumbed out a business card with the skill of a Vegas blackjack dealer. "In case you ever want to get together in the future. You can usually reach me on my cell."

Winston took the card. "Thanks, I just may do that." He watched Conner move on to pay his condolences to the Frozen Dyke, stealthily checking out how tasty Conner looked in his tailored suit, and decided he'd definitely be dialing Conner Blivett's cell phone number in the very near future.

* * * * *

In his best game show host voice, the DJ announced: "And now, boys and *gurlz*, the moment you've all been waiting for! The diva who's eager to please even when she's not on her knees! Won't you give a hot Hotlanta welcome to The One! The Only! *Miiiiiiss Hon-eeeeey D'JOHN!*"

Miss Honey D'John sashayed out, lip-synching to Deborah Cox. A towering blond wig perched on her head, her man's body forced into the feminine contours of a sparkling blue gown. Martin almost swallowed his bourbon and ginger in one gulp. Of course — can't have a gay event in this town without a fucking drag queen.

Task, sitting beside him, looked around the room, trying to spot Rand. They hadn't seen him, but got a glimpse of the man suspected to be the reason for Rand's disappearance: Dane Kensington, standing in a doorway, looking right at them. And then, he was gone.

The song ended. Now it was time for the jokes.

"Y'all hear about that protein diet everyone's talkin' about?" Honey D'John trilled, a voice that was a nasal whine, too high pitched to be masculine, but not the voice of a real woman either. "Gurlz, *I've* been on the protein diet since I was in junior high school. But I had to take a break from it — I was gettin' scabs on my knees!"

Bah-dum-dum!

The crowd laughed. Martin's cocktail was long gone, and he contemplated getting another one, but didn't want to wade through the crowd to get to the bar. He looked over at Task, watching Honey D'John, not laughing, making Martin think that maybe he misjudged the guy.

Or maybe Task didn't get the jokes.

Honey D'John said, "Y'all hear about that tornado that tore across Alabama last week? It did a hundred million dollars worth of improvements!"

Bah-dum-dum!

Martin checked his watch. It was 8:27 p.m. and the show was just getting started. *This is going to be the longest goddamned night of my life.*

* * * * *

Getting into Martin's house was laughably easy. On a hunch, Rand checked beneath welcome mats and flowerpots. He picked up a ceramic frog crouched among the plants bordering the sun porch and heard a rattling inside. He upended the frog and a brass colored key tumbled out its mouth.

The key opened the front door. Though the interior of the house looked the same, it felt different now that he was entering illegally, its stillness making goose bumps rise on Rand's forearms.

Now he sat on Martin's bed, open box in his lap, studying its contents.

Rand didn't know what caliber the gun was; whether it was a .22, 38 or .45 made no difference to him. Only reason he knew it was a Smith & Wesson was it was imprinted on the handle, and figured it was a revolver, not a pistol (a revolver had the spinning chamber thing, right?). All he knew was it could kill someone, and when he walked out of this house he had to be prepared to do just that.

Question was: Was he?

After leaving George's house that morning, he made his way back to the adult video store where he hooked up with the other trick from last night, the one who took off with his duffle bag. He thought, maybe, if he waited long enough he'd see the guy as he returned his DVD. But then he saw the sign out front boasting three-day rentals. Wasn't likely his suburban closet case was going to return his secretly-rented porno any earlier than he had to. *Shit!*

He risked going inside again. The cunt with the jowls was gone and in her place was a bored-looking black guy, watching Jenny Jones on a little portable TV on the end of the counter. Maybe he'd have more luck this time.

He didn't.

No tape, no leverage, no money.

The gun in Martin's closet could change that. It would make things a bit more confrontational than he'd like, more like armed robbery than blackmail, but it would have to do. In his haste to leave the other day, the gun slipped his mind, and later he cursed himself for forgetting. Now he was glad he forgot. Otherwise that gun would be in his bag, with the tape, in the back of the suburban closet case's SUV — or tossed on the side of the highway somewhere.

Forgetting the gun was about the luckiest thing that had happened to him in the past two days.

Rand picked up the gun from the metal box, a prickly sensation bubbling beneath the palm of his had as it pressed against the handle. He wondered why holding the gun made him so anxious. It wasn't like he planned on killing anyone, hoped he didn't even have to pull the trigger, in fact. Being involved in one murder was enough for one lifetime. Then again, he'd always heard it got easier after the first one.

* * * * *

Contestant No. 1 was introduced as Tango Cash, needlessly explaining in the contest's "interview segment" that he got the name from the Stallone movie, *Tango & Cash*. Dane Kensington said, "You don't say."

Tango was naturally stocky, the type of body that could easily turn to fat, but he'd spent some time at the gym to keep that from happening. He couldn't tone the muscles in his face, though. From the neck up the guy was big and round: big round head, lips like two sausage links and a round, pug-like nose. Standing on stage wearing just an electric blue thong and a broad, goofy grin — his only facial expression — Tango said he wanted to be a porn star because he liked to fuck.

Tango also was a big ol' girl, with a voice that was somewhere between queeny and effeminate. Hearing the word "fuck" in that voice cracked Task up. Laughing, he looked over at Martin to see if he thought the girlie wannabe porn star was funny, too.

Martin puffed on his cigarette, exhaling an impatient sigh with a cloud of smoke.

Tango's favorite thing to do sexually: "I like to give head ... and fuck!" He said he was a top. That got a chuckle from the crowd. One guy shouted: Bullshit! Tango's goofy grin wavered.

Martin leaned across the tabletop that was no bigger than a large pepperoni from Pizza Hut and asked Task: "He's not here. Do we have to sit through *all* of this?"

"You got something better to do? 'Sides, don't you wanna talk to Dane after?"

"I don't really want to, no, but I guess we need to."

They heard Tango say, "I once gave blowjobs to two guys behind El Azteca on Ponce. At the same time!"

Martin asked Task, "How many contestants are there? Five?"

"Seven, I think."

He retreated across the table. Glaring at the stage, he took another drag on his cigarette.

"Great," Martin said.

* * * * *

The gun sounded like a firecracker going off. A firecracker to the power of ten.

"SHIT!" Rand shrieked and hit the floor.

A minute later, he stood up, nervously. The revolver lay on the bedroom floor, where it landed, after slipping from the waistband of his shorts, traveling down his leg and escaping his shorts entirely, firing when it hit the floor.

Rand approached the weapon cautiously, as if it would spring to life and start firing on its own. He picked it up by the barrel. Still warm.

The gun went into his right front pocket. It was heavy enough to pull his shorts down off his right hip, and it bulged obviously against his thigh. Checking himself out in the bedroom mirror, he thought of the Mae West line, is that a gun in your pocket, etcetera, etcetera. He took one of Martin's Oxfords from the closet and tied it around his waist. That helped.

He wondered if any of Martin's neighbors called the cops and listened for sirens, but heard nothing. Not much of a Neighborhood Watch program, evidently.

Rand was both grateful and perplexed that he had trouble finding the spot where the bullet hit. At first glance, nothing appeared to have a hole in it that wasn't supposed to. Five minutes later, he found the spot, a small chunk taken out of the wall near the closet, about four inches above the baseboard, bits of plaster scattered on the floor in front of it. Nothing that would be noticed at first glace. Martin would probably notice his shirt was missing before he noticed the bullet hole in his wall, or that his gun was stolen.

Downstairs, he stopped by the kitchen. He was already leaving with a gun and a shirt, might as well get something to eat while he was here. From the illumination of the range hood light, Rand got a clue how Martin was spending his spare time recently. A bottle of Jim Beam, almost empty, sat on the kitchen counter. By the sink sat a tall, quart-sized stadium cup, Atlanta Braves logo emblazoned on the sides, an inch of watery, pale amber liquid inside. Rand picked it up and sniffed. A bouquet of stale bourbon and a flat ginger ale. In the sink, a couple more stadium cups, and a gnawed pizza crust poked out from between the rubber teeth guarding the garbage disposal.

That his leaving drove Martin to liquor and carbohydrates brought a wan smile to Rand's face. It was kind of funny, really. So why did he feel guilty?

Rummaging through the refrigerator and pantry yielded Rand a meal of a bruised apple, a can of Pringles and a Diet Coke. The clock on the microwave read 9:10.

I need to get the fuck outta here!

Carrying the soda in his left hand, the Pringles tucked under the same arm, and clenching the apple between his teeth, Rand started to head out the kitchen door.

And then he stopped.

On the kitchen table rested a digest sized magazine, one of the local fag rags. It was open to a full-page ad.

Green text jumped out at him: "Have you ever dreamed of becoming a PORN STAR?"

In the corner of the ad, the smiling picture of Dane Kensington.

In Rand's chest, a tangle of emotions and memories tore through him like a bullet.

* * * * *

County ordinances regarding nude dancing forbade simulating sex acts, spreading one's ass cheeks on stage and dancing while sporting a hard-on. Contestant No. 3, Saber, freely violated all these ordinances, humping the stage, massaging the obvious chubby in his star spangled G-string, and, in a move that got him the loudest cheers, laying on his back and curling his legs over his head, nearly folding his smooth, wiry body in half.

"Damn!" whooped Task. "Bet he can suck himself off. Whatta you think?"

"Is our fucking waiter gonna come back to this side of the room?" Martin groused.

"Dunno. Hey, you ever try that?"

"Try what?"

"Sucking yourself off? I tried it a few times, nearly broke my back. Most I could do was cum on my own face."

Martin shot him a disapproving glare. "Thanks. I needed to know that." But Task was pretty sure he was trying to picture it.

"Tell you what, I'll go up to the bar and get us some refills," Task offered. "Just want to see this guy take off his thong first."

Saber whipped off his G-string moments later, proving to the crowd he was aptly named. Grabbing his thick, semi-hard cock, he began to stroke it while swiveling his hips in time to the driving beat of the music. The crowd went wild. Management went apoplectic. Dane Kensington hopped on stage. "Thank you, Saber! We'll let you finish your act later tonight..."

"Mmmm-MMMM!" Task stood up, shaking his head. "Love to get me a piece o' that! I'll go get our drinks now. Can you loan me ten dollars?"

Martin's irritation nearly glowed in the bar's dim lights. "Loan? You're going to pay me back?"

"Hey, I'm saving you the trouble of pushing through that crowd. Try and enjoy the show."

Martin handed Task two fives, grumbling all the while. Task thanked him and started shoving his way through the forest of patrons, getting a few "hey, cuties" and butt-grabs on his way to the bar. By the time a bartender took his order, Contestant No. 4, some little swishy guy calling himself Dickson Hardy, was halfway through his routine.

"No charge, sweetie," said the bartender, the one they called Crix, the only bartender at The Tackle Box who liked him. Liked him more now, after Task slipped him one of those tablets he stole from Dario's gym bag.

"Thanks, dude," Task nodded, picking up the two cocktails, not bothering to leave a tip.

Now back to sourpuss. Jesus, he'd never seen a gay guy so determined not to have a good time looking at naked men. And Rand hung out with this guy for nearly a week? Couldn't see how he stood it. Martin was attractive, no doubt, but he needed to lighten the fuck up.

Maybe he needed a little help in that department.

Before heading back to his and Martin's table, Task took a detour to the men's room. Both stalls were taken — one by three guys loudly snorting up something to stimulate their evening, the other by a guy taking a crap. Task waited against the far wall, hoping the cokeheads (or tweakers, or whatever they were) vacated their stall first. They did. Task swooped into the empty stall and latched the door.

He set the two drinks down on the cracked porcelain lid of the toilet tank and pulled a wadded-up napkin from the front pocket of his jeans. Inside were the last two tabs of Ecstasy he'd stolen from Dario. Placing one of the blue tabs on the tank lid, he pressed his thumb against it, trying to crush it, only succeeding in breaking it into three pieces. He took out his room key — the Swisher Suites still used regular keys, not the electronic locks you opened with a card — and mashed it against the broken tablet, grinding it into smaller pieces. More like crumbs than a powder, but it would have to do. Holding Martin's bourbon and ginger just beneath the lip of the toilet tank lid, he swept the chalky crumbs into the cup and stirred them into the cocktail with his index finger. Confident the liquor would dissolve the more obvious pieces swimming around the drink, Task unlatched the door. Standing outside the stall was Dario, waiting with some grinning queen with a weak chin and bulging eyes. The dancer gave Task a threatening look as he and the weak-chinned queen entered the stall.

"Motherfuckin' thief!" he spat just before the queen latched the door.

NINETEEN

It began with the photos...

Rand spread his legs wider and pulled at the leg of his basketball shorts. "Can you see my balls yet?"

Task's roommate Alex said, "Barely. Maybe hike the shorts up a bit more on your left leg, spread your legs apart more. Yeah, that does it."

Click. Flash. Temporary blindness.

Rand stood up unsteadily, the spots in his eyes, coupled with the lingering effects of the bowl he smoked twenty minutes ago, unsettling his sense of balance. "How 'bout a couple ass shots now?"

"Sure thing," Alex said, waving the photo regurgitated by the Polaroid in the air before laying it on the coffee table next to the others.

"Figured we could do one with my shorts down partway, showing some crack," Rand said, turning his back to Alex. "Kind of a tease, you know? After that I'll lose the shorts."

Rand pulled his shorts down until they were halfway down his butt. "How's that?"

"Say cheese."

The shorts came off. Rand climbed back onto the sofa, knelt on the seat and leaned over, hands pressed into the armrest. He arched his back, pushing his ass upward, and spread his legs further apart. "That look good?" he asked.

There was a pregnant pause before Alex answered, "Mmmm, yes."

The camera flashed, whirred and rolled out another photo. Rand flipped around and reached for the Polaroid. "Lemme see! You never really get a good view of your ass in a mirror 'less you got one of those three-sided things."

He pinched the corners of the photo between his fingers, watching the image of himself materialize in a reverse fade, his butt-cheeks appearing first, glaring from where the flash hit them on their rounded peaks, the rest of his body pitched forward into shadows. It was like looking at a photo of a stranger, seeing himself at this seldom-seen view.

Rand tossed the photo onto the coffee table and eased back on the plaid sofa. "Now for some full frontal," he giggled. He batted his cock, draped heavily over the silky pink pillow of his ball sack. "Should probably be hard for these."

Alex had been trying to act professional, like he was a real photographer, not just asked because he happened to have a Polaroid. He was finding it difficult to act detached now, his face coloring as he smiled, nodded, looked away and then looked back again.

Rand was smiling at him suggestively. His dick was slowly raising its sleepy head.

Alex passed the camera over to his other hand and not-so-subtly reached between his legs to adjust himself.

The tension in the air thickened as the silence grew longer. Then Rand said, "Bet you could help make me hard."

"Looks like you're not having any trouble doing that on your own."

Rand's cock had grown noticeably in the past two minutes. "That's 'cause I'm looking at you."

The coloring of Alex's face got deeper, his smile broader, and he looked away again. Even though he was a walking sexual fantasy, Task's roommate always seemed slightly embarrassed to be reminded of his own attractiveness, which only made him that much more irresistible. The semi creeping around inside his gray gym shorts didn't hurt, either.

"C'mere," Rand said.

"You think we should be doing this?" Alex asked, even as he was setting the camera down on an end table, even as he was stepping closer.

Rand didn't answer, just waited until Alex was in range. Close enough to grab.

Roughly, he hooked his fingers in the elastic waistband of Alex's shorts and pulled.

Alex's cock had been a near obsession of Rand's for months, ever since Task first introduced him to his roommate. Even when compared to Rand's exaggerated imaginings, Alex's dick was not a disappointment. Rand closed a fist around the shaft, and, while pulling on it gently, turned his face up to Alex's, letting him see his awed smile.

A second later, Rand had Alex's dick deep in his mouth. Alex had his hands on top of Rand's head. His body rocked, his breathing was heavy.

Rand sucked and licked every inch of Alex's rod, caressing its hardness with his lips and tongue. He reached up and cradled Alex's low-hanging balls in his hand. He nuzzled his face against Alex's nut-sack, the coarse, curly hairs raking against his skin, his natural musk filling Rand's nostrils.

Alex's breathing got louder and shallower. "Oh, yeahs" and "oh, gods" escaped beneath his gasping breath. His orgasm was imminent.

But Rand pulled away.

"Take my picture now."

"Wha ... what?"

"Now, while I'm all hot," Rand insisted, leaning back against the seat cushions.

Alex, shaking his head as if to say, "I don't fucking believe this," reached for the Polaroid. Crouching down on the floor for a straight-ahead shot, he said in a tight voice: "Tell me when."

Rand grabbed his cock — now stiff and raging — and pushed it toward the camera. "Now."

A click and an explosion of white. Rand's prick was captured on film.

He brought one knee up, digging his heel into the seat cushion. Rand's other foot remained on the floor. He took his hand from his dick and placed it on his chest, his fingers tracing the curve of one of his pecs.

"Okay. Now."

Alex stood up for the next shot, the camera looking down on Rand as he played with his cock, a look of genuine pleasure on his face. Alex snapped the photo.

"Hey! I didn't say 'when'."

"Thought it was a good shot. You'll see," Alex said, putting the photo and the camera down on the coffee table. Getting down on the floor, he said, "I think that's enough photos for now."

His body was warm and firm on top of Rand's. Their tongues battled against each other, their hands groped and grabbed, pinched and pulled. Their cocks produced an excruciating friction. Alex's mouth slid down Rand's neck, traversed the ridges and grooves formed by the taut muscles of his torso, not stopping until he reached Rand's turgid dick.

One gulp later and Alex had swallowed Rand's cock down to the hilt.

Writhing, panting, grunting, Rand thrust his hips forward, his rod pushing against the waves of Alex's tongue. That tongue then covered the contours of Rand's scrotum, playing with the balls within. "Mmmmms" and "ooohhhs" slipped out of Alex's mouth between licks. Rand scooted his hips forward, hooked a leg over Alex's shoulder. Pressing a hand against the top of his head, Rand urged Task's roommate further down between his legs.

Down Alex went.

"Ohfuckyeah!" Rand hollered, his body rising off the sofa. Alex's tongue spiraled its way into his butthole, fighting against his contracting sphincter.

Rand's body curled and twisted, working against the probing of Alex's tongue. His hand gripped his dripping dick, compulsively stroking it as Alex's tongue-fucked him.

His nut-sack constricted, his balls close against his body. An electric-like current crackled through his shaft.

"Oh! Oh! Oh, yeah! Oooooh!"

Alex's mouth returned to Rand's dick in time for the second big spurt. He held Rand's cock in his mouth until the very last drop of jism oozed out.

A moment later, Alex was standing over him, one foot up on the sofa, his engorged cock aimed at Rand's face. Rand leaned forward, mouth open wide, tongue sticking out. But the load he was ready to catch, when fired, splattered against his forehead. He grabbed Alex's dick, pulled down on it like a lever, adjusting his aim, getting a blast of cum right across his nose in the process. Finally, he just stuck Alex's cock in his mouth, though by then Task's hunky roommate was pretty much spent.

Laughter followed. "You're a mess," Alex chuckled, wiping some of his jizz off Rand's face with his fingers.

"And you can't shoot straight."

More laughter, dying down to a heavy quiet.

"When does Task get off work?" Alex asked, stooping down to pick his shorts off the floor.

Rand looked over at the clock on the VCR. Just after nine. "Not till midnight, at least."

"Still, better hurry and get cleaned up. People get off early, come home unexpectedly. Hate for your boyfriend to catch us like this."

Rand said, "Task isn't my boyfriend."

The next day the photos and a letter were mailed to DanKen Studios. A week later, Dane Kensington himself — not an assistant, not one of the directors he employed — called and set up a meeting, suggesting Rand come out to his house in Sherman Oaks.

* * * * *

The sky finally made good on its threat of rain. The sporadic tapping of water drops pelting the windows, the sharp *ping* the drops made as they hit a drainpipe outside the kitchen window, jerked Rand back to the present.

Maybe I should steal an umbrella while I'm at it, he thought.

Rand set the can of chips and the soda down on the kitchen table and took a bite of the apple. It felt mealy and slightly mushy in his mouth, so he didn't take another one. Dropping the apple in the trash, Rand headed into the foyer, thinking Martin kept an umbrella there.

The doorbell rang.

Rand froze. He was at the entrance into the foyer. While panic curdled his blood and tap-danced through his bowels, his mind tried to make a decision based on the adrenaline-fueled thoughts whizzing through it.

It's Martin — no, can't be Martin. Martin wouldn't ring his own fucking doorbell, like, who'd he expect to answer it? Gotta be someone else. Probably just someone stopping by, someone trying to lead Martin to the path of righteousness via the Church of the Latter Day Saints or maybe just a neighbor wanting to borrow something. If I stay here, stay real, real still they'll think no one's home to convert to the Church of Latter Day Saints, borrow a cup of sugar or whatever.

The doorbell rang again, and this time a man's voice accompanied it. "Hey! Martin! You home?"

If I keep real still...

The guy pounded on the door. "Martin!"

Or maybe...

The doorknob rattled, then turned.

I should run like hell!

The front door opened. "Hey, Martin, you left a key in the fr— well, hell-o!"

Rand turned to bolt before seeing the man's face. *Just run for the back door and keep running! The back door isn't even ten feet away — the longest fucking ten feet ever, but you can make —*

Something solid caught him on the side, just above his hip, and he ricocheted off course, into the kitchen table, stumbling forward and falling over, taking a chair down with him.

Nothing was broken. He wasn't paralyzed, but with the wind knocked out of him and fear hijacking his central nervous system, he might as well have been. Nevertheless, he made a valiant effort of trying to get back on his feet.

The kitchen light came on, singeing his irises until a shadow fell across him.

Rand looked up into the teeth of a predatory grin. "So you're Martin's twink," the man said, nodding. "Yeah, it makes sense now. I'd skip work to stay home and fuck you, too."

TWENTY

It was raining when Nine got out of the cab, a half-block past where he intended to go. He ran from beneath one awning to the next to keep from getting soaked. At the corner, his destination: A restaurant, with a sign out front advertising complimentary valet parking, an arrow pointing down a narrow side street. Behind the restaurant, a small parking lot with a little hutch for the valet. Looked like only one guy was working, and he was busy holding an umbrella over a woman alighting from the passenger side of a pewter-colored Mercedes.

Perfect.

Nine hung back from view as the woman and her husband or boyfriend turned their car over to the valet and headed for the restaurant's front entrance. He kept his head down as he passed them, though they were both huddled under a single umbrella and likely didn't see him. Once the couple rounded the corner, out of sight, Nine sprinted into the parking lot, seeing the tail lights of the Mercedes glowing at the end of the lot. The lights went off and Nine ducked down between two parked cars and waited.

The valet — early twenties, probably a college student, young Republican-attractive — came trotting past where Nine crouched, umbrella resting on his shoulder. He was singing something to himself. Sounded like "Oops! I Did It Again."

Silently, Nine stood up and fell in step with the valet. When he was within a few feet, he called out, "Hey!"

The guy turned, obviously startled. "Wha…"

Nine's fist slammed into the valet's face. "This is for the keys to that Mercedes."

The umbrella and car keys slipped from valet's hand. Blood began to trickle out his nostrils. In his last few seconds of consciousness, he managed to sputter out the question, "Wha' the fuck ya' doin'?" He started to raise his fists to defend himself.

Nine punched him again. The valet dropped to the ground, his head falling back into a pothole filled with muddy, oily water.

"That second one was for singing a Britney Spears song," Nine said, squatting to pick up the Mercedes keys. "Jesus, *Britney Spears*? Maybe when you come-to you'll have some taste."

* * * * *

The winner of the Porn Star Search was Contestant No. 3, Saber, who could bend his body in half, who started jacking off on stage, who said his wildest sexual experience was being gang-banged by ten men at a pool party.

Martin applauded when Saber was announced the winner. That's when he knew he was drunk.

No, not drunk. *Altered.*

He looked over at Task. "You put something in my drink, didn't you?"

Task didn't hear, or pretended not to, clapping and hollering as it was announced Saber's shameless exhibitionism netted him $500 and an all-expense-paid trip to Los Angeles to appear in a new DanKen Studios production. Other participants got a DanKen T-shirt and a copy of *SkinPicks #4*, a compilation DVD featuring "some of DanKen Studio's raunchiest scenes."

He should've known his drink was spiked. It didn't taste right, a foreign bitterness lingering beneath the cocktail's familiar tangy sweetness. He made a comment about how his drink had a funny flavor, but kept drinking it. After having to wait nearly twenty minutes for Task to return from the bar — "You have to distill the bourbon yourself?" he'd asked — Martin didn't feel like fighting his way back through the crowd to complain to the bartender and get a replacement cocktail.

He tried asking Task again: "What did you...?"

Martin didn't finish the question. He realized, at this moment, he felt too good to care.

Dane Kensington was center stage. Flanked by his two co-hosts and fellow judges, Honey D'John and Todd Trulaine, and with all the contestants lined up in a row behind him, he thanked the crowd for coming (pausing for the titters produced by his double entendre) to the event and reminding people to stick around.

"Todd has in his hand thirty invitations" — Todd raised his handful of said invitations as if Dane's statement required a visual aid — "to a private party later tonight, hosted by *moi*, at my penthouse suite in the Wilkes Overlook Hotel in Midtown. For the next thirty minutes, Todd will be circulating through the club, selecting invitees. You don't have to do anything to be invited, but if you ask him for an invitation you're definitely not invited, so please, no begging, no bribing. Just get yourself another drink, sit back, enjoy our fine entertainment and maybe — just maybe — tonight will be your lucky night."

A Tori Amos song, remixed beyond recognition, drowned out the excited buzz of the crowd.

Task shouted above the beat, "Ya' wanna try and talk to Dane now?"

Martin was too busy giving his inhibitions a good-bye hug to answer Task right away. When he did think to answer, he'd forgotten the question.

Task flashed a knowing smile. "Feelin' better?"

"I ... what did you put in my drink?" Not accusing or angry now, just curious.

But before Task could answer, Todd Trulaine appeared before their table, wearing a pair of shiny red hot pants so tight you could see the outlines of the hair on his balls. Todd thrust an invitation toward Task.

"Mr. Kensington personally requested you attend," he said. Looking over at Martin, who was intently studying his crotch, Todd pulled another invitation from the stack he clutched in his other hand. "You should go, too," he said, giving Martin an invitation and a promising smile.

"We'll be there," Martin beamed.

The porn star ambled away, moving his ass just so. "Looks like Dane wants to talk to us, too," Task said, turning the invitation over in his hand.

Martin said, "You see that? That Todd Tru-guy was coming on to me."

* * * * *

Alan Bryson paced outside The Pheasant restaurant in Midtown Atlanta, getting soaked by the rain but too pissed off to care. "Just great. I finally get a Mercedes and it fucking gets stolen. Didn't even have it a full year," he said. "That's what we get for coming into the city."

"Goddammit, Al, this could've happened anywhere," Grace said.

He cut his eyes toward his wife. It was her idea to have dinner at The Pheasant, even though there were plenty of perfectly fine restaurants in Duluth, where they lived. She stood with her back to the restaurant, alternately looking out at the parking lot and at Alan. In one hand she held an umbrella, and with the other hand she clutched her lacy shawl around her bare shoulders. "I guess so," he sighed, unclipping his cell phone from his belt. "Tell me what happened again before I call the police."

"Not much to tell. I went out here to get my cigarettes out of the glove compartment and reached the parking lot in time to see some guy drive off in our car. I shouted for the valet, but he wasn't anywhere around, so I came in and got you."

Alan shook his head as he dialed 911. "So much for secure parking," he said, bringing the phone to his ear. "Oughta' sue this fucking place."

"Al, wait. Don't call the police yet."

"What?"

"I said hang up."

Alan shut off the phone. "What's the problem?"

"What kind of trouble would we be in if the cops find the car and there's a gun in it? An unregistered gun."

"Why would they find an unregistered gun?"

"Remember when I drove up to Tennessee last month to visit my mother? Well, Wesley..."

"Your brother the felon. I should've known this would involve him. Surprised *he* didn't steal the car."

"Let me finish," Grace snapped. "He gave me this little handgun, said it was his ex-girlfriend's, and he sure as hell wouldn't use it. He said I might need it for protection, living in Atlanta and all ... you know how my family is."

Yeah, he knew how her family was. That's why he told his wife he'd let her drive the Mercedes if he could stay behind in Georgia and play golf. It was worth letting her take his car if it meant not having to deal with any of his wife's knuckle-dragging kin. Alan brought a palm to his forehead. "This is too fucking perfect."

"I was going to get rid of it, Al. I just stuck it under the passenger seat and, well, just sort of forgot about it."

"Until now."

"Until now," Grace said, looking away.

"Guess if the cops find the car and the gun we could just say the gun belonged to asshole who stole it."

"I don't know, it was a pretty girlie-looking gun ... one of those Lady Smith & Wessons, I think."

Jesus, she may have some nice tits, but sometimes he wanted to punch her. He hit the redial button on his phone instead. "So the thief has a girlfriend. Car's probably at a fucking chop shop by now, anyway."

Alan listened to the phone ringing on the other end, wondering if the 911 operator was ever going to pick up. He headed for the little hutch at the parking lot's entrance, where the valet should've been, to get out of the rain. As he got closer to phone booth-sized structure he heard moaning. "Al, did you hear that?" Grace asked, following him. "Sounds like it's coming from behind one of those cars."

"Probably some homeless fuck who woke up without any booze," Alan said, stepping under the hutch's roof. Christ, he hated this city.

The moaning got louder, and then he heard Grace scream. From behind the car parked nearest to the hutch crawled a man in a yellow rain slicker. His face was covered with blood and mud, and his left eye was swollen shut. It was the valet. He tried to speak, but his words came out a gurgle.

The 911 operator finally answered and Alan said, "About goddamn time. I want to report a stolen car, and you better send an ambulance, too. Guy here's hurt pretty bad."

"What's with you? You seem kinda' nervous about something," drawled Todd Trulaine, sprawled out on the limousine's plush leather seat like it was his living room sofa.

Dane pulled the joint from his lips, tilted his head back and closed his eyes while the intoxicating smoke burned in his lungs. He answered and exhaled simultaneously, his voice a raspy wheeze. "Not nervous. Just got a lot on my mind." Dane handed the joint back to Todd. "Organizing an orgy isn't as easy as you might think."

Todd's giggling bounced through the air. He brought the joint to his lips with one hand while his other hand slid over his flat stomach, down to his money-making package. "All you need to think about is this," Todd said, squeezing his crotch.

"That's always on my mind, trust me," Dane answered mechanically, while inwardly he berated himself for appearing anything less than cool. The killing hadn't started yet, and he was already acting like a suspect.

The jay was passed back to his waiting fingers. Dane sucked in another deep hit. Just let the cannabis work its magic, he told himself. He took Todd's advice and thought about cocks: about Todd's cock, about his own cock, and about all the other cocks that'll be bobbing around his triple-X-rated soiree.

He imagined breaking in a few of tonight's contestants. Saber, definitely — that guy was more than deserving of first prize, even if his stage act could've gotten the club shut down. Of all the contestants, his was not the best face, closer to average than handsome, and his body, though nicely toned, was not quite as built-up as Dane preferred. And the name! *Saber*, for the love of God. Sounded like someone who got shot out of a cannon. But the man did have a saber-like dong and a perfectly fuckable butt, not to mention he was a throbbing mass of sexual energy, an enthusiastic exhibitionist, and limber to boot. Dane pictured Saber sucking himself off while he fucked the newbie's hot ass. As the mental image took shape in his brain he could feel his cock getting ready to party.

"Hey, Dane, baby, stop Bogarting the weed."

"Oh, sorry." He held out the roach, ashes tumbling onto the seat as Todd pinched it between his thumb and forefinger. "Just thinking of all the fun we're going to have."

"Fuckin' A."

Dane had the driver pull the limo to the hotel's side entrance. The only additional clothing Todd put on before leaving the club was a body-hugging black tank, and while Dane could really give a shit what anyone thought, he figured it best not attract any undue attention from the hotel's management by striding through the main lobby with a scantily-clad boy-toy in tow. Just inside the entrance stood a bank of newspaper boxes, featuring the day's news as gathered by the *New York Times, The Wall Street Journal,* and *The Washington Post.* Dane, who had so much to do today he hadn't bothered to get a paper this morning, gave the headlines a once-over. A headline on front page of the *Atlanta Journal Constitution* made him stop in his tracks.

TWO SOUGHT IN CANDIDATE SHOOTING
Suspect: Hired to rent motel room by two men

Dane felt as if his insides were being dropped down a mine-shaft. Curiosity made him want to fumble in his pockets for change and buy the paper, read every incriminating word. Denial made him turn away and pretend he'd never seen the damning headline.

This can't be happening! This can't be happening to me!

That the two men the Miami police were trying to track down would be dead by morning was small comfort.

"Hey, baby?" Todd called, holding open the doors of an elevator. "You comin' up or what?"

* * * * *

Kylie Minogue was blasting as they left The Tackle Box, Martin singing along. Task never really cared for Kylie, but he definitely preferred her singing to Martin's shredded falsetto.

"You feelin' good?" he asked Martin, mostly to get him to stop singing.

"You bet," Martin said, putting his arm around Task's shoulder as they stepped outside. It was raining, but they didn't quicken their pace. "I think this is the best I've ever felt. It's like ... I'm in love with everybody."

Task nodded. "Good way to feel." He had popped one of the stolen E tablets himself just before they left the club, and hoped to be in love with everybody soon, too.

Martin asked, "You know what these things are supposed to be like?"

"The X?"

"These parties. Dane's parties."

"Never been to one, but heard they're pretty wild."

"Like, how wild?"

"Like, we might not be wearing our clothes for long, wild."

"I see," Martin chuckled and gave his shoulder an affectionate squeeze, which would not have been his reaction, Task was pretty sure, if he weren't high. He even held the car door open for him and when Task dried off his wet skull with the hem of his T-shirt, exposing most of his torso, Martin reached other and tickled his belly. "Very nice," he giggled.

"Shit, man, save it for the party."

A muffled electronic beeping sounded from somewhere inside the car; Martin opened the glove compartment and pulled out his cell phone. He checked the caller's identity on the phone's digital screen.

"I'll let voice mail get it." Martin dropped the phone back into the glove compartment and then started the car.

"C'mon," he said. "Let's party!"

TWENTY-ONE

The man switched off his cell phone. "No answer. Just voice mail."

"So, what now?" Rand asked. "Are you going to call the police?"

The man made a face and shook his head. "Don't really like getting too involved with the police," he said, setting his phone down on the coffee table.

"Why?"

"Let's just say I've had a few bad experiences."

The man leaned back on the sofa and crossed his legs, resting his right ankle on his left knee. His free hand — the one formerly occupied by a cell phone — dug at his crotch. The other hand still held the gun, pointing it across the living room, where Rand sat.

Rand tried not to look at the gun, or the man holding it. If he didn't look at them, he didn't have to think about the man pulling the trigger. Instead, he looked at the clock hanging over the mantle of a seldom-used fireplace, surprised it was after 10:30, surprised so much time had passed since he got caught.

Pain was another distraction. There was the pain that had taken up residence in his skull, getting Rand's attention as it hacked its way through his brain, breaking off little chunks of gray matter at a time. When he shifted his weight, he could think about the suffering his lower back endured, the pain throbbing in his kidneys so bad he thought he might throw up.

And he still his thoughts returned to the man pointing the gun at him.

It was almost an hour ago when the man pulled him up from the floor, grabbing the wrist of his right hand and pulling it behind his back, wrenching it backward and making Rand cry out. He tried to work himself free, but that only made the man bend his arm harder, the agony more intense. Rand tried reaching back with his free arm, swatting at the man spastically. It was like a housefly trying to fight off a lion. Then he made a grab for the gun, trying to get the gun out of his right front pocket with his left hand. All that accomplished was drawing the man's attention to the bulge in the right leg of his shorts, the man saying, "What have we here?"

Then Rand had a gun pointed at his head.

The man said his name was Conner, introducing himself as he guided Rand into the living room, the barrel of the gun digging into the back of Rand's neck. "And your name again?" he asked, as if it mattered.

Conner was about Martin's age, somewhere in the neighborhood of 40, and fairly cute, in an aging circuit boy way. The way Conner's dark suit fit made Rand curious about the body beneath.

The guy's aiming a fucking gun at my skull and I'm checking him out, Rand chastised himself.

Force of habit.

Conner didn't make any phone calls at first. Just asked questions. Wanted to know what Rand was doing in Martin's house, what he was planning to do with the gun. "Just what is your story?" he asked.

Rand tried the string of hazy half-truths he'd fed Martin, but Conner wasn't buying. It was a lot harder to bullshit a guy when you didn't have his dick in your hand. Harder still when the guy had a gun.

"You're *real* story," he said, cocking the hammer on the revolver.

That was when Rand stopped looking at the clock on the wall above the mantle.

"It's true, I am from California," Rand said, the emphasis on "I am" coming out a girly whine.

Conner said, "Okay, that part I can maybe believe, just because of your voice. You have one of those non-accents like they have out there. But I'm not believing that bullshit about you just came all the way out here to just 'visit friends,' and when they weren't home just fucked Martin for free room and board. What, you didn't think to call these friends first, tell them to expect you before you set off across the country?"

"All right, all right. It's not like that," Rand said, shaking his head, his mind racing, trying to think what he could tell Conner that would satisfy his curiosity yet not give away anything. He tried pleading.

"Look, the part about fucking Martin — letting him fuck me — for a place to stay, that much is true. But what's the harm in that? He wasn't complaining." He turned towards Conner. "I wasn't planning to hurt him, or involve him in anything. Honest."

"Honest? So why break into his house? Why the gun?"

"I just needed... I was ... I was hungry. I was just here to take some food."

"And what? If Martin was here, take it at gunpoint?"

"No! I took the gun..."

Conner pounced the moment the words leaked from his mouth. "You *took* the gun. So this belongs to Martin." He turned the revolver in his hand, as if looking at it for the first time. "I didn't know Martin had a gun. Seemed too much of a softie for firearms. Surprised he didn't shoot his..."

Rand leapt from the chair and broke into a sprint. He heard Conner shout, "Oh, no you don't!" The sound of a crash and Conner's cussing followed Rand into the foyer. The front door was just three feet away. His hand was swooping down to catch the doorknob.

And then an explosion made his brain rattle around inside his skull, making him miss the doorknob and making him fall forward, slamming his face against the door.

He made another grab for the doorknob. Another explosion, this time ground zero was his lower back. Excruciating pain radiated through his kidneys, making him double over and fall on his knees.

"That was my fault," Conner said after dragging Rand back to his chair in the living room. "Should've known better than to take the gun away from you."

Rand was back to staring at the clock then, his tears making it look like he was staring at its face through frosted glass. Thought the blurry hands were telling him it was ten o'clock. And then he thought about the pain he was suffering and the gun pointed at him.

And then he went back in time, a month ago. Back in Los Angeles, in Sherman Oaks...

The house was a couple of stucco and glass boxes, topped with a flat, white gravel roof. Probably considered modern at the time it was built, but to Rand the house had all the appeal of a Chrysler dealership.

Dane Kensington opened his door personally (Rand had expected to be let in by a scantily-clad houseboy). Handsome and immaculately groomed, the scent of CK-One wafting off him, he made middle age look appealing. No one would mistake Dane for being younger than forty, but no one would guess he was as old as fifty. He wore a navy blue knit shirt and flat-front tan slacks, the fit just right to pique interest in the fit body beneath. Rand had seen Dane before — his photo frequently appeared in *Frontiers* — and knew he was a good-looking guy, but in person he was breathtakingly sexy.

Definitely not like one of the flabby geezers he'd blow in the alley behind Boner's for an extra twenty bucks.

"Nice place," Rand lied as he was let inside.

"Thanks, but this is nothing," Dane said, taking Rand down a glossy-tiled hallway leading to the rear of the house. "There are guys in this city who buy bigger houses for their mistresses. But I like it."

Dane went to fetch them drinks, leaving Rand alone in the living room. "Expensive" and "impersonal" seemed the operative words in the decor. Boxy, black leather furniture was scattered around the room and abstract paintings, likely chosen on their couch-matching merits, hung on the walls. Rand felt as if he were awaiting a consultation with a plastic surgeon, not hanging out in the home of a pornographer. Only a life-sized bronze cast of a ripped male torso hanging on a far wall gave any hint of the owner's true nature.

Dane returned as Rand was inspecting the bronze torso. "Like that?" he asked, handing Rand a frosty glass of dark beer. For himself he'd gotten a glass of ice water. "Had that done a few years ago. There's this artist in Chicago who does them. Met him at the erotic art festival the Tom of Finland Foundation has. Really nice work."

Rand took a sip of beer. "Whose body is that?"

"Mine."

Rand almost said wow, but gave an appreciative nod instead.

Dane placed a hand on his back. "C'mon, we're here to discuss your body, not mine," he said, guiding Rand toward the sofa.

"Should I take my clothes off?"

"Not yet," Dane chuckled.

Instead, they talked, Dane asking him questions like why did Rand want to be a performer — Dane didn't say "porn star" — and did Rand realize it was not a decision to be taken lightly. He even asked to see Rand's I.D., saying you couldn't be too careful. Then, satisfied Rand wasn't a fifteen-year-old who looked eighteen, Dane asked him to strip.

Rand was surprised to feel a twinge of self-consciousness flutter through him, as if it were the first time he'd disrobed for a stranger. No need to be nervous, he reminded himself. This was the easy part.

He stood before Dane, the pornographer looking him over without comment, just sipping from his water as if he barely noticed him. Rand no longer felt nervous; now he felt awkward and a little silly. Finally, Dane said: "Quite nice. Now turn around and bend over. Spread your cheeks apart, let me get a look at your asshole. Very nice. Do you always shave or did you do that because you thought it was porn union rules?"

"There's a union?"

"That was a joke."

"Oh."

Rand turned back around. "Very, very nice," Dane said, nodding and fingering his goatee. "You look a lot like that singer ... whatsisname? Was with one of those horrible boy bands..."

Rand supplied the name. "I get that a lot," he added. *Like every other night.*

"And you've got to be the only man in L.A. under thirty who doesn't have a tattoo."

"Got my ears pierced instead." He pulled on one of the small silver hoops hanging on an earlobe.

"So, you are gay?"

"Um, yeah." His tone made it sound more like "duh!"

"Good. Those gay-for-pay types are a pain in the ass — no pun intended."

Rand mimicked Dane's chuckle, despite the staleness of the unintended pun.

"HIV?"

"No."

"Last time you were tested?"

"About three months ago, around then."

"Good, but it wouldn't hurt to go in for another test," Dane said. "Top or bottom?"

"Uh..." Rand never really considered it. "Both, I guess, but bottom, mostly."

Dane kept nodding. "We don't do bare-backing, scat or blood play. Outside of that, anything you won't do on camera?"

Rand hadn't considered that, either. "Fisting. I won't even do that off camera."

"Not an issue. Only a handful of our performers..."

"No pun intended?"

Dane grinned, showing off his even, bright-white teeth. "No pun intended, yes." A brief pause, then he said, "You're relaxing some, good. Guess now's as good as time as any to see what your cock looks like hard."

The butterflies returned to Rand's stomach. "Oh, yeah. I guess so." He eased himself down on the sofa, tentatively, as if expecting Dane to scold him for putting his bare ass on the expensive leather upholstery. But Dane said nothing, just watched.

Rand pulled on his dick like it was taffy, trying to think of something arousing. He thought of the afternoon he posed for the photos that got him this audition, of messing around with Alex. That elicited a pleasant tingle in his groin and got his prick to perk up – a little.

He thought of the night he, his two roommates — one an "exotic dancer" like Rand, the other a waiter who sold a little dope on the side — and Task did 'tina and fucked all night long. That perked his cock up a bit more.

Then he thought of how Task would respond when he found out about Rand's auditioning for Dane Kensington.

His dick began to deflate.

Never in his life had he had trouble getting hard, even with some of the trolls who paid him to put his dick in their mouths. He thought of all those ads on TV for medicines to relieve "erectile dysfunction," how he always laughed at them. They didn't seem so funny now.

"You want some visual aid?" Dane asked. "I've got plenty of porn."

Moments later, Rand was kneeling before the porn king, unbuttoning the fly of his pants. It was an idea Rand had considered earlier — and summarily discounted as being too stupid and possibly counter-productive. But regarding his flaccid cock, the idea once again popped to the forefront of his brain.

All Dane said was: "You don't have to do this, you know."

"I want to," Rand said, pulling out the older man's cock, already semi-hard. No erectile dysfunction here.

He took Dane's cock all the way down his throat, his tongue massaging the shaft. Dane caressed the top of his head and moaned softly, finally bringing Rand's cock to life. After a few more minutes of slurping on Dane's pole, Rand was relieved to finally be sporting a quivering boner.

A few minutes later, Dane gently pushed him away and stood. Rand remained on the floor, waiting, watching. Dane pulled his shirt over his head, puffing out his chest as he brought his arms down in a slow, wide arch, like an eagle landing. He kicked off his dark brown loafers and slipped off his pants. Now nude, he reached down and pulled Rand to his feet.

What was meant simply to be a career-advancing blowjob escalated into full-scale lust. They kissed — the rough, hungry kind of kiss that had nothing to do with romance. They pawed each other clumsily, hands moving impatiently from shoulders, to back, to buttocks — Rand discovering Dane's ass was nearly as firm as his own. Slowly, Dane returned to his seat, his mouth traveling down Rand's smooth torso as he lowered his butt down into his chair. He swallowed Rand's cock whole, making Rand gasp and thrust his hips forward.

Rand felt a finger wiggling between his butt cheeks and nudge his asshole. A pleasurable tremor pulsed through his body.

Moments later he joined Dane on his chair, straddling his lap. Rand pushed his butt against Dane's hard-on, the thick shaft rubbing up and down the divide of his splayed ass while Dane chewed on one of his stiff nipples.

Reaching behind his back, Rand seized hold of Dane's cock and pressed the moist head against his puckered hole. "Ya' wanna fuck me," he hissed. A statement, not a question.

Dane let out a deep moan in reply, thrusting upward, his cockhead knocking at Rand's ass-lips. Knocking, but not entering.

They paused long enough for Dane to retrieve a condom and lube, erotic supplies he kept conveniently on hand in a drawer of a dark-stained credenza at the far-end of the living room. "You never know when the opportunity will arise," Dane said with a wink as he rolled a rubber over his dong. The two men resumed their rutting on the floor, Rand on his back, legs in the air; Dane on top, slowly pushing his cock into Rand's chute.

Dane fucked him in full, rhythmic thrusts. Each time Dane sank his cock up his ass, Rand felt the burn of the carpet rubbing his back raw. He responded by leaving marks of his own, dragging his jagged, bitten nails down the taut terrain of the pornographer's back. Dane snarled and rammed him harder, lifting Rand's body off the floor, fucking him with jackhammer force. Rand rubbed his own rigid cock against the other man's hard torso, begging for more.

Rand announced his orgasm in a screechy wail. Warm jism oozed between their bodies. A few thrusts later, and Dane was crying out, his cock pumping deep in Rand's gut.

A week later, he said goodbye to his roommates and the crappy North Hollywood apartment they shared, then quit his job at Boner's. He was Dane Kensington's boy, full-time.

* * * * *

"Trying to think of an escape plan?"

Rand turned to Conner and shook his head. "Just wondering how long before Martin gets back."

"What, think he's gonna save your sorry ass?" Conner sneered.

"Just wondering if he'll be gone long enough for me to suck your cock."

Using his wits failed. Time to use his body.

One half of Conner's mouth tugged upward, an ugly, mocking half-smile. "You're serious?"

"Yeah."

Rand was pretty sure his captor would take him up on the proposal — Conner didn't strike him as the kind of guy to turn down a blowjob, no matter how ludicrous the circumstances. To his surprise, however, Conner shook his head.

"Right, and then before I cum you bite my dick off and run. Nice try, but I saw that movie. We'll wait."

TWENTY-TWO

From the stage, Honey D'John could almost pull off a reasonable facsimile of Old Hollywood Glamour, albeit in her own self-parodying style. Up close she looked like the bloated, alcoholic wife of a televangelist. Or John Elway done up as Jayne Mansfield for Halloween. Either way, a rough sight for dilated pupils.

Didn't look too happy in her role as greeter to Dane Kensington's party, but forced a smile as Martin and Task approached the penthouse door. "You boys have fun," she trilled as she took their invitations. "If you're lucky, maybe I'll join you later."

"Sounds like a threat," Martin said as they ambled past her.

The lights inside were turned low, casting the penthouse in a hazy glow. Music pounded in the background, a mellower beat than what blasted at The Tackle Box but just as repetitive, the volume just loud enough to muffle the buzz of conversation. Refreshments were available on two tables near the entrance, light hors d'oeuvres on one, beverages on the other. No caterer or bartender. About twenty guests stood around in groups of two and three, most drinking bottled water, all of them attractive and all of them fully clothed.

I might as well be at an office cocktail party, Martin thought, disappointed.

But there was evidence that a more interesting evening was in store. Placed around the suite were glass bowls filled with condoms. On a coffee table sat an economy-sized bottle of lubricant and a candy dish filled with little blue pills. Atop a credenza against the far wall were an assortment of dildos and butt plugs, on display as if they were sculpture. A guest had picked up one of the larger sex toys — a black rubber phallus the size of a loaf of French bread — and pretended he was fencing with it, much to the amusement of his giggling friends. A porno played on a TV, but no one appeared to be watching it. Instead, eyes kept drifting to a pair of closed double doors at the opposite end of the room, faces expectant.

Task snagged two bottles of water off the beverage table. "You're gonna need this," he said, handing a bottle to Martin.

"Thanks." Martin hadn't realized how thirsty he was until he brought the bottle to his lips. He guzzled half the bottle before he pulled it away from his mouth. "I have to say, I was expecting something a bit more hoppin'," he said, giving the room another quick scan.

Task shrugged. "Give it time."

Honey D'John left her post at the door and trudged through the room, the four-inch stilettos she wore obviously taking their toll. Following the drag queen was a dark-haired man, in his early thirties, with a muscular build — definitely fit within the crowd's sex appeal quotient. He wore the partial smile of someone who knew a particularly juicy secret. Honey led him to the double doors. She rapped three times, and one of the doors cracked open. She announced the new guest, placing a hand on his shoulder as she guided him forward. The door opened wide enough for the man to slip inside. Honey started to say something, but the door slammed while she was mid-quip.

"Fuckin' bitches," she grumbled as she headed toward the suite's entrance, thrusting her fake tits forward and patting her wig.

"Hey, what's in there?" Task called to her, pointing at the double doors.

Honey regarded him as if she'd just stepped in dogshit. "What? I'm a fuckin' information booth now?" she said acidly. Then, in a tantrum, she ripped off her wig and kicked off her heels. "Fuckin' V.I.P. room, my padded ass. I'm a *performer*, not some goddamned *ticket-taker*. You cunts have fun. I'm outta here."

Honey D'John snatched her shoes off the floor and stormed out of the suite, her drama fit earning her the loudest whoops and applause she'd gotten all evening.

* * * * *

Dane was slumped in a chair, nursing his second vodka tonic, when he heard the eruption of whistles and clapping in the main suite. "What's all that commotion out there?" he asked, irritated.

Nine cracked the door and peeked out. "Looks like your orgy is now minus a drag queen."

Dane shook his head. "Serves me right for hiring local talent. Correction: Alleged talent. Besides Miss Thing's hissy fit, anything else of interest happening out there."

"Just cute guys standin' around talking. Could be a Jaycees meeting."

"Great. All I need is for Anita Bryant to show up, and my night's complete."

"Who's Anita Bryant?" asked Saber. He'd been circulating — prancing, more like it — around the room, dressed in a white jock strap and Doc Marten's, giggling with the other contestants, flirting with Todd and Dane, and checking himself out in the mirror.

"You serious?" asked Nine. "You don't know who Anita Bryant is?"

"Is she a porn star?"

Nine laughed and shook his head. "At least you got a hot ass."

Saber sidled up to him. "I've got a hot *everything*," he cooed, rubbing up against Nine's thigh.

"Maybe you could show me later," Nine said, landing a playful slap across Saber's bubble butt.

The bathroom door opened and out stumbled Todd Trulaine and three of the contestants in the Porn Star Search, sounding like a troop of gibbons.

Their mirth grated on Dane's nerves, and he gnashed his teeth, trying to keep his temper in check. After several deep breaths, he beckoned for Todd.

"Yeah," Todd said, grinning and rubbing his nose. "You ready for a blowjob or somethin'?"

"I think it's time to get our party started. Why don't you take our boys here and show these crackers the definition of 'orgy.'"

Todd nodded. "No one wants to be first out on the dance floor, huh? No prob. You joining us?"

Dane shook his head. "Not just yet." He felt about as sexy as someone undergoing chemotherapy. "Later."

"Making a grand entrance? 'Kay." Turning around, Todd waved his arms at the chattering porn wannabes. "All right, guys, time to do like the song says and get this party started."

The shrieking outburst of enthusiasm that followed made Dane wince. They followed Todd, their porno Pied Piper, out of the room, a few of them stopping to squeeze Dane's knee or rub his shoulder, asking if he was joining them. "I can show you some stuff I couldn't on stage," promised Tango Cash. Dane assured him he'd be out later, stealing Todd's explanation of wanting to make a grand entrance.

The only one who remained was Nine, leaning against a vanity, arms crossed over his chest, grinning. "You look like you're about to be audited."

"Did you happen to see any headlines recently?" Dane snapped. "They got a lead in Miami."

Nine hopped forward. "What kind of lead?"

"Some low-life my guys hired to check into the motel, so nothing could be traced to them — or me. 'Course, then it was just blackmail."

"The cops got anything else?"

"I didn't read the article, just saw the headline. They know to look for two young guys now. Shit, they could find another witness ... or worse, the gun."

"What if they do? Not likely registered, doubt it could be traced easily. 'Sides, what's it matter. Those guys won't exist after tonight."

Dane felt his stomach constrict. "Yes. Right."

"So, where are the guests of honor?"

Dane checked his watch. "I expect one in about twenty minutes. The other, let's see."

He pushed himself out of his chair and crossed the room to the double doors, opening one by a couple inches and peeking outside. His party was starting to show signs of life. Several of the guests had lost their shirts, and a couple had stripped down to their skivvies. One of the porn wannabes — a diminutive bleached-blond twink who went by the name Joey Platinum — was already nude, letting one of the guests play with his ass.

"He's here," Dane whispered, motioning for Nine to step closer. "See that guy with the shaved head, bobbing it up and down like an idiot? Wearing a red T-shirt? That's him. That's Task."

"Not bad," Nine said, looking over Dane's shoulder. "Hate to put a bullet in such a fine bod, but business is business."

"Sssshhhh!" Dane slammed the door. "Will you fucking stop talking about it?"

Nine stepped back, allowing Dane room to pace. "Tell you what," he said, unbuttoning the shirt. "I'm going out there to mingle, get to know our pal Task a bit better. The other one gets here, send him out to me."

He pulled off his shirt, revealing a ripped torso covered with dark hair. The sight of Nine's bare chest was nearly intriguing enough to pull Dane out of his anxious funk. Nearly.

Nine winked at him and slipped out the door, joining the party.

Dane went into the bathroom and took a Viagra.

* * * * *

Conversations tapered with the introduction of new — and uninhibited — flesh. The scantily clad Porn Star Search contestants circulated around the room, coaxing guests out of their clothes and making lewd invitations. One runner-up, a sinewy man with skin the color of milk chocolate and who had a tribal design branded into the center of his back, picked up one of the dildos — a realistic-looking replica of co-host Todd Trulaine's cock, it turned out — and gave guests a demonstration of his fellatio technique. Tango Cash flitted about the room, hooking his hand between randomly selected legs. "Need a fluffer?" he asked as he rubbed the crotch of the startled guest.

Another contestant was now naked, wiggling his bare ass before a small group of admirers who, at his insistence, fingered his butthole.

Saber had pulled the front of his jock aside. With his schlong swinging between his legs like the trunk of a baby elephant, he approached guests asking, "You wanna touch it?"

This was more like it, Martin thought as he watched the action unfold. His cock, which had been tingling with anticipation on the elevator ride up to Dane's penthouse, began to swell. Surveying the roomful of attractive guests, he considered all sorts of sexual possibilities. Trouble was he didn't know how to initiate any of his lusty thoughts. Martin had participated in a couple threesomes in his lifetime, but for the most part, was a one-on-one kind of guy. Orgies were beyond his realm of experience, and now that he was at one, he wasn't sure how to join the fun.

Where to begin?

He looked over at Task, standing a few feet away, nodding his head in time to the trance music slithering through the air, seemingly oblivious to what was happening around him. Not the brightest bulb, but Task did possess a certain rough sexiness Martin always found, at least on a fantasy level, very appealing.

Task raised his bottle of water to his lips and gulped, draining the bottle. As he pulled the bottle away, he let out a satisfied breath. His wet lips glistened in the room's low light, and a few errant drops hung in the stubble on his chin. The thought how good those lips would feel around his cock caused Martin's hard-on to throb.

Why not?

Martin set his own bottle of water down on an end table and took a step toward Task, thinking he'd just slide an arm around the trashy young man's waist, pull him close and see how he responded. But before he could get close to Task, Todd Trulaine intercepted him.

"Hey, *bay-bee*," the porn star said, planting his hands on Martin's chest. His fingers immediately set to work unbuttoning Martin's shirt.

"Hey!" Martin replied, grinning ear to ear. He could think of nothing else to say.

He didn't have to. Seizing Martin's shirt in his hands, Todd pulled him forward and kissed him, plunging his tongue into Martin's mouth. Martin responded likewise, enjoying the way Todd was rubbing up against him. Todd's mouth tasted of spearmint and smoke.

"Ooooh, yes!" Todd gasped as he pulled off Martin's shirt. "I love guys with hairy chests."

Todd tossed Martin's shirt carelessly on the floor and started unbuckling his belt. "I love guys with big, hard cocks even better," he said.

Martin stood there, motionless, as Todd unzipped his fly. "So do — ahhhh!"

Needle-like fingers of pleasure scurried beneath his skin as Todd Trulaine slipped his hand inside Martin's underwear and grabbed his drooling dick. "I bet you do," Todd whispered, gently squeezing his swollen shaft.

Martin looked past Todd and saw Task, standing behind them, a lecherous smile on his face, pinching one of his own erect nipples poking through the taut fabric of his T-shirt. He looked like he was thinking about joining them, and Martin would've gladly welcomed him. Maybe Task and Todd could both lick his dick like he'd seen done so many times in videos — seen, but never experienced, even the few times he was part of a threesome those many years ago.

Then he was being pushed backward, Todd guiding him toward the long sofa dividing the room. Martin flopped down on the sofa and Todd crouched down, pulling off his shoes. He raised his ass off the sofa's seat so Todd could pull off his pants and underwear. A crowd began to gather, and while Martin was aware of the audience, he didn't acknowledge them, focusing instead on the bulbous package in Todd's shiny red shorts. He heard a few complimentary murmurs — "Oh, daddy" and "He shoulda' been in that contest" and "I'm next" — and felt a few anonymous hands squeeze his shoulders before DanKen Studios superstar Todd Trulaine knelt between his spread thighs and swallowed Martin's cock whole.

The orgy had begun.

* * * * *

Task had seen Martin looking at him, just before the porn star guy pushed Martin onto the couch (apparently Todd Trulaine really was coming on to Martin back at the club). It looked to Task like Martin wanted him to join in the fun.

He did a quick scan of the room. No Dane Kensington, no Rand, but the double doors at the end of the room were still closed. Maybe they were in there. Maybe he should check it out.

Task looked back at Martin, naked on the sofa, getting blown by the porn star.

Maybe he'd try the doors later, he thought, pulling off his shirt.

Other guys were stripping off their clothes, too. Some were slow about it, making out with whomever was standing nearby, letting the stranger help him out of his clothes. Others shucked off their clothes hurriedly, like they were about to go skinny-dipping. Lots of cut bodies, lots of cut cocks, though a few were uncircumcised. All were worth sucking. One of the guys was grinning at him. It was the guy the drag queen ushered in right before throwing her shit fit. The man was shirtless now — nice, muscled torso, covered in dark fur — but still in his dark gray pants, just snug enough so you could get an idea of what he was packing underneath.

The man caught him looking, and the grin became a lecherous smile.

Task looked back at Martin. He had his legs hooked over Todd Trulaine's shoulders, Todd now rimming him and Martin gasping, "Oh, Jesus fucking Christ yeah!" One of the other guests — thick with muscle, tan torso waxed smooth, high-lighted hair, bangs held upright with pomade, your standard circuit boy look — was now on the sofa with Martin. He was holding his cock over Martin's face, pulling on it while he watched Todd eat Martin's hole.

He was trying to decide whether to join Martin on the couch, maybe get on the other side of him so Martin could suck his and the circuit boy's cocks at the same time, or approach the smiling guy.

A hand grabbed his ass. "You look overdressed."

It was the smiling guy, beside him now. "So do you. I was just watching these guys, thinking about joining them."

"Or we could start up a show of our own," the guy said, squeezing Task's butt.

Just then, Saber hopped in front of them. "Hey, guys. Wanna touch it?"

He grabbed his cock, still soft, and shook it. Task reached out, curled his hand around Saber's dong. "How big's it get hard?"

"Why don't you get me hard and find out?"

Task looked over at the smiling guy with the fur-covered torso, as if to ask if it was okay. The guy — should really ask his name, Task thought — told him, "Go ahead. Like I said, start a show of our own."

Getting down on his knees, Task lifted Saber's cock up to his lips and started sucking. He felt hands on top of his bare skull and heard the guy with the furry chest say, "Like a fish to water, huh? The way he sucks cock."

* * * * *

Martin sat up, panting, his broad chest heaving. Todd Trulaine was standing, squeezing his crotch, the little red shorts barely containing his mammoth cock. Sitting beside him, to his left, was the man whose cock Martin had been sucking. Martin didn't exactly go for the circuit clone look, but he'd enjoyed sucking the guy's dick. Another guy, one of the guests, not one of the contestants, climbed over the back of the sofa, taking the spot on Martin's right. He had a bit more body hair than the guy on his left, who even shaved his pits, and the hair on his head was longer, worn in a shaggy cut, streaked four different shades of blond. He was paler than the circuit clone, with a slimmer build — an updated interpretation of late '70s sexy.

"I'm Barry," said the guy on Martin's right. "You're hot!"

Barry's dick was standing tall, a respectable seven inches. Didn't look like he trimmed his pubes, but his balls were shaved.

Before Martin could introduce himself, Todd grabbed his hand and guided it to the front of his red shorts.

"You ever suck off a professional?" Todd asked Martin.

"Not that I know of."

"Now's your chance."

Martin pulled down Todd's hot pants, and the porn star's cock popped forward. Big, but not as big as he expected, what with Todd being a porn star and all. The thick shaft bowed out toward the top, tapering down to a dark pink crown. He leaned forward and took Todd's bottle-shaped cock into his mouth.

He felt hands — assumed they were Todd's — moving over the top of his head. He heard guys saying, "oh, yeah" and "suck that dick." He heard other guys moaning. Hands pushed his legs apart, and someone worked his way between Martin's thighs. Martin felt his cock slide into someone's warm, wet mouth (Barry's, maybe). He shuddered, then swallowed Todd's prick whole.

Martin's hands moved over Todd's ass, pulling his butt cheeks apart. He was going to finger the porn star's asshole, only someone else got to it first, rimming the porn star while Martin pulled apart Todd's buttocks, Martin's fingers coming in contact with a stabbing tongue. Martin wondered who was eating Todd's ass, then his cock hit the back of Barry's (or whoever's) throat, and he didn't care, he felt so goddamn good.

"Whoa, there, baby," Todd said, pushing Martin back. His dick bounced as it popped from Martin's lips, slinging spit. "Don't slow down, and I'm gonna cum down your throat."

And Martin said, "That doesn't sound too bad to me," leaning forward again to resume blowing the porn star. First, though, he gave a quick glance between his legs, see who was slurping on his prick, to see if it was Barry. It was.

* * * * *

Nine couldn't decide if the guy Task was sucking, the one with the freakishly huge cock — eleven inches, maybe — had a semi or if he was fully hard. Some guys with the really big dicks, like, say, John Holmes, with thirteen inches, never seemed to get completely stiff. Probably pass out, all the blood it took to make that thirteen-incher rock hard. Nine was glad he didn't have that problem. Truth be told, nine inches was what his cock measured hard, which, to him, was the only time a prick was worth measuring anyway. Soft, Nine was more like seven and a half.

Measure his cock now, it would be nine inches.

Around the room, guys finally started acting like they were at an orgy. All the guests were nude or close to it, most sporting hard-ons. In a corner a twink with bleached-out hair was bent over, grabbing his ankles, while another guy, stocky with olive skin, munched his butt. In a chair, a black guy with his short hair twisted into little nubs, the beginnings of dreads, was working a big, black dildo up his ass, getting assistance from a white guy who sort of looked like that Australian actor, the one who looked hot in a gladiator costume but reportedly was a prick in real life. Another corner of the room, a guy with a round head and beefy body was on all fours, moaning while a man with a military buzz cut and ropy muscles smeared lube around his asshole. The buzz cut guy was waving his cock, already covered with a rubber, and telling the round-headed guy, "You ready for me to fuck you now?"

Task stopped sucking the tripod guy to get some air. That's when Nine decided to unzip. "Here, suck on this awhile." He nearly smacked Task in the face with his cock.

"Shee-it," Task drawled, reaching for the monstrous member and jerking on it.

Saber reacted as if he'd just unwrapped a birthday present. "Omigod! That's almost as big as mine!" he squealed.

Nine saw a few eyes turn their direction. Probably more attention than needed to be drawn his way, but he wasn't worried. As he told Dane: Guys at this party weren't going to remember his face.

Saber joined Task on the floor, and soon Nine had two mouths working on his cock. Saber sucked on the head while Task licked the base of the shaft and slurped on his balls. The wannabe porn star tried to deep throat him, managing to swallow three-quarters of Nine's cock. When Saber pulled his mouth away, syrupy strings of spit hung from Nine prick. Task took over, gulping down the wet, throbbing cock all the way down to the root.

"You hot little cocksucker," Nine moaned, pushing his hips forward, forcing his cock deeper down Task's throat.

A shame he had to kill him.

"I can suck myself off," a jealous Saber announced.

"I bet you can." Nine wondered if that other guy, Rand, had shown up yet? Wondered if he was as talented a cocksucker as Task. He had every intention of finding out.

His cock was suddenly bobbing in the open air. Nine opened his eyes just in time to see his rod disappear between Saber's lips. Task was standing beside him now; still had his jeans on but had the fly unzipped with his hard-on sticking out. A lot closer to average sized than either Saber or himself, Nine noted, but a tasty-looking cock all the same.

Through the bliss of Saber sucking on his schlong, Nine heard Task say: "You know that Dane guy, right?"

"Uh-huuuuuh!"

"Maybe we could go in that room where he's holed up, join him."

Task's fingers went dancing down his spine, a pleasant ticklish feeling augmenting the hot ecstasy burning through Nine's crotch. "Ah... I dunno 'bout that."

Saber stopped sucking Nine and said, "Yeah! If he's not gonna come out here, let's bring the party to him."

Nine said, "Shouldn't you be concentrating on sucking my dick?"

But Saber already had hopped to his feet. "C'mon," he said giddily, grabbing Task by the arm and pulling him toward the closed double doors at the rear of the room. "He'll let me in. I won the contest."

"Sweet suffering shit," Nine groaned, stuffing his cock, still moist with Saber's saliva, back into his pants. *I might shoot this Saber guy, too. For free.*

TWENTY-THREE

"Really? In a parking garage?" Conner sounded impressed.

Rand nodded. "He was scared shitless, at first, afraid we might be caught."

"Then you started sucking his dick, and he forgot all about being seen." Conner was chuckling and shaking his head. "Showed him how to enjoy his midlife crisis, for a little while at least."

Hanging out together for about two hours now, they were talking like frat house buds, except Rand had his wrists and feet tied together, Conner saying he was tired of keeping the gun aimed at him. Had Rand hunt for the rope used to tie himself up, Conner following behind, gun pressed to his back. They ended up using a couple of phone cords they got out of the downstairs bedroom Martin used as an office, one taken from his DSL modem. Conner said, "Don't think we'll be doing any web surfing tonight, do you?"

Rand fiddled with the cord binding his wrists for about fifteen minutes before giving up. For a PR rep, Conner was pretty good with knots.

Conner wanted to know what else Martin liked to do in bed. "No kinky shit, if that's what you're getting at. Not like he wanted me to piss in his face or anything like that," Rand said. "But he's not boring. One time, I got him to fuck himself with a dildo while he fucked me. You two ever fuck?"

Conner laughed like the question was totally preposterous. "Me and Martin? Shit! Don't get me wrong, he's a good-looking guy and all, but a bit too straight-laced — no pun intended — for me. Also bit old for my taste."

"Isn't he the same age as you?"

"He's older than me by a few years," Conner said, sounding kind of touchy about it.

Rand shrugged. "Older's not bad. That Dane guy I told you about? He's, like, fifty and still pretty damn hot. Like this one time…"

He was going to tell him about spending the weekend with Dane in Palm Springs when Conner's cell phone rang. Conner held up one finger, telling him just a moment before he picked up the phone. "I don't fuckin' believe this," he chortled before answering. "This is Conner. Oh, hi!"

It didn't sound like it was Martin, and Rand was crestfallen. He found himself wishing Martin would hurry up and get back. He'd be pissed, yeah, but Rand was pretty sure Martin would just let him go in the end. With this Conner guy, he didn't know what would happen to him.

Hearing him on the phone now, it sounded like a booty call, Conner purring into the phone, his hand straying to his crotch, fumbling with his dick, saying something about "you need some special grief counseling?" Then he heard Conner give out the address. "You're coming from, where, Morningside area? Get on Ponce, take it down to Clairemont and make a left..."

When Conner hung up, Rand said, "We're going to have company?"

Conner stood up. "I am. You're not invited."

* * * * *

"Nice pants," Nine said.

Dane wasn't sure if he was trying to be sarcastic or if it just came out that way. He had just put on his black leather chaps, with the lace-up sides, and was deciding whether to put on the matching codpiece or show off his hard-on (the little blue pill worked fine, thank you) when he heard the pounding on his suite door. Before he had time to ask who it was, Saber came bounding in, dragging Task behind him. Nine followed shortly after that, making the crack about the chaps.

"Part of that 'grand entrance' I planned to make," Dane said, glaring.

"Don't think you'd need to wear anything to make an entrance."

That sounded sincere, and the compliment took the edge off Dane's anger. Five years ago he posed for a photo spread that ran in *Honcho* magazine to promote *Daddy Cums Home*, a video he starred in — his first in nearly 20 years — with the heading: "THIS is what 45 looks like!" Another photo spread ran in *[2]* magazine, featuring Dane simulating (in the published pictures, at least) sex with his *Daddy* co-star, Ray Harley. It was great publicity, and it headed off an encroaching midlife crisis.

Saber slinked up to him, getting close enough so their cocks crossed like swords. "We got tired of waiting," he giggled.

"Looks like."

But then Task stuck his hand out. "Hey, I'm Task."

"Yes, I know," Dane bristled, reluctantly taking the young man's hand. His eyes dropped down to check out Task's cock, sticking out of his open fly. Tempting, he thought.

"You hear from Rand?"

"Who's Rand?" Saber asked.

Dane shook his head. This he didn't need. "No, I haven't."

"Maybe later we can talk ... after the party, I mean," Task said.

"We'll see."

"No seeing about it. We've got business to..."

"Oka-ay!" Dane hooked an arm around Saber's waist. "Come with me, baby. I want you to demonstrate your special talent for the crowd." He led his newest discovery toward the door.

Task called after him: "And then after...?"

"Yeah, yeah, we'll talk." Dane shot Nine a threatening look. "I promise."

The orgy in the main room of the penthouse was in full swing, so much so that only a handful of guests — those who weren't yet sucking or getting sucked, fucking or getting fucked — noticed Dane's entrance. They flocked to him the moment he stepped into the room, Saber at his side, eager to be in the presence of a celebrity, even one whose fame was restricted to the subculture of gay porn. These admirers were partially clothed, most still wearing pants, but a few had disrobed down to their skivvies (the boxer brief appeared to be the underwear of choice). Some of the men were shy, unable to look Dane in the eye when he said hello, and blushing when they looked down at his hard cock jutting forward. Most, however, flying on the effects of some chemical or other, greeted him with lewd compliments and obscene offers, grabbing for his prick and fondling his ass.

Dane made no move to stop them.

Things were rather lively on the couch, Todd Trulaine riding the cock of a muscular, hirsute man. Two other men stood on the seat cushions on either side of the hairy hunk, taking turns feeding their dripping cocks into his hungry mouth. A moment of staring, and Dane recognized the man fucking Todd. It was the older guy who accompanied Task to the club. He had seemed rather sullen at The Tackle Box, Dane remembered, but was certainly into the spirit of the occasion now. A very hot scene, Dane noted, watching Task's friend (or whatever he was) thrust his cock up into Todd's quivering butt. Very hot and very convenient.

A couple of the guests, a grinning pair with gym-molded bods, bleached white teeth and identical haircuts, the hair styled into a peak on top — Dane mentally dubbed them the Circuit Twins — were playing with Saber's over-sized dong, the guys daring each other to take it up the ass ("You know I'm a top," protested one, a purse nearly falling out his mouth). Dane slipped a hand between his future star's butt-cheeks and leaned in to whisper in Saber's ear. "What was that you said about being able to suck yourself off?" he asked, wiggling his index finger into Saber's sweaty asshole.

The young man shivered. "I can show you," he giggled.

Dane thrust his finger in deep. "I was hoping."

Saber leaned into him, moaning softly. "But if you want to keep doing that, that's okay."

"We'll have plenty of time to play," Dane replied, slowly pulling his finger from Saber's butthole. He brought the moist digit to

Saber's face and plunged it between the horny young man's parted lips. "But first I want to see you suck your own cock. And I'm sure these guys do, too." He tilted his head toward the small group of men circling them.

Dane stepped away and urged the group to give Saber room to show off his "special talent." Hovering in the periphery of the group he saw Nine whispering something to Task, his hand stroking Task's hard-on. When he caught Nine's eye, Dane jerked his head toward the front door. *Get the bastard out of here.* A subtle nod indicated Nine understood. Rand, if he ever showed up, would need to be dealt with later.

Saber pulled off his jock, tossing it at one of the onlookers who made a show of sniffing the pungent garment after catching it. Lying down on the carpet, Saber threw his legs up over his head, curling his body into the shape of the letter "C." With seemingly little effort, he was able to take the head of his own cock into his mouth. The demonstration elicited cheers and whistles, the small audience acting like drunken frat guys at a strip club. Their cries soon faded into a mesmerized silence as Saber slurped on his own dong, the guys showing their appreciation by fondling the pronounced bulges in their crotches. Men in their underwear exhibited tell-tale wet spots at the front of their briefs.

Dane watched, as enrapt as his guests. There was more to appreciate than just the novelty of his limber, horse-hung discovery fellating himself. He was equally turned on by the sight of Saber's upturned ass, gently bobbing as he sucked his own cock, legs parted enough so the asshole — shaved, the skin around it a darker shade — was visible. Looking at that ass now sent a surge of excitement through Dane's cock that no drug could simulate. This was pure lust.

Dane knelt down in front of Saber, between the young man's dangling legs, systematically blocking the view of Saber's self-sucking display with his own still-hot-at-50 butt. No one complained. He brought his face down to that raised ass, sinking between the fleshy pillows of Saber's buttocks. The young man's natural scent was strong, but not unpleasant. Dane's tongue tickled the pulsing sphincter, feeling the hard ring beneath the delicate skin. Gently, almost affectionately, he licked Saber's asshole. Beneath him, Dane heard Saber mewling; his sounds of pleasure a wet hum escaping around the barrier of his thick meat pole.

With his thumbs, Dane pried apart the porn hopeful's ass-lips, opening them to expose the dark pink entryway to Saber's chute. After a brief moment to admire the orifice, he spit into it. The silvery gob of saliva landed at the wrinkly, outer lip of Saber's sphincter, then oozed into the open hole. Dane chased after the slick stream with his finger, the wet hums beneath him becoming more pronounced. He twisted his finger around the damp walls of Saber's ass, enjoying the way it made the young man tremble.

Removing his finger, Dane brought his mouth back down to Saber's butthole. This time, he attacked, jabbing his tongue past that defensive ass-ring, plunging it into Saber's spit-lubed anus. Saber's body shook, and his muffled cries became more urgent. The studpup's reaction hit Dane right in his groin, his cock seemingly harder now, pre-cum flowing like a mountain creek. As his arousal increased, so did the forcefulness of his ass munching. Dane stabbed his tongue deep into Saber's hole, wiggling it around inside, fighting against the twitching sphincter and winning.

Around them, men were taking off their clothes and freeing their cocks. Dane felt an anonymous hand caress his ass, fingertips lightly tracing his fuzzy hole. A tongue replaced the fingers, sending a ripple of pleasure through Dane's body. He pushed backward, grinding his butt into his admirer. The mystery tongue burrowed deeper; Dane shuddered and groaned. Hands toyed with his cock. The anonymous tongue glided down to his balls.

The added stimulation spurred Dane's erotic needs. He wanted to stuff his cock into Saber's hole, fucking him while the talented young stud sucked himself off, the way he'd imagined earlier in the evening, until his mood was crushed by that newspaper headline. This time his lust was too strong to be quelled. Pushing the headline from his mind, Dane sat back on his haunches, disrupting his devoted rimmer in the process. Saber uncurled his body until he was lying flat on the floor, giving his back a break. Horny men surrounded them, their little show inspiring many of the guys to act upon their urges. One of the Circuit Twins knelt on the floor, his mouth alternating between his Doppelganger's dick and the bowed rod of another guest. Another threesome was arranged in front of him: a beefy man with pierced nipples and a bushy thatch of black hair stretching across his chest lay on the floor, his face obscured by the short, compactly built young guy sitting on it; between the beefy man's legs a generically attractive blond feasted on the guy's equally beefy cock.

From across the room, in the vicinity of the sofa, a deep voice groaned. "Yeah, drink that load." Dane looked in the direction of the voice, but his vision was blocked by a dazed-looking man, idly masturbating while staring down at Dane and Saber, waiting for their show to continue.

Dane felt the heat of another man's flesh press against his back. "Man, you're so goddamned hot." The rumbling whisper was punctuated by the wet stroke of a tongue along the nape of Dane's neck.

Turning, Dane saw his admirer was a twenty-something multi-ethnic beauty: slightly upturned eyes and flat nose suggested Asian blood; full lips and caramel colored skin likely contributed by black genes. The firm muscular body was that of a god, and he had the cock of a thoroughbred.

"I could say the same for you," Dane replied. "And if you're the same guy who was eating my ass, you're pretty goddamned talented, too."

The mixed-race hunk smiled demurely.

"What is your name?"

"Jalen, but I go by Jay."

"How about a kiss, Jay."

As forceful as Jay had been eating Dane's ass, his kiss was amazingly tender. "Sweet," Dane chided when their mouths broke away. Then he attacked the young man's full, brown lips like a tiger pouncing on its prey. His hand clamped onto Jay's well-proportioned, uncut cock, stroking it roughly as his tongue stabbed inside Jay's gasping mouth.

Saber, feeling left out, reached up and took hold of Dane's cock. "Are you going to fuck me?"

Dane pulled away from Jay's lips, but maintained his grip on the sultry stud's dick. "Of course," he assured Saber. Turning back to Jay, Dane said, "Get us some lube and rubbers, will you?" Only then did he release Jay's cock.

As Jay sprung to his feet to get the necessary accoutrements, Dane once again scanned the room, seeing wall-to-wall naked bodies, men sucking and fucking, groaning and grunting. He tried to pick out Nine and Task among a forest of the stiff cocks and undulating asses, but they were nowhere to be found.

* * * * *

The bitter taste of cum washed over Martin's taste buds.

"Oh, man, take that load," groaned Barry, even though it wasn't his load Martin gargled. It was the Circuit Clone's load, but C.C. was too busy trembling in ecstasy, his head rolling, to say much of anything.

Swallowing the stranger's juice seemed to fortify Martin's erotic energy, and he thrust upwards into Todd Trulaine's chute with renewed gusto. The porn star leaned down to slip his tongue into Martin's mouth, the two men sharing the remnants of the Circuit Clone's jizz. Martin heard Barry's frantic, breathless announcement: "God! I'm gonna shoot!"

Even before the words left Barry's mouth, Martin felt the warm, heavy drops of spooge splatter down onto the side of his face. Todd pulled his lips away long enough for Barry to slide his spurting cock between them, resting the throbbing shaft across Martin's open mouth. Todd covered the topside of Barry's prick, trapping it between his and Martin's lips. Barry gently pumped his rod between their mouths, their massaging lips forcing out the last drops of jism. Slowly, he pulled his cock back, pausing for Martin and Todd to lick the creamy residue from his cockhead.

Barry fell away, beside them on the couch, and Martin continued to fuck Todd, digging his fingers into the porn star's hard buttocks. Todd arched his back and rolled his hips, one hand pinching one of Martin's erect nipples, the other pulling on his own red, weeping dick. He was making noises like a seal about to be fed its daily bucket of fish. A harsh, rasping cry and Todd was spraying his jizz all over Martin's belly.

Todd's orgasm prompted Martin's own. An explosion within him rocked his body, his muscles twitching as if electrocuted. His mouth was open wide, but the only sound he made was a breathless croak, like a dying breath. Martin's cock felt white-hot as it fired, his balls drawing up tight against the base of his shaft, as if squeezing out every last drop of cum.

The groan stuck in his chest finally escaped, coming out so forcefully Martin startled even himself.

Through halting breath, Martin said, "Damn, I haven't cum like that since..."

...fucking Rand.

"Since when?" Todd asked, squeezing his butt around Martin's still-pulsing cock.

"Since a while ago."

Todd eased himself off Martin's lap, Martin's sheathed cock popping out of the porn stud's ass and landing on his stomach in a moist splat. The condom's reservoir tip was filled to capacity, the weight of his cum making the condom's nipple-shaped cap slump to one side. Todd took hold of Martin's dick and yanked the jizz-filled rubber from it with the mindless dexterity of a factory worker on an assembly line.

"I'll go get us something to clean up with," he said, twirling the sticky condom around his index finger.

Martin nodded, watching Todd skip away to the bathroom. On either side of him, Barry and the Circuit Clone had melted against the sofa's cushions. Barry gave Martin a sleepy smile. "That was awesome," he sighed, reaching over to play with the spooge congealing in Martin's belly fur. The Circuit Clone was practically comatose, staring from heavy-lidded eyes at the porno playing on the TV, the scene a harshly lit daisy-chain fuck occurring in an empty warehouse.

Watching filmed sex hardly seemed necessary at this stage of the night, Martin thought as he looked around the room. He'd been aware of the antics occurring around him while he had his fun on the sofa, yet only after being satiated could he take in the action happening around him. All the men in the penthouse were nude or close to it. Everywhere Martin turned, he saw stiff cocks being stroked or getting sucked and splayed asses being eaten or fucked. On the far side of the room, the party's host, Dane Kensington, had finally left his lair and was busily tonguing the asshole of the auto-fellating winner of the Porn Star Search. Another man — dark-skinned and hard-muscled — crouched behind the porn mogul, munching his butt. Martin looked around for Task, but couldn't spot him.

A thick, bright white hand towel landed on Martin's abdomen. "Look like you could use that."

The voice didn't belong to Todd Trulaine, but a deity — at least, that's how the man standing before Martin appeared. A Roman nose, sharp cheekbones and impish eyes sat on a long, oval face, the lower half shadowed with dark stubble. His tall, narrow frame was armored with thick, ropy muscles. Tattoos decorated his biceps and small, silver bars accented his nipples. The hair on his rippling abdomen formed a goody trail leading to neatly groomed pubes and a thick cock at half-mast. A heavy silver ring hung from his dick's plump crown.

"Thanks," Martin said, taking the towel and wiping Todd Trulaine's cum off his belly, his eyes fixed on this gorgeous stranger.

"I was watching you," the man said. His deep voice had a vague accent Martin thought might be French, but he couldn't bring himself to ask if it was. "Got me and a lot of the other guys horny."

"I do what I can." He wiped the jizz off his face and held up a hand. "I'm Martin, by the way."

"I'm Arno."

They shook, then Arno said, "There's a bed in the other room no one's using. Want to break it in?"

Though his hard-on hadn't abated, Martin was still recuperating from fucking Todd. However, turning down Arno's offer was not an option he dared consider. He was spent, but Martin was still horny.

"Sure," Martin said, dropping the DNA-dampened towel on the floor and pushing himself to his feet. "It'll just take a moment for me to get my energy back. I'm not eighteen anymore." He winced at his own joke.

"I think I can revive you," Arno replied.

He took Martin's hand and led him, through the writhing bodies littering the room, to the vacated V.I.P. room, leaving behind

Barry and the Circuit Clone, both now sound asleep on the sofa, their cocks now flaccid and curled between their legs like puppies.

TWENTY-FOUR

"So this is where you live?" Winston LaGrabe asked, checking out the living room's conservative decor, all earth tones and dark woods. He figured Conner as more of a chrome-and-leather kind of guy, with framed Tom Bianchi prints on the walls.

"This place?" Conner snorted. "Naw, just house sitting for a friend. I live in Midtown."

Winston nodded, wondering if they were going to just start fucking right away or if Conner was going to offer him a drink first. Vodka would be nice, but seeing Conner now, coat off, his white dress shirt hugging his sculpted frame — and, Christ, was that bulge at his thigh his cock? — fucking right away was good, too.

"You're an actor, right? You're not gonna believe this, but I've seen some of your shows. There was something on Skin-a-max a few weeks ago with you in it. Some type of thriller. What was it called? *Deadly* something-or-other."

"*Deadly Passions*. God, I can't believe you actually watched that." Secretly, though, Winston was thrilled.

"Caught it fifteen minutes into the movie, saw you in that shower scene and kept watching. Christ, you had a hot ass."

"Had?"

"Looks like you still do, the way those pants fit," Conner said, circling Winston, still standing in the living room. "'Course, I'd rather take a look at it without the pants."

Winston grinned. So they were going to just start fucking. Fine by him. Ever since Nine stopped by for the money that afternoon, teasing him like he did, Winston had been craving cock. The urge just got stronger when he met Conner at the funeral home. He was grateful that only a few people stopped by the house after the visitation, none staying past 10:30. Winston was even more grateful when one of the Log Cabin Republicans gave the Iron Cunt and Frozen Dyke a ride to their hotel. Alone by eleven o'clock, it seemed almost pre-ordained that he and Conner Blivett hook up that night.

"Would you like a look at it now?" Winston asked coyly, waggling his butt in Conner's direction.

Conner moved in beside him and placed a hand on Winston's ass, mapping its shape with his open palm. "Does a bear shit in the woods?" he said, hand cupping the underside of Winston's left buttock and squeezing, making the blood rush to Winston's cock.

"I don't know much about wildlife, but I'm going to take that as a 'yes,'" Winston giggled, leaning back against Conner's chest. Winston hands smoothed the front of his shirt so his pecs stood out, hoping to draw Conner's attention to the fact he was in great shape above the waist as well.

But Conner wasn't particularly interested in his chest and grabbed for Winston's belt. As he worked to unthread the belt from Winston's waist, Conner rubbed his pelvis against the actor's backside. Winston could feel his hardness pressing against his ass, right along the crack, and pushed backwards, grinding his butt against Conner's hard-on. Then he felt something else — something *very* hard — digging into his right butt cheek. It was most definitely a cock he felt against his ass crack, so what was the thing jabbing him in the right cheek?

He thought about asking, but then Conner got his pants undone and was reaching inside the fly. "This all for me?" Conner said, fondling Winston's dick through his silk boxers, turning his semi into a full-fledged boner. Knowing what was poking his ass cheek no longer seemed so important.

Winston sighed and reached behind him, clumsily groping for Conner. "You can have anything you want," he exhaled, body shaking as Conner's hand slid inside his boxers, fingers massaging his cock.

Conner nibbled the back of his neck. "You sure? I can be a greedy bastard."

Winston didn't doubt that for an instant.

His pants fell to his ankles. His boxer shorts followed, Conner having to jerk them down hard to get them past Winston's stiff prick. Conner followed Winston's pants and underwear to the floor, kneeling behind him, his face at Winston's ass. Conner's hands grabbed the full globes of Winston's butt and pried them open, exposing Winston's asshole to the cool open air. He heard Conner whisper, "Oh, yes," and then Winston felt his mouth at his hole, his tongue digging inside him.

The sensation caused Winston to pitch forward. There was nothing in front of him to brace himself against, so he bent over and rested his hands on his knees. Conner hooked his hands over Winston's sturdy thighs, pulling the actor's ass against his face. His tongue wiggled inside Winston's chute, pinched between his ass-lips. Winston shivered and moaned, and his cock quivered and drooled. He heard Perry's voice say: "I can't get enough of this ass."

"Stop it," Winston whined.

Conner stopped long enough to say: "Huh?"

Winston moved, crab-like, over to the paper-bag colored sofa and knelt into it. "Nothing," he said. "Just ... keep doing what you were doing."

"Sure thing." But Conner stood up, pulling his shirt out of his pants and unbuttoning it at lightning speed. Once the shirt was off, he undid his trousers, and they dropped to the floor with a loud *thunk*.

"What was that?" Winston asked, looking back over his shoulder at Conner, now only wearing a pair of designer-label white briefs, every bit as hunky as he'd imagined.

"What was what?"

"That noise?"

"Nothing," Conner chuckled. "Just my gun."

And then Conner stepped out of his briefs.

* * * * *

From where he'd been stashed, in a closet in the downstairs bedroom/office, Rand couldn't hear what Conner and his guest were saying, but the occasional a loud moan or lusty "Oh, yeah!" would travel to the back bedroom, making it clear what they were doing. Rand tried to imagine the details: Conner getting his dick sucked or sucking the other guy; maybe the two of them in a sixty-nine. Maybe they were eating one another's asses. Could be fucking, but it seemed too soon — Conner's friend got here only fifteen minutes ago — unless they weren't into foreplay.

He tried to picture Conner's "friend," but the only images he conjured were his own fantasy men: that actor from Texas who got arrested for playing drums too loud at night; that baseball player who was rumored to be gay, said he wasn't, but was fucking hot no matter what; or that foul-mouthed Irish actor who was better known for boozing and whoring than for any of his movies.

Rand's cock started getting hard.

And here I am with my hands tied behind my back.

Again, he thought back to that weekend with Dane in Palm Springs, the one he started to tell Conner about before the phone call. He was forced to the sidelines then, too, though at least he got to watch and, ultimately, participate.

* * * * *

They were at a gay resort, someplace called Rosy Palms. Everyone in the room was naked, but his were the only hands held behind his back by a pair of fleece-lined leather cuffs, the kind marketed to bondage enthusiasts.

"Just sit here and watch," Dane said, gently pushing Rand into a burgundy-upholstered armchair facing the bed. On the bed sat two of Dane's stars, Scott Pullitt and Colby Callister. Scott was the younger of the two, a clean-cut looking blond guy with a lean, athletic body, a big, meaty cock and a sweet Southern drawl ("He's from Georgia," Dane said, as if it were a handicap to be politely overlooked). The other guy, Colby, was in his mid-thirties. Rand remembered he was fairly popular in the early '90s, a bleached-blond, smooth-bodied stud. He left the business and moved to Eugene,

Oregon, to open a health food store with his lover. The store and relationship failed a couple years later, and Colby returned to Los Angeles and porn, his hair its natural brown, his face bearded and his torso covered in a thick, wiry pelt. A colorful tattoo of Ganesh spanned his back from shoulder to shoulder.

Dane joined his stars on the bed, his ass looking damn good, not like any of the 50-year-old asses Rand had seen — hell, better than a lot of 30-year-old asses. Dane slid between the two men and they began kissing and groping one another, making Rand's cock snap to attention immediately. Colby's mouth traveled down the side of Dane's neck, and he gently pulled on the silver ring hanging from one of the pornographer's pencil-eraser nipples. Scott and Dane's arms crossed, each man's hand grabbing the other's cock.

None of the men said much, just grunted and sighed and slurped. If they spoke, it was a barely audible whisper. There was none of the hollering and shrieking and barked commands like "suck that big dick" that you heard in Dane's videos, and that made it all the sexier to Rand. He rolled his hips in the chair, squeezing his ass-cheeks together, the movement creating a pleasurable tension within his groin. Pre-cum oozed from his cock, coursing down his shaft and collecting in the folds of his nut-sack.

Colby sucked Dane's cock, and Scott rose up on his knees so Dane could blow him. Dane deep-throated the horse-hung porn star easily, which didn't surprise Rand but impressed him nonetheless. Colby took Dane's dick into his mouth in full, rhythmic gulps while his hands massaged the older man's balls.

Dane flopped back onto the mattress and Scott climbed aboard his face. Rand's eyes darted back and forth between Colby sucking on Dane's cock and balls and Scott riding Dane's face, the pornographer's tongue stabbing between the pink globes of his buttocks.

"Ya' wanna fuck me, Daddy?" Scott drawled, his ass bouncing atop Dane's mouth, muffling any verbal response.

Dane pushed the Southern-born porn star off his face. When he spoke, he sounded like a high-diver who'd just returned to the water's surface. "I want you guys to jack off onto my cock."

"Ya' sure?" Scott questioned, one hand idly stroking his hefty boner while the other caressed Dane's heaving torso.

"We have all night to fuck," Dane said, running a hand over the top Colby's head, still bobbing between his legs, before pushing the older porn star away. "Right now I want you guys to shoot all over my cock and balls."

Colby took the request in stride, but Scott appeared to still question Dane's agenda, shrugging and shaking his head. Dane sat up, perched on the end of the bed, facing Rand, while his two stars stood on either side of him, jerking off. His hands caressed their butts and his fingers toyed with their assholes. Occasionally, he took one of the men's cocks into his mouth, sucking them closer to orgasm. He'd bat his tongue against the red crown of Colby's cock or lick the underside of Scott's veiny shaft, his eyes, shining with a devilish glint, focused on Rand the whole time.

Scott came first, his load as thick as vanilla yogurt, splattering Dane's abdomen and pubes. He bent at the knees, aiming his cock like a fire hose as it pumped out a few more healthy squirts of jism, this time hitting the assigned target. Colby, his teeth bared and his face beet-red and sweaty, followed a minute later, his watery load splashing down onto the head of Dane's dick.

"Bring Rand over here," Dane said, nudging Scott away.

Scott seemed to have forgotten Rand was still in the room, and appeared embarrassed now that he'd been reminded. He looked at the floor as he approached Rand, giving him a sympathetic smile when he saw Rand's purple-headed hard-on.

"Take the cuffs off," Dane said after Scott delivered Rand. Once the restraints were removed, Dane took Rand's hands in his own, looking up at him, that same devilish gleam in his eyes. Letting go of one of his hands, Dane pressed an index finger against the dewy head of Rand's cock. He pulled the finger away and brought the wet tip to his mouth, glossing his lips with Rand's pre-cum.

"Now you," he said.

"Now what?"

"Cum on me. Looks like you're going to any second, anyway."

Rand looked from Colby to Scott, though he wasn't sure why. Colby, now sitting on the bed beside Dane, gave Rand an encouraging nod. Scott gave Rand another sympathetic smile and looked away.

A fizzing sensation bubbled beneath his skin as Rand wrapped his hand around his aching prick. Pleasure, so intense as to be unbearable, rocketed through him as his jacked off. He felt like he was teetering on the edge of a cliff, each stroke threatening to push him over the edge, crashing on the rocks below. But when he did finally go over the edge, it was more like blowing up than falling, his body flying in all directions, his brain floating above. When he regrouped, Dane's chest, stomach and cock were covered with thick splats of jizz.

Dane looked up at Rand's flushed face, his smile a mixture of admiration and mischief.

"Lick me clean," he said, absent-mindedly finger painting with dollop of cum pooled at his sternum.

Without protest, Rand got to his knees, but was hesitant when confronted with Dane's pulsing cock, decorated with silvery drops and creamy white strings of cum. If he hadn't jacked off first, he'd be lapping the spunk off Dane's body like it was dinner at Spago. Now he felt drowsy rather than horny, and sucking Dane's jizz-drenched cock didn't seem all that appealing.

"Go on," Dane insisted. "Lick my cock clean."

Rand took a deep breath, then leaned forward, quickly, inhaling Dane's pole. The cum was gooey and had a metallic-chemical taste with an underlying sweetness. He sucked the thick mixture of semen into his gullet noisily, eliciting a deep groan from Dane. Rand took his mouth off Dane's cock, and Dane stuffed three of his fingers into his mouth, feeding him the jism he'd raked up from his belly.

He looked at Dane, saw the mischievous look was gone. Now he seemed dazed, his mouth slack, his eyes directed at Rand but focusing on something far away. Rand stroked the porn mogul's dick, and Dane's head fell backwards, his whole body shaking. He stroked the man's cock some more, enjoying the spasms it produced in Dane's body.

"Once you got their cocks, you got control," J.T. had told him, years before, showing Rand the ropes of hustling. Rand thought of that now, his fist going up and down Dane's sticky shaft, making Dane convulse.

But Dane wrested that control away, grabbing Rand's wrist and pulling it from his dick. "Suck it," he grunted through clenched teeth, hand clamping down on Rand's shoulder and guiding him forward. "I want you to suck me off."

Rand complied, swallowing Dane's cock, massaging the shaft with his tongue as slid down his throat. He cupped Dane's balls, gummy with drying cum, and fondled them gently between his fingers as his mouth traveled up and down the length of the older man's dong. Dane shivered, letting out a fluttery moan. "Any second..." he rasped, thrusting his cock forward into Rand's hungry mouth.

Dane shoved Rand backwards and rose off the bed slightly, crouched in a position that was somewhere between sitting and standing. "Open ... your ... mouth," he hissed, his hand yanking his cock at a frenetic pace.

Rand closed his eyes, tilted his head back and opened his mouth wide, sticking his tongue out for good measure. They'd played this scene out before, alone, back at Dane's house in Sherman Oaks. Dane loved to cum in his mouth, almost as much as he loved fucking him. He heard Dane cry out, then felt the pornographer's hot load splash down on his forehead, nose and tongue. Scott and Colby chorused their admiration for Dane's cumshot, while Dane shook the final drops of jizz off his cock and into Rand's mouth.

A pair of hands hooked under Rand's armpits, and he opened his eyes, just in time to see Dane's face coming toward his. They kissed, snowballing Dane's tangy spunk. By the time they're mouths separated, Rand was hard again. So was Scott, and Colby had a semi.

"Maybe it's time we get better acquainted," Scott said, leading Rand back to the burgundy armchair. Scott sat down and Rand kneeled between the porn star's nearly-hairless thighs. "That's it," Scott drawled as his fat rod slid between Rand's moist lips. "Give us some of that star treatment."

Later, after they'd all gotten off a second time and had showered to wash off the sweat, cum and lube, Dane asked Rand to join him outside. They sat in plastic deck chairs on the small patio outside the suite. The night air was cool, and Rand wished he'd put on a shirt. Dane left the sliding glass door open, and they could hear Colby extolling the virtues of Eastern religion to Scott, who said he grew up Baptist himself. On TV Homer Simpson throttled Bart.

"You're incredible," Dane nodded, teeth gleaming in the moonlight. "Don't tell the other guys, but you're far and away one of the best cocksuckers I've found in awhile."

"I've had a lot of practice," Rand said, only half-joking.

"Yeah, when you get back from Miami, you're going to be a big star."

"Miami?"

That's when Dane told him about the trouble he was having with this guy in Atlanta named Perry Snopes, a business owner who didn't like it that Dane and some partners had opened a gay strip club near his antique store. The guy didn't have an issue with the club being gay — he was gay himself — but thought dick dancing going on so close to his shop was scaring away clients. "Like the guys are doing shows in the parking lot," Dane said. The guy even organized a protest group to pressure the city council to enact tougher zoning laws. So far, the guy had just been a pain in his ass, but no real threat. But now he had announced his candidacy for city council, and if elected he could do some damage.

"He could lose," Rand said.

"I don't want to take that chance. That's why you're going to Miami next weekend."

Dane started giving details. "It seems our upstanding citizen Perry is just as weak for cock as any other fag, just very discreet about it. Chris in there" — Dane jerked his head toward the open door — "fucked him several years ago."

"Chris?"

"Scott," Dane corrected himself. "Sorry, I sometimes alternate between guy's real names and porn names. Gets confusing. Anyway, Scott had fucked Perry years ago when he lived in Atlanta and was known as Chris. Perry went after him when he found out his husband, this washed up actor, was already screwing around with Christopher.

Real fucked-up situation. So, anyway, Scott was in Atlanta last week, promoting his latest DVD, and whom should he run into at a restaurant but Candidate Snopes. Said Perry looked at him like he just stepped in dog shit, then goes into candidate mode, shaking his hand and saying that I-hope-you-remember-me-in-November crap. He gives Scott a business card and says to call him, only he doesn't say the words, just mouths it, like he's afraid some waiter might hear and give two shits.

"So Scott — who knows all the trouble I'm having with Perry — gives him a call, and they get together at Scott's hotel. Scott said Perry showed up in a baseball cap and glasses, real cloak and dagger. This is when he found out Perry was going to be in Miami for a seminar — after they fucked, of course. I have someone make a few calls, tell a few lies, and now I know what the seminar is and what hotel he'll be staying at. And you're going to be there waiting."

"What am I supposed to do?"

Dane explained the business about the camcorder. Rand was supposed to keep an eye on Perry, hang out in the hotel bar waiting for him. "He's going to come down for a drink, eventually. You convince him to go to your motel, shouldn't be too hard to do. Keep the condoms and lube in the same drawer as the camera. As you get them out, switch on the camera. If you're lucky, he'll want to use the bathroom first, you can do it then."

Rand said, "Why not get Chris — Scott — to do it?"

"'Cause he knows Chris, knows he now works for DanKen Studios and, therefore, Dane Kensington. I don't want any of this coming back to me. Besides," Dane grinned, "I like a challenge. It'll be fun."

Easy for you to say, Rand thought. "I dunno. That thing with the camcorder in the drawer? Sounds complicated."

Dane said, "For five grand, it'll be a piece of cake."

* * * * *

Now I won't even see my $5,000, let alone $1 million, Rand thought bitterly.

He shifted his weight inside the closet. His wrist scraped across something hard and sharp, cutting into his skin. Rand cried out, but a pair of Martin's bikini briefs stuffed in his mouth – Conner thought that was funny – muffled it. The pain was immediately dulled by hope. Rand leaned forward and felt carefully for the thing that had cut him, finding it in seconds. It was a nail, sticking out nearly an inch from the baseboard.

It was doubtful the idea that popped into Rand's mind — an idea gleaned from various TV shows and B-movies — would actually work. The sharp part, the part that dragged across Rand's wrist, was where the nail head had broken off. Perfect for stabbing, not for slicing. But it was an idea worth trying. It was the only one he had.

TWENTY-FIVE

"You want to do this *here*?"

The guy — said his name was Steve — had parked his Mercedes behind a shabby looking office building located at the end of a dark side-street, about two miles from the Wilkes Overlook Hotel. Steve said, "Yeah, here. What's wrong? It's secluded."

"Just thought we were going to a hotel, is all," Task said, looking out the passenger window, past the water drops on the glass, at the cracked, graffiti splattered cement block wall abutting the office building's crumbling parking lot.

"I like sex in cars. Turns me on. 'Sides, you're getting paid, aren't you?"

Task shrugged. "Whatever." This was reminding him of when he used to work the Boulevard.

"You going to suck my cock or you waiting for an engraved invitation?"

Task began regretting his decision to leave the orgy. But Steve had said he'd pay Task $500 to have him all to himself, so Task said okay. He figured he could get Steve off, then get back to the hotel and talk to Dane about Rand, see about getting his money for that deal in Miami.

He unzipped Steve's pants and pulled out his semi-hard cock. Task stroked it a few times before leaning down to flick his tongue against the head. Steve was impatient — didn't matter how much money they had, tricks were all the same; couldn't wait — and told Task to put it in his mouth already. He took Steve's semi into his mouth in one voracious gulp, like a fish chomping down on a baited hook. Steve's dick stiffened in his mouth as he sucked and slurped and prodded it with his tongue. Steve leaned back against the driver's seat, making noises that reminded Task of a sleepy tiger he saw at the Fresno Zoo.

"Get out of your clothes," Steve rasped, pushing Task away. The anemic glow of a security light above one of the office building's back doors streamed into the car, hitting Steve's huge hard-on, the spit making it glisten with a silver sheen.

Task pulled off his T-shirt and started untying his boots. "Aren't you going to take your clothes off, too?"

"Who hired who? Your job is to do as I say. Didn't they teach you that in hustler school?"

"I don't usually do this sort of thing," Task said, kicking off his boots.

"Right. Me neither."

Steve was starting to remind Task of that Jerry asshole who ran Boner's back in L.A., or that shithead John at The Tackle Box.

Despite his dislike for the man, when Task shucked off his jeans he was showing Steve a cock that was rock hard and drooling.

"Now we're talking," Steve said, his voice losing some of its edge. He took Task's dick into his hand and pulled on it, and Task closed his eyes, grooving on how it felt. Task opened his eyes when he felt Steve's fingertips at his lips.

"Taste yourself," Steve whispered, pushing his fingers into Task's mouth. Sucking on the invading digits, Task recognized the subtle flavor of his own pre-cum. He grabbed Steve's wrist, holding the fingers in his mouth, his moaning and lip smacking almost sincere.

"Get in the back," Steve ordered.

Task climbed over the front seat, pausing when he was halfway over to let Steve fondle his ass. Steve made *mmm-mmmm* noises as his fingers swirled around Task's butthole, Steve saying he couldn't wait to have some "real fun with that ass." Task flopped onto the backseat. Lying on the leather-upholstered seat, his legs spread, Task waited for Steve to climb over and begin the real fun.

But then Steve got out of the car. He walked to the car's rear door on the driver's side. From where Task lay, all he saw through the car door window was an anonymous torso with a huge cock sticking out. It made him think of a trick he had back on Santa Monica. The guy had one of those low-to-the-ground sports cars, a Z3 or Corvette, and Task stood outside the driver's side window, letting the guy blow him from the car. A drive-thru hustler.

The car door opened and Steve climbed in, saying he wasn't going to risk crushing his balls climbing over the front seat. Once he closed the door, he told Task to put his feet up in the air. "I want to eat that ass," he said.

Task raised his legs up, bringing his knees up over his head and his ass up in the air, pushing his sock-covered feet into the plush headlining of the Mercedes. Steve was blocking most of the light coming from outside, but apparently could see Task's butthole well enough that he took a minute to admire it. He stuck the thumb of his right hand between his lips, and then brought it to Task's upturned ass. "Sweet little hole," Steve murmured, pressing his wet thumb against Task's ass-lips.

He then put his face between Task's legs and pushed his tongue past his pulsing sphincter. Task groaned and squirmed, flexing his ass muscles as Steve's tongue slithered up his chute. Pre-cum dribbled from his piss-slit and landed lightly on his bent torso. "Yeah, man, tongue-fuck that hole," Task hissed through clenched teeth. Tricks loved to hear that porno movie shit, but this time he almost meant it.

Steve thrashed his tongue inside Task's anus, making his entire body quiver. Steve raised his head, the lower half of his face glazed with his own spit, and said, "You want me to stuff my cock in that hole? You ready to get fucked?" Then he stabbed his tongue back into Task's asshole. He did that a few more times, alluding to the fuck Task was going to get, then returned to rimming him.

"I can't wait to ram that ass."

Lick, poke, slurp.

"I'm gonna fuck you good."

Lap, prod, thrust.

"You ever had nine inches before?"

And Task thought, "They all say they've got nine inches," but in Steve's case that looked to be true.

"Yeah, man, give it to me," Task panted.

Steve sat up and took off his shirt, but he didn't take off his pants — at least, not entirely; he just pushed them a little further down his thighs. Task started to bring his legs down, give his back a rest, but Steve said to keep his ass up in the air. He leaned down and spat against Task's hole, using two fingers to spread the gob of spit around his sphincter, then pushed the two saliva-slick fingers inside his chute. Task squeezed his butt muscles against the invading digits, wanting to hold them inside.

Steve hocked up another gob of spit into his palm and used it to coat his throbbing cock. "I've got a rubber in my pants pocket if you don't got one," Task said.

"It doesn't matter," Steve said, an icy smile cutting across his face.

Task had only barebacked twice — once because he was forced by a trick, smacked around until he agreed, and another time because he was flying on crystal and didn't care. He'd gone to county health to get tested, the tests coming back negative both times. He was riding an X high now, but he wasn't so far gone that he was willing to risk a third time.

"Um, look, I don't do it without a rubber."

"And I don't pay five hundred to wear one."

Before Task could protest further, his ass-ring was forced open by the spit-covered head of Steve's cock.

"No, wait... not...oooohhh!"

Steve's dick filled his chute and a pleasurable pain filled his body. Consequences suddenly didn't matter, and Task was into the moment. Pinned to the seat, with Steve's sweat dripping down on him, Task writhed and jerked with each full thrust. Pulling on his cock, his erotic and chemical high worked in tandem, heightened by one another. The car rocked like a boat on choppy water as Steve rammed Task's ass, Steve calling him a "dirty cock slut" and Task saying, "Oh, yeah, fuck me harder."

Task's breath stopped in his throat and his cock pulsed in his fist. Warm, heavy drops of jism splattered onto his chest and splashed onto his chin. He looked up at Steve, his face twisted into a mask of exertion, seeing gnashed teeth, flared nostrils, narrowed eyes. The insistent stabbing of Steve's cock became more determined, until he let out a loud groan — practically a roar — and heaved a final thrust into Task's hole. Steve's load filled his insides, and Task pinched his the butt-cheeks together, trying to milk out every last drop with the walls of his ass.

Through gasping breaths, Steve said that was fucking hot. He pulled out, and Task's asshole snapped shut. Flopping into a seated position, Steve wiped the sweat off his forehead with the back of his hand, then picked his shirt up from the floor.

"Get dressed and I'll drop you back off at the hotel," he said, opening the car door.

Task brought his legs down and his body up, a tingling dizziness buzzing through his brain from the shift in positions. "What about my money?"

"You'll get your money," Steve said, not looking at him as he stepped out of the car.

Task opened the car door on his side and got out, the wet asphalt soaking his socks, his body covered in the humid night air. He opened the front passenger door and leaned in, kneeling on the floorboard on one knee, his bare, sticky ass exposed to the outdoors. Task grabbed his T-shirt and used it to wipe off the jizz that clung to his face and chest. Steve was getting behind the wheel. Task looked up long enough to see he'd put his shirt back on, unbuttoned, and was now fiddling with something between the seats, like he was feeling for lost change. Task dropped his cum-soiled shirt onto the seat and reached for his pants and underwear, his hand hitting something shoved beneath the front seat. He reached deeper beneath the seat, his hand grasping the object, recognizing its shape by touch but still saying, "What's this?" when he pulled it out into the dim light.

The tiny revolver looked like a toy, silver with a pearl grip, the barrel barely two inches long.

"Whose faggy gun is this?" Task chuckled, curling his hand around the decorative grip.

"I dunno. I prefer something a bit more masculine. Like this."

Task looked up, right into the nine-millimeter pistol Steve had aimed at his head.

TWENTY-SIX

With Saber curled into his self-suck position, Dane slowly pumped the aspiring porn star's smooth, overturned butt. Occasionally, he looked down to watch his cock sliding in and out of the pink-rimmed hole, splitting apart the full globes of Saber's ass. He watched himself fucking the young man like he was one of the voyeurs gathered around him, near the action but not part of it. Then Jay's uncut cock would slap him in the face, demanding attention, reminding Dane of his host duties.

Beneath him, Saber trembled; the dual stimulation of sucking his own mammoth cock and getting his ass plowed rapidly pushing him toward orgasm. Dane conjured the image of Saber cumming in his own mouth, the thought sending a hot jolt of excitement through his body like an electric current. He only wished he could see it for real; the way they were positioned, Saber's head was between Dane's thighs. Damn! He wished he was videotaping this, like he did back in the day before everyone got so fucking litigious and you could film your orgy without worrying about whether all your guests signed a release.

He felt the walls of the Saber's ass constrict around his dick, and heard the young man make anxious noises beneath him. Dane pulled his mouth away from Jay's cock long enough to gasp, "Yeah, baby, cum in your own mouth."

The few men watching concentrated their attention on Saber smoking his own pole, anxious to see the moment he came. Dane felt the young man's sphincter contract and his body quiver, immediately followed by a sharp grunt. The naked audience made louder noises.

"Oh, shit — right into his mouth!"

"Eat it up, baby! Swallow you're own load."

"Fuck, that's *hot*!"

Jay let out his own exclamation, an unintelligible yell. Dane pulled his mouth away from the exotic stud's cock just in time to see it erupt, catching him on the chin and splattering his chest with its creamy, white man-juice. Jay returned his dick to Dane's mouth, and the porn mogul sucked out the last remaining drops of jizz lingering in his piss slit.

Dane couldn't stand it anymore. He pulled his cock from Saber's hole, relishing the sight of his reddened ass lips spitting out a foamy glob of lube. Saber brought his legs down and Dane saw his cum-streaked face. Saber's eyes looked dreamy behind heavy lids, and his jizz-frosted lips were parted. At that moment, he was the hottest thing Dane had ever seen. He pulled the condom from his dick, tossing it carelessly onto the floor, and began pumping his raging hard-on with his fist.

"Hungry for more?" he snarled through gritted teeth.

Saber said nothing, but his eyes brightened in anticipation. He opened his mouth to receive Dane's load.

A fierce, guttural cry erupted from Dane's throat. His body tensed, his lips drew back from his teeth, making him look enraged. His cock exploded, sending viscous white streams of cum into Saber's open mouth, as well as on his face and neck.

Around them, men cheered, sounding like Tourette's sufferers at a Baptist revival.

"Goddamn!"

"Jesus fucking Christ!"

"Holy shit!"

One of the men in the crowd, a short Latin guy with a tightly built body, his legs and ass carpeted with woolly black hair, stepped forward, stroking his cock over Saber's face. A series of high, whiny gasps announced his orgasm. A second later, he was firing his load onto Saber's forehead.

Other men followed the Latin guy's lead, moving in to jack off onto the young man's face. Saber received each load as if it were a warm summer rain, cooing happily as strangers covered his face and chest with spooge.

When the last man stepped away, holding his spent cock in his hand, Dane reached down and helped Saber to his feet. He took a moment to study the porn star wannabe's face, so covered with jism he looked like a melting candle. Taking Saber's head in his hands, Dane leaned in for a hard, probing kiss, tasting the salty-metallic flavor of semen on the young man's lips and tongue. With that kiss it was made official: DanKen's newest porn star was born.

The raunchy scene was immediately followed by nervous chuckling and averted eyes, as if the men were embarrassed by the events they'd so happily participated in minutes earlier. Dane hooked an arm around Saber's neck and brought him close, kissing his sticky forehead. "Next time, we'll try that in front of the camera," he promised.

"I can't wait," Saber said, beaming.

DanKen's newest discovery announced he was going to take a shower and headed to the bathroom, Dane slapping his pert bubble butt before he trotted away.

It was after 1:00 a.m., the penthouse suite of the Wilkes Overlook Hotel was a cacophony of sighs, moans, grunts and obscene exclamations. Every corner of the suite was occupied by men engaged in — or about to engage in — some form of sexual activity; the only men who were not were those recently spent and who now lounged in a dazed state, waiting for their cocks to recover, so they could jump back into the writhing mass of man-flesh.

I'd still be hard even if I hadn't popped a Viagra, Dane thought, taking in the scene around him.

"That was incredible," said Jay, sidling up to Dane, placing a hand on his butt. "That's the hottest I've had it in a while."

"You're not done yet, are you?"

Jay shook his head. "Just taking a breather. You look like you're ready for another round." He fondled Dane's hard-on to emphasize his point.

"That's what being surrounded by gorgeous men like you does to me," Dane replied with a wink.

He told Jay not to leave without getting his business card, and then the two men parted company. Dane stepped around one of his porn star contestants — he forgot his name — bent over the hors d'oeuvres table and getting fucked by a guy with a homely face but a rocking body. On a neighboring table, bottled water and beer were offered in tubs of ice. Dane grabbed a bottle of water and headed across the room to his bedroom suite, the V.I.P. room.

The V.I.P. room had lost its exclusivity. Dane entered to discover his bed occupied by a tangle of bodies. This was to be expected, but it still irritated him. He was glad he had thought to lock up his valuables in the room safe.

He ducked into the bathroom. The door was open, but the room was occupied. Dane entered just in time to see Saber, kneeling on the floor of the shower stall, get pissed on by Todd Trulaine.

"I didn't know this was the kind of shower you had in mind," Dane remarked.

Saber didn't reply, too busy writhing beneath the warm stream of urine to acknowledge anything or anyone around him.

"If you got to take a leak I'm almost done," Todd said.

"Uh...okay." Golden showers weren't really Dane's thing, but Saber seemed to be getting off on it. He set his bottle of water on the sink's marble countertop and stepped up to the edge of the shower stall as Todd was shaking the final drops of pee from his semi-hard dick.

Without saying a word, Saber moved over to where Dane stood, leaning back on his hands, arching his back, ready to get pissed on by the porn king. Grasping his stiff cock and lowering it as much as he was able, Dane started to pee. He pissed in a high arch, hitting Saber right in the face. His first impulse was to apologize, until he saw Saber open his mouth to catch the pungent water.

"Got ourselves a hot little piggy here," Todd drawled, pulling on his dick as he watched Saber gargle with piss.

His bladder drained, Dane snatched up his bottled water and left the bathroom. Back in the bedroom suite, he approached the mass of undulating flesh on his bed, sipping his water as he watched the heated activity. There were four men, one of whom he recognized as Task's friend, the older guy with a nice, hairy body. He was worshiping the cock of an absolutely beautiful man (Dane loved the Roman nose); two other men busied themselves with the cock and ass of Task's friend.

Thinking of Task's name made Dane wonder if Nine had taken care of him yet. And would he return in time to take care of Rand, should he ever show up?

The thoughts twisted Dane's stomach into a knot. He looked at the men on his bed, concentrating on them to force Task, Rand and Nine from his mind. The anxious thoughts would never be erased completely, only buried temporarily. And Dane knew precisely where he wanted to start digging the grave.

Taking a deep breath, forcing himself back into the moment, Dane set his bottle of water on top of the dresser and joined the intertwined bodies on the bed.

* * * * *

Winston arched his back, looked up at the ceiling and sucked in a lungful of air. "Oh, yeah — fuck me harder!" he said. Or meant to say; what came out of his mouth was harshly panted gibberish: "Oh! Yah — fu-u-u — m'hard!"

Conner understood, nevertheless, tightening his grip on the former TV star's legs and slamming his cock into Winston's ass with increased force, making the bed shake. Winston rolled his head back to Conner, saw his handsome face red and contorted in an ugly grimace, his eyes wild. Sweat dripped down Conner's muscular body as he fucked Winston — putting a lot of energy into it, Winston liked that. He punctuated each thrust with an angry grunt, the type of noise men made when they hit each other.

Winston made some more noises of his own, drawn out moans and groans. He rocked his pelvis and squeezed his butt-cheeks together, trying to tighten his hole as much as he could, wanting to feel with the walls of his ass every raised vein on Conner's shaft. Though he didn't equal Nine's endowment, Conner had a good-sized dick, and Winston wanted to get as much pleasure from it as he could, not an inch wasted.

Then Conner let go of his legs and fell forward, his sweaty torso meeting Winston's. He pounded Winston's ass in long, full strokes. Winston writhed beneath him, growing weak from getting fucked and the weight of Conner's body pressing down on his, his cock rubbing against Conner's moist abs. He clawed at Conner's back, begging for more. Conner's face dove forward, his tongue spearing Winston's parted lips. Winston's hands flew to the back of Conner's head, holding it in place as their mouths were pressed together, not wanting the kiss to end too soon.

Not wanting it to end at all.

But all things must end, and their kiss ended with Conner violently jerking his head away, grunting, "Oh, fu-uck!"

Winston could feel Conner's dick pulsing against his sphincter, pumping out its load. He reached down to his own red, drooling cock, jacking off hurriedly, wanting to cum while he still had Conner's dong trapped inside his ass. His pleasure escalated to rapturous heights, then shot into hyperspace.

Winston returned to earth far too quickly, discovering the modest load he fired puddled beneath his navel.

Panting, Winston said, "That was … incredible."

"That was hot," Conner replied, flashing a sly grin.

Winston was hoping for another kiss, hoping to feel Conner's weight on him again. But his dead lover's PR man immediately turned his attention to pulling his cock out of Winston's ass without losing the rubber.

As soon as he pulled out, Conner scooted off the bed and pulled the condom off his sagging cock.

"I was going to take a quick shower," he said, holding the slimy, cum-filled prophylactic delicately between two fingers. "Want to join me?"

"Sure." Winston hoped his response sounded casual. He hoped he didn't come across as overly grateful for the invitation, even though he was.

His hopes for continued intimacy were dashed when he joined Conner beneath the warm spray of water. Conner allowed a few brief kisses, but when Winston's hands cupped his ass, he turned away.

Conner began to lather up his chest. "I can do that for you," Winston said, holding a hand out for the soap.

"That's okay. I got it."

Winston had served his purpose.

After a brief turn beneath the water, Winston stepped out of the shower. "I'm going downstairs to get something to drink," he said as he patted himself dry with a damp towel, the only one on the rack.

"Sounds good," Conner said from behind the shower curtain. "Could you bring me up a beer? If there isn't any in the fridge, water's good."

Winston said, "At your service," and left Conner alone in the bathroom.

In the bedroom he glanced over at the bed, the rumpled bedspread damp with sweat and smudged with snail trails of dried pre-cum. Good luck explaining that to your friend, Winston thought, turning on his heels and, still nude, padding into the hall.

He started for the stairs, then stopped in his tracks.

— He heard footsteps.

Coming from the first floor.

Then he heard the front door open.

Fuck!

Walking tiptoe, Winston made it back to the bedroom in three long strides. When he entered the master bath Conner had just cut the water and was reaching for the now-soaked towel. Winston was too panicked to appreciate the sight of Conner's wet, naked body.

"Is this the only towel? Shit." Seeing Winston, he said, "Hey, could you check around, see if you can find me a fresh towel? This one's sopping wet."

"Not now!" Winston said in a stage whisper. "I think your friend is back."

"Huh?"

"Your friend! The one you're housesitting for? I think he's back. I heard someone downstairs."

Conner rolled his eyes and let out a heavy why-am-I-always-dealing-with-idiots sigh. "Well don't pee all over yourself about it. I'll handle Martin."

He stepped out of the tub, swabbed the wet towel across his shoulders and chest, and then pushed his way past Winston, tying the towel around his waist as he walked.

Winston stopped in the bedroom to put some clothes on — it was bad enough he'd helped sully a stranger's bed, but to meet the bed's owner unclothed would be especially humiliating — but only his socks had made it to the second floor. All his other clothing was downstairs on the living room floor. Desperate, he went to the chest of drawers and opened the top drawer and grabbed a random pair of underwear. Black boxer briefs, and — thank the Lord! — they fit perfectly. With luck, Conner's friend wouldn't recognize them as his own.

He stepped into the hall in time to hear Conner say, "Oh, shit!"

Winston started rushing down the stairs. He could see Conner standing in front of the front door, shaking his head. "What is it?" he called out.

But Conner didn't respond, and by the time Winston made it to the first floor he was gone. Winston looked at the front door. It was left ajar.

From a room in the back of the house he heard Conner shout, "Fuck! Fuck, fuck, FUCK!"

Winston started to head in the direction of Conner's voice, but only managed two steps before Conner burst out of a room at the rear of a short hall beside the stairs. "This is not good," he was muttering as he charged up the hall.

"What is it?" Winston asked again.

Conner ignored him, rushing past him, losing his towel in the process. Winston followed him into the living room, seeing him pick his pants up off the floor. Winston thought he was going to put them on, but Conner was checking the pockets.

"No, no, no, shit-goddamn-motherfuck-NO!"

Winston saw his own shirt on the floor, wadded up and dropped near the archway opening up into the foyer. There were stains on it. Brownish red, looking like ...

No, it couldn't be, Winston told himself, trying to stop the thought in its tracks, but it was too late ... blood!

"Conner, what's going on?" Winston pleaded.

But Conner looked past him, his face colorless and his eyes wide with dread. His nudity no longer seemed sexy; now it just made him appear vulnerable. He seemed to age ten years instantly, like watching someone transform into a monster in a movie, Winston thought. Only Conner was not turning into a super-powerful creature; instead, he was degenerating into a helpless one.

"I am so fucked," Conner said weakly.

He dropped his pants. This time, there was no loud thud when they hit the floor.

TWENTY-SEVEN

There were two cars parked in front of Martin's house, a 1997 Infiniti Q45 and a newer Audi TT Quattro. Rand chose the Audi.

The car's interior smelled of leather and cologne. Rand eased the car door closed gently. His hands shook as he put the key in the ignition. A wailing diva, backed by a nerve-jangling synthesizer riffs, blasted him when he turned the key, the music so loud he couldn't tell if the engine had caught. Though desperate to get away, silencing the car stereo became top priority. Only when he'd muted the CD did he hear the purr of the motor. Putting the car in gear, Rand punched the accelerator and the Audi leapt away from the curb. Only when he'd turned off Oakwood Drive did he switch on the headlights.

The blood was coagulating now, feeling sticky against his skin. He tried to inspect his wounds in the glow of the dashboard lights, seeing the dark tendrils of drying blood and the tiny, jagged petals of ripped flesh. The nail had only scratched the skin's surface, not punctured a vein or anything. Nothing serious, he was sure, but it still looked like he'd tried to slash his wrists with a cheese grater.

It was his blood, ultimately, that had freed him. He blindly tried to hack through the phone cords lashing his hands together, rubbing them against the nail sticking out of the baseboard, stabbing his wrists more often than not. The pain was sharp at first — he nearly bit his lower lip off trying not to cry out — then settled into a dull, persistent soreness. The stabs started to feel like stings after awhile. Enough blood had poured out of him to lubricate his hands, and the cord had loosened enough, that he was able to work his hands free.

Rand hadn't left the closet right away, not sure where Conner and his fuck buddy had gotten off to, if they were still in the living room or what. He sat in the closet, silently, rubbing his wrists, and listening. Loud moans and forceful grunts filtered down to his ears from upstairs. He had his moment of opportunity. Nevertheless, he opened the closet door slowly, wincing as the hinges squeaked.

Out in the hall he heard them talking, then heard water running. He had to hurry.

He made a brief stop in the living room. Rand snatched a shirt off the floor — didn't know who it belonged to and didn't give a shit besides — and used it to wipe the blood off his wrists and hands. There were two pairs of pants on the floor, and he went for them, hoping, if nothing else, the wallets were left in the pockets. One of the pairs of pants was unusually heavy when he picked them up, and he smiled, knowing what he'd find in the pockets.

Armed, $43 richer and possessing keys to two possible getaway cars, Rand headed for the front door. He looked at his wrists again, seeing blood blooming out from his shredded skin. Upstairs, the water was still running, and he thought about returning to the living room to grab the shirt he'd bloodied moments ago, but didn't want to waste any more time. He opened the door and slipped out into the humid night, not bothering to close the door behind him.

Though he'd stolen both Conner's and his friend's car keys, Rand checked the rearview mirror every ten seconds, just to make sure he wasn't followed. There might be a spare set of keys in the Infiniti, maybe kept in one of those little magnetic boxes you could stick in the wheel well. But no one appeared to be following him, and after several anxious miles, Rand turned his attention from getting away to reaching a set destination: The Wilkes Overlook Hotel.

He had no idea how to get there, and no idea where he was. Car dealerships and grungy strip malls catering to an Indian clientele marked the landscape. The street flowed into a six-lane roadway, and Rand was heading past Indian restaurants and more car dealerships. He saw a Quik Trip gas station up on the left, open 24-hours. *I hope to hell whoever's working tonight knows how to get to the Wilkes Overlook,* Rand thought as he pulled onto the QT's paved apron.

The rain had stopped, leaving behind freshly washed air. Rand stepped out of the car and headed into the brightly lit convenience store. Surprisingly, the guy behind the counter was not Indian, but a white guy in his mid-thirties. *Almost cute if you can get past the mullet haircut and scraggly mustache,* Rand thought. The man greeted Rand far too cheerfully for the hour, wanting to know if he could help him.

"Can you tell me how to get to the Wilkes Overlook Hotel?"

"In Midtown?"

"I guess. If I knew where it was I wouldn't be asking directions."

Mullet Head's tone of voice was a third less cheerful when he gave directions. Rand was ten miles in the opposite direction of where he needed to be.

"Anything else?" Mullet Head asked.

"Yeah, where's your restroom?" Rand needed to wash the blood off his hands.

* * * * *

Martin's mouth glided down the shaft of Arno's cock, his tongue playing with the silver ring hooked through the sultry hunk's cockhead. Arno's hand stroked the top of Martin's head, moaning softly. *Even his moans sounded vaguely French,* Martin thought.

Anonymous mouths busied themselves between Martin's legs. He'd glimpsed the men briefly as they joined Arno and him on the bed, one with a broad nose, full lips and dark, curly hair; the other was younger, with more carefully drawn features, ginger hair and a chin strap beard. Both men had the requisite buff physiques (no one at this orgy, it seemed, had more than five percent body fat), though Chin Strap had the slighter build. Without so much as an introduction, they dove between Martin's splayed thighs, Big Lips feasting on his butthole while Chin Strap gobbled down his cock.

The mattress dipped and rocked as someone else climbed onto the bed. Martin pulled his mouth away from Arno's cock long enough to look over his shoulder. Dane Kensington, wearing black leather chaps, his hard-on jutting forward proudly, was joining them. The briefest instant, Martin recalled the evening's original mission: to talk to Dane Kensington, find out if he knew where Rand was. This could be his chance.

But that instant passed, the thought of Rand disappearing the moment Arno said, "Eat my ass," the command coming out a smoky purr.

Arno rolled over and got up on his hands and knees. Martin positioned himself accordingly, letting Big Lips, Chin Strap and Dane deal with the new arrangement as they saw fit. With his face at Arno's ass, Martin pried his butt cheeks apart, admiring the furry divide, his pink-lipped sphincter twitching enticingly from beneath the dark hairs surrounding it. He spit onto Arno's asshole, rubbing his saliva around the rosebud, letting a finger slip into the opening. As he did this, a tongue — he didn't know whose — pushed into Martin's hole while his balls were cupped in someone's hand. For a moment, he paused and closed his eyes, letting the pleasure of the anonymous tongue and hand circuit through his body. He trembled and his cock fairly vibrated, anticipating more intense sensations.

Then Martin pushed his face between Arno's muscled butt cheeks and speared his tongue deep into the beautiful man's hole.

Arno's reaction was forceful and immediate. His body convulsed, and a long, throaty moan burst out of his mouth, sounding as if it had been knocked out of him. Martin's fingers pressed into the firm flesh of Arno's ass, holding on as he burrowed deeper. Arno's scent filled his nose, a heady mix of soap, sweat and man-musk that triggered an animal response. Martin's tongue ferociously stabbed Arno's butthole. He ground his face into that hairy trench, Arno's ass-hairs feeling silky against his cheeks. He dropped his mouth below the asshole then slowly dragged his tongue up the beautiful man's taint until he returned to his quivering pucker, attacking it like a cougar sinking its fangs into deer. He might've even growled.

A finger slipped inside Martin's ass, and his body stiffened. His ass-lips gripped the invading digit, squeezing it as it probed his chute. Above the fleshy horizon of Arno's butt Martin saw Chin Strap kneeling in front of the sexy stud, his hands on top of Arno's head as he fed him his dick. Jealousy nipped Martin's insides — an inappropriate emotion for an orgy, he knew, but one not easily squelched. *Arno was* his, *dammit.* It was his cock, not Chin Strap's, that should be buried in Arno's mouth.

Three fingers stretching his hole returned Martin's mind to more physical sensations. His body jerked as the fingertips pressed against his prostate. He was fairly certain his cock was drooling all over the sheets. Dane Kensington, his voice low, asked someone — Big Lips, maybe? — to get him a condom and some lube. Moments later, he felt a cool stream of lubricant, thicker than water, lighter than syrup, course down his butt crack and around his hole. The fingers, now most assuredly belonging to Dane, moved in and out, swabbing his sphincter with lube. Martin said nothing, just kept his mouth busy tonguing Arno's hole, willing to allow events to take their course.

The head of Dane Kensington's cock pressed against Martin's ass-lips. There was that oddly pleasurable tension just before the cockhead punched through, knowing it could hurt like hell, but knowing, too, that it could feel fan-*fucking*-tastic. To Martin's surprise, Dane entered him gently, slowly working the head of his cock past his sphincter, pausing to let Martin's ass acclimate to its larger diameter before pressing on. There was no pain — his asshole was recently stretched by a replica of Eric Hanson's cock, after all — only a pleasing tightness, like an arrow being drawn back in a bow, as Dane's rod filled his chute. Martin found himself easing his body backward, meeting the pornographer as he pushed forward.

Martin raised his face from Arno's butt and grunted loudly as Dane sank his cock to the hilt. Dane's body stuck to his ass, cemented by sweat, and Martin felt the other man's balls press against his butt crack. They were still for just a second, long enough for Martin to remember the rare times he bottomed — not for Ron, but another former boyfriend, back a hundred years ago, when he was 27 or 28. The guy's name was Jeff, a few years older than Martin, with a tan, beefy body, a boyish grin and a sexy mustache (at the time Martin had a thing for mustaches; now he associated them with cops and the 1970s). Jeff had a meaty cock that curved to the left, and he loved to slide it into Martin in a sideways position. They'd lie on the bed, in a spoon position, with Jeff's curved cock buried in Martin's ass, barely moving. Jeff wouldn't thrust so much as undulate. He'd work his dick around inside Martin's chute while playing with Martin's cock, moaning into Martin's ear how his ass felt so good. It wasn't the wild, frenzied fucking Martin had been conditioned to expect from a man, but feeling Jeff's body pressed against his back, his rod deep inside, never failed to give Martin the most incredible orgasms. Martin tried to use Jeff's technique on later boyfriends, but they didn't have the patience for it, demanding Martin pound their asses like a jackhammer, which was exactly how Dane began to pound Martin's ass. Martin held onto Arno's butt to steady himself Dane fucked him. Occasionally, he managed to flick his tongue against Arno's rosebud, but mostly his mouth was occupied with ecstatic moans.

A cock batted him in the face from the left and Martin turned to confront its red, engorged head. Looking up he saw the dick belonged to Big Lips, now staring down at him, his mouth open, that faraway, dreamy look in his eyes. Big Lips stroked his cock and brought it down on Martin's face, leaving a dewy kiss of pre-cum on Martin's cheek. Before he knew it, Martin had Big Lips' big dick in his mouth, sucking it hungrily as the porn mogul plowed his ass.

From the right another dick poked his face, this one belonging to Chin Strap. The shaft was long and kind of on the skinny side, capped with a bell-shaped head. Chin Strap's cock was still moist with Arno's spit, and because of this Martin immediately transferred his mouth to it, wanting to taste Arno, even if it was on another man's cock. Chin Strap gasped and panted, his hand brushing the top of Martin's head. Martin then heard the wet smacks of Chin Strap and Big Lips exchanging a sloppy kiss above while he sucked cock below.

He thought he heard Dane ask: "You guys close?" Then he felt Dane's weight rest on his back, his skin warm and damp. Martin was slurping on Big Lips' dick when he felt Dane's lips brush his left earlobe.

"You ever have a cream pie?" the pornographer asked, Dane's deep voice making Martin's tremble almost as much as his probing cock.

Martin made a noise that was neither a negative nor affirmative.

"These guys're gonna make you one, and you're going to eat it all up."

Martin said nothing, his mouth jumping back over to Chin Strap's dick. Dane kept fucking him, though his thrusts were more measured now, as if he were pacing himself. He could hear Big Lips beating off, the flabby sound like someone spanking a Jell-O mold. Grunts, moans and shallow breathing filled the air around him. Martin heard Dane say, "Oh, yeah! Onto that hot hole!" and suddenly got a clearer idea of what a "cream pie" was.

Big Lips didn't cry out when he came. Martin heard him suck in a lungful of air, and then silence, holding his breath as he shot. From the corner of his eyes Martin saw his load splash into the valley of Arno's beautiful glutes, the spooge making a slow crawl down the fur-lined channel of Arno's ass. "Oh, yes," Dane hissed, punctuating his words with a sharp stab into Martin's chute.

Chin Strap pulled his cock away and Martin's mouth started to chase after it. But Chin Strap swatted him away. Glancing upward he saw Chin Strap's face frozen in an expression somewhere between a grin and a grimace. The young man jerked off in long, full strokes. In a sudden spasm, he came, firing his load — twice as copious as Big Lips' — onto Arno's butt, hitting the bull's-eye of his asshole. By the time Chin Strap squeezed the last drop of juice from his dick, Arno's fur-ringed hole was nearly obscured by creamy white goo. A cream pie indeed.

"Eat it," Dane rasped in Martin's ear.

Martin brought his mouth down to Arno's cum-frosted asshole, the slightly chemical odor of jism stinging his nostrils. Hungrily he lapped it up, the taste of the two men — one mild and slightly sweet, the other bitter — mixing on his tongue as it slid down his throat. Someone — Big Lips, Chin Strap, he didn't know who — said, "Oh, man!" Dane Kensington's breath hit the back of his ear in hot gusts as he rode Martin's ass.

The heady taste of semen intoxicated him, turning his body into one big conduit of erotic sensation. His muscles twitched. The walls of his ass quaked as Dane's cock pushed against them. Martin's dick, painfully hard and weeping pre-cum nonstop, threatened to erupt at the merest disturbance of air currents. In this state he'd forgotten all about the respectable-try-to-do-the-right-thing-Martin. Now his id had taken over, and he became oh-yeah-fuck-me-harder-Martin, with cum dripping off his chin and sweat beading on his skin. Martin dove once more between Arno's parted butt cheeks and poked his tongue into the gorgeous man's sticky hole, relishing Arno's cries as he speared his anus.

Arno suddenly moved away and Martin had the urge to grab his legs and pull him back, like a Neanderthal dragging his bitch back to the cave by her hair. But then Arno was in his face again, this time presenting his spectacular pierced penis, throbbing and glazed with its own juices. Martin closed his mouth over the head, his tongue prodding the silver ring looped through the glans. Arno's hand worked the shaft as he moaned all the while, letting out a stream of *oh-oh-ohs* in that musical accent of his. Martin tried to concentrate on Arno's cockhead, but Dane's insistent fucking kept pitching his body forward, causing him to gobble down more than he'd intended (more than a few times he feared his uvula would get hung up on Arno's Prince Albert). Arno's moans grew louder, and he panted a few *I'm-gonna-cums* in with *the oh-oh-ohs*. Martin pulled his mouth away and let Arno's hand take over, his eyes moving from Arno's face to his cock. The moans grew into howls, and Big Lips and Chin Strap were uttering bits of encouragement: "Oh, yeah, man, cum on his face," and the more succinct, "Shoot that load."

Arno's breathing became labored, his chest heaving, his lips drawn back, squinting his eyes.

Martin opened his mouth wide, stuck out his tongue and waited.

Arno's entire body began to spasm. The howling stopped abruptly, caught in his throat.

"In his mouth," encouraged Big Lips.

Martin nodded and waited.

A wrenching cry forced its way out of Arno's mouth. Jism gushed out of his cock, hitting the side of Martin's face and splashing down on his tongue. Big Lips and Chin Strap voiced their approval. Dane's breath became harsh and frenzied. He said to Martin: "Don't swallow."

And then Dane was pulling out of Martin's ass, and Martin thought he was going to jack off on his back, like one of Dane's own videos. Martin was pushed over on his side instead, Dane grabbing his ankles and maneuvering him into position, on his back. Martin barely had a chance to look at Dane — his gym-sculpted physique, his chest hair flecked with gray, his sheathed cock standing tall — before the pornographer was on him, plunging his dick back into Martin's hole, ramming his tongue between Martin's wet lips.

They snowballed Arno's tangy load as Dane pumped Martin's ass. Martin twisted beneath the older man, his body humming with pleasure as Dane Kensington's taut belly rubbed against his over-excited cock. Dane suddenly let out a harsh, throaty cry. He drove his cock deep into Martin's chute and held it there, his body frozen, as his balls emptied their pent-up load.

For a moment, Dane remained on top of Martin, the rise and fall of his chest pushing against Martin's. With another man — Rand, perhaps — Martin might have appreciated the romance of the moment. But now all he wanted was to get off. He pushed against Dane's shoulders, urging him to sit up. The porn mogul rose up and rested on his haunches, his dick still buried within Martin's butt. Big Lips, Arno and Chin Strap kneeled in a semi-circle around his head, caressing his forehead, stroking his chest, pinching his nipples. Martin reached for his red, pulsing dick, only to have his hand slapped away by Dane. Dane spit into his palm and curled his lubricated hand around Martin's cock, pulling on his cock in rhythmic strokes.

Martin's response to the stimulus was borderline violent, his body shuddering as if he'd been electrocuted. Gasping, grunting and yowling, he announced his orgasm. Milliseconds later, he was lost to an overwhelming euphoria as his cock fired, his load shooting over his torso in a high arc and landing in the center of his chest.

Onlookers — not just Big Lips, Arno and Chin Strap, but other men who'd gathered around the bed — cheered like Martin had just scored a touchdown. He heard Dane say — no, *roar* — "Oh, fuck yeah!" Above the din, he heard Arno's mellifluous voice, just low enough that he couldn't make out his words, but they sounded sweet all the same.

Cum continued to fire out of his prick, each spurt taking Martin higher. He felt as if he were floating away, the voices around him becoming distant. He closed his eyes and drifted, letting the pleasure rippling through his body carry him away.

TWENTY-EIGHT

Shooting people was easy work.

Nine learned that with his first hit, three years ago, when a yellow-haired queen named Landry paid him $15,000 to kill a business partner who was plotting to strike out on his own, and in direct competition. It was just shortly after Nine got out on parole and tried to go straight — in the legal sense, at least. He was working as a doorman at a seedy queer bar in the Valley called Scandals. The pay was crappy, and Nine swore if he heard Cher's song "Believe" one more fucking time he was going to tear the DJ's head off with his bare hands. Fifteen grand for a night's felony seemed too good to pass up.

Doing the hit was ridiculously uncomplicated. Landry's double-crossing business partner had a weakness for anonymous sex and would often cruise Griffith Park for tricks. It took all of five minutes to get the guy off in the bushes with the promise of a blow-job, then put a bullet through his brain. Nine took his wallet to make it look like a mugging — exactly how the cops investigated it. And because the victim was gay, the cops didn't investigate too hard.

His other hits were just as simple: Get the guy in a secluded area, using sex and/or drugs as a lure, shoot him, take the wallet and then leave. The murders were assumed to be robberies or drug deals gone bad and homophobia, pervasive in most police departments, ensured that detectives wouldn't lose too much sleep trying to track down the killer.

What made the hits so easy was the element of surprise was usually in his favor. Most people — unless they were Mafia, gang members or law enforcement officers — didn't anticipate getting shot, ever. The people he was hired to get rid of were business rivals or cheating boyfriends, people who, by and large, wouldn't be carrying guns. That's why, when he pulled the gun on Task, he didn't figure he'd be the one taking a bullet.

It happened so fast he didn't realize anything happened at all until it was over. Task asked something about a faggy gun and Nine, not knowing what the hell Task was talking about, pulled his Sig Sauer from its hiding place between the seats and said he preferred something more masculine. Next thing he knew, there was a bang and the car stank of gunpowder. He squeezed the trigger of his Sig, heard Task cry out, but he kept moving, out of the car and out of view. Nine started to get out of the car and chase after him. That's when he realized his left flank was spurting blood.

Jesus butt-fucking Christ! The little shit shot him! Just his luck, he had to steal a car with a gun stashed under the seat.

Didn't look like anything vital was hit, so Nine started up the Mercedes and pulled out onto the street, one hand on the wheel, the other holding his gun, looking for Task. His search lasted three blocks before he changed priorities. The seat was wet with his blood, and a burning pain began creeping through him. Bandages and painkillers became more important to him than an escaped target.

Nine headed back to his motel, mentally listing what he needed to do as he headed down West Peachtree: (1) Ditch the car; (2) bandage the wound; (3) change clothes; and (4) hunt down that fucker Task and kill him.

Of the items on his "to do" list, getting rid of the car was the most challenging. He couldn't just park it and walk off, not with the interior covered with DNA; it would be like leaving a forensics team his forwarding address. There weren't any large bodies of water nearby, so driving the car into a lake or river wasn't an option. He considered looking for a car wash and hosing the car down, but who knew how long it would take to find one. There was a third option; it wasn't ideal, but it would have to do.

Nine cut down a side street, two blocks from his motel, crossed Spring Street and made a sharp left into litter-strewn vacant lot. There wasn't much cover, just a couple unhealthy looking trees and some underbrush, but the area was unlit. The building across the street looked to be vacant, a big "For Lease" sign in the window and its beige stucco walls tagged with gang graffiti.

He grabbed his gun, popped the door to the gas tank and slowly eased himself out of the car, gnashing his teeth as a burning pain sliced through him. Carefully, Nine pulled off his bloody shirt and tore it in half, tears coming to his eyes as another wave of pain ripped through him.

Nine stuffed one half of his shirt in the open gas tank. He didn't smoke, so he had to use the car's cigarette lighter, a huge hairy pain in the ass. First attempt the shirt didn't catch fire, just smoldered and smoked before going out. The second attempt was aborted when he was stopped by another wave of pain, the lighter cold by the time the wave calmed. As for the third time being a charm, it wasn't. The fourth time didn't appear too charmed either, making Nine wonder if he might have better luck rubbing two sticks together. Then he saw it: a tiny flame.

Halle-fuckin'-lujah!

Backing away from the car, Nine watched as the flame grew, consuming the fabric as it moved toward the open gas tank. He turned and walked briskly toward the street.

The explosion made him jump. An orange-yellow light fell over him, and he could feel the heat of fire against his back. Across the street, he saw flames reflected in the windows of the vacant beige stucco building. Off in the distance, he heard a man shout, "Wha' the fuck?"

Nine didn't look back. His hand pressed to his wounded side, he walked, as quickly as he was able, toward his motel, hoping he could make the two blocks without being spotted.

Yeah, that should be easy. Nothing's more inconspicuous than a bare-chested guy covered in blood, carrying a gun and walking like a drunken crab, lit by the flames of a blazing Mercedes.

Minutes passed like hours as he walked up the street, ducking out of sight — into shadows, behind parked cars, behind shrubbery — whenever cars passed. He was climbing the back stairs to the motel's second floor when he heard sirens. A fire engine was charging up Spring Street as Nine was opening the door to his room.

Once he washed off the blood he saw the bullet had gone clean through, the entrance and exit wounds less than an inch apart. Didn't hit bone, but a little more to the right, and he might've been reduced to one functioning kidney. Nine used mouthwash to disinfect the holes in his flank, which felt slightly better than getting a catheter inserted by a palsied hand. Using a hand towel and a torn up pillowcase he fashioned a bandage, then popped a couple Vicodin to stave off the pain.

He was slipping into a clean pair of pants when his cell phone rang. He answered on the fifth ring with a terse, "Yeah." Nine listened without comment as the person on the other end spoke, panicked but trying to hide it.

Nine asked the caller, "What did you say the guy's name was?"

The man repeated the name and Nine said: "Don't worry. I know where he's headed."

He hung up and finished getting dressed. From his suitcase, he removed a silencer and fitted it on the end of his Sig. After checking himself in the mirror, adjusting his shirt to make sure the bulge from the gun wasn't visible — one of the few times he tried to hide a bulge in his pants — Nine grabbed the keys to his rental and left his room.

* * * * *

The air enveloped Dane like a warm, damp blanket as he stepped out onto the terrace. At the far eastern corner of the rooftop patio, leaning against the four-foot-high cement wall, stood two men sharing a joint. Dane recognized one as the short Latin guy who jacked off onto Saber's face earlier. The other guy was African-American, with a nice, tight body — might've been a contestant in the Porn Star Search, but Dane couldn't remember. Both guys had their pants on now and seemed a little embarrassed when they saw Dane, whose hard-on — which hadn't abated since he'd popped the little blue pill nearly four hours ago — remained exposed for easy access.

Jonathan Asche

"Wanna hit?" asked the black guy, holding the smoldering roach toward Dane.

"No thanks." He held up a fresh bottle of water. "Just came out here to re-hydrate, is all."

He didn't step outside for a conversation, either, and ambled away from the men, taking a pull from his bottle as he looked out at the city. Though it was early Saturday morning, many lights were on in the surrounding skyscrapers, and Dane wondered if any of his neighbors were able to see the goings on in the Wilkes Overlook penthouse. He imagined some low-level clerk, working late to meet an asshole boss's deadline, looking out an office window and doing a double take when he saw the raunchy activity happening in the neighboring hotel. Maybe he'd even pull his dick out and start jacking off — fuck that deadline. The imagined scenario aroused a chuckle from Dane.

He eased himself down in a patio chair at the west end of the terrace, the wet wire mesh of the seat cold against his exposed ass. Sirens wailed in the distance, and Dane tried to decipher if they belonged to police cars, fire engines or ambulances. Long ago, before he became Dane Kensington and was Darren Kennert, a salesclerk at Mervyn's, living in an Oakland neighborhood on the border between dicey and downright dangerous, he could tell the difference between a police siren and an ambulance siren, having been serenaded nightly by emergency vehicles. But now, decades later, he could only guess, and with no real confidence, that the sirens in the distance came from fire trucks. Or maybe ambulances. Not police cars, Dane was sure of that. He needed to be sure of that.

Shit, is this what my life's going to be like from now on? Paranoid every time I hear a siren, sure it's for me?

Once again anxious, Dane reconsidered taking a hit from the joint offered to him minutes ago. He looked back over his shoulder toward where the two guys were standing, but they were gone, either returning inside to get off one more time or, like more than half the guests already had, calling it a night. Dane was alone on the terrace.

He let out a grave sigh. His hand went to his cock, still stiff and ready for action. Dane flicked his boner a couple times, in the same detached fashion he had when he was a kid, ten or eleven years old, when erections seemed more like a physical quirk — like farting, something to snigger about with other boys at school. Now, at this moment, that's all his cock seemed: a physical novelty, a testament to the powers of medicine. His desire, though, had gone limp.

A sliding glass door opened, and the soft moan of house music escaped into the night air, only to be silenced when the door closed. Dane didn't turn to see who was joining him on the terrace, afraid his curiosity might be mistaken for interest. He still wasn't in the mood for conversation, and a blowjob under the stars, while preferable to talking, would only prove frustrating in his current state.

Then he heard breathing, heavy and close — only a couple feet away. It wasn't the type of heavy breathing he was used to hearing, borne of torrid sex or a strenuous workout at the gym. This breathing was weighted with equal parts fear and anger, and immediately Dane knew who had joined him on the terrace.

A turn of the head confirmed his visitor's identity.

Dane said, "I was beginning to think you wouldn't make it."

TWENTY-NINE

He should've taken a cab that day, two weeks ago.

He had the money — Dane gave him $1,000, cash, and told him to go shopping, get some nice clothes for his trip to Miami. But Dane also said he could keep the change, and Rand wanted to keep as much of that $1,000 as he could. He'd kept his shopping spree under $600, and wasn't going to waste any of the wad on a cab ride.

At a stop on Van Nuys, a few miles away from Ventura, Rand regretted his decision to take the bus. Climbing aboard was Task

Los Angeles was a big city. L.A. was a small town.

He'd changed his hair, got it cut short and spiky; his once chestnut brown locks now bleached platinum. Everything else was as he remembered, including the facial hair, left its natural color. Rand watched Task move up the bus' center aisle, wearing a ratty turquoise tank top that exposed his muscular, tattooed arms, and threadbare blue jeans that clung like a second skin, and felt a tightening in his chest and a curdling in his stomach.

Rand scrunched down in his seat, trying to make himself smaller, hoping Task's eyes, hidden behind a pair of wrap-around sunglasses, hadn't seen him sitting there, trying to hide behind the heavyset Mexican woman sitting next to him. Task passed his seat without comment, not even a nod hello, and for a moment, Rand thought he might not have been noticed.

But of course, he was.

"I've been trying to call you, but it says the number is no longer good," he heard Task say from the seat behind him, leaning over his shoulder so close Rand could feel his breath on the nape of his neck. Not accusing, just stating facts. There was no trace of anger in his voice.

"Um, yeah," Rand said weakly.

"Those guys you live with? They said you'd moved out, went to Palm Springs."

"I, uh, did go to Palm Springs, but I didn't, y'know, *move* there."

"Asked Jerry when you'd be coming in to work, and he said you quit."

"He's an asshole."

"Yeah, but the money was okay. You always seemed to do all right dancing."

Rand folded his arms across his chest defensively. "Just got tired of it, that's all."

"So ... what? You're now a banker or something?"

The blood was rising to his face. "I'm getting by."

Jonathan Asche

Task pinched Rand's shirt collar and tugged on it. "Abercrombie & Fitch? Brand new? Fuck, that's more n' getting by. You got yourself a sugar daddy or something?"

"Leave me alone!"

The Mexican woman looked over at them, treating them to her sour expression before she returned to staring out the dirty window.

The bus came to another stop. A few people got off, a couple more got on. Rand said, "I need to get off in a couple stops."

The bus moved jerkily back into traffic, and Task said, "I've missed you."

Using a tone that was at once thoughtful and seductive. And hard to resist.

Rand shook his head. "Don't ..."

Task placed a hand on his shoulder, squeezing it gently. "You got something going, I'm okay with that. Just don't try and disappear. Like last time."

It was getting difficult to breathe. Rand said, "I just want out," the words coming out of his mouth like a helium leak.

"Wanna stop by the duplex? Maybe smoke a bowl and ..."

Task didn't finish, just started chuckling mischievously.

Rand closed his eyes. "Stop."

Then Task brought his face closer, cupping a hand over Rand's ear, shielding his teasing tongue from view as it traced Rand's earlobe. He whispered words so low that even at close range they were barely audible, yet their meaning went directly to Rand's cock.

When they reached the run-down Hollywood duplex, Rand was grateful to learn they had the place to themselves. Last time he saw Task's roommate was just before he went to meet Dane Kensington, and then he boasted he was going to build a life without Task in it. Now, following Task back to his bedroom, he didn't want any witnesses to his weakness.

Task hadn't made any investments in bedroom furniture in Rand's absence: A mattress thrown on the floor, a plastic milk crate serving as a night table, and a wobbly metal shelving unit holding random stacks of clothes, CD's, drug paraphernalia and crinkled copies of Mandate, Indulge and Spin. Discarded clothes formed little piles on the floor around the bed; Rand and Task quickly made a new pile with the clothes they were wearing.

They tumbled onto the mattress together, Rand rolling on top of Task, feeling the warmth of Task's semi-hard dick pressed against his own. They kissed hotly, Task's mouth tasting mildly of peppermint, stronger of smoke. Rand brushed a hand over the top of Task's head, the white-blond spikes of hair gummy with styling product. Task's hands coursed down Rand's back to his ass, prying his

254

cheeks apart, a finger poking the pursed lips of his sphincter. Rand gasped, nipped at the side of Task's neck, panted out an offer — no, a need — to suck his cock.

Task obliged. Leaning back against the flat pillows, hand on top of Rand's head between his legs, Task groaned that his mouth felt so good, and he missed feeling it on his dick. Rand kissed his balls, then dragged his tongue back up the shaft, up the torso, across a nipple and back to Task's mouth for another kiss, hard and sloppy. When they pulled their mouths away, strings of saliva still connected them. Task grinned, said, "You missed me, too, huh?" and squeezed Rand's ass while he said it.

He rolled on top of him, grinding his hips against Rand's, rubbing their weeping cocks together. It didn't take long for Task's mouth to make it to Rand's dick, gulping down his hard-on lustily. His mouth was warm and wet, drool leaking from between his lips and dripping down on Rand's balls. Task stuck a couple fingers in his mouth, brought them out slimy with spit, and then eased them inside Rand's hole.

Rand arched his back and said, "Oh, god-DAMN!"

Task's mouth went lower; Rand's legs went higher. Rand clutched the sheets, last changed God-only-knew, holding on as Task's tongue snaked deeper into his asshole.

Rand bottomed, as he usually did. Task bottomed for other men, said he liked it almost as much as topping, and had bottomed for Rand a couple times, for variety. But the Task-topping-Rand arrangement seemed more natural to them; and now, as in the past, they took their positions without discussion over who was going to do what.

They fucked doggy style. Task rammed him in measured thrusts, putting a lot of pelvic action into it. He leaned over Rand's body, steadily pumping his ass, telling Rand he was so fuckin' hot and Rand just gasping in reply. Task reached under Rand's body, grabbed his drooling cock, his strokes matching the rhythm of his fucking. The electric pleasure buzzing through them got ratcheted up a few thousand volts. Their cries got louder.

Rand's load joined the other sperm samples spackling the sheets.

A round of frantic gasping and grunting, and Task was cumming, his cock throbbing against Rand's ass-ring.

Together they fell onto the mattress, Task still inside him. They were still, Task gently toying with one of Rand's erect nipples. A neighbor's radio, turned to a classic rock station, blared outside. Metallica was playing — Rand couldn't remember the song but knew he sort of liked it — and that's when Task said it:

"I love you, ya' know that."

Rand knew, but hearing it made his stomach harden and his dick soften.

"I ... Can I take a shower?"

Task said: "Go ahead," not pushing his declaration of love. But then, Task seldom pushed. He knew he didn't have to.

When Rand returned to Task's bedroom, still damp, a ragged towel tied around his waist, Task was sitting up on the bed, thumbing through the $400-and-some-odd dollars, money that was in Rand's pants pocket. The pants were now up on the bed, beside Task.

"Picked up your pants by mistake. This fell out," Task said casually.

Rand didn't bother calling him on the lie. "So just put it back."

"Lot of cash to be carryin' around, 'specially with you giving up dancing and all." He waited a beat, then said: "So who is the sugar daddy? He a celebrity? Someone I might've heard of?"

"Maybe," Rand said. "Just put my money back."

Task nodded. "Sure, no problem." He fondled the money a few seconds more, peeled off a hundred — "You don't mind? Tips have been shitty this week" — and then stuffed the remaining cash in the pocket of Rand's jeans.

Rand started dressing, and Task picked up a shoebox lid from his milk crate nightstand, the lid a makeshift tray for his pot-smoking accoutrements. "What's the daddy's name, if I 'maybe' heard of him?" he asked as he sorted through buds and stems.

Lying would've been easy. Rand could've made up a name and said he was a movie producer, someone behind the scenes whom Task wouldn't have heard of and wouldn't be checking out. That would've been easy.

But Rand blurted out the truth. "Dane Kensington."

Task furrowed his brow, like he was trying to place the name. "Name sounds familiar..."

Again, he could've lied, just said Dane was a movie producer and left it at that.

"He does porn."

"A porn star?"

"No. He makes porn. Has his own studio and everything. We've seen some of his videos, I think. That one with Colton Ford we liked so much? Forgot what it was called. He did that one."

"You're the porn star."

"Um, no. Not yet."

Task's brow furrowed again. "What's he waiting on?"

Lying would've been so easy...

Rand said, "He wants me to do something for him in Miami first."

* * * * *

Nine walked through the lobby of the Wilkes Overlook like he was just another guest. He had no reason to be nervous or paranoid; the desk clerks only saw was a well-built man, early-thirties, dressed in all black. Maybe they thought walked a little stiffly, like he was sore, but didn't think much of it. Maybe they thought he was hot, and dwelled on that instead. They did not see a man hiding a gunshot wound and a nine-millimeter beneath his baggy shirt, heading for the bank of elevators with murder on his mind.

And if Nine's walk across the lobby aroused the slightest suspicion in any of the desk clerks, the Vicodin he took twenty minutes earlier enabled him to not give a flying fuck.

He rounded the corner, to the alcove where three elevator cars waited. The doors to one elevator were already open, and a young man with a shaved head and wearing a red T-shirt was stepping inside.

No fucking way!

Nine reached for his gun and quickened his pace. He was only a yard away from reaching the elevator when the doors closed.

Shit!

He hit the closed doors with the side of his fist, leaving a smudge on their gleaming silver surface. His frustration vented, Nine then calmly pressed an "Up" call button set in the wall between the elevator doors, and waited for the next car to open up and take him to the penthouse suite.

* * * * *

Rand walked around Dane's chair until he was standing in front of him, facing the pornographer.

"I got sidetracked," he said to Dane.

Dane, wearing a sly smile, said, "You're late, but there's still some fun to be had. I think tonight's winner is still in there. Goes by the name of Saber — a cheesy name, I know, but it's starting to grow on me. Once you see his dick, you'll realize it suits him. And he's a total pig — more than you, even."

"I'm here for my money."

Dane forced out a chuckle to go with the smile. "Since when have you been all business."

"My money," Rand repeated, struggling to keep his voice even – struggling to sound in control.

"Perhaps you and I could have some fun." Dane spread his leather-chapped thighs and fondled his hard-on. "Seems like ages since I had my cock in that sweet little mouth of yours."

Rand allowed his eyes to drop to Dane's stiff pole for half a second before returning them to the older man's eyes and repeating, again, "My money."

"I still see your face, covered with my cum... Remember the fun we had in Palm Springs?"

That's when Rand pulled the gun from his pocket and aimed it in the vicinity of Dane's chest, holding it with both hands so it would stay steady. Dane's smile evaporated.

"The money."

Dane's smile returned, this one was less confident. "Come on, you're smarter than this, Rand. You don't want to shoot me. Where will that get you? And shooting me here, with all those possible witnesses." He waved a hand toward the penthouse behind him. "Not a wise move."

"Everyone in there is either fucking, fucked up or sleeping. Doubt they'll even hear the gunshot."

"And if I'm dead, how're you going to get your money?"

"You're only going to be dead if I don't get my money. The choice is yours."

"Wasn't I supposed to get something for my money?" Meaning the videotape.

"Being allowed to live should be enough," Rand said.

Dane shook his head. "You don't have the tape, do you?"

"Just. Get. My. Fucking. Money!"

A sliding glass door opened. Rand lowered his pistol. His heart, already hammering at full throttle, added a few more beats-per-minute.

Task charged out onto the terrace.

Rand thought, *I can't fucking win!*

For a moment, their eyes locked, communicating shock, disappointment, fury.

Rand wondered when and why Task shaved his head, and observed — he couldn't help himself — that the look was even sexier than his bleached-blond post-punk look. Other than the shaved head, though, Task looked like he'd spent two days living on the street, the red fabric of his T-shirt was dark in places, either wet or stained, and his jeans were smudged with dirt. His right arm had raw, bloody patches where it had been scraped, as if he'd skidded across cement.

Task's mouth began tugging in different directions, preparing to say words his mind couldn't conjure. He finally managed to sputter an accusing, "You!"

Tears welled in Rand's eyes. He shook his head. "Stay out of this."

Task raised his scraped-up arm, extending it toward Rand. The hand at the end of that arm held a short-barreled pistol.

"No, *you* stay out of this." Task abruptly swung his gun toward Dane's head. "That guy I left with, Steve, tried to kill me. That was your plan, wasn't it?"

"I have no idea what you're talking about," Dane said. His voice was remarkably calm, but his eyes, darting rapidly from Rand to Task, like a speed freak watching a tennis match.

Rand raised his gun again, this time training it on Task. "Put the gun down." The command came out a whimper. The tears broke free, spilling down his cheeks.

But Task kept the gun aimed at Dane's head, his trigger finger starting to twitch.

"This fucker tried to have me killed!" Task shouted.

Blood, bone and brain tissue sprayed out the front of Task's head. His mouth went slack, his eyes, seeing nothing, softened. He crumpled to the ground in a heap.

Behind him stood a dark-haired man dressed all in black, holding a gun outfitted with a silencer.

"That's one," the man said.

THIRTY

He was still floating, lost in the afterglow of the deliciously raunchy dream. He had given himself over to strangers, letting go of his inhibitions, doing whatever lust dictated, the dream so vivid he could almost believe it happened. He could almost believe the bitter taste lingering on his tongue was from the loads he'd lapped up so enthusiastically in his dream.

Martin's eyes slowly opened to discover his head was resting on a pillow of warm skin and hard muscle. One of his hands lay just above a thatch of pubic hair, matted with dried spooge. Curled over a sinewy thigh was the thick, pierced cock Martin remembered sucking in his dream.

A dream that really happened.

Martin rolled his eyes upward, toward the striking face of the very real man upon whose chest he rested. The man caught his gaze, and a smile cut across his gorgeous face.

Arno, that was his name.

"I thought I imagined you," Martin said dreamily, returning the smile.

Arno held his smile. Then he said, "I've got to take a piss."

Reality slapped Martin in the face.

Martin sat up. Arno climbed off the bed, and Martin watched, admiring his ass as he crossed the room. Once Arno disappeared into the bathroom, Martin got off the bed as well, thirst being his motivating factor. He stepped over naked bodies supine on the floor and passed one of his "dream men" — Big Lips — inhaling a line of white powder off the top of a dresser.

In the main suite, the orgy had dwindled considerably. Many of the guests had gone, and those remaining seemed to be fading fast. Two men slept on the sofa, and another sat in an easy chair, looking catatonic as he stared at the muted TV, now turned to the Travel Channel. The only sexual activity going on that Martin could see was in the far corner of the room, where a beautiful man of mixed race was getting a listless blowjob from one of the runners-up in the Porn Star Search.

Martin's watch was still the only thing he was wearing. He checked it: nearly 3:00 a.m.

At the refreshment tables, he grabbed a bottle of water and gulped down half its contents right there. He checked out the snack table, the deli trays thoroughly picked over and what remained — drying ham slices, bruised cherry tomatoes, sweaty cheese — didn't look all that appetizing. And did someone actually shoot a load onto the carrot sticks? *Jesus!*

He considered doing one more pass around the suite; maybe see what sort of mischief he could get into. Maybe Arno would be interested in another round.

But his high from whatever Task had slipped him was waning and sleep suddenly seemed more appealing than sex (there's a "You know you're old when" moment, he thought ruefully), and Martin realized what he really wanted to do was go home. He also realized he hadn't seen Task – hadn't seen him for much of the evening, in fact.

He could just leave, Martin reasoned. He owed Task nothing, not even a ride. If he was able to get out to Georgia from California by himself, surely he could make his way back to wherever he was staying without Martin's help. Probably in a motel now, fucking like mad with some guys he met tonight.

He could just leave ...

Martin was born and raised in Madison, Georgia, about an hour's drive east from Atlanta, and a world away. There he was taught to take his hat off when indoors, to respect his elders, to open doors for women ("Women's liberation doesn't exclude you from being a gentleman," his mother said), and to extend every courtesy to guests, even if they were only acquaintances. Though his mother never addressed the situation, Martin assumed "every courtesy" included giving your guest a ride home from a cum-soaked gay orgy.

He would try to find Task.

Martin turned from the unappetizing hors d'oeuvres and began hunting for his clothes, somewhere on the floor, his intention being to get dressed and hunt for Task. He was stepping into a pair of khakis that he hoped were his when a voice made him pause.

"Stay out of this."

The voice had drifted in from the outside patio, through the open sliding glass door. He didn't recognize the voice immediately, though it sounded familiar. What struck him was the tone, pleading with a tinge of desperation.

He took another step, not sure if he should head for the terrace right away or get dressed first. Or just stay the hell away, not wanting to get involved in someone else's drama.

The next voice he heard he recognized. Task saying — shouting — "No, *you* stay out of this." He said more, but the TV was suddenly un-muted, a bubbly woman twittering on about the "rockin' and raucous" nightspots of Rio de Janeiro at full volume. Martin swung his gaze toward the guy in the chair, aroused from his stupor long enough to hunt for the remote. The guys on the sofa didn't stir.

Martin almost didn't notice the man dressed in all black crossing the room, walking stiffly, as if sore or injured, but with intense determination. A man on a mission. Something about the man in black made Martin uneasy, and when he saw the man was heading right for the open sliding glass door, he zipped up his pants and followed.

Cautiously, he poked his head out the doorway. The sight at the opposite end of the terrace struck him like a hard slap to the face.

Rand.

He stood there, looking like he was about to sob. Tears were already spilling down Rand's face, his wet cheeks shimmering in the light cast from the outdoor lamps.

There were three other people in the scene. Standing, his back to the door where Martin stood, frozen, was Task. Sitting in a chair between the two young men was Dane Kensington, his figure mostly obscured by Task, recognized by Martin only by his leather-clad legs, one of which was beginning to jackhammer something fierce.

Creeping up behind was the man in black, his arm raised, holding a...

Jesus Christ, no!

He wanted to call out a warning, and had opened his mouth to do just that. All that came out was a barely audible croak.

Shock and fear held his vocal chords hostage only for a second. In that second, he heard Task shriek, "This fucker tried to have me killed!"

In that second he heard a quick, sharp noise — something between a *whoosh* and a *zing* — slice through the air.

In that same second, he saw Task fall to the ground, blood from his shattered skull spreading onto the wet cement.

The man in black said something, his voice very low. Then he raised his gun again, aiming it Rand.

Martin's voice remained paralyzed, but the rest of his body sprang into action. He leapt out of the doorway and onto the terrace, his eyes fixed on the man in black. Any reservations or second thoughts were washed away in a flood of adrenaline.

His eyes darted toward Rand, seeing his beautiful face made ugly by fear and some other emotion Martin couldn't place. Rand had a gun, too, and was pointing it — not too steadily — at the man in black. Even though he'd likely miss if he pulled the trigger, brandishing the revolver made the man — the killer — hesitate. That hesitation gave Martin the milliseconds he needed to close the distance between him and the killer. He was four feet away when the man in black noticed him, turning slightly —

Three more feet...

— and giving Martin a you've-got-to-be-kidding smile.

Martin lunged, arms outstretched, bringing them down on the man dressed in black.

The man's smile disappeared.

They tumbled to the ground together. Two shots were fired; one bullet silenced, the other, not.

Shouting and screaming followed. Martin was on top of the man in black, sitting on his chest. The man in black howled, his face twisted into a grimace. Martin rammed his fist into the center of that grimace, splitting it into an expression of stupid surprise.

Martin brought his fist down again.

In the background, the screaming melted into gasping sobs. "Oh God, oh God, oh sweet fucking Christ!"

Rand.

The man in black sent a fist into Martin's rib cage, enough power behind it to make Martin wince from the pain, but not hard enough to slow him down.

Martin's fist slammed into the man's nose, making a wet crunching noise.

From the doorway, a man shouted, "Call nine-one-one!"

A hand on his shoulder stopped Martin from bringing his fist down again.

"We've got to get out of here!" Rand screeched.

The face of the man in black was a gory mess. Blood and snot poured out his broken nose, forcing him to draw in shallow, gurgling breaths through his split lips. Martin, who hadn't been in a physical altercation since he was a freshman in high school — when he was, in fact, the proverbial 98-pound weakling — stared at the man's pounded face in disbelief. *I did that?*

"Get the fuck up!" Rand shouted, pulling on Martin's arm.

He stood, letting Rand lead him back into the penthouse. They had to push past the few onlookers who stood gawking at the door. Inside was a flurry of activity, as men swarmed around hunting for the clothes they had shucked earlier. A few, Martin noticed, didn't even bother getting dressed, just bundled their clothes in their arms and bolted naked out the door. The scene looked like a department store clearance sale for nudists.

Martin pulled away from Rand.

"What're you doing!"

"My clothes," Martin said, scanning the floor. "I've got to get the rest of my clothes."

"Goddammit, there isn't time!" Rand shouted.

"I'm getting my shoes, at least. I paid two-hundred bucks for that pair!"

"Cheap-ass queen!" quipped one of the men in the clothes-gathering fray.

Martin found his shoes near the sofa and scooped them up. He saw Arno, wearing a pair of white briefs now, pulling on a pink and purple paisley nightmare of a shirt. Martin felt a twinge of longing, despite all that had happened in the past five minutes, and despite Arno's hideous shirt. He wanted to get Arno's phone number, or at least say goodbye.

"I'm gone!" Rand barked.

There wasn't time.

Rand was at the door to the emergency exit stairs when Martin ran out of the penthouse suite, holding his shoes in his hands. He pushed his way past the half-naked men standing in the hall waiting for an elevator, making it to the stairwell door just before it slammed shut. Rand was already a flight ahead of him, and he tried to bridge the distance taking the steps two at a time, praying he didn't trip doing so. Remarkably, no one followed them down the stairs.

He called out for Rand to wait for him, but the younger man maintained his pace, refusing to let Martin impede his escape any more than he had. Only when he reached the ground floor — fifteen flights of stairs later — did Rand wait, stopping at the scuffed black exit door until Martin came huffing and puffing down the final flight of stairs.

"Got ...to quit ... smo ... king," Martin wheezed. "Again," he added a breath later.

Rand pushed open the door. "Where's your car?"

"Par ... king garage. Next ... door."

They ducked out the hotel's back exit, startling a couple bellboys taking a smoke break. The two men kept running, their panic escalating as the sound of sirens grew louder. Martin, still barefoot, stepped on a sharp piece of gravel, sending an even sharper pain through his foot. Suddenly he wasn't running but doing a lopsided hop, clenching his jaw against the hurt. Too close to stop, he told himself, trying to keep up with Rand.

In the parking garage they at least had the luxury of taking an elevator. Rand held the door open, asking Martin what level as he hobbled into the elevator.

"I ... have no idea."

"That's just fucking great!" He slammed his fist into the wall. "We're gonna get arrested because you can't remember where you parked your goddamned car!"

"Well excuse the fuck out of me for thinking my night wouldn't end in gunfire!" Martin shot back. "Hit four," he added.

He was parked on level five. "Remember the last time we were in a parking garage together?" Martin asked as they approached his car.

Rand made a passing attempt at a smile. "Yeah."

"That was more fun."

Martin fumbled in his pocket for his keys, hoping that he'd find them in his front pocket, that they hadn't somehow fallen out when he tossed them on the floor earlier, or that he hadn't put on someone else's pants by mistake. Right, he chided himself, some stranger just happened to be wearing khaki pants in your exact same size. But the way his night was going he wasn't going to rule out any unfortunate happenstance, no matter how farfetched.

To his relief, there was a set of keys in his front pants pocket, and they were his own. He unlocked the passenger door first, holding it open for Rand (even when fleeing the police, he was a gentleman) before stepping around to the driver's side. The engine caught on the first turn of the ignition key. Another relief; Martin worried the battery would be dead or the starter would have burned out, thinking of all the cheesy horror movies he saw in the '70s and '80s in which teens hop into a car to escape an knife/axe/chainsaw-wielding maniac only to have the engine stall.

"Can't you go any faster?" Rand carped as Martin negotiated his way through the maze of the parking garage.

"Yeah, I can. Can burn rubber as we tear out of here if you like — bust out of here like we're in *Smokey and the Bandit*. I'm sure that won't look suspicious."

Rand kept quiet, turning his gaze out the car window.

At the exit, Martin had to stop to pay the parking attendant. He hadn't checked himself out in a mirror but was sure he was a sight, a sweaty, bare-chested guy with someone else's blood caked on his hands. The parking attendant, whose expression suggested she'd welcome an early grave, barely looked in his direction as she took Martin's money and made change.

The mechanical gate raised and Martin pulled forward. A line of police cars was parked in front of the Wilkes Overlook, blue and red lights bouncing around the street. An ambulance was backed up to the front door, two medics wheeling a gurney inside the hotel. A Channel 2 News van pulled up behind the row of police cars, and a cameraman with Fox 5 News was already scoping out the scene. Martin recognized a couple men from the penthouse, men who, like him, had been writhing around naked, sucking and fucking in wild abandon barely twenty minutes earlier. Now they were dressed and looking solemn while a uniformed police officer questioned them.

No one — not the cops, not the news crews, not the bystanders — noticed Martin's Acura pull out of the neighboring parking garage and head toward I-75/85.

"Rand."

"Yeah."

"I need to know what's going on."

A heavy silence was broken by Rand's heavier sigh. "I know," he said, his voice almost lost in the purr of the car's engine.

After that, all Martin heard was Rand's plaintive sobbing.

THIRTY-ONE

Rona McGurin opened her room door to find a uniformed policeman standing on the other side.

"Yes?" she asked, sweeping a lock of highlighted hair back behind her ear.

"Sorry to wake you ma'am," the officer said. "I'm Officer Taggert. Just needed to ask a couple questions."

Officer Taggert was a young guy with a lanky build, a military buzz cut and no hair on his pale, narrow face. Must be a rookie, Rona thought: no mustache. She liked the way Officer Taggert's eyes kept drifting down to her chest. Rona was 35 but a slavish devotion to tanning had her looking closer to 45. A fondness for beer and Mexican food was quickly eroding her waistline. Her affair with her boss had ended recently (the bastard dumped her *after* he divorced his wife). Any male attention, even if it was from a green cop admiring her tits at 4:00 a.m., provided a much-needed boost to her self-esteem.

"Questions about what?" Rona asked, pulling at the front of her University of Alabama nightshirt, so Officer Taggert could get a better view. She checked his hands. No wedding band.

"There was an incident on the top floor, in the penthouse. We're looking for the suspects. We're just asking everyone in the hotel if they might have seen anything unusual, anyone acting suspiciously."

"What happened?" Rona asked.

"I'm really not at liberty to say, ma'am. We're looking for three men..."

Officer Taggert launched into his cop-like descriptions. Everything was approximate: Approximately 25 years of age, approximately 5-foot-8-inches tall. Only hair color and clothing were stated with any certainty. When the policeman mentioned a Caucasian male, approximately 30 years of age, approximately 6-foot-2-inches tall, dark hair and dressed in all black, Rona swallowed and forced her eyes to stay on Officer Taggert's watery blue irises.

Rona shook her head. "No, I haven't seen anyone like that. Haven't seen anything at all. I've been asleep."

"I understand, ma'am..."

"Call me Rona."

Officer Taggert almost smiled. "Okay, Rona. Just routine, asking everyone in the hotel."

He produced a business card and handed it to her. It was a generic Atlanta Police Department card. "I'll call if I happen to see anything later," Rona said helpfully, trying not to smile too broadly to keep the crow's feet at a minimum.

Officer Taggert's face colored a bit. "Thank you, ma ... Rona."

Rona closed the door and let out a relieved breath. Turning, she walked back into her room.

"You did perfect," said the man in black, something resembling a smile appearing in the mass of lumps, bruises and cuts that was his face. He kept his gun trained on Rona as she returned to her chair.

Rona didn't have a gun, but she had a look that was nearly as deadly. It was a look that, in part, had earned her the reputation among the employees she supervised at Kitchens Transport in Troy, Alabama, of a fucking cunt. She treated the man in black to that look now. He was unfazed.

She sat down and he said, "My ride should be here in about twenty minutes."

Rona pulled a cigarette from a pack of Merits sitting on the table beside her. "Are you going to kill me then?" she asked, trying to sound tough but her hand shook as she lit her cigarette.

The man in black didn't answer, and her hand shook so bad she almost dropped her cigarette.

* * * * *

"Let's test it," Task said giddily, unzipping his jeans

Rand said okay, switching on the camcorder and closing the dresser drawer.

Task was still soft but that was part of the fun, making him hard. It only took a couple minutes. Then Task was fucking his mouth, thrusting forward as Rand's mouth was on a downward plunge. Rand pulled Task's pants down further, down to the knees, and encircled his ball sack in his hand, his thumb and forefinger meeting just above his nuts. He pulled on Task's strangled balls, just enough tension to heighten the pleasure of his blowjob.

Task moaned, but he did it while he was gulping in air instead of while exhaling. A reverse moan.

He moved from playing with Task's balls to playing with his ass, fingering his hole while gulping down his cock. This produced an even louder reaction, Task gripping the top of Rand's head and grunting *oh yeah, oh yeah, oh yeah.*

"Lick the head!" Task said through excited breaths. "Lick it like an ice cream cone."

Rand did as he was told, flicking his tongue against Task's engorged cockhead, catching every drop of pre-cum he squeezed out of the slit. A minute or two later, Task took over, gripping his dick and stroking it furiously, panting, "I'm so close." Rand closed his eyes.

He felt the thick, warm drops of cum land on his face a second before he heard Task's wrenching groan. Opening his eyes, he was confronted by the head of Task's cock, a heavy, white drop of spooge clinging to the tip.

"That was great, man," Task gasped, pushing his dick down, wiping the drop of jizz onto Rand's nose. "Now let me do you."

Later, sprawled out on the bed in their motel room, they watched themselves on the camcorder's little playback screen. The picture quality wasn't the greatest, and the edge of the hole Task cut in the dresser earlier blocked off the left quarter of the screen, but otherwise the video was all right. You could tell what was going on, even if it was fuzzy in places. Though Rand was fucking around with a pornographer, he had yet to see himself having sex on screen (Dane kept assuring him that would happen after the job in Miami). Live-action was a bit more uncomfortable than looking at nude Polaroids of himself. Watching himself now — especially watching the replay of Task splattering his face — was more embarrassing than exciting.

"Oh, yeah, man!" Task hooted, shaking his head as he watched himself shoot a load onto Rand's face. "That Dane dude's gonna have himself a star!" he added, kissing Rand on the forehead, acting like a proud stage parent.

Rand felt his blush deepening.

Task, of course, exhibited no embarrassment watching himself suck off Rand. He even had Rand position himself for more cinematic effect, bending over the bed, his ass pointed at the camera. Task was sitting between his legs, deep-throating his cock and finger-fucking him simultaneously. Rand could watch this a bit more comfortably since his face wasn't in the picture. He could've been anybody — anybody with a perfectly formed ass.

"Woo-whee!" Task whooped, just like he did when the plane took off from L.A., as Rand's on-screen self covered his goatee and T-shirt with jizz. "Goddamn, that's getting me hot all over again." He shook his hard-on-in-progress to emphasize his point.

"I'm hungry," Rand said, getting off the bed. "I'm going to take a shower. Then let's go get something to eat."

They ate at Subway, down the street from their motel.

"How much money your sugar daddy give you?" asked Task between bites of his meatball sub.

When Dane dropped Rand off at LAX that morning, he gave Rand $3,000 cash in his pocket. A round trip for Task took care of $700, cab fare was $60, and they had to pay for four nights at a motel that was somewhere between run-down and architecturally significant — not just paying for the room but paying some Cuban or Mexican guy (Rand couldn't tell which) to go into the office and register them, so no one could trace the room back to Rand and in turn trace it back to Dane. Now Rand had $800 in his pocket; he left $300 hidden in his bag in the room.

Jonathan Asche

"Enough to get us through the weekend," Rand said. "And he's not my sugar daddy."

"He give you enough that maybe we could get some 'tina or some weed? Maybe both?"

Rand expected this, but rolled his eyes nonetheless. He had to beg Task not to bring his stash from home, Task saying he knew a way to sneak it past airport security. "Maybe, but don't forget we need to get you some clothes that don't look like they came from Goodwill. 'Sides, where you planning to get this stuff?"

"Shit, man, that's the easy part. We're in Miami, remember?"

They went to a hole-in-the-wall bar and grill, someplace called Estrella where classic rock and Latin pop got equal time on the jukebox. They weren't there thirty minutes before a wormy looking guy wearing an over-sized T-shirt and baggy jeans that hung onto his bony ass for dear life approached them. He said his name was Mario, and he told Task he could get them some "good shit." Mario told them to follow him out the back exit, they'd complete the transaction behind the bar.

Instead of drugs, Mario had two friends — big guys — waiting outside. One got Rand in a chokehold, the other pushed Task to the ground and kept him there by kneeling on the small of his back. Mario produced a .22 pistol and reached into Rand's front pocket, pulling out the wad of bills, knowing right where to look because he saw Rand pull out the money when he paid for their beers earlier.

"Hey, what about the stuff!" Task shouted as the three guys took off in separate directions, disappearing into the night.

Rand wished Mario had just gone ahead and shot him.

"Fuck! I knew it was a mistake to bring you along!" Rand fumed, clenching and unclenching his fists while trying to decide if he should take a swing at Task. "You had to fuck this up, didn't you?" He wasn't about to tell Task about the $300 he left back in the room.

"What? It's not my fault we got robbed. We'll get some more money."

"Oh, yeah? How the fuck we do that?"

"Same way we usually do."

"What, you expect us to suck like fifty cocks in one night?"

"There's worse things," Task said.

He spun on his heels and started walking, not caring what direction as long as it was away from Task. But Task tried to chase after him, putting a hand on his shoulder and telling him to wait up. Rand pulled away violently, shouting at Task to stay the fuck away.

"Where're you going?"

"Away from you!"

"You coming back?"

Rand kept walking, not turning back. He was so deep in his anger that he was oblivious to the world outside himself — the oppressive sultriness of the air, the passage of time, the distance he traveled. When he did stop to consider such things, he felt like he'd been kidnapped in his sleep and dropped someplace at random. He knew nothing of Miami except what he'd seen on TV, and so far the real thing paled in comparison. Now, however, he seemed to be getting closer to the city's more glamorous side, the architecture, landscaping and people looking more like the made-for-TV Miami.

He paused in front of an art gallery on Lincoln Road. The gallery was dark — closed for the night — but for track lights just behind the plate glass windows in front, trained on four large paintings facing the street. Two of the paintings were of little interest to Rand, abstracts that looked like nothing more than splotches of red, yellow and lime green. Big fucking deal. The other two pieces, the ones that made him stop, were much more provocative. They weren't paintings at all, but digitally altered photographs. One depicted a nude man against a dark background, hatching from an egg from which white stuff — *was it supposed to be cum?* — oozed. The other work featured two nude men, one black and one white, embracing, the black guy touching his impossibly long tongue to the tip of the white guy's chin. The background was covered in ying and yang symbols of varying sizes, only within the symbiotic black and white symbols were the same nude men. All the men were hot, girded with rippling muscles. Neither of the pieces showed full frontal, but you could see the pubes of the guy hatching from the egg, his dick obscured by a piece of eggshell.

"Somethin' else, ain't it?"

The comment was made in a deep, country twang, personified by a man who took his fashion cues from *Urban Cowboy*: Black cowboy hat, Chambray shirt and snakeskin boots. All he needed were spurs and a lasso.

"Which ones?" Rand asked.

"These ones here," the cowboy pointed at the photographs, "how they can get away with showing them right up front like that, where anyone can see. Back where I'm from, they'd shut a place down for showing these at all."

"Sounds like you should move."

The guy chuckled and said he was on the road most of the time anyway. Rand nodded and thought about moving on, not really looking to make friends. But the cowboy didn't seem in a real big hurry to be anywhere, and Rand got a vibe that it was more than art appreciation that was making him linger.

"You out by yourself?"

A smile cut through the man's silver-frosted beard. "For now. Night ain't over yet."

The cowboy's name was Shep — of course, Rand thought — and his hotel was nearby. It was one of the city's newer hotels, but not one of its fancier ones – no ocean view and no spa. They took the back stairs up to Shep's room instead of using the elevator in the lobby.

"What's all this?" Rand asked when they entered the room. Stacked around the room were rectangular cases — six total — made of blond wood, covered in scuffs and scratches. They looked like oversized briefcases, each about four feet long by two and a half wide.

"Just for my work," Shep said dismissively, taking off his cowboy hat. Rand expected him to be bald on top — guys who wore hats usually were, he had noticed — but Shep's head was covered with wavy, dark brown hair going to gray.

Rand dropped the subject of the wooden cases and asked: "So, what do you want to do?"

Shep hooked his thumbs in his jeans and rocked on his heels. "Weh-hell, now, let's see. I can think of all kinda things..." He didn't look at Rand as he spoke. "You said a blowjob is how much?"

"Twenty-five."

"And to fuck?"

"Thirty if I fuck you, fifty if you fuck me — you wear a rubber, no exceptions."

He was hoping Shep would just want a blowjob; those were quick and relatively safe. But Shep wanted a flat rate for one hour, so Rand told him $100. Shep agreed without negotiating and Rand immediately wished he'd tried for $150.

Rand got undressed first, Shep saying he wanted to "check out the goods," whistling when Rand stepped out of his pants. Shep fondled Rand's balls and pulled on his dick, shaking his head like he couldn't believe he was being allowed to do so.

"Now let me check you out," Rand said, unbuckling Shep's belt.

Shep was in the neighborhood of forty and his body was a bit on the thick side, not fat but stocky. Good looking, Rand thought, but not what he'd call hot, and the cowboy thing was just too Village People for his taste. The guy did sport an intriguing package in his 501's, though, and Rand was eager to see the cause of that enticing bulge.

The pleased gasp Rand emitted when he unbuttoned Shep's fly was genuine. The guy had a hefty eight-incher, partially erect. "They do grow 'em big in Texas," Rand cooed, taking Shep's cock in his hand.

"From Oklahoma, actually," Shep said, "but thanks."

Rand sat on the edge of the bed and Shep thrust his cock between his lips. His tongue prodded the plump head and teased the piss-slit before gliding down the veiny shaft. "Oh, shit," Shep said in his hickory-smoked drawl, meaning it in a good way — the only way he could mean it with his dick buried in Rand's throat. Rand sucked his cock and played with his balls, noticing one of Shep's nuts was bigger than the other and wondering — briefly — what was up with that. He wasn't going to ask, though, especially not now.

"Oh, man, I wanna fuck that cute butt of yers," Shep said, sliding his prick to and fro over Rand's tongue, not in any big hurry to change orifices.

"Whatever you want," Rand said playfully, wetly kissing his cowboy trick's cockhead.

Shep pulled a half-empty bottle of Wet out of his suitcase and tossed it to Rand. Rand squirted some lube over his fingers and laid back against the pillows, spread his legs and slid a lubricated index finger into his asshole. "Oh, sweet Jesus," Shep drawled, shaking his head again like he just couldn't believe it. He stood watching Rand finger himself, his cock trembling visibly, the pulsing head looking dewy. Only when Rand inserted a second finger did Shep pull his eyes away and finish undressing.

"Hand me the lube," Shep ordered, tearing open a condom packet. He was kneeling at the front of the bed now, naked. His body was in better shape than Rand first surmised, his belly plated with a six-pack. Shep's torso was covered with fur, like his pubes were left to spread like vines, over his abdomen, across his chest and up to his shoulders. No hair on the back, from what Rand could tell in the mirror on the wall behind Shep. The ass was all right, if a bit on the flabby side.

Shep rolled on the rubber and positioned himself between Rand's spread legs. "Man oh man," he said over and over, one hand taking over where Rand's fingers left off, the other stroking Rand's cock. "Yer somethin' else."

"And you haven't even fucked me yet."

Shep said, "Man oh man."

The cowboy eased his dong inside him. Rand closed his eyes and gnashed his teeth, steeling himself against the sphincter's first protest. Then he relaxed, freed by the rush of pleasure that followed when Shep's cock filled his chute.

Shep leaned on top of him, his weight pressing Rand into the mattress. He fucked Rand in jerky thrusts, his huffing and puffing blending in with the noise of the air conditioner. Rand hooked his legs around Shep's waist and rose to meet the older man's plunging prick, grinding his cock against Shep's abdomen.

Breathing became heavier and frenzied. Shep was really ramming his ass now, gasping oh yeah, oh man, oh fuck. He pushed his body up, threw his head back and let loose with a roar. He held that pose, his shoulders jerking as his cock pumped out its load. When his orgasm had faded, Shep fell back on top of Rand, grunting in his ear.

He pulled out, carefully holding the loaded condom at the base. "Man, that was good," Shep drawled, head turning side to side, pulling the condom off his dick. He then went to the bathroom, delicately holding the rubber between two fingers.

Rand remained on the bed, stroking his hard-on, waiting for Shep to flush the condom and return to finish him off. He heard the cowboy taking a piss, heard the toilet flush and then heard him start running a shower. Rand stopped waiting.

He rolled off the bed and reached for his pants. As he got dressed he got curious about the contents of the wooden cases stacked around the room. The third case Rand tried to open was unlocked.

He was sitting on the bed when Shep stepped out of the bathroom. "What's in these cases?" Rand asked.

"Guns," Shep said off-handedly as he stepped into a pair of white cotton briefs.

"Really?

"I'm a dealer. There's a gun and knife show at the convention center this weekend. I bring 'em up to my room, so I can keep an eye on them. Don't like leaving them in my truck unattended."

Rand stood up. "What kind of guns?"

"Handguns mostly, a lot of twenty-twos and forty-fives, but I carry a bunch of calibers."

Rand nodded and said, "Interesting." Shep paid him — Rand had to remind him it was $100, not $75 — and he left, running as soon as the door closed behind him. He wanted to get away from the hotel as fast as he could, before Shep discovered he was missing inventory.

* * * * *

"Why did you want the gun?" Martin asked.

They were in Martin's living room, sitting side by side on the sofa, Rand drinking his second Diet Coke and Martin working on his third glass of water. Smoke hung in the air from countless Marlboro Lights. It was nearing five o'clock in the morning, but sleep was not an option.

"I don't know," Rand sighed heavily, realizing the answer was a cop-out even though it was truthful. "I just thought that maybe I'd need it. I liked the idea of having it. I'd have to sell it before we flew back to L.A., anyway."

"You had no intention of using it?"

"Shit, what do you think I am?"

Martin shook his head. "I have no idea."

Rand had no response, realizing Martin was right. He wanted to come clean, tell Martin the truth — most of it, anyway.

"It was the next night you picked up Perry Snopes?" Martin prodded.

"Yeah." Rand looked around the room, making a mental sweep. Earlier, after they left the hotel, when he realized Martin was taking him to his house, he worried Conner and his fuck buddy, might still be there. But the Q45 he'd left behind in favor of the Audi was no longer in the driveway, and nothing appeared out of place inside. Looking around the room again, he still saw no evidence of his earlier visit during Martin's absence.

"We waited in the bar of his hotel the next night, about two hours, trying to stick to sodas, so we weren't too trashed. Plus, their drinks were fucking expensive. I mean, draft beer was six bucks. We figured he'd come down eventually, and he did, 'cept he passes the bar, and I saw him head to a side door. We get up and follow him, get to the door in time to see him get in a cab. Fortunately there's another one waiting behind it — some Iranian dude was driving, thought it was funny when we told him to follow the cab that just left." Rand paused to take another gulp of his soda, the can almost empty. "I'm hoping like hell wherever this guy's going it's not too far because we only have so much cash. Fuckin' Task traded our return plane tickets for drugs — all happy 'cause he got some Viagra in the bargain, too, saying there's nothing like doing 'tina and having a four-hour hard-on."

"Sounds like fun," Martin said dryly.

Rand rolled his eyes. "Whatever. He thought I was being stupid for getting pissed, said we could hitch back to L.A., or at least make enough to take a bus. That's Task: Nothing's a problem. Least he didn't find the few hundred I had stashed in my bag. Anyway, that Snopes guy goes to one of those fancy discos, Head, Hero — something that starts with an 'h.' Had a fifteen dollar cover charge, can you believe it?"

"I can believe it. Go on."

"Well, we find the guy, drinking by himself, and the rest was pretty much as planned. We go, 'Would you like to go have some fun?' And he goes, 'Sure!' He's glad we're going to our hotel because he doesn't want anyone at this workshop he's in to see him with a couple guys he's picked up, not because they'll find out he's gay but because it could get out he's cheating on his husband. That's what he called his boyfriend, 'my husband.' I mean, I'm queer and it still sounds weird, guys saying they have husbands."

"Weirder than blackmailing politicians?"

"It was a fucking job to me, all right?" Rand shot back, reaching for the pack of cigarettes on the coffee table. "Five thousand dollars for doing something I usually only get fifty bucks for, at the most, plus a paid weekend in Miami. You were me, you'd jump on it, too."

Martin drained his water glass and shrugged, like he'd have no idea what he'd do if he were Rand.

Rand lit up and continued. "Anyway," he said, exhaling a grayish-white cloud, "we get the guy back to our room, everything going as it should. One of us keeps the guy busy, playing with his cock, while the other switches on the camera. We do the guy, and we think we're done. I go into the bathroom to wash up and that's ... that's when I hear the shot."

Martin didn't say anything, just sat hunched over, hands clasped between his knees. He was turning the words over in his head, Rand could tell. His silence wasn't going to last long.

"Why did he shoot him?" Martin asked. For all the water he consumed, his throat felt dry.

"Because he found the camcorder. That's what he said." Rand took another drag of his cigarette. "I believed him."

"That was his reason for killing the guy?" Martin asked, incredulous.

"Task isn't ... wasn't ... one to think things through. Shouldn't surprise you. You said you met him."

"He was no mental giant, but I didn't think he'd kill for no reason."

"People have killed for less," Rand said, tapping the ash off his cigarette, missing the ashtray by three inches. "We wiped off everything we thought we touched, grabbed the videotape and got the fuck outta there. Took a cab up to another hotel — just told the driver to take us to the cheapest hotel he knew, don't know where it was. All I remember is it had this fuckin' ugly bright blue shag carpet. Anyway, we check in for the night, and we smoke a joint, trying to calm down. Task kept saying don't worry, no one knew we were staying there. That always got me about him, he never panicked, like whatever happened, happened. He could actually go to sleep, knowing he shot some guy, while I'm practically pissing in my pants."

He stubbed out his cigarette and went on. "I knew I needed to get away from him. While he was asleep, I got my stuff, got the tape and slipped out. It was, like, nine o'clock in the morning. Got a ride from a trucker who was heading to Atlanta. I knew Dane Kensington had a club there, so... "

"And then you met me," Martin sighed. He picked up the pack of cigarettes, started to pull one from the pack, reconsidered, and then brought the cigarette to his lips.

"And then I met you."

"That's some story," he said, lighting his cigarette.

Rand felt his face getting hot. "It's true."

"Yeah, I almost believe you."

"What? You're pissed I didn't tell you this in the beginning? Even Task wouldn't be that dumb."

"I trusted you in my home." Martin's voice was low, but there was a violence gathering beneath his words. "I thought I was helping you out."

"You were!" Rand snapped. "I needed a place to stay, and you gave me one. But don't forget: You got something in return."

Martin spun his face toward him, looking as if he'd been slapped. "I expected nothing! I made you sleep on the couch that first night, remember?"

"Yeah, I remember. I also remember you didn't fight too hard when I got in the shower with you the next day. The only reason you let me get in your car — the only reason you believed my bullshit — was you wanted to fuck me, admit it."

"That's not true."

"Bullshit! Tell me, Martin, if I was twenty years older, missing half my teeth and sitting in my own shit, would you help me then?"

Martin looked away and drew on his cigarette, saying nothing.

"Thought so. So don't fuckin' act like you're so kindhearted and pure, that I was just one of the many homeless people you help on a regular basis. Yeah, in the beginning, I was using you, but you wanted to be used."

Martin whirled back around to face him. "I didn't want to harbor a fucking fugitive!"

"I didn't want you to! I never wanted" — his voice broke — "you involved. Believe it or not, I wanted to protect you. That's why, when I found out Task knew where I was, I bolted. I didn't want you to get in any deeper in this shit than you had already."

"If only you thought to run from Task before you went to Miami," Martin said acidly, like it wasn't something Rand thought about daily.

Rand's eyes dropped to the floor. "I tried before, but ... it's not that easy."

"You were stupid to get mixed up with Dane, too, but I can understand that one a bit more, your judgment was clouded by greed." Martin took another puff. "But Task — what was the pull, anyway? He was cute, yeah, in a rough-trade sort of way, worth a one-night stand, but beyond that ... I don't know."

"I couldn't just break up with him."

"Now who's talking bullshit? Of course you could."

"It's not that simple," Rand tried to explain. "There's more to me and Task than just..."

"What? You're going to tell me you two were soul mates or some such shit?" Martin was still in full *I-told-you-so* mode. "Yeah, I thought I found my soul mate, and he ran off with a fucking college boy!"

"Will you shut the fuck up and listen!" Rand exploded. "Task wasn't my boyfriend. He was my brother."

THIRTY-TWO

Rand's words had the impact of a lead pipe to the back of the skull. "But I thought..."

"We were lovers? We were that, too."

Martin felt hollow inside. He didn't want to be judgmental — he'd done enough of that already — but Rand's admission of an incestuous relationship made him uncomfortable. Martin recalled a debate he had with his ex, Ron, sparked by a Website Ron found claiming to feature sex between brothers. Ron thought the idea was hot, but Martin said he thought it was creepy. Ron had said, "It's not like one of them is going to get pregnant and give birth to a wall-eyed half-wit. If they want to do this as consenting adults, I don't see the harm." Ron spoke as if to disagree with this argument was to align oneself with the likes of Jerry Falwell and Anita Bryant. But Martin would think of his younger brother — now living in Prague, of all places, teaching English — and was revolted by the idea of anything sexual between them. Ron had two sisters, no brothers.

He stubbed out his cigarette in the overflowing ashtray and immediately lit another. He wasn't sure what to say, or if he should say anything. It was Rand who filled the growing silence.

"If it helps you, he was my half brother — Mom was actually married to his dad. My dad, who knows? Growing up, we called him J.T. — his name was Jason Task. Task was mom's maiden name, I think. I had a crush on him as far back as age twelve, I guess. I don't know. He was older, and I just remember being fascinated by his body, always wanting to see him naked and shit like that. I never wanted anything to happen ... I mean, I wanted it but figured it couldn't happen.

"He did some time in jail, got caught at school with a few joints and a couple tabs of acid. He did about a year and a half. Didn't even tell us he got out of jail, just one day I went to visit and was told he was released. Called me after he'd been out a few months, said I should join him in L.A. So I did."

Martin said: "And that's when..."

"Yeah," Rand nodded, not looking in his direction. "That's when we started fucking."

The statement hung in the air with the smoke from their cigarettes.

"We lived together for a year, in this shitty garage apartment Task had in North Hollywood. People thinking we were just roommates, brothers sharing an apartment."

Martin felt warm ash tumble over his hand and realized he'd let his cigarette burn down to the filter. "Your friends didn't suspect?" he asked, brushing ashes off the seat cushion.

"We didn't have friends. We had guys we hung out with for drugs and guys we saw for money."

"Hustling?" Like that was a surprise.

"No, selling AmWay. We held a few legit jobs, but not for very long and nothing that really paid anything. You can't really survive in L.A. on minimum wage. Task — he was still J.T. then — was already working the streets when I got there. Told me it was easy, he didn't deal with too many freaks. Mostly, the guys just wanted blowjobs. You had to be more careful of cops than the johns, he said."

Rand paused to get another cigarette. "Only a few left in this pack," he said, tossing the box back on the coffee table.

"When did J.T. become known as Task?" Martin asked.

"After I tried leaving the first time." Rand took a long drag of his cigarette, looking across the room thoughtfully. "I was getting weirded out by our whole set-up — us two fucking, and turning tricks. Then we started working together, asking guys if they wanted brothers, either as a three-way or watching us do it. It got... I don't know. It was like all of a sudden I realized what I was doing and didn't want to be like that anymore. That's when I took off."

"But not for good."

Rand let out a weighted sigh. "I lasted maybe six months. I was living on the street for four of them. That's when I realized there were worse things than living with Task."

He didn't elaborate, and Martin didn't ask him to, not sure if he really wanted to know.

"It took a few days to find him. He'd moved out of that shithole we were in, and half the people we knew seemed to have disappeared, probably arrested or dead. Finally found out he was working as a dancer at Boner's. When he saw me, all he said was, 'You look like shit.' Wasn't even mad. Like he just knew I'd be back.

"We picked up where we left off," Rand continued, still not looking at Martin. "A different arrangement, this time. He'd started going by Task, said we could just tell people we were boyfriends. Said we didn't have to live together, though we did for a while, I didn't have anyplace else to go. I ended up sharing a place with one of the other dancers and another guy. I didn't have to hustle anymore, either. Got a job dancing at Boner's, did pretty well. I'd do a trick now and then, but nothing like before, walking up and down the street, giving guys head in an alley."

Hearing Rand's story, Martin felt a numbness coming over him, like he was armoring himself against any deeper emotional reaction. So much of what Rand was revealing about his past could've been a TV movie-of-the-week, or at least fodder for Jerry Springer's show, and at first he questioned its veracity. Rand had lied to him before, why not again? But the way Rand told of his past with the shamed expression on his face, the way he couldn't even bear to look at him, made Martin believe him. The emotional toll of a hard-lived life wasn't so easily faked.

"I sent pictures to Dane, wanting to become a porn star," Rand continued. "Thought that would be a way out. I didn't want to involve Task, actually managed to ditch him for a few weeks. But then we hooked up again — he happened to get on the same bus I was on, if you can believe that. Motherfucker wasn't even mad I'd skipped out. I went back to his place and ... that's when I told him about what Dane wanted me to do in Miami. It was my idea for him to come along. Stupid, I know, but I was nervous, doing it alone."

Rand sniffled, and Martin, seeing his eyes getting moist, felt a pang of sympathy. Even after all the lies and felonies, his heart went out to the young man next to him on the couch, and that made him vulnerable. For that reason, though he still had questions, Martin kept quiet. He didn't think either of them had the strength for further revelations.

They remained silent as Rand finished his cigarette and Martin turned over what he'd heard in his mind. The first bluish rays of dawn were starting to seep through the drapes of the living room window.

Rand put out his cigarette and then turned toward Martin. "So, what now? You going to call the police?"

Martin exhaled slowly, heavily, as if he'd been holding his breath. "I think," he said, standing up, "I'm going to take a shower and go to bed before it's daylight."

THIRTY-THREE

They both took a shower — separately. By the time Rand turned off the water and was toweling himself dry, Martin was already in bed, dozing. Rand, naked, climbed into bed beside him.

And slept.

Sunlight cut through cracks in the drawn drapes, making Martin wince as he opened his eyes. He didn't know how many hours rest he got, but he could tell it wasn't enough. His head felt heavy, and his body felt heavier, every muscle its own mass of aches and pains. Even breathing caused his muscles to protest. Yet although he craved more sleep, he couldn't sleep any more.

Not when his cock was hard and throbbing, pressed against Rand's bare ass.

This wasn't just run-of-the-mill morning wood; he was horny. He pushed his body forward, his hard-on sliding against Rand's butt crack, the friction causing his aching body to crackle with need. Incredible, Martin thought, to want sex after the night he'd had, a night that was both physically and emotionally draining. But here his cock was demanding more.

Like the first night he brought him home, Martin considered Rand's body off limits, only now for different reasons. After all Rand put him through — lies, violence, crime — Martin couldn't imagine fucking Rand. Betrayal wasn't sexy.

Rand shifted his weight, wiggling his ass against Martin's dick. His desire grew more urgent.

I should just go to the bathroom and jack off, Martin thought. But that thought was followed by the memory of Rand's words: *I was using you, but you wanted to be used.* It was well past time for Rand to return the favor.

He rolled over and pulled open the top drawer of his night table, reaching for his bottle of lube and condoms but not finding them there. They were instead sitting on top of the table. He hadn't remembered leaving them there but didn't waste time pondering the matter — his cock was waiting. Martin tossed the sheet back, admiring Rand's body as he covered his hard-on with lube. After he rolled a rubber over his prick, he turned back onto his side, facing Rand's back, and slid his lubricated fingers between the warm cleft of the young man's buttocks.

Rand stirred slightly, making a low mewing sound in his sleep. He didn't open his eyes as Martin massaged his asshole, and Martin wondered if he thought this was some part of a wonderful dream. Only when a finger made its way past his ass-lips did Rand's eyelids flutter open.

"Wha...?"

"Sssshhhh, just relax," Martin whispered, his finger going deeper.

Rand let out a sharp gasp and pushed against Martin's probing finger, inviting a second one into his chute. Martin said nothing, just breathed hotly against the nape of Rand's neck. His cock throbbed impatiently, waiting for its turn to enter Rand's hole.

"Yes," Rand panted, answering an unspoken question. He rolled back against him, his eyes were closed again, and Martin wondered if he was dreaming again.

Martin withdrew his fingers and gripped the base of his cock. He pushed forward, entering Rand in a sideways position, having only to apply the slightest pressure to squeeze past the younger man's ass ring. Rand grunted and twisted his body slightly, raising a leg so Martin could slide his dick into him more easily. With one satisfying thrust, Martin sank his pole into Rand's chute, all the way to the hilt.

Martin fucked Rand in slow, easy thrusts, and Rand responded by pushing his ass backwards, meeting Martin on his upward plunge. It was just the way Martin was fucked by Jeff, the boyfriend from way, way back, and it was just as exciting now as it was then, the pleasure building in small, agonizing increments. He reached for Rand's dick, finding it pulsing and oozing. With his thumb he manipulated the younger man's cockhead, smearing around his natural lubricant.

"Harder," Rand implored, rolling his hips.

Martin gnashed his teeth against the rush Rand's movements produced. "I want it slow," he insisted, but his cock was losing patience.

Rand refused to cooperate, rocking his body violently, slamming back against Martin and squeezing his ass muscles around his throbbing pole. Martin gave in, plowing into Rand's hole with equal intensity, until the mattress was shaking like a boat caught in a storm.

They communicated through animal-like grunts and harsh breaths. Martin bit into Rand's shoulder as he rammed his cock into the depths of his gut. Rand reached between his thighs and covered Martin's tightened nut-sack with his hand and gave his cum-engorged balls an encouraging squeeze.

Martin stroked Rand's drooling dick, his breathing becoming shallower and more urgent. The words "I'm cumming" barely left his lips before he was spewing his load, onto his thigh and all over Martin's fist clasped around his shaft. And as Rand had done to him the first time they fucked, Martin brought his jizz-coated hand to the other man's lips. Without having to give the command, Rand lapped up his own load off Martin's hand, holding his wrist as his tongue sought out the tendrils of cum that seeped between Martin's fingers.

A jolt of pleasure shot through Martin, and he clamped his arm around Rand's firm torso, holding him tight. He sank his dick deep into Rand's asshole, holding it there as the muscles in his body tensed. His orgasm was like a dynamite blast, set off in his cock and exploding throughout his body. He trembled, his prick pumping out white hot cum.

"Does that mean you forgive me?" Rand asked.

"No," Martin said, pulling out of his moist hole, "it means I was horny."

He was in the bathroom taking a piss when the doorbell sounded. Hearing the chimes he felt nothing more than annoyance, like getting a phone call at 5:00 a.m., though in this case it was the intrusion and not the hour — when he checked the clock he was surprised to discover it was after 1:00 p.m. — that irritated him. It was only after he stepped out of the bathroom and saw Rand's anxious expression that he considered the doorbell could be announcing something more ominous.

Rand was sitting up in bed, his muscles tense, looking as if he were ready to spring up from the mattress at the slightest provocation. His eyes darted rapidly from Martin to the bedroom door, as if deciding whether to stay or flee.

The doorbell chimed again.

Martin sighed and opened a dresser drawer. "I'll go see what they want," he said, pulling out a pair of shiny blue basketball shorts.

"Don't go down there!"

"What? Probably just Jehovah's Witnesses, or my neighbor looking for her goddamn Chihuahua that gets out all the time." Martin stepped into his shorts and hiked them up, snapping the elastic around his waist. "I'll go see."

Rand said, "Don't. It could be the police."

"It's probably nothing," Martin said. "Besides, the police have no idea who we are or where we are. They couldn't. It's not like I signed a guest book. They don't even know I was at the hotel."

"But people saw us there!"

"People who probably don't remember my name or what I look like above the waist. Doubt a description of my cock would lead the police to my doorstep. "

"Someone could've seen us drive away and gotten your license plate number." Panic stretched Rand's voice tight. "The police could've traced it... or..."

"Or what?"

The doorbell sounded a third time.

"Just don't answer it," Rand urged.

"You're being paranoid," Martin said, trying to reassure himself as much as Rand. "Just wait up here, and I'll go see what it's about. I'm sure it's nothing."

The doorbell chimed twice more in rapid succession as he headed down the stairs, the visitor getting impatient. Martin checked through the door's peephole and instantly relaxed.

"Where the fuck did you get off to last night?" Conner asked when Martin opened the door. "I came by but you were gone."

"Oh, yeah. I forgot, you said you might stop by," he said sheepishly, looking down at his feet and scratching the back of his neck. "I just had to get out for a little bit. Going stir crazy."

"Understand," Conner said, nodding vigorously. His eyes were hidden behind a pair of rimless sunglasses. He was dressed in gym wear: a yellow tank top with red drawstring shorts, just tight enough, so you could see which way his dick hung.

"You on your way to the gym or over to the Ansley Kroger to cruise?"

"Cute. Just checking up on you. Heard you had a pretty eventful night."

The air suddenly got twenty pounds heavier. "How's that?"

"A friend of mine, visiting from out of town, said he met you at this thing, over at the Wilkes Overlook?"

"I don't know what..."

"Don't remember him? He's with me now." Conner looked off the side of the front porch and motioned to someone out of Martin's field of vision. "Hey, why don't you come over here and say hello."

A moment later, Conner's friend stepped into view.

Martin stepped back. "No..."

"Martin, this is Nick, a friend of mine from way back. Remember him now?"

The man smiled tightly at Martin as he climbed the front steps, his teeth barely showing beneath his split lips. "I think it's coming back to him," the man said.

The man in black was now black and blue, and heading right for him.

Fear not only chilled Martin's blood, it froze his muscles, too. He stood in his foyer, motionless, watching as Conner's friend, Nick, neared the front door — just watching as if it were a scene in a movie, not something that was happening to him. But it was happening to him, and he had to do what he could to stop it. Martin rushed to close the door.

Conner blocked him, stepping inside and pushing Martin backward with surprising force. "Martin, buddy! I'm surprised at you," Conner said, a malicious smile on his face. "That's no way to treat guests."

And then they were in his home, Conner throwing one of his well-muscled arms around Martin's shoulder. "Don't worry, this'll be over quickly."

The back door was a straight shot from where Martin stood, just a dash through the kitchen.

Conner seemed to sense what he was thinking and brought his forearm up so it rested uncomfortably against Martin's Adam's apple. One sudden move and his windpipe would be crushed in the crook of Conner's arm.

Conner, his friend from work — his friend who was going to assist in his murder.

"You didn't tell him my nick-name, Con," said Nick, the tight smile still on his bruised, swollen face.

"No, I didn't, did I? Know what they call Nick, Martin? Nine. Wanna know why?"

"Does it matter?"

"Two reasons," said Nick-who-they-called-Nine. He reached behind his back and appeared to fumble with the waist of his pants. When his hand returned to view it was holding a gun. "One reason is I use a nine-millimeter when I kill people. 'Fraid you won't get a chance to see the other reason."

"Fucks 'em with a nine-inch dick and kills 'em with a nine-millimeter gun. Sounds like it could be a movie, doesn't it?" Conner chuckled.

"So where's your little friend?" Nine asked.

"My little friend?"

Conner's arm tightened around his neck. "That's what he asked. Where is he?"

Martin had to push the words out of his mouth. "I... don't know what... you're talking about."

Nine began slowly moving his gun through the air, from left to right, up and down. "Can't decide: An arm, kneecap or foot? What do you think, Con?"

"I think you should remember I'm right beside him."

"Hey, my aim's good. I'm a professional, remember?" Nine took a step closer, grinning when he saw Martin flinch. "C'mon, tell me where that little fuck's at, and we won't make you suffer before we kill you."

Martin nearly whimpered. "I don't know. He took off a couple days ago."

Nine brought the gun up to Martin's nose. "You saw him last night. I'm sure you got a good look at him before you fucked up my face."

"He took off, I swear."

I swear? Even to his own ears, Martin sounded pathetic.

The cold steel of the gun barrel touched down beside Martin's left nostril. Conner whispered, "C'mon, don't make this any harder than it has to be."

"He's not..."

Conner brought his arm in a little tighter against his throat. Nine pushed the gun down harder against his face.

"Don't make this any harder," Conner repeated. "Just tell us where that little shit is."

The pressure against Martin's windpipe was unbearable. He spoke in an asthmatic whisper. "I don't..."

Martin brought his knee up — fast, directly into Nine's crotch.

The guy might've had a nine-inch cock, but he didn't have cast-iron balls. Surprise, shock and agony registered on Nine's bruised and swollen visage within the span of a microsecond. His hands veered outward and his gun went off.

"Fuck me!"

Conner leapt away from Martin, spewing a string of curses, telling Nine to watch it with that fucking gun. But Nine wasn't listening. He'd dropped the gun and was now cupping his bruised nuts, retching and coughing out anguished breaths, his black and blue face now turning bright crimson.

Martin felt the wetness on his neck before he felt the pain. He put his hand up to his ear, discovering he now was missing an earlobe.

"Holy shit." Never had he imagined — even in those years when he'd just come out and believed fag bashers lurked around every corner — that he'd ever get shot. It wasn't, in fact, until now that he considered the risk of kicking Nine's balls up into his throat. They obviously planned to kill him anyway, so what did he have to lose? Considering he only lost an earlobe, Martin hadn't lost much at all.

But he wasn't safe yet. His eyes went to Nine's gun, resting on the hardwood floor of the foyer. Unfortunately, Conner saw it, too. The two men scrambled for it, Conner pushing Martin down and out of the way. Martin recovered quickly, riding the crest of an adrenaline surge, and lunged for Conner just as he was wrapping his hand around the nine-millimeter's grip. They both fell to the floor in a heavy thud. Martin rolled on top of Conner and cuffed his hands around his former friend's wrists, struggling at once to keep Conner pinned to the floor and keep him from aiming the gun at his face.

The two men grunted and writhed, their faces contorted in expressions of extreme exertion. Their muscles were tense, bunched up in sharp relief beneath sweat-shiny skin. So far Martin was staying on top, but Conner was just as strong, and Martin had to use all his might to maintain his tenuous position of dominance. He straddled Conner's hips and pressed all his weight down, forcing Conner's hands down to the floor.

Martin felt something beneath him. His thinking clouded by panic, it took him a moment to realize what it was.

"You have a hard-on?"

Conner smacked his lips. "Wanna have some fun before we kill you? Just tell us where that Rand guy's at and that big cock's all yours, baby."

"You're incredible." Just as incredible was that for a flash of an instant — a moment he'd never admit aloud — Martin was tempted by the offer. Women were right: Men are so easy.

Martin didn't take Conner up on his offer, but it provided just enough diversion for Conner to overtake him, capitulating him onto the floor and climbing on top of him. In thirty seconds they'd traded positions, Conner on top of Martin, sitting on his chest, kneeling — painfully — on Martin's arms. Martin's eyes went first to the jutting tent between Conner's legs before confronting the gun pointed between his eyes.

"I've gotta hand it to you, Martin," Conner rasped, "I never thought you had it in you. Now, one more time: Where the fuck is Rand?"

A shot exploded through the air. Martin shuddered and closed his eyes tightly. He opened them a second later, amazed he could still do so.

The next sound heard was the sound of Nine's body hitting the floor.

"Here I am," Rand said from the stairs.

Conner was on his feet: "I fuckin' knew it!" He started to raise the nine-millimeter up toward Rand.

Martin pushed himself up off the floor, hoping he could tackle Conner before...

Another shot rang out.

"Mother *fuck*!"

The nine-millimeter clattered to the floor. Conner, holding his gut, stumbled backwards.

Rand finished descending the stairs. He was dressed now, holding a revolver, keeping it trained on Conner.

Conner came to a stop in the archway leading to the living room, resting his back against the doorjamb. "Motherfucker shot me," he gasped incredulously as he slid down to the floor.

"I think you'll live — for now," Martin said dryly before turning his attention to Rand. "Where did the gun come from?"

"You don't recognize it?"

"What do you mean...?" Then the realization came to him. The .45 revolver was given to him by his father nearly a decade ago, when he was living in the fringes of Midtown, then just beyond the reach of the area's gentrification. "Just 'cause you're queer don't mean you shouldn't protect yourself," his dad said, one of the few times he'd ever referenced his son's sexuality out loud. Martin tried to refuse the gift, but his father insisted. Martin took the gun to a firing range a few times and had shown it to a cop with whom he'd had a one-night-stand, but otherwise the gun stayed in a lockbox tucked away in his bedroom closet.

"When did you find that?"

"Does it matter?" Rand asked, standing before him now. "It saved your life."

"If only my father was alive. He'd be so proud," Martin said. "Now give it to me."

Rand put the gun in his hand. "What're you going to do?"

Martin ignored the question. "Do you have any money?"

"Huh? I — forty dollars, I think. Why?"

"My wallet's on top of the dresser. Go upstairs and get it."

Rand charged back upstairs and Martin turned to check on the carnage now littering the foyer. Conner remained slumped against the doorjamb in the living room entrance, hands still pressed against his gut, his yellow tank top darkened by a red stain spreading across his midsection. His tan face now looked sickly, and his breathing was labored. Their eyes met, and Martin quickly looked away. Nine lay sprawled out before the front door, a pool of blood oozing beneath his head. There was a glistening red hole where his throat had been, and Martin had to turn away lest he puke. Nine would not be wielding his nine-millimeter gun or his nine-inch cock ever again.

"Here you go," Rand said, bounding down the stairs, holding Martin's wallet out to him.

He took the wallet from Rand and, still holding the .45, opened the wallet and thumbed through the cash inside.

"Here, take it," he said, plucking the bills from the wallet and handing them to Rand. "It's not much, but it'll help. And take this, too." Martin pulled out a MasterCard. "There's a Greyhound station about three miles from here, on Commerce Drive." Hastily, he gave Rand directions there from his house. "Use that card to get a ticket, I don't care where. Back to L.A., it doesn't matter. Then get rid of it. In twenty-four hours, I'm going to report it as stolen."

Rand turned the card over in his hand. "But what about...?"

"I'll take care of it," Martin said forcefully. "No get your ass out of here."

Their eyes met. Rand's were red and framed with tears. "I..."

Suddenly Rand was in his arms. Their lips pressed together, their tongues probing. They held each other so tight Martin thought their bodies might fuse together. He felt a rush of an emotion he hadn't felt in some time. That's when he felt his own tears spill down his cheeks.

Martin pushed Rand off him. He'd dropped his wallet when they embraced and now he stooped to pull something else from it. "One more thing," Martin said as he stood up, "I want you to call me when you get to wherever you're going."

He handed Rand his business card.

"Use my cell phone number," Martin added.

Rand stuffed the cash, credit card and business card into his front pocket and threw his arms around Martin. "Thank you," he whispered.

"Go," Martin said, the command sounding more like a sob than an order.

An eternity later, he heard the front door slamming shut behind Rand.

"That was beautiful, a moment made for the Lifetime channel. If I weren't so busy holding my guts in I'd applaud."

The sound of Conner's voice dried Martin's tears instantly. He turned and pointed his gun at the man he thought was his friend. "Why?"

"Why what?"

"Why were you fucking trying to kill me, for starters? Why was Rand so important? Just what the hell was this all about?"

An ugly smile crossed Conner's handsome face. "You want me to sum it all up for you, Martin? Like they do at the end of a TV cop show? Shit, that's stuff I wouldn't tell the police, why would I tell you?"

"'Cause I got a gun aimed at you."

"Like you'd use it," Conner snarled.

"Are you sure? I've surprised you before." Martin cocked the revolver and took a step in his direction. "How do — did — you know Nine?"

Conner took a deep breath, grimaced from the pain then let out a sigh. "We used to work together in California, at this cheesy club called Scandals," he began. "I'd been fired from my advertising job and was bartending for a while ... used to do it in college ... 'til I found something else. Nick ... he wasn't Nine then, not yet ... he was a bouncer/doorman. He wasn't as beefy as they liked their bouncers, but he'd just gotten out of prison so they figured he was tough enough for the job. There was one guy who came in the club all the time, with poofy blond hair and wearing all these rings n' shit ... a real queen but he had great blow. He wanted to take care of his former business partner and wanted to know if I knew anyone who could do the job. That's when I thought of Nick.

"We formed a partnership, of sorts. I'd send him referrals and get a small percentage of his fee. I got a job a few months later with this small PR outfit in Burbank. Nick thought I'd have trouble

Jonathan Asche

drumming up business for him then, but he didn't realize I'd run into more scum in an office than we ever thought about meeting at a second rate queer bar. Of course, you already knew that, didn't you, Martin?"

"Is that how you guys got involved with Dane Kensington?" Martin asked. "When you were out in L.A.?"

"Hell, I never met the guy. That was strictly Nine's gig, sort of. Ended up relating to one I set up here."

"Why did you come to Atlanta?"

"No one suspected anything in L.A. until about a year ago, when one of our clients cracked under pressure and pointed the cops in my direction. He's an ex-client now, Nine saw to that. While the cops were busy with the disappearance of their lead witness/suspect, I thought it would be a good time to change my name and my location. Figured if Atlanta was good enough for Whitney and Bobby, it was good enough from me." Conner chuckled, his laughter quickly becoming a groan of pain.

Martin said, "So you never were in Memphis."

"Yeah, I lied on my resumé, too. What can I say? I'm a bad guy."

"So why did Nine kill Task? Why did you guys want to kill Rand?"

Conner said, "Yeah, that was kinda' funny. See, I initially got Nine this gig in Miami. I put him onto the lover of one of my PR clients..."

"Perry Snopes," Martin whispered.

"You get an 'A' in math. Yep, that was our deal, though Nine actually set it up. I just suggested he corner Perry's pathetic actor husband. But see, that one didn't quite go as planned; Nine follows Mr. Perry Snopes, self-proclaimed shining example of Gay Monogamy, to a nightclub and watches him leave with two hustlers. Care to guess who those two hustlers were?"

The names leaked out of Martin's lips. "Rand and Task."

"The man gets another 'A.' Yep, the same. Hope knowing that doesn't spoil your wedding plans. So, Nine follows our upstanding politician to this second-rate motel and waits for the hustlers to do their thing and leave so he can do his thing. After they leave, Nine here goes up to the room only to find Snopes' brains splattered all over the wall. No problem, it's an easy twenty-five grand. Except," Conner continued, "cops find a video camera on the scene, but no tape. So now we need to find those hustlers and that tape before our client finds out it wasn't Nine here that took care of his troubled relationship. What we thought was an easy job turns out to be a huge pain in the ass. That's when Providence intervened."

"How so?"

"Hey, if you don't mind, could you drop the *Murder, She Wrote* bit and just call fucking nine-one-one?" Conner sniped weakly. "I'm losing a lot of blood."

"As soon as you tell me what you mean, 'Providence intervened'?"

Conner made an exasperated noise and said, "Nine gets this call from Dane Kensington, wanting to meet about a problem he has, says he'll meet him in Atlanta. When they meet, Kensington tells him about how he had this scheme to blackmail Perry Snopes, get him to drop out of the city council race so The Tackle Box, which he owns, can operate in peace. But the dumb bastards up and killed him and Dane wanted Task and Rand out of the picture before anything could get traced back to him, and before anyone could get the goddamned video tape. By the way, you wouldn't happen to know where that tape got off to, would you? Not that it matters now..."

"No clue," Martin said. "So you just needed to kill me because..."

"Jesus Christ, do I have to spell the whole thing out? You were in the way, that's all. Nothing personal. You'd be out of it completely if you'd not gone after the little fucker when he left you. Now could you call an ambulance now? I really..." Conner was interrupted by a spasm of coughing "...really need to get to a hospital."

"Yeah, sure. I'll call now," Martin said. He started to back away, but then stopped suddenly. "One more thing."

"What the fuck now?" Conner whined.

Martin squeezed the trigger.

Conner attempted to speak, but the bullet ripping through his heart stopped his last words from ever being uttered. His face was a mask of surprise, going slack as his head fell forward, his chin resting on his open, bleeding chest.

Martin went into the kitchen, got a dishtowel and returned to the foyer. Using the towel he picked up the nine-millimeter and went over to Conner's lifeless body. He'd never touched a dead body before and tried not to think about it now as he put Nine's gun in Conner's hand, curling the still-warm fingers around the grip. Instead, Martin thought about what he'd tell the police when they arrived.

When he was sure he'd arranged everything properly, he returned to the kitchen to call 911.

THIRTY-FOUR

Winston tightened his grip on the sheets and gritted his teeth, the feeling almost too much to bear.

He'd been dealing with Perry's death for a week, but now, a day after his funeral, with the house empty of family and friends expressing their condolences, Winston was faced with life alone. Eyes closed tight, he shook his head from side to side. "Oh, God, oh God," he whimpered. He inhaled sharply, the air hissing against his teeth. A tear leaked out of his left eye, rolled down his face and seeped into the pillowcase.

The feeling became more intense, and Winston moaned louder.

Good-bye, Perry Snopes.

He opened his eyes. Between his spread thighs, peeking over his tight nut-sack and stiff cock, were the pale blue, heavy-lidded eyes of Edward, one of the employees of Schackelford & Sons Funeral Home.

Hello, freedom!

Winston was free of more than just Perry. Nine also was gone, killed by some guy in Decatur. He'd almost overlooked the story in the Sunday edition of the *Atlanta Journal Constitution*, wouldn't have noticed it at all if it weren't for the subhead: *Possibly linked to pornographer shooting.* Now that had been something, the murder of Dane Kensington and some other guy — Winston didn't remember the name, but the paper said the guy was from California — during his party (the paper didn't call it what it was, an orgy) at the Wilkes Overlook penthouse suite. Even the Log Cabin Republicans at Perry's funeral were talking about it. Nine (Nicholas Carpetti, a.k.a. Nine, was how he was identified in the paper) was allegedly shot in self-defense by Martin Richter, according to the article in Sunday's paper. Conner was killed, too, only Conner was an alias, police said; his real name was James Kledson. Winston scanned the rest of the article to see if there was any mention of Nick "Nine" Carpetti being linked to Perry's murder. Finding no reference to his late lover, Winston moved on to the paper's entertainment section.

No more Perry, no more Nine and no suspicions linking the two. It was enough to make him forget his anger over his car being stolen. A shame that Conner — or James, or whomever he really was — got killed, too. Not really a nice person, but he was a hot fuck. Well, there would be others, Winston reasoned.

And then he got a call from Edward, wanting to know how he was holding up. Winston sighed into the phone, fingers toying with one of his nipples as he thought of how sweet Edward had been at the funeral home, and how well he filled out his charcoal gray suit. "Okay, but I'd feel better with some company," he said wistfully. Edward said he was off work and could come over that afternoon if Winston would like. Winston said he would like.

Truth be told, Edward didn't have the most attractive of faces, his crooked nose, slight overbite and weak chin making him appear a bit of a country bumpkin in Winston's eyes (the thick Southern accent didn't help). The body, however, was solid, as was Edward's cock, and, God-almighty-damn, could the guy eat ass!

Edward's tongue twirled inside his asshole. "Oh, God!" Winston wailed again.

Edward wagged his face back and forth between Winston's splayed butt, a pig at the trough. He raised Winston's ass further in the air as his tongue simultaneously dug deeper into his chute. All Winston could do was cross his feet behind Edward's head and hold on for dear life. Pre-cum dripped onto his belly and collected in his navel, and his balls had drawn up so tightly they'd practically retracted back into his body. He knew if he touched his swollen, seeping cock like he so desperately wanted to do, he'd pop his load in three seconds.

He gathered up another few folds of the sheet, pulling one of the corners free from the mattress.

"Fuck me," Winston panted. "Oh, God, fuck me now."

Edward didn't respond to the request right away, having too much fun fucking Winston with his tongue. That tongue then left Winston's quivering sphincter, washing over his balls and sweeping up his pulsing shaft. Edward licked his cockhead just long enough to make him shudder, then his tongue continued traveling up Winston's torso, pausing along the way to slurp the pre-cum out of his navel.

"Oh, Jesus, I don't know if I can stand this!" Winston cried.

Edward silenced him with a savage kiss, rubbing his cock against Winston's butthole while his tongue darted between his lips. Winston tasted his own juices on his trick's tongue, and on his face smelled the heady blend of florid cologne and his own sweaty stink. He dug his fingers into Edward's muscular back and moved beneath him, hoping he could hold off cumming until Edward entered him.

"Where're your rubbers," Edward drawled, pushing himself up from Winston's heaving body.

Winston pointed with his left hand. "Table ... cabinet," he babbled, too horny to form complete sentences.

"So how ya' want it?" Edward asked a couple minutes later, holding his lubed and sheathed prick in his hand. "From the front, from behind? Maybe sit on it? How's 'bout all of the above?"

"Oh, baby, I don't think I can last that long," Winston said, the Georgia twang he'd worked so hard to get rid of creeping back into his voice. "Just fuck me."

Edward grabbed his thighs. "From the front, then. I like to see guys faces when I fuck 'em."

He closed his eyes as Edward slid his fat rod into his hole, going in a bit more easily than he expected. (Then again, he had gotten fucked more in the past week than he had the entire three months preceding Perry's death). Fortunately, his ass muscles made up for the fact that his sphincter wasn't exactly virgin-tight, squeezing Edward's cock as it burrowed deep into his chute. Edward rolled his hips, and Winston wiggled his, the movement of Edward's dick inside him eliciting long, loud moans.

Edward leaned down for a kiss — a lick, actually, running his tongue along Winston's lower lip before pulling away. Winston circled his hands around Edward's waist, using the other man's body as leverage as he raised his hips off the bed to meet Edward's probing cock. His own prick pressed against Edward's granite abs, the friction hot and electric. Their bodies worked against each other, Edward pushing down and Winston pushing back. Winston undulated his hips, his weeping cock scrubbing Edward's washboard abs, his ass squeezing Edward's dong as it plunged inside him. Their grunts and groans got louder, their movements forceful and jerky, as if they weren't quite in control of their own bodies. Winston heard a distant pounding, drummed out by his own harsh breath.

In one hot rush he came, his gooey load getting smeared around like mayonnaise on bread from Edward's thrashing on top of him.

Edward leaned back, so he was sitting on his haunches, and Winston saw the wet glaze of his own jizz streaking his trick's rigid abdomen. "Aw, yeah," he breathed, giving Winston his lopsided smile that didn't seem to involve his lips turning upwards so much as it did his face attempting to turn itself sideways. He clamped his hands onto Winston's thighs and began pumping his ass in fast, hard thrusts, his fingers biting into Winston's flesh the harder he fucked him. He groaned and hollered while stuffing Winston's hole, but suddenly went silent when he shot his load, as if cumming knocked the wind out of him.

The distant pounding was heard again, only it didn't seem as distant now. It certainly seemed louder.

"Sounds like ya' got company," Edward said, his fingers caressing Winston's balls.

Dammit, he needed to get that front doorbell fixed. "Maybe if we ignore it they'll go away." Winston wondered if he'd locked the door after letting Edward in.

Whoever was at the door pounded again, calling out as they did so. From the upstairs bedroom Winston couldn't make out what was said, but he heard one word distinctly.

"Did he say 'police'?"

"Sounded like," Edward concurred, concentrating on pulling his dick out of Winston's ass without the condom slipping off.

Winston felt as if his heart had just taken a ten-story drop into his stomach. "I can't imagine what they'd want," he said, still lying on the bed, hoping he didn't look as ill as he felt.

Edward stood up. His cock was at half-mast, the end of rubber sagging from the weight of his load. "Why don'tcha go down an' see. You said yer car got stolen the other night, right? Maybe they found it."

Winston sat up slowly. "Yes, maybe that's it." He hoped to God that was it!

He slipped on a pair of gym shorts and went downstairs. Upon opening the front door Winston saw two men crossing the front yard, heading for a blue Crown Victoria parked at the curb. "There he is," said one, a tall, lanky guy, wearing a brown sport coat. His partner — older, shorter, wider and wearing a hideous melon-colored blazer — turned and looked back at Winston, his eyes like those of an iguana. The older guy pursed his lips and headed back toward the house, his partner following closely behind.

"You Winston LaGrabe?" asked the older guy as he started up the front steps.

"Yes?"

"I'm Detective Meyers, with the Atlanta Police Department."

The lanky guy appeared beside Myers and held out his hand. "I'm Detective Shawn Creighton. We'd about given up on you."

Creighton was actually quite attractive, with a lot more muscle on his gangly frame than Winston first thought.

"I was... taking a nap," Winston said, wondering if he'd wiped all the spooge and lube from his hand as he shook Creighton's.

There was nothing cute about Meyers. "Mind if we come in?" he asked, his voice a tobacco cured rumble. "It's a sauna out here."

"Um, what's this about?"

"Just a few questions," Creighton said, offering a quick smile. "Please?"

Winston wanted to refuse, insist they get a warrant or that he didn't want to talk without a lawyer present. *Yeah, and while they're getting that warrant I can get the word "guilty" tattooed on my forehead.* Best thing to do was cooperate. He opened the door wider and stepped aside, gesturing for the detectives to enter. He hoped like hell Edward kept quiet upstairs.

He guided them to the living room, offering them something to drink knowing they'd probably refuse (they did). Winston sat on the sofa and Creighton sat in an ornate armchair across from him. Meyers remained standing. All three men looked out of place amongst the frilly antiques and Baroque artwork. Winston couldn't wait to unload all this old lady shit and get some furniture from the current decade.

After a few stilted pleasantries about the unbearable summer heat and the niceness of the house, Creighton said, "We believe we found your car."

Winston brought a hand to his chest and let out a relieved breath. "Oh, wonderful! Was it in one piece?" He was still hoping he could get some insurance money out of it, maybe get a Z3 or perhaps an SUV, like a Lincoln Navigator or Cadillac Escalade.

"Want to know where we found it?" Creighton asked, ignoring Winston's question.

"The Wilkes Overlook Hotel parking garage," Meyers said.

"Okay." Winston didn't see the significance but didn't like Meyers' tone.

"Place has been in the news a lot past few days," Creighton said.

Winston tilted his head, giving the detective a quizzical look. He could win an Emmy for playing dumb.

"Two murders? A queer — *gay* sex party? You had to have heard about it," Meyers said. "The TV news has been all over it."

"Oh, right," Winston nodded. "You'll have to forgive me. My partner's funeral was this weekend. I've been a bit ... pre-occupied."

Creighton nodded. "I can imagine, losing a loved one and your car getting stolen, both in the span of a week."

"Whose car is that outside?" Meyers asked, hands in his pockets, eyes focused on the painting over the fireplace. "Didn't look like a rental."

"Uh, it's a friend's car."

"That friend here now?"

Winston's nerves stretched tighter. "Oh, no. He's just letting me borrow it for a few days."

"Nice of him," Creighton observed.

Meyers turned away from the painting. "So you're here by yourself?" His iguana eyes bore down on Winston.

Winston dropped his gaze to his lap. "Of course," he said, pulling at the hem of his gym shorts.

Creighton, in his role as the good cop, nodded like he believed him. "Do you happen to know a Nicholas Carpetti?"

Winston's insides began disintegrating. "Who?"

"Maybe you know him better as 'Nine.'" Meyers suggested.

"Why... why would I know him?"

"I don't know. Why would you? Why would your number be programmed onto his cell phone?"

Winston's lower lip started to quiver. "Excuse me?"

"This Nine guy was killed Saturday, at a guy's house in Decatur," Meyers continued. "Guy said he shot him in self defense, which may or may not be true — I don't care, that's not my case. But when the Decatur detectives found your number on his cell phone they were nice enough to give us a call. You know what else they found out?"

This can't be happening!

"Found out Nine was wanted for questioning back in California regarding a couple murder-for-hire schemes. Your boyfriend was murdered, wasn't he? Shot while staying in Miami, while you're here by your lonesome in Atlanta? And here your number turns up on this suspected hit man's cell phone. Awful lot of coincidences there, don't you think?"

Winston kept his eyes on his lap, his knees pressed tightly together to keep them from shaking. The detectives waited for him to say something, waited until the silence in the house became heavy and oppressive. When Winston finally spoke, his voice was soft and reedy. "I think... I think I should get..."

Upstairs, a toilet flushed.

Meyers' iguana eyes widened. "Alone, huh?"

"I need to get a lawyer," Winston croaked.

Creighton said, "Yeah, you do."

EPILOGUE

One Month Later

He stood beneath the security lamp, holding the business card in one hand and the borrowed cell phone in the other, dialing with his thumb. A cool breeze blew through the alley, A cool breeze blew through the alley, making him wish he had a jacket. He put the phone to his ear and listened to it ring on the other end. He shivered and brought an arm across his chest, and it had nothing to do with the chilly breeze.

The phone rang five times before an annoyed voice said hello.

"Martin?"

"Yeah?"

"It's Rand."

"Hey!" Enthusiastic now. "I've been waiting to hear from you. Kind of wished it wasn't in the middle of the night, but still..."

"Oh, yeah, forgot the time difference. It's almost nine o'clock here."

"And where's 'here'?" Martin asked.

"San Francisco."

"L.A. wasn't expensive enough for you?"

Rand chuckled and kicked the pavement. Standing across the alley, about ten feet away, a couple of guys — both in their mid-thirties, both with goatees, one guy Latin-looking — laughed as they passed a joint back and forth. The Latin guy wore a flannel shirt, unbuttoned in the front, exposing his tan torso. The other guy wore a black tank top, showing off arms that were all tattoos and muscle. Neither seemed bothered by the breeze.

Rand looked at the men and said into the phone, "I'm getting by."

"Doing what?"

"Working at this coffee shop in the Castro," he said. "Doesn't pay for shit, but it's a start."

"You're not hustling, are you?"

"No Dad, I'm being good." He changed the subject. "What about you? How'd things go after I left?"

"You haven't seen the papers?"

"Not much of a reader. 'Sides, the papers out here are more into the death of Dane Kensington, Gay Porn King. One fag rag actually called him a porn legend. I saw one article something about that Nine guy, getting killed, but the cops weren't sure if it was related."

"I was arrested ... after a trip to the ER to get my ear looked at ... fingerprinted, jailed, all of it. Want to know who I first thought of calling to bail me out? Conner. Habit, I guess. I got another friend to get me out, and then I got a lawyer. Luckily, they ruled it as self-defense. I don't think the cops investigating it believed me entirely; didn't help that my neighbor said she saw you leaving my house."

"Oh, shit."

"Yeah, exactly. But lucky for us, she's in the early stages of Alzheimer's. She changed her description of you three times, one of those times saying it was a girl who left my house." Martin said. "Another time, the cops talked to her she couldn't remember the day she saw you."

"But they dropped it?" One of the men across the alley — the Latin guy in the flannel shirt — looked at Rand and smiled.

"They did. I mean, I wasn't lying completely ... that Nine fucker did shoot off my earlobe. And when they found a link between him and that Snopes killing..."

"What?"

"Yeah, it seems Conner — not his real name, by the way — sent Nine to Perry's lover, convincing the lover to pay I-don't-know-how-much to kill off his husband. They charged the lover, a has-been actor named Winston LaSomething, about three days after Perry's funeral. Media here's going apeshit over it."

"Holy shit."

"And," Martin continued, "ballistic tests showed the bullets that killed Task and Dane were the same ones belonging to the nine-millimeter Conner was holding when they found his body. I guess the cops figured I was doing them a favor and agreed it was self-defense."

"Conner had the nine-millimeter?"

"When the cops found him, yes."

Rand didn't press for details. "So now...?"

"Now, what?"

"What else are you up to?"

"Working my ass off for one thing. I thought I'd get fired because... well, because I got arrested. Even if you're innocent, employers don't like that sort of thing, especially if it's in connection with something splashed all over the papers. But whom do they turn most of Conner's clients over to? Me. Plus, I'm a minor celebrity now. People are calling up requesting I handle their advertising campaign. Shit, I almost *wish* they fired me."

From the brick building behind Rand a black, steel door opened and a dark-haired man with a stubble-shaded face poked his head out. "Guys, we're about set up."

Rand said, "I gotta get back to work."

"Stuck on the evening shift, huh?" Martin said. "They always give the newbies the shitty hours."

The older guys crossed the alley, heading for the door. The

tattooed guy in the black tank top paused, looking at Rand. "Um, Martin?"

"Yeah?"

"Just wanted to say I... um, I..."

Martin broke in. "I know."

The tide of emotion receded. The tattooed guy was waiting. "I really need to go now."

"I understand. Just one quick question, though, while I'm thinking of it. That videotape you had of... from Miami? What happened to it?"

Rand answered with the truth, "I have no idea."

Martin started to ask another question, but he cut him off. "I really got to go now. I'll call you again later. Love ya'." Rand disconnected before he could hear Martin say goodbye.

The tattooed guy was grinning at him. "Awww, ain't that sweet." He looked menacing, but had the voice of a show tune lovin' queen.

Rand held the cell phone out to him. "Thanks for letting me borrow it, Mike."

"Anytime, hon'," Mike said, taking the phone. He held the door open for Rand, patting his ass as he stepped past him.

Inside, he saw the stubble-faced guy again, standing in a doorway holding a gallon-sized bottle of lube and talking to the Latin guy who was out in the alley earlier. In the studio beyond the doorway lights were being adjusted, orders being barked. Someone said, "Could we move that cage over to the left?"

When stubble face saw Rand he said, "Hurry up and get ready! We want to start shooting in five."

"Okay, okay." Rand didn't see the hurry. They'd been waiting around for two hours; what were a few minutes more?

A tall man with a goatee — almost every other guy here had a goatee — slid an arm around his shoulder. "Hey, doll, need some help?"

The guy's name was Brady, but he was better known as Kit Reed, three-time Grabby winner. Rand looked up at him. He was a good foot shorter than Brady, a.k.a. Kit. "What, taking off my clothes?"

"There's more than just taking off your clothes, you know that," Brady scolded, guiding Rand into narrow room that served as both a lounge and dressing room. "I assume you've douched?"

Rand rolled his eyes. "Yeah, like when I first got here." He pulled off his shirt.

"Good boy." Brady sat down in an armchair the color of a mustard stain. "Now let's get that hot cock ready for its big debut."

Rand unbuttoned and unzipped, and Brady took over from there. He watched his dick slide into the other man's mouth — a mouth that had been awarded for sucking dicks — but felt no arousal. Brady paused and looked up at him, holding Rand's limp, saliva-covered cock in his hand. "You nervous?"

"Maybe a little," Rand admitted.

"Just relax," Brady said, his voice soothing. "Relax and enjoy it."

Brady went back to work, slurping on Rand's cock and fondling his balls. Rand got a flash of Martin, on his knees in the parking garage, swallowing his prick. Afraid of getting caught but more scared of not giving Rand what he wanted.

That's when his cock started to stiffen.

* * * * *

The reading lamp over the headboard had been switched on when Martin returned to the bedroom.

"Sorry, I was hoping that didn't wake you," Martin said, setting his phone down on the bedside table, next to his watch.

A voice with an almost musical accent asked, "Who was it? Your young friend?"

Martin started to chuckle, but it came out his nose as a harsh snort. "Yeah, my 'young friend.' He's in San Francisco now. Didn't consider the time change." It was after midnight in Atlanta.

"So he's all right?"

The accent, Martin had learned, was French Canadian. "Like you care?"

"I care if you care."

Martin shrugged and pulled back the covers. "He says he's doing okay," he said, sitting down on the bed, much lower to the floor than his own. "But he said a lot of things in the past that weren't true. I'm just going to hope he wasn't lying this time."

Arno's hand found his thigh. "You miss him?"

His touch sent a current up Martin's leg, right to his groin. Hanging on the wall across the room was a painting of a nude man, reclining by the pool, his dick soft but a good size, Martin liking the way the head rested on the guy's thigh. "Well, yeah, I guess," he said, eyes focused on the painting.

"Miss the sex, maybe?" Arno teased, his hand gliding further up Martin's naked thigh, making his cock twitch. "Miss fucking that hot, young ass?" Arno said it like "hot, yong awz."

Martin looked over at Arno, his mouth twisted into a playful grin. The grin was familiar to Martin now, having been seeing it for the past three weeks, ever since Arno gave him a call, and he heard that unmistakable voice say, "Remember me?" Said he was afraid

Martin got away. "Good thing your picture was in the paper and on TV."

"Oh, yeah, being in the spotlight's been great," Martin laughed. "Hearing from you, though, is good."

And now here he was in Arno's apartment, a place near the Georgia Tech campus, with its low-to-the-ground bed and erotic artwork, for the fourth night this week, and Arno was giving him that playful grin — again. The grin, Martin quickly learned, was almost always a prelude to a fuck.

"You know what?" Martin threw the covers back, exposing the Frenchman's nude body. Arno's pierced cock was already three-quarters hard. "I think I like this a lot better."

Arno started to say something, but Martin's hot tongue blocked the words. Martin rolled on top of him, his body fitting neatly between Arno's spread thighs. Arno cupped one hand behind Martin's head and clamped the other on his bicep while Martin's tongue slid deeper into his mouth. Heat buzzed between their bodies, generated by their now-fully erect pricks. Martin rocked his hips, rubbing against Arno's cock, his own cockhead butting against the silver ring looped through his new lover's dong. A purr vibrated in Arno's chest, and the hand that cupped the back of Martin's head slid down his spine, making a beeline for his ass.

Martin's mouth moved to the side of Arno's neck. Between nibbles he growled nasty thoughts as Arno's fingers slid between his butt-crack and jabbed his hole. Then Arno brought his legs up and Martin's cock was sandwiched between his splayed cheeks, rubbing against the asshole he'd plowed into only hours ago.

"I wanna suck you," Arno breathed, the swivel of his hips igniting a tingling pleasure that rode the length of Martin's cock.

Martin toyed with one of Arno's nipple rings. "Yeah?" he panted. "You don't want me to fuck you again?"

"I want to taste you."

"Then, by all means."

He straddled Arno's chest and leaned forward, placing his palms against the wall behind the bed, facing a Tom of Finland print, staring at a square-jawed leather daddy with an improbably huge cock while feeding his more proportionate member into Arno's mouth. Then he saw nothing, blinded by the rush of ecstasy stirred by Arno's talented tongue.

With Martin's cock buried in his gullet, Arno slipped a couple spit-lubed fingers up his ass and rubbed Martin's prostate. Martin hissed and grunted, his hips jerking up and down. He closed his eyes tight and saw Rand on that first night he brought him home, when he insisted he sleep on the couch. He saw him with his smooth ass up in the air, lit from the blue-white glow of the television, fingering his hole, knowing Martin was watching. His memory hopped forward, to the last time Martin saw Rand's face, just before he stepped out his front door. In that single last glance, he saw beyond the beauty of his features, struck more by his eyes, brimming with sadness and gratitude and possibly something more.

He cried out and opened his eyes in time to see his load spew into Arno's open mouth and splatter his face. He saw his French-Canadian stud smile up at him as he squeezed the final drops of jizz from Martin's cock, catching them on his tongue and swallowing them greedily.

He no longer saw Rand.

* * * * *

Charles Hadley stood at the dining room window and watched from behind shear curtains as his wife, accompanied by his perpetually smirking sister-in-law, backed her Lexus RX 300 out of the driveway and headed out of their Alpharetta neighborhood. Then he waited, making sure a good fifteen minutes went by in case they had to come back because they forgot something. That happened once, and he almost didn't make it into the bathroom in time before his wife opened the bedroom door.

He went out to the garage, opened his toolbox — a Christmas present from his wife, even though they hired a handyman to take care of all household repairs — and removed the videotape from it. The tape was a mini-DV made for a camcorder. Charles had it for a month, finding it in that bag that hustler left in his SUV. Charles kept the tape and tossed the bag into a dumpster behind a Circle K. His fingers still tingled holding it.

Upstairs in the bedroom Charles got his camcorder out of the closet, plugged it up to the bedroom TV and slipped the tape into the video camera. He turned on the TV and hurriedly pulled off his clothes. Christ, he was getting hard just thinking about watching it. He got his wife's bottle of cocoa butter lotion, set it on the nightstand and lay down on the bed, pillows propping up his back, only to get up again when he realized the remote wouldn't operate the camcorder. With the "play" button hit on the camcorder, Charles settled back onto the bed, his hand fondling his cock in anticipation.

Static filled the screen, and then, abruptly, he saw that blond hustler from that porno store on Cheshire Bridge. The hustler was on his knees in front of some guy, seen only from the waist down, holding the guy's dick in his hand. A dark, blurry shape curved around the bottom left corner of the screen, like something was in the way of the camera lens, but you could still see most of what was going on. The hustler slid the guy's cock into his mouth, and Charles Hadley's own prick snapped to attention. He pumped some of the sweet-smelling cocoa butter lotion into his hand and started stroking.

The guy getting blown by the hustler swung a hand into view, revealing part of a tattooed forearm. There was sound, but it was muffled, like pressing your ear up to someone's door, and Charles couldn't understand what they were saying. Didn't matter what they said, watching the cute hustler suck that mystery dick and remembering how good it felt, getting blown by the guy a month ago was enough. Charles thought of that hot mouth and stroked his cock at a faster pace.

A flash of static and then the scene changed: three guys, clothed, only visible from their waists to their knees, all the really sexy stuff happening out of camera range. Didn't have to wait long for the clothes to come off, though, and for the guys to fall onto the bed. It was the hustler and another young guy — probably the same guy getting sucked off earlier, judging by the tattoos. The third guy was older, about Charles' age, it looked like, and still looking pretty damned good (for a fleeting moment Charles reminded himself he needed to be using his gym membership more frequently than he had been). The guys moved about the bed, but the camera stayed in one place, recording it all from a set distance. There were no close-ups of mouths swallowing cocks or tongues flicking assholes, but somehow it seemed so much hotter, it being "real" guys instead of porn stars. The guy with the tattoos (he also had blond hair and a dark goatee) was sucking the older guy's cock; the older guy — who looked vaguely familiar, though Charles didn't know why — was slurping on the cute hustler's dong.

Jesus, if that was me... Charles vowed that next business trip he was going to splurge on two hustlers, hoping the opportunity presented itself soon.

The older guy was eating the hustler's ass. Couldn't see it in detail but you knew what he was doing. Charles licked his lips and briefly closed his eyes, imagining it was his tongue up the guy's butt, not sure if he'd ever do such a thing if he had the chance. He couldn't take a sip from another person's glass; licking a guy's butthole seemed out of the question, but it was still exciting to watch.

He was getting close to cumming now and had to force himself to control his frenetic strokes, keeping his hand still but holding his throbbing dick.

The two younger guys on the video were working on the older guy's cock, their heads kind of obscuring the action. Then the hustler — Charles thought of him as *his* hustler — got on all fours and was fucked by the older guy. The guy with the tattoos was underneath the cute hustler getting fucked, the guys in a sixty-nine while the older guy rammed Charles's hustler. Charles's hand started moving up and down his cocoa-buttered shaft once again. How the fuck could he *not* jack off to what he was seeing?

The guys on screen changed their position, Charles's hustler on his back now, legs curled up into the air, the older guy fucking him while the tattooed guy kneeled next to them, pulling on his cock. His favorite part was fast approaching, and the sensation humming through his dick intensified in anticipation. The tattooed guy with the goatee grabbed his hustler's stiff pole, stroking it and saying something barely decipherable above the muffled hiss of the video's soundtrack. Charles could only make out the words "want," "cum" and "face."

Then his hustler moaned and his body jerked. Even though the picture was grainy and the color a bit flat, the hustler's cumshot was plain as day, splashing down on his muscular pecs. The tattooed guy reached down and scooped up the jizz off the cute hustler's chest and fed him his own load. Seeing that caused Charles's balls to draw up.

But the part that really got to him — the part that made him shoot the single other time Charles had watched the video — was next. The tattooed guy rose up on his knees and started jerking off at a frenzied pace, much like Charles was now. The tattooed guy groaned loudly, thrust his hips forward and covered the hustler's face with cum. Seeing that brought Charles to a level of arousal that equaled the intensity of his first time with a guy, when he was a junior in high school and his pal Lee, on the track team, said he'd suck Charles's dick if he promised not to tell anyone. He tried to prolong the moment by thinking of his wife, but her upturned nose and highlighted hair were quickly pushed out of his mind by the mental replay of the hustler getting fed his own jism and then getting a facial.

Charles's body shook convulsively, his orgasm ricocheting through him like a pinball before firing out his cock, a big creamy eruption.

His first impulse after cumming was to immediately eliminate any possible evidence. There were murderers who covered their crime scenes with less care. Charles would clean up — take a shower, even, if there was time — and make sure his wife's lotion was returned to the bathroom (that almost gave him away one time, his wife wanting to know why the bottle of lotion was on his nightstand). First and foremost, though, the tape was rewound and rushed back to its hiding place. Charles's biggest fear was he'd forget to take the tape — or the DVD's he sometimes rented — out of the player and it be discovered by his wife or, even worse, one of his kids.

But he stayed put this time, knowing he had the house to himself for the entire day, his wife off shopping; his son, a college junior someplace in the Caribbean, working his summer job on a cruise ship; and his daughter, still in high school, on some church youth group trip to Disney World. He could relax.

Charles spent his post-orgasmic daze swirling a finger through the slimy puddles of spunk that dotted this belly. His cock was still hard, his erection just beginning to fade. Maybe, he thought, he'd watch the tape again. He then realized the tape was still playing and turned his attention from his dick to the TV screen. There could be more raunchy action, and he'd never bothered to check it out.

There was only one of them on the bed now, the older guy, lying down on his stomach, resting on his elbows. Damn, he looked familiar, and Charles tried again to place the guy. On screen, the older guy was looking at something to his right, out of camera range, an expression on his face like he just smelled shit. He turned and looked directly into the camera, looking bored now. His bored expression became one of perplexion. His brow furrowed, the older guy swung his legs over the side of the bed and sat up.

Perry Snopes, that's who that was. Charles remembered seeing his picture several times this month, in local news broadcasts and in the *Atlanta Journal Constitution.*

"What's this?" Perry said, moving closer to the camera lens now. The room behind him disappeared, and all Charles saw on screen was his flaccid cock getting closer.

His hand reached forward and the picture shook, Perry's crotch getting closer in a clumsy zoom. He turned, light pushing past his stomach and showing his dick in silhouette (even looks good soft, Charles thought). Something else was said and a noise — sharper than a "thwack," not as crisp as a slap — cut through the tape's blurry sound. Perry crumpled to the floor out of camera range.

Charles Hadley sat up in bed and leaned forward, closer to the TV screen. Another figure came into view — his hustler, he assumed; just got a view of him from thighs to belly, but there were no tattoos and the guy had a towel around his waist. An argument ensued, the hustler yelling while the tattooed guy, partially in view now, tried to calm him down. Charles couldn't understand most of what they were saying, but the word "fuck" was used repeatedly.

His hustler darted out of view, and the tattooed guy called after him, then stopped, backing up. Charles thought he heard him say, "Put that down," but wasn't sure. He said something else, raising his voice this time. There was more movement, Perry Snopes getting to his feet, wobbling like he was drunk. Talking like it, too.

Perry lunged for the tattooed guy, the two guys pushing against each other, moving back and forth in front of the camera's unblinking eye.

The pop that sounded was unmistakable, even with the tape's shitty sound.

The tattooed guy hopped backwards, cursing. Perry Snopes fell to the floor again, not getting up this time.

The last image on the tape was the hustler — no longer Charles's hustler — sitting down on the bed, gun still in his hand, sniffling.

He said, "I wasn't..."

The tattooed guy, off camera, said, "Yeah, I know. You missed."

The screen filled with digital snow.

Charles Hadley sat there on the bed watching static, his body still while his insides twisted into knots. He wished he'd rented a DVD instead.

ABOUT THE AUTHOR

Jonathan Asche's fiction has appeared in the magazines *Playguy, Honcho, Torso, Inches, Men* and *In Touch for Men*, as well as the erotic anthologies *Friction 3, Three the Hard Way, Manhandled, Hot Gay Erotica, Buttmen 2 and 3, Best Gay Erotica 2004, Best Gay Erotica 2005* and *Best Gay Erotica 2007.* His first novel, *Mindjacker*, was published in 2003. He lives in Atlanta, Georgia, with his husband Tomé.

FILTHY NEVER LOOKED SO GOOD.

HOT HOUSE EXCLUSIVE
ROBERT VAN DAMME